DREAM A LITTLE DREAM

ANTOINETTE STOCKENBERG

St. Martin's Paperbacks

ISBN: 0-312-96168-5

Printed in the United States of America

St. Martin's Paperbacks edition/June 1997

St. Martin's Paperbacks are published by St. Martin's Press, 175 Fifth Avenue, New York, NY 10010.

10 9 8 7 6 5 4 3 2 1

for Ciocia Claudia

Thanks to Dr. Howard Browne, who rode to the rescue more than once; to Kristine Rolofson, castle connoisseur, for her suggestions; to Nancy Richardson at Connections for the travel lowdown; to George Martland for the insurance skinny; and, as ever, to Jennifer Enderlin for her sure but gentle guiding hand. Hi, Bob!

Prologue

$\mathcal{I}$t loomed on the hill like a Disneyland dream: Fair Castle.

He felt a dull ache of pleasure at the thought that it was still intact, still standing—despite the fact that it was standing a few thousand miles too far to the west. Grateful that its American owners hadn't broken it up for salvage or turned it into condos, he lifted his binoculars for a better look.

It seemed bigger than in the photographs, smaller than in the paintings. The word that sprang to mind was *pleasing*. It had good bones. From its soaring facade to its small domed turrets, Fair Castle was a satisfying mix of harmony and oddity.

He swept his glasses in a broad arc to the south and then to the north. He had to admit that the Americans had chosen their site well: a high knoll with sweeping views of the mid-Hudson valley, itself on fire with early autumn color. He could easily have been standing at the edge of a wood in England.

He focused his glasses on the main entrance, marked by a massive arched door. Centuries of ancestors—*his* ancestors—had passed through that door. As always, the thought was bitter. He put it aside. He was about to get into his car and drive around to some other vantage point when the door of the castle swung open and a young girl burst through it, her laugh carried high on the wind.

She was ten or eleven years old, with auburn hair and

a gait like an ostrich. Clutching something red—a plume?—she ran down a path that led to a side promenade, then hid behind a huge stone urn, waiting.

He swung his glasses back to the entrance. Out strolled a taller, older, calmer version of the girl. Mother? Sister? From that distance, it was hard to tell. One thing was certain: The two were related. He watched as the older one cupped her hands to her mouth and, in a voice that echoed through the valley, called out to the younger.

"Izzzz-a-belle . . . Isabelle!"

She yelled something else, but he couldn't make it out.

It drew the girl out from the long shadow of the urn. After waving the red plume through the air like a victory banner, she handed it over to the woman, who smacked her on the head in return. Then the two went inside, clearly still friends.

A grim smile played on his lips, then died. *The heirs,* he thought. *Pity.*

Wrapping the strap of the binoculars around the hinge, he slipped the glasses back into their case and laid them on the rear seat of his car. He was about to drop behind the wheel when he drew out the glasses again for one last look. *Fair Castle.* There it was. Dramatic. Potent. Irresistible.

His. Whatever it took.

From the battlement they watched together as he threw the binocular telescope onto the front seat of his vehicle and then made away.

"Will he be up to the quest, my love?" she asked in a pale echo of her former voice.

"He is determined to have it. I see it in his face."

"Aye," she agreed. "There is a ruthlessness there that he would do well to disguise, or it will defeat his purpose, and ours."

"He will not be defeated."

"I believe you. He has come at last, the issue of our desire. Flesh of our flesh, blood of our blood, he has walked till now in darkness. We will make that darkness flare."

"*It galls me that it must come to this. I should not have failed you the first time, my sweet.*"

"*Shhh. Too late for that; too late. You loved me with all your heart. Eventually you gave up your soul. A woman cannot ask more than that.*"

"*You deserved more than that. Much more.*"

"*Shhh.*"

The cloud of dust raised by the wheels of the vehicle began to thin. Eventually it settled back into the dirt from which it rose.

"*We have waited a small eternity,*" *she mused,* "*for him to claim his birthright.*"

"*And now,*" *her mate said,* "*his time—our time—is come.*"

Chapter 1

"*H*and me the vambrace."

"You bet." Elinor lifted the small piece of armor and looked it over carefully. "Huh. No dents on this one either, Chester," she said. "There goes my theory about our man being left-handed."

Her stepfather hardly heard her. Chester Roberts was focused completely on the task at hand: assembling a complete suit of armor—the first in his collection of knightly odds and ends—for display in the great hall of Fair Castle.

Chester had gone more insane than usual at an auction on the day before, plunking down a huge sum for half a dozen boxes filled with what he hoped were carefully wrapped pieces of a suit of armor. For all of last night and most of the morning, he and Elinor had been working feverishly to get the steel contraption up and standing before the arrival of their first tour group.

But it wasn't as though a sixteenth-century suit of armor came with a set of directions. Did the fan plate go on before or after the knee cop? Did the tasset hook directly to the tace? And why didn't the chain mail fit?

"The suit's a composite, no doubt about that," Chester had told his two stepdaughters as the three of them unpacked the boxes on the night before. "But the auctioneer absolutely, positively guaranteed that all the pieces will fit."

Too bad it wasn't in writing. Nearly done now, they

seemed to have several pieces left over—which was fine with them—but it was obvious that part of the chin piece was missing. Without the chin piece, the thin rod of the mannequin's neck showed through, completely ruining the illusion of strength.

Chester sighed as he fit the vambrace over the wooden forearm that should have been a knight's warm flesh. "I suppose I shouldn't carp. A little tweaking, and that German chin piece of mine should work just fine."

"Besides, they did give you the extra pair of gauntlets," said Elinor, nudging her stepfather's mood back up. Big, balding, and bearded, Chester Roberts was still a kid when it came to emotions.

She watched him slip first the left, then the right gauntlet over the mannequin's wrist-stumps. Almost done.

"Too bad Izzy's in school today," she added. Her ten-year-old sister had been nearly as excited as their stepfather on the night before. "She's missing the best part."

"Mmm," Chester answered, hardly hearing her. He went back to the box, reached down to the bottom, and came up grinning. "And now, the crowning touch!" he said, holding the visored helm in both hands for Elinor to see.

With utmost care, he climbed to the second rung of the stepladder with it. Carefully, slowly—ecstatically—he began to lower the gleaming orb of steel over the featureless head of the mannequin.

"Oh, wait!" Elinor suddenly cried. "We forgot the plume!"

"You're right! We forgot the plume!"

Chester set the helm on top of the ladder and Elinor handed him a magnificent red ostrich plume, all too new, which he tried with fumbling hands to fit into the slot designed to hold it.

No luck. The quill was too large. Frustrated, Chester jabbed at the helm so awkwardly that the thing jumped from the ladder and hit the floor with a horrendous clang, skidding to a stop at the feet of Elinor's mother and the small group of tourists she'd just led into the hall.

"Chester!" her mother snapped, jumping back. "You've scared us half to death!"

Oblivious to his wife's annoyance, Chester ran to the helm and picked it up as if it were a puppy run down by a truck. "Oh, *no*," he said, shocked by his clumsiness. "If I've damaged it . . ."

"Chester. It's armor," his wife said with a quick lift of one eyebrow. "Do think about it."

"Still and all . . ." He ran his hand over the gleaming skull, feeling for dings. "It'd be tragic."

"Not as tragic as spending every last cent—" She bit off the rest of the sentence and swallowed hard. Susan Roberts would much rather die than argue in public.

But Susan Roberts, stunned by her husband's latest extravagance, was clearly still fuming over the suit of armor.

"Elinor—dear," she commanded her daughter, "would you mind escorting our visitors from this point? I've just remembered I have a desperately urgent call to make." She swept past the group with a graceful shrug, headed, no doubt, for the aspirin. "I shan't be long."

Shan't. Someone in the tour must be European, Elinor decided. Her mother never dragged out her *shan'ts* for Americans anymore.

"Sure. I'll be glad to," Elinor said cheerfully, dismayed by her mother's mood. With every return visit to the castle that she made, she found that her mother seemed more bored, more weary. Was it with Chester? After only five years? Could it be with Fair Castle itself?

I'm beginning to lose touch with them all, Elinor realized. She was becoming caught up in her blossoming career as author and illustrator of children's picture books. And with the big-city distractions of New York. And, of course, with Tom. But Tom was over now. It was time to come home; time to reenergize. Without Fair Castle, without her family, there would *be* no children's books. All of the inspiration for her medieval stories was right here, smack dab in the castle.

Putting her fears and worries aside, Elinor turned to the five women and three men who were waiting patiently to hear how the hell an English castle ended up on the banks of the Hudson River.

"Well! Hello, everyone!" she said, making herself sound chirpy. "As I'm sure you've learned," she began, "we're a family-run castle. As a matter of fact, there are three generations living under this roof: my grandparents, my mother and her husband, and my sister. I was raised here, too, and still come up from New York City to visit whenever I can."

She swept them all with a good-natured grin and added, "Yes, it's a little eccentric—but not by sixteenth-century standards. Besides, we're all in the arts. People expect us to act this way."

Most of them chuckled, instantly put at ease by her friendly, confidential manner. Elinor said, "We're very good at pinch-hitting, so let me pick up where my mother left off. You know that Fair Castle was one of the last ones built in England, right? Good.

"Though the castle is English," she said, slipping into a tour guide's voice, "it resembles the tower houses being built in Scotland during what's now regarded as the golden age of castles over there.

"The walls aren't as thick as Scottish tower houses, and obviously there are too many entrances for Fair Castle to be impenetrable. But the original owner was still a conservative man by English standards. After all, by the 1550s no one in England was building strongholds anymore."

She went on with her spiel, sizing up the group while she talked: three ladies with gray hair and sensible shoes who looked like seasoned travelers, a young couple holding hands who were clearly there for the romance of it, and a ponytailed college kid in hiking books and backpack who'd no doubt stumbled onto the castle by chance.

And, of course, the European. He wasn't German; not Italian. Not Dutch, Slavic, or French. British? Could be. He wore a tweedy jacket and an air of reserve. Or maybe he was a Scot; there was something stern and unforgiving in his blue eyes as he swept the vaulted hall that loomed around and above the group.

Elinor had been giving tours of the castle for fourteen years—ever since she was sixteen—and was very, very good at reading people.

"Ta-dah!"

Everyone turned toward Chester, who'd finally got the plume in the helm and the helm on the mannequin. Fair Castle's knight in shining armor was ready for battle—or as ready as he was going to be, until he got his German chin piece and a mace or a halberd in his grip.

Chester had his ham-sized fists planted firmly on his hips and was beaming like mid-May sunshine.

"As you can see," said Elinor, flashing her stepfather a victory sign, "we've just acquired a wonderful new addition to our collection of armor and weapons. The suit dates from the sixteenth century, although some of the components are not original to it. The armor is in very fine condition—the guy who owned it must've been in the reserves," she quipped.

Apparently her flippancy annoyed the fellow in tweed. He decided to set the record straight. "Actually," he said, "by the end of the century the use of armor in warfare had declined."

All heads swung toward him. Elinor said, "I'm sorry?"

The man's smile was thin, aloof, superior. "The reason the armor is in such fine condition," he said in a clipped accent softened by a burr, "is that by the mid-sixteenth century, military strategy had changed from the medieval period. Armies had to be capable of long marches and quick maneuvers."

"Oh!" she said, taking it in. "In other words, by then armor was becoming—"

"Obsolete," he said as he glanced around the cavernous hall.

Uppity son of a gun, Elinor decided. She pursed her lips while she searched her brain for a snappy comeback. Not a one came to mind.

"I haven't had time to research that particular subject," she answered, feeling the color rise in her cheeks.

"Of course," he said absently. "Please continue."

"Thank you."

Just what she needed: a know-it-all. Every once in a while someone like him came bopping along, an expert on some tiny little niche of history who just had to let everyone in on it.

Smiling gamely, Elinor resumed the tour. "We tend to think of the great hall as the place where the lord ate with his knights and their ladies," she said as their heels echoed on the slate floored hall. "But by the 1550s, that practice had all but ended. A nobleman ate apart in other rooms from his entourage and appeared in the great hall only on ceremonial occasions."

One of the gray-haired women said, "Why even have a great hall, in that case?"

"Status," Elinor said. "Consider this the forerunner of the modern two-story foyer. Great halls did have other uses, of course. Servants were sometimes fed there, and once in a while the host would put on a play or celebrate a feast in one."

She glanced at the blue-eyed expert, expecting him to put in his two cents. But the man was listening quietly. Apparently she'd misjudged him.

"It's so old, so big, so . . . old," said the young woman, snuggling into her boyfriend's side. "Is it haunted?"

It was the number one question that tourists asked.

Elinor gave her the usual answer. "All castles are haunted," she said with a mischievous smile. It was what visitors wanted to hear, but her sense of honesty made her add, "If you're asking if any of us has ever seen a ghost, the answer—darn it—is no."

A sympathetic chuckle rippled through the group. Elinor had no intention of confessing that she absolutely, positively, did not believe in ghosts. It would be bad for business.

"Hey! Those are pretty cool," said the boyfriend, pointing to Chester's antique sword collection mounted high on the wall above the vast stone fireplace.

The weapons were mounted high for one reason: safety. Two years earlier the castle had been broken into and three of the swords stolen. Nothing else had been taken. Elinor's mother was certain that the swords were now being used in black masses and other unspeakable rites.

Elinor's grandmother, who *did* believe in ghosts, had another theory altogether. She was convinced that the original owners had simply come to claim their stuff.

Elinor was tempted to toss in those tidbits—just to get a rise out of the surly guy in tweed—but she kept to the standard story line. "The sabres and backswords and rapiers are from the period," she said, then added lightly, "but the dress swords and the boarding cutlass are just impulse buys."

A few more impulse buys like the swords and the suit of armor, and Chester will be the rest of the way into the poorhouse. The thought came and went like a shooting star, but it fed Elinor's growing sense of unease that all was not well financially at Fair Castle.

"What's that weird one on the end?" the young man asked.

Elinor said, "It's Asian, I think. Some sort of ceremonial sword."

"African," argued the man in tweed. "An executioner's sword."

Elinor blinked. How would he know *that*, for Pete's sake?

"Our visitor from—Scotland? England?—sounds pretty sure of himself, so it must be true." She gave him a cutting glance. Just where was her mother, anyway?

"England. Near Berwick-on-Tweed."

"What? Oh. Well, that's a border town," Elinor said flippantly. "It's practically in Scotland."

"Don't tell that to my ancestors. They fought hard to keep it in England." By now there was a militant glint in the man's eye.

Elinor suspected that he used both his good looks and his cultivated accent to intimidate poor, ordinary Americans. Well, tough. He could be English, he could be Scottish, he could be the devil himself, for all she cared. His high-handedness annoyed her intensely. Intensely.

Turning deliberately away from him, she began pointing out the simple detailing in the rough-hewn, drafty, but still imposing hall. Fair Castle was no sissy country house, she explained, back on automatic now. Though fairly comfortable, the castle was the last of a breed: a four-story tower that was immune to fire, anarchy, raiders, and neighbors with grudges.

Better. She felt in control of the tour again. It was much easier when her back was to the man; she was almost unaware that he was there.

Almost.

"On this floor," she said, "we'll tour the chapel, the buttery, and the kitchen. On the next level we'll view the great parlor, the dining chamber, and the library. And we'll peek in the archives room, which houses a growing collection of works on English history—in fact, an eighteenth-century scholar will begin a stay at the castle tomorrow to do some research," she said, unable to resist a smug glance at the Englishman.

"After that we'll stroll down one of the unusual features of Fair Castle, an outdoor gallery. And finally, we'll go up to the roof and enjoy the wonderful view from a delightful turret where you'll all be served tea."

It was that cup of tea in the turret that made Fair Castle such an unusual tourist attraction. Elinor had come up with the idea herself and had designed their brochure around it; she was very proud of the whole thing.

Ah—but today they had an Englishman in their midst. Nuts! He'd have his own ideas about a proper tea. Nuts! They didn't even serve clotted cream. And that high-school kid they stole from McDonald's to serve the tea—oh boy. If the Brit was expecting a sweet little lass from the Cotswolds, he was in for some first-rate culture shock.

Elinor looked around without much hope for her mother, then began taking the group along the ceremonial route to the great chamber.

She paused before a wall hung high with half a dozen portraits, four of them acquired by Chester at auctions. "Portraits came into fashion in the sixteenth century," Elinor explained. "Generally they were displayed in an indoor gallery, but since we don't have one, we've hung them here."

She pointed to the fourth portrait of the group. "See the woman with blond ringlets wearing the dark panniered gown and rakish feathered hat? That's Lady Norwood, wife of one of the owners of Fair Castle. Her first name was Elinor; she died in 1780. The portrait of her was one of the possessions that got thrown in with the sale of the castle; so was the one of Lord Norwood—her husband, Charles—to her left. The baron died much earlier than she—but then, life spans were short back then. The paintings aren't by Gainsborough or Reynolds, obviously, but we think they're wonderful."

One of the women in sensible shoes said, "Didn't you say your own name was Elinor, dear?"

Elinor grinned. "My grandfather liked the name so much that he got my mother to name me after her. Except for the hair and the eyes and the nose and the body, I think we look identical, don't you?" she quipped.

"Elinor! Hateful woman! I am jealous of her still."

"She meant nothing to me."

"I know; I know. And yet I cannot rid myself of the notion that somewhere, somehow, she is smug in her triumph."

"It is because of the family who flaunt their possession of the castle. They are the ones who keep alive the vile myth."

"Fie upon them, then! They shall feel my wrath."

"No. Not yet. We must wait. And watch."

"But we have waited generations! How much longer—?"

"You have little patience. In that, you are not changed."

"And you, my love, are too at ease with eternity."

Chapter 2

*T*hey proceeded up the stairs to what the British liked to call the first floor, with Elinor dutifully pointing out sixteenth-century architectural features worth noting.

"You can see that the stairs are made of stone," she said, rattling on. "Wooden staircases began to be built right around this time, and they became all the rage. Stone stairs like these were actually ripped out and replaced with wood ones—if you can imagine."

Everyone seemed properly scandalized, including, she thought, the Brit. Finally. He was being nice.

But not for long. In the great chamber the two of them got into a testy exchange over the social nuances of plays versus masques. In the withdrawing room they argued over whether servants slept there or masters ate there. In the library—the *library,* for pity's sake—they came to near blows over the bricks.

"I'm sure they're original," she'd said.

"No, they're not."

"Yes, they are."

"No. They aren't."

Are too. Are not. God! It was embarrassing!

Elinor was forced to bite her lip and move on.

The gallery—a long, roofed-over walkway that was open on one side to a view of her grandmother's garden below—was one of Elinor's favorite places to be. But not today. Suddenly she was tired of Fair Castle, tired of the tour, tired most of all of the Englishman who kept scrutinizing every fact she uttered. So what if those facts weren't a thousand percent accurate? They were mostly accurate. You were able to get the idea. What was his problem?

Elinor wanted suddenly to go back to her apartment in New York, put up her feet, and watch TV. Instead she was celebrating her completion of a book deadline by— what? Jousting with a hostile tourist? For this she'd caught the early train?

The morning's euphoria had gone completely. She listened to her voice drone on.

"It may surprise you to learn that in the sixteenth century physicians began preaching the importance of daily walks for good health," she told the group. "Open galleries like this one, designed for exercise in decent weather, became very popular. And the views from them were often pretty."

On cue, they all looked over the balustrade at the garden below, where the last of the season's mums were making a stand along with a few never-say-die roses. So brave, so pointless: One hard frost would slay them all. Like her grandmother Camilla, Elinor hated to see the garden wind down.

The Brit nodded toward a wild mass of towering greenery beyond the garden. "Might that once have been a maze?" he asked with that insinuating politeness of his.

"Yes. It might," Elinor answered, ashamed for no reason. "My grandfather wanted a hedge maze like the ones that were fashionable in the sixteenth century. But he decided that Fair Castle was too rugged for so formal a project. It didn't look right."

"And besides, they're a lot of work," said the Brit with an ironic smile.

"That, too," Elinor admitted. What a royal pain in the armor he was!

"What kind of hedges are they?" asked one of the women, cheerfully oblivious to the voltage in the air. "Maybe I'll start one when I get home."

"Um, let me think," said Elinor, frowning.

"Ligustrum," the tweedy one said.

Too much. She rounded on him and said, "Oh, my. A horticultural expert as well? *You're* the one who should be living in the castle. You're a regular Renaissance man."

A hit. A direct hit. His handsome face turned a surprising shade of anger as he returned her grim smile. "Maybe I should."

"Hey, excuse me . . ." It came from the college kid with the backpack, the one who had seemed only vaguely interested in the tour. "I don't know about anyone else, but I really would like to know how this castle got here. Or is that a stupid question?"

"Oh, I'm sorry," said Elinor. "Somewhere I lost the thread of my narrative."

And I know where, she decided.

Frustrated, she took a deep breath to clear her mind of the man and said, "Let me back up a bit. Fair Castle was built in a town called Dibble, situated alongside the Tweed—"

She stopped, went blank, resumed. "—River. Fair Castle was actually the second castle built for the owner. The first one, little more than a fortified tower and called a pele, was made of timber and burned to the ground."

She paused for effect and said, "The reason? The tower was part of a network of signal stations along the border between Scotland and England. This is how the system worked: When either country detected a raiding party headed their way, they'd light a series of signal fires on the sides of hills or the roofs of their houses or castles."

With a rueful smile she finished her tale. "Yep. You guessed it. The good news is, the baron managed to rally his allies and keep the marauding Scots at bay. The bad news is, he burned down his house doing it. But Lord Norwood was a wealthy man; he built himself a bigger, better castle. Fair Castle."

The kid with the backpack couldn't believe it. "They lit a frigging fire on the roof of a wood tower?"

Everyone laughed, including the ladies; but the Englishman's smile was tight-lipped. He was taking the laughter personally, Elinor decided. Hail Britannia, and all that.

He'd been leaning against the balustrade with his back to the garden and his arms folded across his chest as Elinor spoke. He was a man nearer to six feet than much over it, with ruddy skin, a Roman nose, dark hair flecked with gray, slate blue eyes, and an aura of strength that was more implied than stated.

Why did she have that sense of him—that he was so powerful? He wasn't that big a guy. Was it the square chin? The thick hair?

He was quite aware that she was watching him. His voice was low, almost taunting as he said, "The signal system you mock was actually very effective. One fire burning meant that raiders were on the way. Two, that they were moving fast. Four, that they were coming in great numbers."

He was making that up. No one knew that kind of detail. Her grandfather was passionate about sixteenth-century England and he'd never said a word about how many fires meant what. And there was another thing... some other thing...

Filled with sudden, irrational dread, Elinor edged one step away from the Englishman.

He noticed it and said with a bland smile, "But I'm keeping us from our tea in the turret."

On his lips the event sounded unbelievably dumb and American, a marketing gimmick only one step removed from free action-toys at Burger King.

"No, first we have to go to the dining—"

"But how did the frigging castle get here?" It was the young man with the backpack, clearly convinced that he wasn't going to get either the answer or the tea.

"Here you all are! Still!"

Elinor's mother had a let's-get-moving look in her eye. "I'll take it from here, dear," she said sweetly.

Elinor pretended not to hear. "Actually," she said, "how the castle got here is a very romantic story. I love to tell it. Back in the Depression my grandfather, who's an artist, was poking through a flea market in Maine and stumbled across a fabulous find.

"It was the kind of discovery an artist can only fantasize

about," she said with a sigh, speaking from experience. "My grandfather, Mickey MacLeish, bought a landscape painting by a minor artist named George Potter and took it home with the intention of reframing it. When he removed the Potter canvas from its frame, he found another canvas, in perfect condition, on the reverse: an up-till-then-unknown oil by Cezanne."

Her eyes misted up and her voice caught in her throat as she said, "It was—what can I compare it to?—it was like stumbling onto a new play by Shakespeare, written in his own hand. The story created a sensation at the time; it was written up in *Life* magazine. Maybe you've read about it?"

She scanned their faces. One of the graying women said good-humoredly, "Don't look at us; we're not *that* old."

"No, that's not what I—well, anyway. The Cezanne was far too valuable a possession for someone of my grandfather's means. He put it up for auction, got a fabulous sum, and then had to decide how to spend the money."

Her British tormentor said dryly, "Because he was a thoroughly practical chap."

"Okay. So my grandfather has a whimsical side," Elinor conceded with an icy smile. "It makes him all the more *special*."

"No kidding?" said the boyfriend, figuring it out at last. "He got a whole castle for the price of one crummy painting?" He looked around him and snorted. "No way."

Elinor shrugged; his reaction was typical. "He also had some money of his own."

"So he went over to England castle-shopping?"

"No, he'd been on a tour of the British Isles with my grandmother," Elinor said. "That's when he fell in love with one of the sights they saw: a small castle with a handwritten for sale sign on it. They fell in love with the whole idea of it."

Her mother was impatient to get on with the tour, so Elinor finished her tale. "*Any*way, it turned out that the English owners were really desperate for funds. Near bankruptcy, in fact. There had already been a scandal . . . a suicide . . . a court battle."

By now Elinor was afraid to speak too ill of anything English, so she cut short her explanation and said, "Personally, I think my grandparents were the best thing that ever happened to Fair Castle. They've lived in it ever since its reconstruction, and they're fiercely devoted to it. We all are."

She glanced at her mother, suddenly uncomfortable with the notion that her family had more or less plundered a chunk of Olde England and carried it off to the Colonies.

"Where exactly is Dibble?" asked the backpacker. "I've walked the north country. I don't remember seeing any signs for Dibble."

Susan said, "It's not surprising. Dibble is a tiny hamlet; it's near Berwick-on-Tweed."

Aha! That was it! Elinor rounded on the Brit and cried, "*You're* from Berwick-on-Tweed!"

He said, "From Dibble, actually."

"Are you really!" said Elinor's mother, delighted. "What a coincidence!" She gave him her most gracious smile and said, "Perhaps you know the family who once owned Fair Castle?"

"I do," he said. His own smile seemed to Elinor more grim than engaging. "The woman who sold the castle to you is my grandmother, Lady Norwood."

"*Really,*" said Susan. She turned to Elinor with a speechless look, then laughed a little giddily and said to Lady Norwood's grandson, "And have you come to take your castle back?"

The Englishman never got the chance to answer. From the great hall below them came the shocking, thunderous sound of steel colliding on steel, of armored mannequins engaged suddenly in battle.

Elinor, jumpy already, let out a yelp of fear and broke away from the group, sprinting down the stone steps that separated her from the sickening sound.

At the foot of the stairs she was appalled to see their newly assembled knight scattered in bits and pieces on the floor, and Chester Roberts, the sorcerer who'd put him together, lying sprawled and unconscious close by.

Chapter 3

$\mathcal{E}$linor ran to her stepfather and dropped to her knees, shocked to see that his face was the color of putty. With the help of her mother and the Englishman, she rolled the stricken man to his side. Chester shook his head and moaned, coming to again almost with reluctance.

Susan, her eyes wide with alarm, cradled her husband in her arms. "Darling, what? What happened?"

Oddly relieved by her mother's distress, Elinor said, "Chester? Should we call an ambulance for you?"

"Yes, call one."

It wasn't Chester speaking; it was the Englishman. Susan began to scramble to her feet, ready to do his bidding, but Chester wanted his wife to stay.

"I'm ... fine," he said, which no one believed. "Damndest thing ... I just keeled over ... Damndest ... thing."

"Do you feel any chest pains?" the Brit asked.

"No ... nor before, either. Not the kind makes you think heart attack. I just had a ... I don't know, a spell."

He sat up, looking groggy, but color was returning to his bearded cheeks. "I got all light in the head ... 'n' stuck out my arms to steady myself against the—" He looked around at his Humpty-Dumpty knight and let out a half-hearted sigh. "Against the armor. That was smart."

"I'm calling an ambulance," Susan decided. The panic was gone now, replaced by quiet resolve.

Chester looked up and said plaintively, "I wish you wouldn't."

His wife, ignoring him, headed briskly for the office—originally the steward's room—behind a reception area just off the hall.

The Englishman said, "Right, then; let's get you to a chair."

He helped Chester to his feet, then supported him as they made their way to a Renaissance-style armchair sitting forlornly against the wall. Elinor dashed ahead of them to undo the gold Do Not Sit cord slung between the arms. God only knew if the chair would support her stepfather; he was a bulky man, well over two hundred pounds.

Even with help, Chester lumbered toward Elinor like a drunken bear, sending pieces of armor skittering with his big, unsteady feet. Her heart went out to him. He looked hopelessly disoriented. What on earth had happened? She was sure she'd heard him whisper the words "no, no" after his dragged-out moan as he came to. Could she have imagined it?

"Guess I should've eaten breakfast," he mumbled as they eased him into the armchair.

But the apprehensiveness in his bearded face couldn't have been caused by hunger. He looked afraid.

"What was it?" she asked. "Did you see something, Chester? Did something startle you?"

"No! Nothing. Can I have . . . a glass of water?" he added in a croak.

"Sure, I'll be right back," she said. She glanced at the Englishman, who was watching Chester intently. "Can you stay while I—?"

"Of course."

Troubled by the look on her stepfather's face, Elinor made a beeline for the water cooler in the office. The feeling that someone had slipped unseen into the castle was very strong. They'd broken into Fair Castle in broad daylight once before; they certainly could do it again.

But no. That didn't make sense. Chester may have been a gentle giant, but he wasn't a timid one. He would've confronted an intruder head-on—not passed out in a dead faint.

It had to be medical.

She reached the office as her mother was leaving it. "They're on their way," Susan told her daughter. "How is he?"

"Better. But he seems evasive," Elinor admitted. "As if he's ashamed."

"It's my fault," her mother said in an anguished rush. "We had a terrible argument last night over the armor, I said some really awful things and—" The rest of the sentence got lost in the clatter of her heels on the stone floor as she hurried off to rejoin her husband.

Elinor didn't buy that theory, either. Her stepfather wasn't the brooding type, and in any case, he showed no signs of remorse for having plunked down a good chunk of his pension fund on an oddball suit of armor.

So it had to be medical.

By the time Elinor returned with the water, Chester was on all fours, picking up the armor. Her mother was trying to haul him to his feet, scolding him the whole time.

Elinor's father had died suddenly and violently, traumatizing her mother, and Chester's fall to the floor had clearly opened the ten-year-old wound.

"Susan, I'm fine," Chester was insisting, waving her away. "Don't let's make a federal case out of this, okay?"

He did seem more his old self, which left Elinor suddenly free to remember that she'd left her tour group high and dry. Back up the stairs she dashed, aware that she hadn't invited the Brit to rejoin the tour.

Too bad, she thought. *He can always ask for a refund.*

Eight hours later, Elinor was zipping herself into a little black dress and wondering whether it was too late to fake a broken leg.

Drinks with the Englishman! She had no doubt that he'd spend the entire time picking apart her command of history in general and Fair Castle in particular. Because that's what the English did. They were just so . . . smug. What could her mother have been thinking?

Elinor was mad enough to find out.

She slid into a pair of low-heeled pumps and stormed down the hall to her mother's bedchamber, then knocked before giving the door a shove, crossing the threshold, and demanding an answer.

"I resent this!" she told her mother. "I'll only be up here for three or four days and I do *not* want to spend one whole hour of them making small talk with some high-handed, overbearing, pompous, know-it-all, English . . . *baron*."

Calmer now—even happy—Susan Roberts was gathering her pale gold hair into an elegant twist at the back of her neck. She smiled at her daughter through the gilt-wood mirror and said, "Which reminds me: Since his father is deceased, it's 'my lord' or 'Lord Norwood.' No hey-yous, if it's all the same to you."

Elinor snorted. "That depends strictly on how civil his lordship is with *me*. Frankly, after this morning I think hey-you would do just fine."

Susan slipped the last hairpin in place and said, "Listen to me, please. I've been courteous to a steady stream of less-than-dazzling boyfriends whom you've dragged back to the castle over the years—I assume, out of sheer spite. You owe me your best behavior tonight. You've been brought up with every advantage, Elinor; you've been brought up in a nobleman's home."

"Don't worry," said Elinor, staring at her glum reflection in the mirror. "I'll do you proud. But I'll be doing it under protest. Izzy and I had a big night planned."

"There'll be other nights."

"When? She's growing up so fast—in a couple of years she'll be a teenager and won't want any part of me; you know how they get about grown-ups."

Susan tucked a blond strand more tightly into place. "If you had children of your own," she ventured, "you wouldn't worry so much about Izzy."

Elinor had walked right into it, of course. "We've already been down that road, Mother," she warned.

Her mother was too content for the moment to argue. "Your sister will always love you, dear," she said, touching up her lipstick. "You're like peas in a pod, despite the age difference. I can see you two when you're sixty and forty, giggling together and making fun of me behind my back. How old will I be then? Oh, my: eighty-one. I can't imagine it."

She stuck the crimson tube back in its case and said quietly, "But then, I couldn't imagine having two daughters by the same man twenty years apart. Life is truly . . . truly . . . a little strange sometimes."

She shook off the obvious memory of Elinor's father and said, "Anyway, Lord Norwood is not only noble, but charming. I don't see what you have against the man."

"You didn't have to fence with him through two-thirds of a tour. The man is obnoxious. He—"

"Darling, he *can't* be obnoxious. He's English. They simply don't know how. Did I mention he's staying to dinner?"

"Dinner! On what possible pretext?"

"We were thinking of serving him food," her mother said dryly. "In any case, we could hardly not ask him. His people were the ones who commissioned Fair Castle, for pity's sake."

"Oh, sure. He *says*. How do we know he didn't just read the brochure and make up a name for himself? If the place belonged to his forebears, why hasn't he been to see it before now? What's taken him so long?"

Susan looped a heavy band of gold through one ear and sighed. "You've lived too long in the city, El. It's making you suspicious and hard. A handsome, well-spoken man with a genuine stake in Fair Castle drops right in our lap, and you treat him like some common—"

"Hardly common!"

"It does show, doesn't it," said her mother, her blue eyes shining with pleasure. "The minute I set eyes on the man I thought, well, *finally*. Someone with good shoes and a decent haircut who can speak in whole sentences without two or three y'knows. It's refreshing."

"It's *stupid!*" said Elinor, erupting anew. Her mother's plan was all too clear. Add one English nobleman, and the castle would be completely equipped.

Throwing her hands in the air, Elinor added, "And by the way: *y'know* is *not* a dirty word."

Her mother began to get crisp with her. "I assume we're both referring to that awful man you're seeing? Tom? Well, I'm sorry, but I haven't changed my mind about him. I fail completely to see his appeal." Her voice softened as she said, "You're so bright, so talented, El. Why waste the prime of your life on someone who digs out rotten wood for a living?"

"He's a contractor, Mother. You make him sound like a termite. And anyway, Tom and I aren't seeing one another anymore," Elinor said offhandedly.

The fact was, she'd broken off with him a couple of weeks earlier—no spark—but didn't want her mother to have the satisfaction of knowing it.

But her mother knew it now, and she was plenty satisfied about it.

"Darling, that's *won*derful!" she cried. "Why didn't you say so before this? I know you're used to being on your own and all, but surely you can throw me a crumb of news now and then. If you can't give me reason to hope," she added with a forlorn smile, "then at least give me reason not to despair."

"Very funny, Mother. Have I told you lately what a snob you are?"

"All the time, and it just isn't true," said Susan, slipping a slender arm through her daughter's. "I have nothing against termites. I just wish they had better manners. Come along. It's time to exchange small talk with Lord Norwood. Think of it: an English baron, in our castle. *Isn't* this exciting."

As it happened, Lord Norwood had phoned in his apologies; he was running late and wasn't sure he could make it. The new cook—short, squat, and mean—had taken the call but had declined to pass on the message.

"I'm the *cook,* not the secretary," she said as she brought out paté.

"Then why did you answer the phone?" Susan asked, exasperated.

The cook shrugged. "Thing kept ringin'."

"But ... you do see that there's no point to taking a message if you don't deliver it?"

"I'm the *cook,* not the secretary."

Susan Roberts lifted her chin, took a deep, long breath, let it out slowly, turned to her father, and said, "I think I'll have that drink now, Dad, rather than wait."

"Stiff one, coming up," said Elinor's grandfather, Mickey MacLeish. "But the first one," he said, bowing low to his wife, "is for you, Camilla, my love."

Cocktails were an old tradition at Fair Castle.

The practice went back half a century, to what Elinor's grandparents referred to as their Broadway Period, when Mickey MacLeish, a young artist, and his darling Camilla, a musical actress, entertained their Bohemian friends in a loft overlooking the East River. Martinis used to flow in that loft, and the same drinks now flowed in the castle— except a little less freely.

Camilla, whose brief career on the stage left her with great legs and a dramatic flair, blew her tall, thin, thoroughly distinguished husband a little kiss. With an impish smile she said to her granddaughter, "Elly, have you heard? The British are coming."

Elinor rolled her eyes. "I know."

"Oh, come on, El," she said with a conspiratorial smile. "It'll be fun."

Susan Roberts, on her guard, said to her mother, "I'd love it if you and Elinor would both behave. *Just* this once."

Elinor said, "We'll see," and sidled up to her grandfather. She tweaked his black beret affectionately and tugged on one of his red suspenders. "Anything in that pitcher for me, Grampa Mick?" she asked.

Mickey MacLeish held up the half-full decanter and said, "Maybe just a tot." Taking a small stemmed sherry glass out of the Gothic sideboard, he poured a little liquid into it and handed it to her.

Everyone knew that Elinor "couldn't hold her likker"; she was a family joke that way. By a process of trial and error, Mickey MacLeish had arrived at a harmless dose for his granddaughter: one ounce, no more, no less, of martini.

So there she was, nursing a drink in a Barbie-doll glass and waiting for his highness to appear, instead of hanging out with Isabelle and picking anchovies off a pizza. It made her mood, on-and-off testy all day, just a little more cross.

"Where's Chester, by the way?" she wanted to know. "Shouldn't he be here to welcome his guest of honor?" She tugged irritatedly at her panty hose through the fabric of her dress; jeans and sweats were more her style.

Her mother frowned at her, then added, "Would it hurt you to have put on some lipstick?"

"I did; it must've worn off. I don't see why the doctors didn't keep Chester in the hospital for observation," Elinor said, still troubled by Chester's behavior earlier. "People don't just arbitrarily pass out."

"Of course they do, Elly," said her grandmother, decked out for the evening in a vintage red caftan from Turkey. She waved her ivory cigarette holder—fitted with a tiny cigar—through the air in a figure-S. "It happens all the time."

Suddenly she said, "I really can't stand it," and jumped up to rearrange some flowers that the cook had stuffed in a vase. "*Agnes,*" she said under her breath. "Who else could make flowers look ugly?"

The cook, who walked in just then with a plate of crackers, overheard and said airily, "I'm the *cook,* not the gardener."

Camilla MacLeish was unimpressed. "My dear, if you're the cook, then why don't you *cook?* I mean, canned paté and ordinary crackers? We have a very distinguished guest tonight; you might've at least warmed up the Brie."

The cook made a sullen face. "No one said anything about Brie."

"No, that's right, I didn't," Susan said quickly. "Never mind that now, Agnes. What we have is fine."

The cook marched off in a huff. Susan turned to her silver-haired mother and said, "Will you shush? If we lose this one, FoodTemp has vowed not to send us another."

Camilla shrugged and said, "Fine. Then *I* shall warm the Brie."

"You know Agnes doesn't want us in the kitchen."

"That's because she steals our food," said Camilla, dismissing her daughter's objection with a wave of her hand.

Hard on the heels of the cook, she left the great parlor just as Chester entered it.

He glanced at the empty leather sofa. "What? No baron? I'll be damned. A no-show. Fella seemed better than that," he said as he dropped into a tufted wing chair.

Elinor explained the delay and added with relief, "You look okay again."

"Chester, by God, you do," her grandfather said, pouring his son-in-law a robust drink. "Whereas every time *I* go to that blasted emergency room, I come out in worse shape than I went in. Nothing to do but sit around and wait. And wait. It wears a body out."

Mickey MacLeish had had two minor heart attacks in the past year, which is the reason his martini, like his granddaughter's, was largely ceremonial. Minor or not, the heart attacks had taken their toll on him. He looked thinner, his shoulder-length hair whiter under the black beret.

"I'll tell you," he murmured as he handed Chester his glass, "that hospital gives me the willies. When it's my time to go, it's going to be here, under my own roof."

Chester stroked his salt-and-pepper beard. "I hear you," he said thoughtfully. "I've never been so glad to see the old turrets risin' up out of the trees as I was this afternoon." He lifted his stemmed glass to his father-in-law. "Here's to Fair Castle, then. May it shelter us into ripe old age."

"Amen to that," said Mickey MacLeish.

"I don't understand it," Susan said, restlessly fluffing a tapestry pillow. "He seemed so interested in the place. He was hoping to see all the chambers, not just the ones on the tour. I'm very surprised," she added, obviously hurt.

"You didn't find that a little strange?" Elinor asked her

mother. "They're loading Chester into an ambulance, and the guy is standing around hinting that he'd like to tour the back rooms?"

"It wasn't like that at all, Elinor," her mother said cooly. "Stop it."

Elinor, who felt like an atheist waiting for the pope, put down her empty glass and said, "Well, you rolled out the red carpet and he's not walking down it. I don't know what else you can do. As for me, I'm off to see if Izzy's done with her homework yet, and then we're going out for pizza. That *was* our plan before it got preempted by the royal visit."

"Elinor, I really do wish—" Her mother clamped her lips together, getting herself under control. When she opened her mouth again, it was to say, "This castle is absolutely wasted on you."

Elinor laughed out loud at that. "On *me? You're* the one who would love to—"

Her stepfather, seeing storm clouds ahead, said quickly, "I think someone's at the door."

"Oh, hell!" said Elinor with a snort. "Wouldn't you know it?"

"Elinor! Go welcome our guest. *Graciously.*"

Elinor marched out of the room with a scowl on her face. She was halfway across the great hall when the door knocker came down again. "Hold your horses, your worship," she muttered. "I'm coming."

"This one called Elinor . . . she is a danger to us, Charles."

"She has a volatile nature, it's true."

"Volatile! You regard her from a man's point of view: volatile, and therefore exciting to bed. But I look at her as a woman would. I see an intelligent, attractive female who has reached the age of a score and ten and who still has not loved a man with all her heart and soul. I see a woman who has not yet cried out in childbirth. How can a woman like her have sympathy for our cause?"

"Beloved Marianne, you never lived to see thirty years, and yet you loved with the passion of two lifetimes. Com-

pared with you, there is no doubt. This one does squander her time on earth."

"They all do," she said sadly. "It is the age."

"Fools, all, then."

Chapter 4

$\mathcal{G}$rabbing hold of the massive iron ring on the arched door, Elinor gave it a hard pull. The door swung slowly, with a groan, across the slate floor. A cold blast of October air rolled into the hall, chilling Elinor's exposed limbs and sending a violent shiver through her.

The light bulbs in the outside lanterns, like the fake-flame bulbs of the inside sconces, were overwhelmed by the crushing blackness of the night. The visitor who stood at the threshold of Fair Castle was hardly more than a dark shadow as he waited to be asked inside. Elinor hesitated for one frightened, thoroughly mystifying moment, and then she rallied.

"Lord Norwood?" The name dripped from her lips like melting ice, and so did her greeting, uttered over a deep and ironic curtsy. "Welcome, my lord. To our humble home."

She heard rather than saw his smile as he said, "Miss MacLeish, I'd have to disagree."

She stood back up. "Okay—it's not exactly humble."

"I meant, you're not exactly welcoming."

He stepped across the threshold into the great hall. She gave him a furtive once-over. Gray flannels, navy blazer, museum-print tie. And no topcoat, which amazed her; the night was cold and raw, the first bleak promise of the season to come.

Just to be un-English, she said, "You must've been freezing your buns off out there."

"Actually, my buns were fine," he answered.

He was too blasé by half. The urge to provoke him got stronger.

She remarked, "We're surprised that you bothered coming at all. Your call made it sound unlikely."

"I'm a little surprised myself. Perhaps I was drawn by your charm."

"You wouldn't be the first."

"But if I were the last?"

"I'd be even more surprised."

Ouch. What was *that* all about? They were like two kids swatting one another on the way to the bus stop.

Smarting, she decided to be more civil; anything else would look like he'd drawn blood. And he hadn't. Not really. She told herself.

"Have you been touring the area?" she asked in a consciously pleasant voice. "The Roosevelt house in Hyde Park is a pleasant drive from here and is a nice piece of Americana to see. It's easy to get to. All you do is take—"

"I'm not here to tour," he said, cutting her off. "I had business nearby. It ran on."

"As I'm afraid I must," she said as they made their way into the great parlor. "It's a shame I won't be able to stay. I did so look forward to showing you around," she added with an ironic glance in her mother's direction.

Susan Roberts smiled a qualified approval and took over from there. "Ah, Lord Norwood! We're so glad you could come!" she said, rising from the sofa and gliding toward him with both hands extended.

Elinor's mother was very good at that—at making one feel one was among people of privilege. One would never have guessed that when push came to shove (usually in August, when the college help quit early) she was perfectly capable of scrubbing toilets and mopping floors.

"Please," he said, taking her hand in his. His face creased in an engaging smile. "Call me Will."

Susan inclined her head in graceful acknowledgment. "My lord. You know Chester, of course. And my father, Michael MacLeish. And this is my mother, Camilla."

Elinor's grandmother was fresh from the microwave with her overcooked Brie. "Nice to meet you," she said, holding out the plate of wet cheese. "Try some?"

He glanced at the pool of cheese in some confusion. While Elinor waited, amused, to see how he'd handle the offer, her mother stepped in for the save.

"Something to drink?" Susan said, herding her guest toward the sideboard.

"Gin and tonic, if it's no bother."

"Don't have that," said Elinor's grandfather, waving away the request. "Something else?"

"Eh-h . . . scotch and soda?"

"Nope."

The baron rubbed his chin and said, "I'll have whatever you are, in that case."

"Good." Mickey MacLeish dropped an olive in a glass and filled it. "So you're part of the Braddock clan. How is it we haven't met you before now?" he said, handing his guest the drink. "My granddaughter has her own theory, by the way," he added amiably. "She thinks you're a fraud."

Susan sucked in her breath. "Dad, that is not what Elinor meant. She meant—"

Elinor jumped in. "My grandfather's being a little blunt. What I meant was, why exactly did it take you so long to come see your family's old digs? We're in the book." She went over to the sideboard and poured herself a recklessly large martini, then drained half the glass.

"A very fair question," the Englishman said. "I'll be the first to admit that Fair Castle has always had certain . . . painful . . . associations on which I'd preferred not to dwell."

Here it comes, thought Elinor, slugging her cocktail. *He's going to throw his family's failures in our faces, as if it's our fault that his grandfather squandered their fortune and then did himself in.*

But the baron did nothing of the sort. He said simply, "When you reach a certain age—and a certain level of success—you're able to face painful associations head-on."

"That's the way, Norwood!" said Elinor's grandfather, hooking a thumb through his red suspenders. He raised his martini in a tribute to the human spirit.

"I'm glad you were able to put that whole painful time behind you," said Camilla MacLeish. "After all, you're not a kid anymore." She patted the tufted sofa cushion next to her. "Come sit. Let's have a look at you."

The baron, apparently bemused by his hosts, obliged her. Elinor watched with wary resentment as her grandparents took their measure of the man. It was important to her that they not like him; she had no idea why.

Camilla MacLeish, who despite her years always sat as straight as a pillar, pushed her half-glasses up her nose and peered at the top of the Englishman's head. "You've still got all your hair," she observed. "That's good. Mickey lets his grow long to draw attention away from his thinning mane, and the beret takes care of the rest."

She pursed her lips as she studied their guest more closely. "But you'd do well to drop that frown of concentration. Here . . . and here," she said, touching her fingertips lightly to the inside corner of each of his drawn-down eyebrows. "Much too serious. That's not good. You'll be old before your time. How old are you, incidentally? Maybe you've already got old before your time."

"I'm forty-one," he said with a wry smile. "And you're right; they've been hard-fought years."

Susan Roberts, who'd been trying to signal Camilla behind the Englishman's back, finally said in exasperation, "Mother! The next thing we know, you'll be reading his palm!"

Camilla paid no attention. "I expect it's your job. What is it you do for a living? I hope it's not illegal. That can be very stressful."

"You don't have to answer, if it is," Mickey said generously. "That part's none of our business."

Chester rubbed his beard and said, "Come right down to it, it's none of our business either way."

Elinor, curious herself, said, "Regardless—you'd better tell them what it is you do, or you'll never get fed." She tossed off the rest of her drink. It was strong stuff; her head was spinning.

"There's not much to my story," the Englishman said with self-effacing charm. "I got into the computer game early and managed to hang on for the ride. A few lucky moves," he said with a shrug, "and here I am."

"Bill Gates?" asked Mickey MacLeish, impressed. "Are you another Bill Gates?"

Lord Norwood laughed and said, "There can only be one Bill Gates."

"And you work in England?" asked Camilla.

"Up until recently, I did. But I've just sold the software company I owned, so I'm between projects," he said.

"And you live in England?" asked Camilla.

"I shuttle between a flat in London and a house in Dibble."

"I remember Dibble pretty well," said Mickey Mac-Leish. "Maybe I know the house?"

"I'm sure you do," said the Englishman quietly. "It's the gamekeeper's cottage on the Fair Castle estate."

Silence.

Then Camilla said softly, "You rent?"

This time the baron's smile was less congenial. Elinor saw a definite edge in it, a kind of ever-so-slight compression of the lips that suggested he'd reached the limit of his amusement with them all.

But his voice stayed pleasant as he said, "Actually, I own the cottage, along with several farmhouses and a newer house on the estate."

Elinor's mother said casually, "And the land itself?"

"That, too."

"Well, *good* for you," said Camilla, smacking him on the knee. "We thought your family had lost not only the castle, but everything else! See that, Mickey?" she said to her husband. "It turned out fine, after all."

Except for the scandal and the suicide parts, thought Elinor, weaving perceptibly by now. She'd always been told that the man who'd gambled away a fortune, then shot himself, had been a wild and irresponsible type.

She searched the face of his grandson, looking for either trait, but all she saw was fierce self-control. On the other hand, her focus was getting a little blurry, so who could tell?

"I understand that there was *quite* a lot of land at one time," said Susan, handing him a plate of crackers. "Is the Norwood estate still intact?"

"Pretty much—now."

He may have thought Susan Roberts was merely making small talk, but Elinor knew better. Her mother was putting him through a credit check.

And meanwhile—*whoa*—the martini was hitting Elinor with the force of a freight train. It occurred to her that it was time to go, before she made a jerk of herself. She stood up and fixed her unsteady gaze on the Englishman.

"I would *just* like to say . . ." she began.

The baron looked at her with a smile that she found as taunting as it was genteel. "Yes?"

"I . . . forgot."

It was true; one look into those slate blue eyes and her mind had turned to mush. She felt the rush of blood to her cheeks at the same time that she became aware of an ungodly wobble in her knees. "Excuse me," she said abruptly, and she walked over to the sideboard to put down her glass.

She missed. Missed the whole damn sideboard. The glass dropped through the air to the floor like a crystal butterfly, shattering into a hundred pieces.

Her grandfather shook his head. "That kid's *never* gonna hold her likker."

"It's all right," Elinor said to the company, much too loudly. "I'll take care of it."

She threw her shoulders back and walked with great deliberation from the room and into the upper kitchen across the hall.

"Agnes, I broke a glass," she said, bracing her hands on the counter and leaning over it dizzily. "Could you—"

"Don't look at me. I'm the *cook*—"

"Yeah, yeah, not the bartender. I know. Just tell me where you keep the brush and pan."

"Under the sink. Make sure you put it back." The heavyset woman wiped her hands on her apron, then stepped halfway across the hall and yelled into the great parlor, "C'mon and eat! Let's go! It's getting cold!"

Whether the food was cold or hot, Elinor was never able to say. Once everyone left the great parlor for the dining chamber, she tiptoed back, cleaned up the glass, then hid in her room for the rest of the night and didn't come out till the morning.

Chapter 5

"*H*e wants to what?"

"To buy the castle."

"Buy the castle!"

"And move it back to England."

"Move it back to England!"

"That's what he wants."

"He wants to *what!*"

"Honest. He didn't exactly say that at dinner, though. Mom told me this morning. During dinner Grampa Mick did most of the talking. He was telling Lord Norwood—"

"Don't refer to him as Lord Norwood, Iz! It's annoying. His name is William Braddock. Call him Mr. Braddock."

"Well, Mom calls him Lord," said Isabelle, stung by her sister's sharp tone. She flipped her auburn hair back over her pajama tops and said, "Anyway, Lord . . . Mr. . . . . Norwood was really interested in Grampa Mick's story about how he had the castle moved to here. You know—all that stuff about the masons and how they took it all apart and numbered everything and then put it all back together over here? I just thought he was being polite. But I guess it was more than polite. And then after dessert I went to bed, because I know *those* stories by *heart,*" she said, bending over double on the bed and covering her ears at the thought of them.

She lifted her head and opened her hazel eyes again, wide, as she summed up her amazing news. "They were drinking Grampa Mick's special brandy that he never brings out. I don't know how long Lord—he stayed, but it must have been really late. Because when I went to the upper kitchen for a glass of milk and some Oreos, I could still hear voices. And I know I was sleeping for a long time before I got hungry."

"Izzy, you're nuts," Elinor said flatly. "You were dreaming."

"You didn't hear them? Grampa Mick was really loud."

"Not at all. I slept like the dead."

But Elinor hadn't slept like the dead at all. She remembered now. She'd had dreams. Strange dreams, violent dreams, all night long. As if she were defending herself from attack.

Isabelle, excited but freezing, decided to crawl under the comforter with her sister. "Well, I definitely wasn't dreaming about what Mom just told me. She made me toast. I didn't dream that, either. You'd better *do* something, El, or who knows what," she urged.

"I don't believe this," Elinor said, throwing back the covers. "I skip one meal and all hell breaks loose!"

She bounded out of bed with a shiver—the room was piercingly cold—and wrapped herself in a ratty terry cloth robe the color of guacamole, then slipped into a pair of fuzzy slippers shaped like dinosaur heads. "Where's everyone now?"

Isabelle pulled the rest of the comforter around her, eskimo-style. "They're in the great parlor, having coffee. We couldn't stay in the kitchen because Agnes came and had to make her shopping list. El? Are we going to have to move?" the child asked plaintively. "I don't want to live in some . . . some . . . *house!*"

"You won't have to, Iz. This is all a misunderstanding. Now go and get dressed. As soon as I come back we're going off boot shopping, just the way we planned." She marched off.

Unbelievable. She could honestly say that she hadn't enjoyed a single hour of her stay so far. From the argument over the armor to the scare over Chester, from the snippy tour of the castle to the martini-headache she was suffering right now—from one damn end of it to the other, the visit had been a bust. The air seemed to crackle with hostility, as if Fair Castle were suffering through a bad bout of PMS.

I don't like this, she thought. *I don't like this at all.* The castle had always been a source of magic and inspiration for her. It was a living, breathing, everyday fairy tale. It fed her spirit; it fueled her career as an artist. Bad things never happened in Fair Castle. Not to the MacLeish family, anyway. True, there was the one terrible thing—her father's death—but that had happened a mile down the road. Elinor had always been careful to keep that memory shut away in a separate box of her mind.

As for the Englishman's so-called offer to buy and move the castle, well, that was just bizarre. Elinor didn't believe it for a minute. Too much brandy all around and one too many what-ifs, and now her mother had her hopes up again. It wasn't cheap to own a castle, and her mother had always understood that more than the rest of them. With Chester's money draining away . . .

Well, it wasn't the first time her mother had got her hopes up; and it wouldn't be the last. If they had a dollar for every enraptured soul who thought he wanted to buy Fair Castle, they could build another one right next to it.

Elinor arrived at the great parlor to find a state of pandemonium.

Her grandfather had the least to say and was saying it the loudest. "It's my goddamned castle and it stays right where it is! I bought it fair and square and this is where I plan to die! Goddammit!"

Chester was saying basically the same thing, except in a kinder, gentler way. "Of course, I'm the new kid on the block, but the way it looks to me, this castle is part of the family. Two generations have grown up in it, and if El ever gets off her behind and finds someone to marry her, it'll be three. Whereas, this fella Norwood has never even set eyes on the place before now. I don't see him as having the motive."

"Motive! The man is a peer and we're living in his ancestral home! How much motive do you need?" Susan said passionately. "Can't any of you see that? I don't think he's toying with us at all. Just because he didn't put an offer on the table last night—so what? It seems perfectly reasonable for him to want to know a little more about the condition of the place before he does. I think it was honorable of him to be as candid as he was."

"Honorable? He's a traitor! Drinking my brandy half the night long, listening to my stories . . . Then to have the *gall*—the unmitigated *gall*—to say he might actually be interested in making an offer—goddammit! On *my* castle!"

"My darling Mick, you are headed straight for the emergency room if you keep this up. Try to calm yourself, would you?" asked Camilla, pulling her husband back down next to her.

"I'll stand if I want to stand, dammit!" he said, yanking his elbow up away from her. "Stop coddling me! *I'm* not the one who dropped to the floor like a stone."

"That was just a fluke," Chester muttered. But the instant flush that darkened his cheeks told them all that he didn't believe his own assurances. Once again he looked afraid.

Once again, Elinor felt a bone-chilling cold cut through her.

"Chester," Susan said, alarmed by her husband's manner. "Are you all right?"

Mickey MacLeish rallied back to his son-in-law's side. "He's fine. What the hell is wrong with you two women? When did you turn into little clucking hens?"

"I suppose I can understand Susan," he went on as he paced the room, discussing his daughter as if she'd somehow vaporized. "Susan has never been keen on the castle. But *you!*" he said, stopping and pointing an accusing finger at his wife. "You break my heart, Camilla. You tear at my soul."

"Mickey," said Elinor's grandmother softly. "You've had two heart attacks. Fair Castle is a huge undertaking. An expensive undertaking."

"Like hell it is!" Tall and thin and proud, the artist chopped through the air with the edge of his hand for emphasis. "We've got Chester, we'll have Elinor when her sublet in New York is up. Tell her, El. And we have Izzy! Izzy knows the castle as well as I do. We're growing *more* staff, not less. We *can* afford it. Goddammit."

Like an old lion provoked, he'd felt obliged to follow his roar with a growl, the growl with a mutter, as he circled a chair at the opposite end of the room and then eased himself into it.

"Hmph. Goddammit. *Damn*."

He was exhausted.

Hands plunged in the pockets of her robe, Elinor had been watching attentively to see which way the wind blew before she set her sail. She hadn't missed a thing, from the coffee-ringed yellow pads, scribbled all over with numbers, to the unlit tiny cigar lying chastely in its holder. The dark circles under her mother's red-rimmed eyes; the surprising wanness of her grandmother's cheeks; the furtiveness in Chester's glance—she saw it all.

And what she saw amazed her.

"This is unreal," she said at last, giving voice to her thoughts. "We were one of the happiest families I know— but look at us now. From the moment that *wretched* man set foot in this place, life has been a nonstop quarrel!"

"You're wrong!" her mother cut in. "It began when Chester dragged home his dummy in shining armor!" She gave her husband a scathing, resentful look.

Elinor shook her head. "No, that's not true—"

"Of course it's true!" her mother argued. "Do you know how much that thing cost? Do you know how much of the pension fund is gone now? I might as well be married to a compulsive gambler!"

"Susan, that's ridiculous," her husband protested. "I'm getting value for my money. It's not like I'm throwing it down some rat hole of a slot machine."

"He's right, Susan. You lay off him," growled the old lion from the other side of the room.

Turning to her father, Susan lashed out at him instead. "Why do you think I'm so thrilled by Lord Norwood's proposal? We can't afford this place anymore, Dad—we can't! We're losing ground every year on it. It's falling down everywhere. And I'm sick of it! I'm sick of giving it all my time, all my energy—"

"People, people!" said Elinor's grandmother, rising from the sofa and clapping her hands in a chiding beat. "Elinor's right. We're turning into the Bickersons. Let's all just take a dee-eep breath—"

"We don't have time for a deep breath!" cried Susan. "Lord Norwood has come to Fair Castle now! He's expressing an interest now! We *have* to have a strategy!"

"Oh, Mother, get a grip! Just because some jerk with an accent gets a little drunk by the fire doesn't mean he's going to fork over hard cash—assuming he has the cash to fork over. If he's so rich," Elinor added, turning the old saying on its head, "then why ain't he smart? Only an idiot would buy an old castle that's falling apart, much less ship it overseas."

The room became very quiet. About the time that Elinor realized she'd offended everyone in it, she also realized that no one was listening. They were all too focused on the door behind her.

Please, no, was her immediate, instinctive plea. Wincing, she shifted her gaze from them to the doorway. As she feared: Lord Norwood, in his country tweeds, standing next to their hopelessly clueless cook.

Pretending he wasn't there, Elinor spoke instead to the help. "Agnes, it's seven o'clock in the morning. What were you thinking?"

"Mrs. Roberts told me to send the baron right in when he came at ten. It's ten. He's here."

The cook turned on her heel and plodded off, while Elinor wheeled back around to check the ebony bracket clock on the stone mantel. Ten o'clock. *How?* Her gaze slid past her grandmother, oddly elegant in plaid; past her mother, very *comme il faut* in a black skirt and cowl-neck sweater; past her weary grandfather and her worried stepfather and came to rest, at last, on her dinosaur slippers.

Oh, shit! She stared down at beady tyrannosaurus eyes staring up at her. *Oh, no.* Yesterday the tipsy exit; today, the guacamole robe. It didn't seem possible. Still, it couldn't be helped. He was there, and she was here, and there were more momentous issues at stake than how she was dressed.

Don't apologize; don't explain, she told herself. In a passable imitation of her grandmother, she took up the unlit cigar and the silver Zippo lighter, stuck the ivory holder in her mouth, and fired up.

Elinor had never smoked anything in her life. Her family watched, mesmerized, as she took a deep long puff, held it without choking, blew it out in a decent O-ring, and said, "Lord Norwood. How nice to see you again."

With great flair she seated herself, much as Elizabeth I might have done, in a thronelike chair that rounded out the seating pit. Her family blinked in unison, then burst into nervous conversation.

"Coffee, Lord Norwood?"

"Have you had breakfast yet?"

"What's the weather out there today?"

Mickey MacLeish, who had his own way of bridging the gap of awkwardness, was the last to speak. "Don't mind Elinor," he told the Englishman in a low growl. "She has a bad habit of telling the truth."

And then he got up and walked out, which left them all right back at square one.

"I've come at a bad time," said their visitor with a polite smile. It was clear that he understood that any time would be a bad time. It was also clear, at least to Elinor, that he couldn't care less.

Elinor's mother was quick to reassure him. "You've happened on one of our roundtable discussions, that's all; they can get quite ... lively."

He gave Elinor a bland once-over and said, "Lively is best, I think."

Now she felt the burn. She might've just pulled off a pretty good imitation of her carefree grandmother, but it was only that—an imitation. Inside she was dying of embarrassment, which put her at a major disadvantage for the coming battle.

Chester offered to get coffee, but Elinor's grandmother said distractedly, "I'll have Agnes bring some," and went out, obviously in search of her husband.

Since Chester would be leaving at any moment to open up the castle for the first tour, Elinor had no choice but to remain where she was. She didn't dare leave her mother alone with this man. Susan Roberts would have the castle under agreement in five minutes flat.

The thought had scarcely formed in Elinor's brain when Chester excused himself, wisely taking the yellow pads with him. Elinor filched his half-drunk coffee and dug in her heels; she was staying put.

"I want to thank you again for having me to dinner, Susan," the Englishman said, making himself comfortable in the overstuffed chair next to hers. His voice was low, almost intimate, as he added, "I've never been in more interesting company."

Elinor's mother blushed and smiled and said, "After you left us, I didn't sleep at all, Will."

Susan? Will? What happened to Mrs. and Lord? Elinor sat up, alert, and straightened her lapels of ghastly green.

"It was probably the pork, Mother," she said sympathetically. "Are you feeling any better yet?" To the Englishman she murmured, "My grandfather gets that way, too. Once you reach a certain age—"

"Elinor? Don't you have someplace to go? Don't you at *least* have something to wear?" Susan cast a withering eye at her daughter's flannel heart-print pajamas sticking out from under her robe and said, "I'm all for casual dress, but really, dear."

Crossing her dinosaured ankles demurely, Elinor stretched her arms in front of her, yawned, and said, "Oh, I'm in no hurry." She turned her lazy smile on the annoyed nobleman. "You know how Saturdays are. Lie around . . . watch cartoons . . . maybe do a load of laundry."

She had three things on her mind: *stall, stall, and stall.* Eventually her grandparents would return and she could hand the reins over to them; but in the meantime, she didn't dare leave her mother alone with someone with a few pounds in his pockets.

"So. Tell me about your software company, Lord Norwood. I'm *fascinated* by technology."

His lips twitched in an ironic smile. "Really? I'd assumed your interests lay in the performing arts."

"I am an artist," she conceded, blushing at the dig, "but not a performing one. I write and illustrate children's books—picture books, they're called."

"Ah. I have an acquaintance who has talent that way."

"I'm sure you do," Elinor said offhandedly. "An amazing number of people think they can create picture books."

His smile remained. "Actually, the Duchess has been lucky enough to find a publisher."

Elinor cleared her throat. "Of York? Ah. Well, yes, I guess she has."

Susan's face lit up with delight. "The helicopter books! They're quite wonderful. You know the Duchess, then." She glanced at her daughter, scarcely able to contain her joy.

Elinor stifled a little surge of professional jealousy and said, "But we digress. You were about to tell us what kind of software your company produced. Whatever it was, it must've been pretty popular."

Since you obviously have money to burn, she wanted to add.

"I'm afraid it's hard to grasp. People rarely do."

"Give it a shot."

"You've heard of the Internet?"

"Of course," Elinor said with a breezy shrug. She didn't have a clue how to use it, but she knew what it was.

"I designed the first successful network management software system," he said. "And then I sold it. Many, many copies of it. Eventually I sold the company."

"I see. And now you find yourself on our shores with nothing, really, to do. You're bored—is that it?"

"Elinor!"

Elinor shrugged and said, "It was just a simple question, Mother."

But Elinor had gone too far. Rising with enough dignity for two, Susan Roberts picked up the remote, aimed it at the television, clicked it on, and dropped it in her daughter's lap. "Enjoy your show."

She turned to her maltreated guest and said, "Will? Shall we begin our tour? The rooms should be warmed up by now."

The Roadrunner cartoons weren't nearly as funny as Elinor had remembered them.

Chapter 6

*T*he shopping trip was more or less a bust. In the first place, they couldn't find the way-cool boots that Izzy had set her heart on. The stores were wiped out completely, which is exactly what Isabelle had predicted would happen if Elinor didn't get up from New York before Labor Day.

In the second place, Elinor's concentration was somewhere else than on her sister's feet. How could she possibly have fun prowling the malls with Izzy when the enemy was inside the ramparts even as they shopped?

Elinor told herself that there was no cause to worry. Before she left, her grandfather, still in a pique, had given her his word that the Englishman would be shown the door the first chance he got. And her grandmother (alarmed that the cure for her husband's bad heart might be worse than the disease) had promised to hold the door.

Certainly Chester wouldn't cave; he loved the castle as much as anyone. That left Elinor's mother, who only owned a third of the business and none of the castle.

The problem wasn't with the family's loyalties. The problem was money. He had it. They didn't. Elinor stabbed at her strawberry shake with a straw and tried to think of ways to scare off the Englishman. Maybe she should tell him about the wiring.

"So I'm like, '*Gross;* he picks his nose? And you still want him to be your boyfriend?' And she's like, 'Well, he doesn't do it around me. I only heard it from Lisa.' And

I'm like, 'Why do you need a boyfriend, anyway?' And Cheryl's like, 'Well, duh. Why do you think?' "

Izzy's Big Mac was cold and her fries were limp; she had no time for food, not with all the things she wanted to tell her big sister. The girl had talked nonstop all through the meal, but now, suddenly, she stopped.

"El?" she said shyly. She looked down at her hamburger and began pulling it apart, searching for the pickle. "Will they think I'm a dork if I don't have a boyfriend?"

The question snapped Elinor out of her uneasy revery. "Will they think—? Are you kidding? *They're* the dorks. Just because they try on makeup and claim to have boyfriends doesn't mean they can go out on dates. It's like dressing up as a Power Ranger on Halloween. Big deal: you still don't have the power."

Isabelle thought about it, and then her brow cleared and the sun came out. "I never thought of it like that!"

Elinor loved to look at her sister; loved to see the fresh, freckled innocence in her face. Ten was a wonderful age, anyway: a kind of charming interlude before the hormones kicked in. But even for a ten-year-old, Isabelle was special. She had none of the cynicism of the city kid and none of the boredom of the suburban kid—because she lived in neither place.

She lived in a castle.

It was like living in a history lesson, with books and paper and tablets everywhere to prod the imagination and nourish the mind. Isabelle was what all parents wished their kids could be: a product of a less threatened, less complicated age.

All it took was that castle.

"Hey, kiddo—are you going to play with that, or eat it?" Elinor finally asked. "Because we should be getting home."

"No, no, I'm eating it," said Isabelle, taking a monster-sized bite of her burger. With her mouth still full, she said, "When did you have your first boyfriend?"

Back to boyfriends! "Hmmm. I suppose my first true love was David Andrews in freshman math," she decided.

"Why didn't you marry him?"

Elinor smiled at the earnestness of the question. "He didn't ask, for one thing. And anyway, we didn't have anything in common. I've always wanted to marry an artist. Someone interesting and intense and emotional, like Grampa Mick. Someone I can relate to. Someone who loves Fair Castle the way we do."

"You could marry Lord Norwood! Oh . . . but he's not an artist. He's a computer person. A programmer, you said."

Elinor snorted and said, "Actually, I think his lordship thinks he's God. With a keyboard."

"But he's really rich, right?"

"We assume." Elinor sucked thick shake through the straw. "I wonder if I can look him up somewhere. I still say there's something—I don't know—fishy about him."

Izzy's smile was impish. "You're just saying that because Mom likes him."

Bingo. Izzy was right. Elinor and her mother had exact opposite ideas about what made an ideal man. Despite— or maybe because of—two marriages to men who didn't fit the bill, Susan Roberts put a premium on breeding, manners, and clothes.

What mattered to Elinor was the man beneath the shirt. He could be illegitimate and in rags. In fact, she might prefer it. Poverty was far more romantic than wealth. Was he sensitive; was he genuine; and did he make her heart beat faster? That's all she wanted to know.

She'd been serious with a few men in her thirty years; but except for a wild and naive fling when she was twenty-two (with a guy who turned out to be married and not so genuine), none of them had made her heart beat especially fast.

So here she was: between men again and sitting in a McDonald's with her kid sister on a Saturday night.

"C'mon, snot," Elinor said, suddenly depressed. "Time to go."

They drove in fading light through the valley. Dressed in the evening blaze of October color, the scene was grandly, almost painfully romantic. The woods, the mountains, the ribbon of water that cut the valley in two—it was easy to see why their grandfather had chosen this fantasy site for his fantasy home. It appealed to his outsized sense of romance, both as a painter and as a man.

Mickey MacLeish was an artist with a nineteenth-century mind-set. He liked to tell everyone that he was simply a student who'd enrolled a little late—by a century and a half or so—in the Hudson River School of Painters. He loved their approach, loved the way they portrayed noble scenes with great realism and no pretension.

"Hell," he liked to say. "The light's still as brilliant, the mountains as lush as they were back then. Poetry is poetry. I'll paint what I want to paint, and fashion be damned."

He was Elinor's mentor and hero, the only father-figure she'd ever really had.

Elinor turned at a small sign posting the castle's hours and guided the family truck onto a winding dirt drive. Branches from wild oaks, crying out for pruning, clawed at the windows as she slalomed around potholes, then downshifted for the last little upward spurt. The truck leveled off for a hundred yards before being catapulted from the overgrown road straight into a fairy tale. From out of nowhere appeared Fair Castle, its narrow windows aglow with dim light, its magical turrets piercing the evening sky.

Tonight the castle, cast in a soaring silhouette against the sunset, looked more alluring than ever. The sky behind it was intense: liquid amber, warmed by a burst of hot fire. The scene was so hauntingly beautiful, the colors, so perfectly blended, that it hurt to look at it. If only she could paint that sky! Her grandfather still tried, and sometimes he came close; but Elinor had given up long ago.

"Look!" said Isabelle, surprised. "Lord Norwood's car is still here!"

Reality check. A silver Mercedes—God forbid he should rent American—sat alone in the visitors' lot to the left of the castle.

"I can't believe they haven't thrown him out yet," Elinor said, more uneasy than annoyed. "Doesn't he have someplace to go?"

"Like a motel, you mean?"

"*Wherever.* We've wined him, dined him, shown him around—I wish he'd let us get on with our lives!"

The threat he posed was so real that Elinor found herself flogging the truck to its parking place, a small paved area behind the castle near the walkway to the service entrance. Before Isabelle had unclipped her seat belt, Elinor was out of the car and making a dash for the side door. She hurried through the mudroom, shot through the pantry, turned a corner, and smacked headlong into a stranger.

"Agh!" she cried as her arms went up instinctively between them to buffer the hit.

Taller than she and steadier on his feet, the stranger caught her lightly by the elbows and said, "Sorry! Wasn't watching where I was going, I guess."

"No, no, it was my fault," she said distractedly. "I'm in a hurry. I'm—you're lost," she added, realizing that he'd made a wrong turn somewhere. "The bathroom is down that hall—"

He grinned and said, "I'm not a tourist. I'll be staying here for the next couple of weeks, doing research. Susan Roberts handed me over to Agnes, but Agnes seems to have gone off somewhere. She said she'd be back, but . . ."

He glanced around him haplessly. "I feel as if you've caught me breaking and entering," he said, flushing. "No kidding, Agnes told me to wait right here—"

"Oh, no, I believe you. It sounds exactly like Agnes. What did you want her for, anyway?"

"This is even more embarrassing. I'm supposed to give her my food preferences and intolerances, but I really don't have any, and I won't be eating here tonight in any case. Still, I didn't want to just walk out, so . . ." He lifted his shoulders in a shrug of resignation. "Here I sit."

He was very good looking, in an all-American sort of way: reddish blond hair, green eyes, fair skin. Scattered freckles gave him a Huck Finn boyishness; he had a relaxed air that made Elinor feel instantly at ease with him.

She stuck out her hand and said, "I'm Elinor MacLeish, Susan Roberts's daughter. Sorry I can't stay and chat. I'm sure we'll be bumping into one another; I'm visiting my family for a few days."

"Tucker O'Toole," he said with an appealing, lopsided smile. "Nice to meet you."

She pumped his hand vigorously, then said, "Do you want me to hunt down Agnes?"

He shook his head, but his eyes lit up in gratitude over the offer. "Don't let me keep you. I'm fine."

"If you're sure," she said, reluctant to abandon him. But she did, and returned to her original mission. She found the Englishman in the library—the nicest, most private room in the castle—enjoying a smoke with her grandfather.

"Grampa Mick!" she blurted in a scandalized voice. "What do you think you're *doing*?"

Mickey MacLeish, like most people, did not take kindly to the question. He scowled and said, "This is a private conversation, El."

Stung, Elinor backpedaled immediately. "No, I meant . . . I meant the cigar," she lied, pointing to the fat rolled Havana in his hand. She'd given the cigars to him herself, before the heart attacks. "You know you're not supposed to . . ."

The scowl faded to a guilty smile. Her grandfather held the stogie in front of him and considered it.

"Ah, what the hell," he said at last. "It's just this once. They were just going to waste. Don't tell your grandmother, punkin."

He patted the brass humidor beside him, took another puff, and turned back to his guest. "Back then I didn't have to worry about zoning, thank God . . ."

Dismissed. Elinor's grandfather launched into a blow-by-blow account of the septic system installation to his fascinated guest while Elinor stood there feeling stupid. Ordinarily she was the apple of Mickey MacLeish's eye, but this particular moment had *For Men Only* written all over it. She mumbled something about opening her mail and began to leave.

The Englishman, still in tweed and looking very much like he belonged in the club chair he occupied, glanced up long enough to smile at Elinor, and then he gave her a wink.

It was the wink more than the smile that lodged in her throat like a crust of dry bread. Condescending bastard! Elinor left the library in a fresh new snit, wondering how the baron had managed to win over her grandfather in the space of one short shopping trip.

Her first stop was the kitchen, where Agnes was peeling potatoes.

"Is he staying for dinner again?"

"So they tell me."

"God. Why doesn't he just move in?"

"That's what he's doin'," said Agnes, dropping a quartered potato in the pot. "His suitcase is upstairs."

"*What?* For how long?"

"Couldn't tell you," said Agnes without looking up. "I'm the cook, not an innkeeper."

"Oh, for cryin' out—well, don't make anything for me, in that case. I won't be joining them."

Elinor went off in search of her grandmother. She passed through the great hall and found her stepfather there, standing precariously on the top rung of an aluminum ladder and rearranging his high-hanging sword collection.

"Chester, have you seen Gramma Cam?" she asked from the bottom of the ladder. "She's not in her rooms."

"Try the office," he suggested, then added, "What do you think? Do the partizans look too long for the swords? Should I leave them with the maces and halberds?"

Elinor craned her head back and studied the new arrangement. "Try it that way for a while. See how you like it."

"What about the three basket-hilted swords all in a row?" Chester persisted. "Too much?"

"Maybe a little," Elinor said arbitrarily. Her mind wasn't on the aesthetics of arms and armor tonight.

Eventually she found her grandmother in the conservatory, a drafty, multipaned structure that was tacked on as an afterthought to the south side of the castle. Camilla MacLeish, her plaid skirt protected by a dirty bib apron, was up to her elbows in potting soil, moving a potbound fern into a bigger home.

"You're back, dear," she said, looking up with a hazy, contented smile. "Did you get Izzy her boots?"

"As far as I know, there are none in the state," Elinor said as she dropped into a broken Adirondack chair. She was dog tired—unlike her vigorous, ageless grandmother.

"Why is that man still here, Gramma Cam?" she said, closing her eyes. Her headache was back. Hell. She opened her eyes again, careful to seem calm. "If you don't mind my asking?"

"Not at all," her grandmother said as she inverted the plastic pot and tapped it against the edge of her worktable. "He's here because—"

The fern popped out in a too-solid lump; with her left hand the elderly woman caught it and pinned it against her smock before it dropped to the floor. "Oh, poor baby," she murmured to the plant. "No wonder you couldn't breathe."

"He's here because—?" Elinor prompted.

Camilla began gently disentangling the outer, potbound roots. "Well, let's face it, El. Your grandfather could use a new audience for his castle stories. We're all a bit tired of hearing them. Lord Norwood is fresh meat."

"What happened to Plan A—showing him the door?"

"It became Plan B—insisting he stay." Camilla Mac-Leish looked up with her trademark, roll-with-it smile. Her cheek was smeared with dirt, adding an endearing, childlike touch to her already glowing aura.

"I haven't seen your grandfather this enthusiastic in a long time, Elly," she added. "He looks ten years younger."

"He was aging fast enough this morning," Elinor ventured, leaning back on the chair again and pressing her hands to her temples.

Her grandmother laughed softly as she scooped a hole with her hands in a big dirt-filled pot. "He was apoplectic. After he and Lord Norwood went into the library, I was sure only one of them was going to come out. But an hour later they were like long-lost buddies. Personally, I think his lordship hypnotized him."

Presumably Elinor was meant to smile at that, but the sense of distress she felt ran deep. It was unlike any other emotion she'd ever experienced, almost a form of paralysis. She sat back with her eyes closed, thinking of the two men in the library, deep in conversation.

"He plies his magic on the old man, while this one waits and worries. His sorcerer's tongue speaks many languages. One by one, the family will begin to succumb to his spell. But this one, this Elinor . . . she will resist."

"He will see her as a challenge, then."

"Will he? Is that how you regarded me?"

"It is no matter for jest, Marianne. You know, above all others, how devastated I was by your beauty, your youth. The first time I saw you at your father's side, I knew I would never love another. The thought plunged me into instant despair."

"Because I was common, you mean."

"Common! I despise the very word! You were extraordinary."

"Common, nonetheless, in the eyes of the law."

"It mattered not to me."

"But it did to your father!"

"And thus began our travail. Ah, Marianne . . . we must have it out, after all this eternity. He must vindicate us. And end our despair."

Forcing herself out of her paralysis of distress, Elinor opened her eyes. Her grandmother was contentedly patting soil around her transplanted fern.

"So that's it?" Elinor said to her. "You're just going to let this . . . this Englishman come and take the castle out from under us?"

Surprised, Camilla looked up from her task and said, "No one told you? Lord Norwood has backed away from that idea altogether. You were right, I guess. It was just the wine talking. And in any case, your grandfather has announced that he will not sell Fair Castle unless every one of us, including you, agrees to it. So you have nothing to fear."

Elinor looked unconvinced.

Her grandmother sighed and said, "All the man really wants is to satisfy his curiosity about the place, dear. That's all."

Elinor said softly, "If you believe *that*, Gramma Cam, I have a bridge I can sell you to go with your castle."

"Now, Elly. Incidentally, we had a visitor today," Camilla said, deliberately changing the subject. "The fellow who's going to be researching Chester's book collection dropped in to introduce himself."

"I know. I bumped into him—literally—a little while ago."

"Tucker O'Toole, that's his name. How could I possibly have forgotten it? Tonight he stays with friends, but bright and early tomorrow he plans to set up shop in the archives room. It should be fun, having two guests staying here at the same time. We hardly ever have company anymore."

"What's he like? He seemed a little out of his element."

"Well, who wouldn't be, around us? I liked him. He's about your age, wouldn't you say? He's down here from Ontario, I think. A nice-looking boy. And very sensitive about staying out of our way. Very thoughtful. Well, of course he would be, if he's bookish. I understand he's working on a book of some kind?"

"We didn't get a chance to talk," Elinor confessed, closing her eyes again. "I kind of ran him over and kept on driving."

She heard her grandmother make a tsking sound. "Elly, you came here to relax—so relax, would you, dear? When you get keyed up, you rile everyone around you. It's very nerve-wracking."

Elinor sat up to protest. "That's not—"

"You, my dear, need a trim," Camilla said, pointedly addressing her fern. She took up a pair of secateurs and began circling the plant.

Elinor wasn't very happy about the prospect of another guest, thoughtful or not. One foreigner at a time was plenty. She pondered the sudden glut, then had a thought.

"What did Mother think of Tucker O'Toole?"

Camilla scrunched her nose as she snipped the first string of brown needles from the fern. "Not much. He's no one particular, after all. Never mind that Chester took to him like a dog to a bone. He's a minion, not a baron. Your mother hardly had two words to spare for him."

"Well, good," said Elinor, leaning back. Now she was intrigued. "Maybe I'll be able to stand him, after all."

"I'm sure," her grandmother said with an ironic smile. It was a secret they shared, this gentle mocking of Susan's snobbery.

Camilla focused on making the plant neat and trim, and Elinor was able to study her grandmother frankly.

Five and a half feet of concentrated energy, Camilla MacLeish moved even now with the exaggerated grace of a stage actress. It made her fun to watch, mesmerizing to be around. She looked amazingly vigorous; she *was* amazingly vigorous. Who else could not only maintain a garden the size of a football field, but turn over her own compost pile with a pitchfork?

In the spotty light of the conservatory, Elinor managed to convince herself that her grandmother had defied the march of time. She would never grow old.

"There! Done!" Camilla said with a satisfied smile.

She gave her long gray braid a perky little flip over her shoulder, then muscled the pot with one arm, the plant stand with the other and, over Elinor's protests, hauled them herself to a south-facing window.

After that she washed up at the soapstone sink while Elinor swept up the dried fronds. When she was done, Camilla untied her canvas apron and hung it on a wood dowel nearby.

She turned to her granddaughter and said quietly, "About Lord Norwood—I don't want you running around making trouble, El. Your grandfather has said that he doesn't want to sell, and Lord Norwood has said that he doesn't want to buy. Either way, it's your grandfather's decision. Let him be the one to make it. Trust him. Please."

Elinor wiped the smear of dirt from her grandmother's

cheek. "You want him to sell, don't you," she said, her voice full of reproach.

Camilla MacLeish sighed and lifted her shoulders in a shrug that looked somehow . . . old.

It shocked Elinor to see hesitation in her grandmother's bearing. The transformation was too quick, too unwanted. It was like seeing the Wizard of Oz unmasked.

Elinor shook off the sensation and added, "I have no intention of doing anything stupid."

"Oh, we never actually *intend* to do stupid things," was Camilla's mild response.

Despite her dismay, Elinor had to laugh. She loved that in her grandmother: that laid-back, gently snotty view of life. Still smiling but newly resolved, Elinor slipped her arm around her grandmother's waist and squeezed. "I adore you, Gramma Cam, you know that?"

"I do, sweetie, and the thought always gives me great joy. Now beat it," said Camilla, her independent self again. "I want to be alone with my plants for a while."

Elinor's own preference for relaxing involved loud music, junk food, and a television blaring in the next room, but she fully understood her grandmother's need to spend quality time with her garden. When Elinor wrote and illustrated her medieval children's stories, she always worked in silence, in a sunlit room that was filled with plants.

Back to the kitchen she went, skirting around Agnes to hit the fridge for a carton of yogurt. Another evening alone in her room. It wasn't supposed to be this way.

She passed the chamber that the family sometimes used for guests. The room originally had been a small oratory overlooking the brick-walled chapel below; but during the reconstruction, her grandfather had had it walled in.

Before live-in help became extinct, the help was put up in it. It had just enough room for a single bed, small chest, and row of pegs for hanging one's clothes. Jacuzzi living it wasn't.

From where she stood in the hall, Elinor could see Braddock's leather bag at the foot of the bed. So this is where they put him. Excellent. Spartan at best, claustrophobic at worst, the bedroom was also the coldest one in the castle. He'd be gone by the next nor'easter.

She was about to move on when she spied the identification tag on the handle of the suitcase.

Chapter 7

*O*rdinarily Elinor was a conscientious hostess; but these were not ordinary times. How did they know for sure that the man about to sleep under their roof wasn't a con artist—or worse? He could be an ax murderer. Who would know?

After glancing up and down the hall, Elinor tiptoed into the tile floored room and began fumbling with the tag, trying to read the name. It was cunningly concealed by a flap which refused to flap.

Annoyed, she set her yogurt container on the chest and lifted the luggage onto the bed, then unlayered the flap from the neatly printed tag underneath: Norwood, Dibble, Northumberland.

Oh.

Still, it didn't prove a thing. It didn't prove he was a baron or that he had big money. It didn't even prove he was a Norwood; only that he had some Norwood's leather suitcase. If he'd stolen it, if he'd bought it, if he'd murdered the owner and kept it . . . the tag on the suitcase did not prove a thing.

He is not who he seems. That single, compelling thought nailed Elinor to the spot, trying to puzzle out the mystery of him.

Possibly what was *in* the suitcase might prove something. Papers, currency, clothes that did or did not fit— the contents would undoubtedly reveal clues about the man. Elinor's hands hovered over the bag as she fought an almost irresistible urge to snap open the beat-up brass lock. Probably it was locked. Probably you needed a key. If it was locked, then that was that. If it wasn't locked—

"What do you think you're doing?"

"Yah!" Elinor jumped back from the bag, knocking it over on the bed, and whirled to face the irate Englishman standing in the doorway. "*Don't* go sneaking up on people like that!" she cried.

"Are you joking?" he asked, plainly amazed by her nerve. "What are you doing with my bag?"

"I . . . it was on the floor. I put it on the . . . bed." It was all she could come up with: a stripped-down statement of the facts.

"I can see that, Miss MacLeish. Now tell me why."

"You know, that's really rude, embarrassing me like this."

He laughed out loud at that. "I beg your pardon? It's rude to catch you in the act?"

"It's rude to point it out."

"You have an interesting sense of etiquette. I repeat: What were you doing with my bag?"

"I *told* you; I was putting it on the bed."

"And I *asked* you: Why?"

"Look, if you're going to stand around badgering me—" she said, trying to brush past him.

He grabbed her arm and caught her close. "*Hey.* I'm a guest in a manor, not a felon in jail," he said in a menacing voice for her alone to hear. "I value my privacy."

"Y-you sound like you have something to hide."

"Don't fool with me, Miss MacLeish, and we'll get along fine."

"Will we?" Elinor's heart was upside-down with fear, but it did nothing to check the fury she felt. She was close enough to him to see stubble on his cheek, a tiny spot he must've missed that morning. It gave her an odd sense of relief, even strength: He might be human, after all. She could take him.

"Listen to me," she said, rallying her anger. "I know your game. You want Fair Castle, and you can't believe we aren't forking it over on a platter. You think that all you have to do is back off a little and try us from another direction. Well, forget it, your lordship! I don't know why you want the castle, and you know what? I don't care. I do know that you'll get it only—only!—over my dead body. Now *let me go.*"

She wrenched her arm free from his grip and bolted from the closet-room, not daring to stop until she had the door of her third-floor bedchamber locked safely behind her.

The adrenaline drained away in a rush, leaving Elinor dazed and shaky. She hadn't felt so threatened since the time she got dumped out of a sailboat into the Hudson during a frostbite race in December.

She was queasy. Her room shared a bath with Izzy's room; Elinor rushed to it, dreading the worst. After a tentative eternity, the uneasiness passed and she was able to draw a glass of water from the pedestal sink that stood under an ornate mirror meant to hang over a stuffy Victorian mantel.

Through half-lowered lids she glanced at her image as she downed the ice-cold well water. She saw a face without color, lips beyond pale. Even her auburn hair, normally straight and shining, had a frizzy edge to it—like a cat who's got its dander up.

All because someone didn't like the idea of her prowling through his luggage.

What are you, an idiot? she asked that pale, puzzled face. Granted, William Braddock shouldn't have grabbed her arm the way he did. And granted, he shouldn't have sounded so menacing—he *did* sound menacing, even in retrospect. But the bigger issue, the one Elinor seemed to be having trouble understanding, was really very simple: *It was not an act of evil to want to buy the castle.*

Assuming, of course, that he did plan to buy it. Which Elinor was still assuming.

She heard a knock on the bathroom door from Isabelle's side.

"El? Aren't you done in there yet?"

"In a minute." Elinor ran a comb through her hair and put on some red to counter the pale, then opened the door to her sister's bedroom before retreating to her own.

"Izzy," she called out to her sister. "Why do you suppose someone would want to take apart Fair Castle, brick by brick and stone by stone, and carry it back to England?"

Isabelle had been on her bed, reading yet another scary book by R. L. Stine. She flopped the book on its belly, then made a dash for the freed-up bathroom. After a long and thoughtful pee, she yelled out, "Because he likes it, same as Grampa Mick?"

"No, Grampa Mick's a romantic," said Elinor as she pulled on a black turtleneck to wear over a denim skirt. "Our Lord Norwood is anything but."

"Maybe he knows there's something special in it—like hidden treasure!" said Izzy. "Or a map!" She was in the doorway, pulling up her jeans hurriedly and trying to hop toward Elinor at the same time, when a knock sounded from the hall.

"Miss MacLeish?" came a voice on the other side of the door. "It's Will Braddock."

Izzy's eyes got huge. "Don't open it yet!" she whispered, zipping up in a panic.

Elinor laughed and said, "You could always try closing the door, dope." But her heart was moving to a pounding beat as she approached the door to the hall and opened it. If he was here to pick up where they'd left off . . .

"Yes?" Behind her she heard Izzy carefully closing the bathroom door, undoubtedly to eavesdrop.

Norwood had an odd glint in his eye as he held out a yogurt container by its lid. "You left this behind during your search."

"I wasn't searching, Lord—Mr. Braddock. I told you. I was—"

"Yes. I know. Putting my suitcase on the bed," he said, with a smile that even Elinor had to admit was altogether irresistible.

Damn him!

She took the yogurt from him and said stiffly, "Please accept my apologies for the . . . intrusion."

Again he smiled. "Accepted, with pleasure." The frown

of concentration he wore eased into something like a good-humored squint. "We've got off to an awkward start," he admitted. He extended his hand to her in a peacemaking way. "Try again?"

"Oh . . . sure," Elinor answered, stumbling with the yogurt before she got her hands organized. She had to admit to liking his handshake: not too firm, not too shy. It always amazed her that men could take strange women to bed and yet not know how to shake their hands. Lord Norwood knew how. One point for him.

He made a movement to go and then stopped himself. "I'll see you at dinner?" he asked, glancing at the yogurt.

"No, I—yes, of course," she decided. Why let him make any more hay with her family than he had already? She needed to be on guard for them all.

"Spiffing," he said with a self-mocking smile. His gaze searched hers in vain for signs of friendliness.

No way, your lordship, her own steady look said. *They may not see through you, but I do.*

He became cool again. "By the way," he added, "the bag contains nothing more remarkable than socks and underwear. The case you want is in the trunk of my car; the keys to the car are in my pocket," he said, jingling them for her benefit. "I leave the key ring on the dresser at night—but I'm a light sleeper. Still, you could try giving it a whirl. The possibilities are endless."

"I think I'll pass," Elinor said, coloring deeply.

"*À bientôt,* in that case," he said in his dry way, still jingling his keys; and then he turned and left her.

Elinor closed the door and, like a sailboat that's momentarily lost its wind, remained stock-still, waiting for something to get her moving again.

That something was Isabelle, who came bursting into the room from the bathroom like a little white squall. She had indeed been eavesdropping. "What search?" she asked with innocent eagerness. "What were you looking for in his suitcase?"

"I don't know," Elinor admitted. "I never got the chance to get it ope—" Yikes! What was she admitting to? She added quickly, "Which is just as well, toad. There are more legitimate ways to find out who he is."

Isabelle, arms stretched out wide, let herself fall crashing onto her sister's down-topped bed. "Well, you could look him up in *Debrett's Peerage*," she said, staring at the ceiling. "Mom says he'd be in there."

"But his photo wouldn't."

"Oh. How about if we hired a private detective? Eee-yew; there's a giant spider on your ceiling, El. Really big."

Bugs and nobility were routine topics at Fair Castle. Elinor went back into the antiquated bathroom and spun off some toilet paper.

"The trouble is, he's not an American," she said as she dragged a chair over to a spot beneath the hairy beast. It was her third spider of the day. The weather was turning cold, and creatures were heading for cover. The mice would be next.

"I suppose he could have a record of business transactions in the U.S.," Elinor mused, missing on her first pass. The spider made a dash for the corner of the white-washed ceiling and stuck his tongue out at her; he knew he was safe. "Shoot! I can't reach him now. But we'd need an English detective, I think."

"We need one of those bug vacuums," Isabelle said unhappily. She'd always had a revulsion against spiders, which made the castle a less than ideal home for her in early autumn.

"Don't worry, Iz," Elinor reassured her. "I'll get him. Sooner or later."

Dinner came and went and Elinor was none the wiser about their guest. Baron Norwood had an almost spooky ability to avoid talking about himself. It was more than British reserve; he acted as if he were in a witness protection program. Whenever someone asked him a question, he turned it aside with some exasperating pleasantry.

Camilla MacLeish tried first. "What did you study in school," she asked, "that prepared you for such a brilliant career in software?"

A shrug. "Oh . . . a little of this; a little of that."

"Where did you go to school, Lord Norwood? I'm willing to bet you're an Oxford man," said Chester after that.

A rueful look. "No, not Oxford, I'm afraid."

"How about travel?" asked Mickey MacLeish a little later. "You ever traveled any in the States, son?"

A thoughtful pause. "Here and there."

Elinor's mother, more subtle than the others, took a different approach. "I imagine that you have a tremendous collection of ancestral portraits; were any of them done by artists we'd know?"

A frown. "Actually, it's unlikely."

After every question he'd redirect the talk right back to the castle—to the plumbing, the heating, the wiring, the roof. By the time Agnes brought in tapioca pudding, the unthinkable had happened: Mickey MacLeish had run out of castle stories to tell.

"Norwood, by God, you've worn me out," he admitted, sliding his cup of half-drunk Sanka away from him. He pulled his sweater more closely over his striped shirt, as if he felt a chill, and settled his ever-present beret over his white locks.

"Tomorrow I'll drag out the plans and schematics for you to see; but for tonight, well, I'm ready to hit the hay," he said tiredly. "You'll excuse me, won't you?"

Surprised, three generations of women turned toward him. With a regal frown, he waved away their concern. "Don't you women start," he warned. "I'm just tired. Can't a man be sleepy without you running for the paramedics?"

He signaled the baron to stay as well. "Sit, sit," he insisted as the Englishman stood in deference. "Enjoy your coffee. Good night."

Isabelle, who was about to fall nose-first into her tapioca, was ready for bed, too. She left the table, followed quickly by her grandmother. That left Elinor to linger over coffee with her mother, her stepfather, and their guest of honor.

"See how she watches in quiet fascination, Charles. She knows not who he is, nor can he tell her."

"She will find out soon enough."

"And in the meantime, she is drawn to him like a moth to flame. See it in her eyes, the way she averts her gaze when he looks at her. See it in her breast, which lifts and falls in anticipation as the company grows smaller."

"Very like the way you looked at me, while your father laid down stroke after stroke on the canvas. It was all I could do not to rush from my chair and tear away your clothes. In truth, I had never had to endure such torture before. It was an exquisite agony."

"I remember it well, my poor Charles. So few steps between us, and yet so vast a chasm."

"It made me on fire for you."

"I remember."

"I had to have you."

"It gives me pleasure still to think of it. And yet I derive no such pleasure from seeing these two together."

"Because it will impede our goal. It is too soon. We cannot let her be drawn into his spell."

"What shall we do, Charles?"

"Stop them."

Chapter 8

$\mathcal{P}$oor Chester had been patiently awaiting his turn to talk shop all evening. Now that his father-in-law had packed up his beret and retired, and with the women subdued, Chester found that he had the baron more or less to himself.

Stroking his beard with a ham-sized hand, Elinor's stepfather began to enthuse about his collection of arms and armor. He pointed to the cuirasses that hung on display from all four walls of the dining chamber.

"I do like my breastplates," he said with quiet pride, "but what I'm really after, someday, is a chanfron. The Ottoman versions, now there's the ticket. Rare, beautiful stuff; you can almost see the horse's nostrils flaring behind it. A chanfron is more—El, what's the word I'm after?"

"Evocative."

"More evocative, than any other single piece of armor. Seeing one always gives me chills." He glanced at his wife, then sighed. "But a fine Ottoman chanfron goes at a hundred thousand plus, so I reckon I won't be bidding on one any time soon."

If Chester was throwing out a hint to Elinor's mother, he'd made a mind-boggling blooper. What he'd done was push down hard on her hot button. Susan's glance at him was quick and grim. She laid her napkin on the tablecloth and said with deceiving calm, "I think we've bored Lord Norwood enough for one evening, Chester. Why don't we leave him in peace? If there's anything you need, my lord, just ask."

Elinor felt a pang of sympathy for her stepfather; their bedchamber would be a cold, forbidding place that night.

Chester shuffled to his feet and bade his guest good night. "And if the toilet won't flush right," he added helpfully, "you just take and hold the handle down a little extra. The one on that floor's a little balky."

"I'll remember that," the Englishman said. He seemed carefully unaware of the look of dismay that Susan was sending her husband.

Susan led Chester away before he could embarrass her further. So now it came down to the nobleman and the commoner.

Suddenly shy, Elinor rearranged the spoon on her dessert saucer and said, "I've never known my family to be party poopers before."

"Maybe it's by design," Lord Norwood said quietly. He reached into the inside pocket of his jacket and pulled out a pack of cigarillos, then tapped two or three of them out from the carton and held them across the table. "Smoke? They're your brand; I ran out special for them."

Taken aback by the whimsical offer, Elinor glanced up at him and saw a smile that was altogether new. A little crooked, dimpling his left cheek, it was irreverent, intimate—anything but aloof. It left her brain in a puddle of confusion.

"I'm trying to cut back, thanks," she quipped, but her voice was a little shaky for a wiseacre. She took a deep breath, rallying her wits. She had absolutely no desire to be attracted to him.

She took a sip of tea and tried again. "I've been meaning to ask you—where did you learn about African executioner's swords?" She made no attempt to hide her suspiciousness. "Even Chester wasn't sure what he had."

The baron took a cigarillo from the pack and, after getting Elinor's permission to light up, leaned back and struck a match to it.

He smiled and said, "I confess to having got hold of your Fair Castle brochure. The photograph of the great hall shows some of the swords on the wall. I was curious about the one on the end, so I did a little research."

He blew out a puff of smoke. "We have a pretty good library of our own back home. You didn't get *all* our books," he added quietly.

Elinor had heard nothing past the word *brochure*. Oddly bothered by the fact that he'd reconnoitered the castle through the mail, she said, "So you already knew quite a lot about us before you ever came here. You knew we have to give tours. You knew about tea in the turret, for that matter."

"Which, by the way, I never did get to have." In a voice as light and smooth as silk, he said, "Why don't we take what's left of ours up there? The Hudson must be beautiful at night."

For whatever reason, Elinor wasn't crazy about the idea. "Oh, the Hudson's just like every other river," she said. "Dark. Slithery. Dank this time of year."

But Lord Norwood had already stubbed out his cigar and was gathering their cups and saucers.

"No, leave them," she said, rising quickly to intercept him. "I've nearly finished, anyway. All right, we'll take a quick look, and that will be that. But really, there's nothing much to see."

Elinor would have preferred that they stay in the dining chamber. She felt more in control in the dining chamber. What electricity they had was in the dining chamber.

"We'll need a light," she told him. "The wiring's gone all funny in that turret."

There were hurricane lamps in most of the rooms for the occasional outages that hit Fair Castle, but the lamp on the sideboard was empty of kerosene. Elinor grabbed one of the pair of brass candelabra still burning on the table, taking care not to spill wax on the cloth, and said, "Shall we go?"

She took him to the fourth floor and from there led him up the narrow wood stairwell that ended in a trapdoor. "The tour groups get so expectant at this point," she told him over her shoulder. "I always wonder what it is they hope to see."

"They're on a stairway to heaven," he said behind her. "It's easy to understand."

His words were innocent enough. But Elinor heard meaning beneath the meaning. She turned, sharply, and one of the three tapers in the candelabra fanned out. Elinor let out a a little gasp. She was as jumpy as the two flames left flickering in the holder.

At the top of the stairs she threw back the trapdoor. The last few steps led through the attic and the pitched roof into a small polygonal turret, itself hardly big enough to hold seven or eight people. "We have to limit the total who come up—not that it's often a problem," Elinor explained.

She set the candelabrum with a sharp little thunk on a stone table that filled the turret, then walked around the table to the window with the best view of the river. "Well, there it is," she announced. "If my grandfather were painting it, he'd call it *The Hudson by Night*."

The Englishman came to the window from the other way around, and they stood side by side for a moment without speaking. For a few fleet seconds Elinor was able to look at the view the way a newcomer would.

It was, undeniably, a scene of striking beauty. A waning moon shimmered through slow-moving clouds, casting long, silver shards on the black flow of river streaming silently south. Below the castle, climbing ever taller, creeping ever closer, were woods of ash and oak, spruce and hemlock. There were no neighbors to speak of, no lights within view: only darkness, only wild.

She said softly, "The turret is the first memory I have of the castle. My grandfather took me up here when I was three and perched me on this very sill, so that I could see the river and the valley. It was about this time of year. I think he wanted me to see autumn color; he was already encouraging me to be an artist, I guess. Then he turned to relight his cigar. My mother walked in just then, saw me unsupported, and let out a scream that I can still remember."

"Childhood traumas are like that," he cut in. His voice was low and musing but somehow more grim than hers.

Elinor nodded and added lightly, "Needless to say, she startled me and I fell off the sill and hit my head on the edge of that table. My grandfather swears I have a dent from it . . . somewhere . . . back here," she said, feeling the hollow at the top of her head.

She grinned. "Maybe everyone has one. I don't even know. I don't want to know; it would spoil it for me."

"Let me see," he said simply.

He lifted his hand and brought it to rest on her hair. Elinor didn't breathe, didn't move, as he skimmed his fingers lightly across the back of her head, feeling for her beloved childhood dent. A rumble of thunder rolled through her brain in the wake of his electric touch. She dared not breathe, dared not move: if only he would go on.

"Here?" he murmured. "Ah, wait. Here."

She closed her eyes as he caressed the spot, once, twice, three times. She felt herself sway. It was another time, all over again, and she was unsure, and ready to fall . . . fall hard . . .

His hand slid lower, cupping the back of her head. He shifted his position to face her; she knew that he intended to kiss her. Is this why she had come to the turret, then? To be held powerless in his one hand?

No. It was not. With a wrenching effort, Elinor made herself stiffen under his caress.

"Anyway," she said, taking a deep breath and trying to sound offhand, "my mother is still convinced that I would have been a neurosurgeon if it hadn't been for the fall."

He accepted her quiet rebuff with surprising grace. "Seriously?" he said, following up on her remark. "Your mother isn't happy that you draw children's books? I'd have thought she'd be proud of your accomplishment."

Uh-oh. This was no good, either. Elinor was feeding him information, the one thing she'd vowed not to do. He was clearly committed to the strategy of dividing and conquering the family; to do it, he'd need all the facts he could get. Well, the heck with that.

"My mother's very proud of me," Elinor said with spirit. "It's just that our family's a little heavy in the arts department. What with my grandfather being a painter and my grandmother an ex-Broadway actress . . . my uncle is a film actor on the West Coast, and Izzy wants to be a novelist. . . . Even Chester has turned out to have an artsy side: He's never met a piece of armor he didn't love.

"You can see my mother's point," she conceded. "She'd like a surgeon or scientist to balance our portfolio. Even a lawyer would do."

"Have you given any thought to software engineers?"

"Aaack. I don't want to become a—"

Elinor realized that the nobleman wasn't talking about her at all. He was talking, quite amazingly, about himself. What he was suggesting, she hadn't a clue. She decided to stick with misunderstanding him. "I don't want to become a software engineer," she repeated blithely. "To tell the truth, I hate computers."

"Hmm. You're not alone there." He'd turned his back on the moon and was leaning against the mullion, gazing at her instead of the view.

So much for The Hudson by Night. It was still out there, still enchanting, but it was obvious that Lord Norwood didn't care a tinker's damn for it. He'd merely wanted to get her alone and someplace dark so that he could break down her resolve not to sell the castle.

Elinor had had men try to seduce her before. But their goals had always been more or less straightforward: sex. An end in itself. The baron, on the other hand, was using her to get to Fair Castle. This was new, and it was scary. Was he aware that the castle could be sold only if all of them agreed? Had her grandfather confided the fact to him? Elinor had to guess yes.

She made a move to go; but the baron was in no hurry.

"What kind of business was Chester in?" he asked offhandedly.

"Oh . . . he owned a small factory in Ohio that manufactured some kind of mechanical thing he invented. It was a gadget that made it easier to line up one gear to another. I'm not making it sound very brilliant, but someone thought it was. They bought him out for a fair amount of money. After that he decided to travel. That's how he met my mother. Here, on a tour."

"I gather that your mother was a widow before she remarried?" the Englishman said delicately.

A kind of veil slid across Elinor's voice. "Yes."

"And . . . you seemed to imply that your father was in the arts? Like everyone else?"

"I didn't imply anything about my father, one way or the other," Elinor said cooly. Her father would never be a subject for discussion. Not with him.

"Ah. I'm sorry."

I'll bet.

Suddenly Elinor had had enough of being manipulated. She decided, on a whim, to give him a mountain of information he did not seek. She'd *bore* him out of the turret.

She launched into a numbing account of the successful effort to clean up the river and didn't pause until she'd told him the maximum allowable level of PCBs in bass that were caught there to be eaten safely.

Her tone was serene; but her eyes were narrowed in challenge.

Lord Norwood decided to take up her gauntlet. "No one else in your family seems as upset at the prospect of a sale as you are," he said at last. "May I ask why you're so troubled over the idea?"

"Aha! So I was right!" she cried, rounding on him. "You *do* want to buy it, despite what you told my grandfather!"

"That's not what I said, Miss MacLeish."

"Why are you here, then?"

"Would you believe me if I said, for a really good look around?"

"No."

He shrugged. "Fine. Then draw your own conclusions. But you still haven't told me why you care so much."

"Here we go again!" she said angrily, fed up with his slipperiness. "You're so busy probing for information that you don't listen. I *have* told you. Because I fell from this sill!" she said, banging a fist on it. "Because I hit my head on that stone table! Because this is where my grandfather taught me how to use perspective in drawing. Because my mother taught me how to read here. Because I sang Raffi songs with Izzy here. Because my grandmother showed me how to knit and do needlepoint here. Because—"

Exasperated, she grabbed him by the sleeve of his shirt and dragged him over to one of the side walls of the turret. "See this?"

She lifted his hand to an indentation in the stone. "*Feel* it. It's an *E*. And this is an *L*," she said, moving his hand to the next letter. "I chiseled them in when I was eight, because I was convinced that no one would ever take away something that had my name on it."

She let out an explosive sigh. "Can't you understand? This turret—this whole castle—has all of my heart and a lot of my soul in it. That's why I care! It's filled with memories. It's filled with who I am . . . who my family is. I can't explain it more than that. It's a spiritual connection. It's—it's like a church to me. Surely you, of all people, can understand that!"

And meanwhile, her hand was lying over his on top of her name. With one easy motion he swept her arm away from the wall and caught her around the waist. His mouth came down on her lips—parted in astonishment—in a kiss that was long, hard, and overdue. She reeled under the force of it, stiffened under the power of it, and then her resolve collapsed altogether and she returned heat for heat, fire for fire, ache for ache.

Just as suddenly, he pulled away from her. "It doesn't have *all* of your heart," he muttered, holding her at arm's length. He turned away and walked quickly out of the turret, leaving Elinor, half-undone and gasping for breath, staring after him.

Outrageous. Lord or no lord, William Braddock was truly . . . outrageous. Left alone and spinning from his kiss, Elinor was convinced that he'd stolen the breath from her body. Light-headed and confused, she groped at one of the diamond paned casements and threw it open. An icy gust blew in, lifting her hair, nipping her cheeks, and blowing out the last two candles.

Now she was both alone and in the dark.

"*I remember our first kiss. You came upon me in the gallery. The night was warm. I could not sleep. The first round of sittings was over, and you had already stirred my soul and stolen my heart. You spoke not a word. When you took me in your arms, I knew that we were bound for perdition—that we would be reckless, despite fate's design. Ah, Charles, and I was right.*"

"*I wanted you to come to my bed there and then.*"

"*But it was already too late. Plans had been made, a date set, terms arranged. Your kin were walking the halls in triumph, pleased beyond measure with the match.*"

"*There was no love in that match. On either side.*"

"*No love, but a contract.*"

"*A contract—what is a contract but a scrap to feed the flames?*"

"*Do not say that! A contract is a sacred document.*"

"*Once I saw you, it was you I wanted. You, and no other.*"

"*And you succeeded. Even now I wonder: If my father's horse had not needed a shoe . . . if we had not been forced to stay for one extra night . . . would you have found me?*"

"*Sweet Marianne . . . if your father had carried you off to the farthest reaches of the New World, I would have found you. I was half-mad with desire for you. I would have found you.*"

"*My poor father. I broke his heart. Saddled with a motherless child, he cared for me as a mother would, keeping me ever at his side. And I betrayed him. That night, I snapped the first link in the chain that bound me in trust to him.*"

Chapter 9

$\mathcal{E}$linor waited a moment to calm down, focusing on the night outside rather than the memory of Will Braddock's tongue on hers. But it was no good. Right back to the kiss went her thoughts: she'd never been kissed in the turret before. Her turret. His kiss. Damn, damn, damn! It was a violation of the most personal kind.

If only she had a match. The moon had become obscured by a thick cover of cloud; the darkness was now blackness. Elinor was very conscious that her heart was still pounding unnecessarily hard. She sucked in deep swallows of cold night air, trying to make it right again. After a moment her head seemed clear enough for her to figure out that the kiss had packed a punch because, one, it had come out of the blue and two, it had happened in a magical place.

Somehow it made her feel better to figure that out.

Pulling the casement shut, Elinor locked it against the rising wind and turned to leave. She knew her way around so well that a light was hardly necessary; and yet, like a blind person, she found her hands groping the air in front of her, just to make sure.

But sure of what? That, she did not know, as she moved reluctantly out of the unlit turret and into more blackness: the electric wall sconces had been turned off, and the lone switch that controlled them was at the bottom of the stairs on the third floor. Amazed that Will Braddock could be so thoughtless, Elinor groped the cold stone walls on her way down, her confusion over the kiss now condensed into a small hard knot of tension in the pit of her stomach.

She half expected him to do something terrifyingly stupid, like jumping out at her and yelling "Boo!" But as she progressed step by awkward step, she realized that the prank, if it was a prank, was more elaborate than just the flip of a switch. He'd flipped off more than one: The third-floor hall was dark as well.

She was at the bottom of the stairs. She flipped the switch on. Then off. On. Off. On off. Appalled to think that he might've tampered with a fuse, Elinor tried to convince herself that the hokey wiring in the turret had also shorted out the stairwell lights.

But that didn't account for the hall lamp being off.

No thin sliver of light was shining from under the door of any of the bedchambers on that level; it was always conceivable that everyone was asleep.

But—that didn't account for the hall light being off.

Maybe the problem was from the outside. Maybe the entire castle was without electricity. The wind was rising. A limb could've knocked down a line. That must be it. Pray God.

Again she paused, listening for the sound of his breathing. She was being absurd—she knew she was being absurd—but the sense that someone was aware of her was overwhelming. The hall switch seemed miles away.

Fair Castle had few windows, and they were small; if anything, the darkness on the bedroom level was even more profound. Fighting an awful sense of claustrophobia, Elinor continued to feel her way to her bedchamber, located halfway between the stairs and the light at the far end of the hall. She had a flashlight in her room; she wished it was in her pocket.

The walls of the hall were plastered over roughly; she skimmed them lightly with her hands, cursing the darkness, fearing the spiders. And as for *him*—if he grabbed her now, she'd die.

I won't let him stay, she promised herself. *Not after this. I can make him leave. I know I can.*

The door to Isabelle's room came before her own in

the hall. Elinor stopped in front of it, running her hand across the wainscotted door until she felt the iron latch. Wincing from the effort to be quiet about it, she lifted the latch and swung the heavy door part of the way open.

"Izzy? Are you asleep?"

She was reassured to hear the sound of her sister's untroubled snoring. Isabelle's night-light—a black glazed bust of Darth Vader—was on, its dim red light beaming from the fallen Jedi Knight's eyes and chest piece. Elinor and her mother had both thought it was a terrible concept for a night-light after Chester dragged it home from a flea market six years earlier, but Chester had shrugged off their objections. "It's a knight-light," he'd said, tickled to pieces over the thing. And he was right. Izzy had taken to it on the spot, and ever since then had slept peacefully in its glow.

But . . . it shouldn't be glowing. Not if the hall light was off; they were on the same fuse.

Shit. There went her theory of a fallen limb knocking out the electricity. She was more confused than ever. Definitely disoriented now and definitely more frightened, she swallowed back the lump in her throat and quietly returned the latch of her sister's door into its cradle before creeping the next few feet down the hall to the door of her own bedchamber.

A flashlight will make all the difference, she promised herself. *And when I find out what's going on . . .*

She groped for the latch to her door, then swung the door boldly open. She tried the switch. It was as she suspected. She cringed, because the next move was to walk through impenetrable blackness to the dresser where she kept the flashlight, and she did not want, suddenly, to do that.

She took three or four tentative steps into her room, slashing the air in front of her with her arms. Suddenly the black silence was shattered by a metallic crash from one of the floors below, not unlike the sound of the suit of armor when it got wrestled to the floor by Chester. It was mixed, she thought, with a loud, short cry.

Backing out of her room, Elinor retraced her steps

along the hall in double time, fearless now of anything that might be tempted to go bump in the night. Someone in the house was hurt.

She was halfway down the stone stairs that led to the great hall when the lights went back on and she was confronted by the sight of her stepfather. Again, he was on the floor. Again, he'd been dealt a blow. But this time he was conscious. And stanching the flow of his own blood.

The scene was almost too horrific for Elinor to take in. Chester had his hand clamped to his right shoulder. His hand was covered in blood. His pajamas tops were red with blood. His neck, his beard, smeared with it. Everywhere: blood.

He looked bewildered as he said almost sheepishly, "I've cut myself, El. I forgot about the ladder . . . I knocked it over in the dark . . . and must've caught a sharp edge on it. . . ."

"Chester, oh my God—" Elinor dropped to her knees and took away his hand, heedless of the blood but fighting an urge to be sick. Gently she pulled the collar of his pajama tops to one side. Across his shoulder was a gash three inches long, and deep. Frantically trying to stay calm, she reached under her skirt and pulled off her thin cotton half-slip, then folded it on itself and covered the gash with it, applying pressure to the wound.

Elinor glanced around the room and up the stairs: no one near. She yelled loudly for help, then said, "I'm going to have to call an ambulance, Chester. Can you keep the pressure on it?"

"Oh, yeah, sure," he said. But he seemed too dazed to understand what she meant.

She jumped up anyway to run for the phone and in her haste kicked the executioner's sword halfway across the floor. Why was it on the floor? Elinor didn't take the time to find out, but kept in a headlong sprint for the office. The call was brief—same man, same place—and she was able to return in a minute or two.

She came back to a scene of hysterics. Her mother had arrived, along with the other adults, but Susan Roberts was ill equipped to deal with the sight of blood. It was too much like the other time, the first time. The first husband. The first husband. Elinor rushed to comfort her, as well as to block the view of this second bloodied husband of hers.

"Why, why, why?" Susan cried. "Why is this happening? Why, why, why?" she repeated, over and over and over. It was her mantra—just as before—but it would never bring peace. Just as before.

The thought flashed through Elinor's mind that if the scene were from some episode of "Masterpiece Theatre," she could call the family doctor and he'd be there in no time with a sedative for her mother. But Elinor's family was living only half a fairy tale. They lived in a castle— but they belonged to an HMO. Comfort? Sedation? They'd have to go to the emergency room.

She got her unconsolable mother settled down as best she could while her grandparents saw to their wounded son-in-law. Isabelle, thank God, was still sleeping under the watchful gaze of Darth Vader. As for the Englishman, he was nowhere in sight. Closely observing Chester for signs of shock, Elinor pulled her shaken grandfather aside and asked him what he'd learned.

Mickey MacLeish, shivering in a flannel nightshirt, bent his white-haired head close to Elinor and said in hushed tones, "He says the lights went out just as he was climbing into bed. He figured it was the wind and came down the stairs to start up the generator—didn't want Norwood stumbling around in the dark—but he forgot that the ladder was still propped against the wall, and he knocked it over.

"It must've dislodged the sword; the thing came tumbling down and damn near killed 'im. You know how close it came to the carotid artery?" He held his thumb and forefinger far too close. "He'd have bled to death for sure. As it is, we can thank God the sword wasn't any sharper," he said in consolation. "It would've severed his arm."

Elinor sucked in her breath and said, "Don't tell Mother any of that, Grampa Mick, whatever you do. I'll go with them to the hospital. Would you sleep in my room? I'd feel better about Izzy if you did. Tell Lord

Norwood—if you see him—what happened. Better yet, I'll tell him myself," she said, her voice grim. "Give me a shout if the ambulance arrives."

She charged up the stone stairs from the great hall two at a time, then put on the brakes and stepped silently to the small closet that once had served as an oratory and now housed their guest from hell.

Carefully, she pressed her ear to the door. Silence within. She stood there a moment, uncertain, then tapped the heavy oak barrier between them. And then she knocked. Hard. No one responded.

"Lord Norwood? Hey! Are you in there?"

Of course he was in there; but for obvious reasons he'd chosen not to answer her. Too distracted to be angry, too angry to be determined, Elinor turned away impatiently to rejoin the others. She'd deal with his lordship in the morning.

Eventually Chester got disinfected, sewn up, bundled in gauze, and immobilized. He'd lost a lot of blood; the doctors decided to keep him overnight. Chester, as meek as he was strong, apologized to everyone around him for the trouble he'd caused. It was all his fault, it was dumb to leave the ladder standing, dumber still not to take a flashlight, it was all his fault, would everyone please forgive him.

His eyes, so amazingly blue, were glazed with remorse as he apologized to the nurse, the aide, his wife, Elinor, the nurse, and the aide again after they tucked him in for what was left of the night. The last thing that Chester would ever want to do was cause anyone any inconvenience.

And yet . . . and yet.

Was it Elinor's imagination, or had she seen the same fearful look in his eyes that she had on the day he'd fainted? It was nothing she could hang a label on; but she saw, or thought she saw, something like hesitancy in his face. As if he were second-guessing himself. As if, for the first time, he weren't in that big a hurry to go back to Fair Castle.

Maybe he was simply afraid for his health. He'd turned sixty only four days earlier. Sixty hit some men hard. From sixty, to the fainting, to the near brush with death. Yes, Elinor decided, that would account for the fear in his face. Never mind that Chester was as strong as a bull. It hadn't been a reassuring week.

And in the meantime, there was unfinished business at Fair Castle. Elinor had plenty of time to work herself into a fine rage as she paced the lobby of the small community hospital. Whatever the Englishman's game had been, it had ended up badly, almost fatally. She didn't know whether to confront him—or call the police. She considered asking her grandfather's advice, but the image of his drawn, tired face as they loaded Chester onto the stretcher lingered. She wasn't sure his heart could handle any more stress.

Why would Will Braddock fool with the electricity? What was his aim? Did he think he was going to scare her out of the castle? Could he be that clueless about her? Especially after her impassioned speech in the turret?

Sure he could. His response had been to kiss her. Typical, typical male: He couldn't tell the difference between passion and—well, passion.

Elinor was still pondering her next move when the nobleman walked through the glass door of the sparcely furnished lobby where she and her mother were waiting for their cab. Elinor took one look at him and made up her mind on the spot: *confront the bastard.*

He looked remarkably refreshed for being out and about at three in the morning. Elinor, on the other hand, was fairly sure she looked the way she felt: as if a tractor-trailer had rolled back and forth over her a few times.

Her mother was in much better shape. She sat, quietly now, the sharp-edged elegance of her features softened by tears and lack of sleep. She had thrown on a shirtdress of navy blue, as much to conceal bloodstains as anything else. Her pale hair was pulled back in a simple knot; her mouth, traced lightly with color. Susan Roberts did not endorse the concept of disarray in public places—which

meant that Elinor, with her wild, uncombed hair and di-
sheveled clothing, was making her crazy.

"Here's Lord Norwood—and look at you," she chided
in an undertone as he approached. "You should have realized he'd come."

"Based on *what?*" Elinor retorted, amazed at her
mother's reluctance to let go of the baron as marriage
meat.

Her mother ignored the question and greeted the Englishman with a brave and tremulous smile.

Striking a perfect balance between familiarity and courtesy, he took a seat next to her and expressed sympathy,
surprise, encouragement—all of the things that well-
wishers say, with none of their usual awkwardness. Elinor
watched his performance with a certain amount of admiration: He was a formidable opponent.

He was there, he said, to ferry them home, and Susan
was genuinely grateful. She rose at once when he announced his intention. "You go on ahead with Elinor,"
she told him, "and bring the car around. I'll tell the re-
ceptionist to cancel the cab."

Susan was throwing them together yet again, which was
fine with Elinor; two minutes alone with the baron was
exactly what she needed.

"Why didn't you answer when I knocked on your
door?" she demanded as he held the lobby door for her.

He feigned surprise. "You knocked? I never heard it."

"You know what, your lordship? That's a crock. I
could've brought Dracula out of his coffin, the way I
pounded on that door."

"He'd be out at that hour, I think," the baron answered. He took his keys from his pocket and began leaf-
ing through them as they walked quickly to the Mercedes
parked in the side lot.

She had to jog to keep up with him. "Look, pal, someone was fooling with the fuses last night, and I don't need
a crystal ball to tell me who."

They were at the car now. Before slipping the key in
the door, he took another, loose key from his pocket and
began adding it to the ring.

Elinor noticed it at once. "Where did you get that key?"

"Your grandfather gave it to me."

"He gave you a key? To our *castle?*"

The baron glanced down at it and then at her. With a shrug he said, "I assume it's a key to the castle. It's certainly not the one to your heart."

His quip offended her in six different ways, not the least of which was the tacit allusion to his kiss in the turret. She said, "Give it to me."

Even he was surprised. "Are you serious?"

"You shouldn't have a key," she said in a shaking voice. "It's not right." Her sense of the wrongness of it ran deep.

His laugh was derisive. "Well, I'm sorry you feel that way."

Impulsively, she lunged for the key ring. Angry now, he swung it out of her arm's reach and said, "What an annoying human being you are!"

"At least I *am* a human being!" She grabbed at the ring again; he swung it away again.

He was half a foot taller and longer of limb; there was no way that Elinor was going to be able to reach the keys in his hand. And what would she do if she could? "Fine," she said. "I'll take it up with my grandfather."

She was as close to him as she'd been in the turret: staring straight into those slate blue eyes, torn between fear and contempt, filled with an appalling urge to find out whether the second kiss would be anything like the first.

"Damn you!" she said under her breath. Her right arm was still extended parallel to his chest, toward the key ring. Disgusted, she recoiled from him by doubling her arm back on itself, jabbing her elbow into his sternum.

"Ow! What the devil—!"

"*Sorry,*" she said. The movement had been at least half-accidental.

From behind him Elinor heard Susan Roberts call her name.

"We're over here, Mother," she answered over the baron's shoulder.

"I can see that," said Susan as she approached. She sounded cold and tired and not in the mood for any more drama. She turned to the nobleman and said dryly, "And you were? Practicing Tai Chi, perhaps?"

He laughed a little harshly, then stretched his arm full-length again over his head. "I, ah, was working out a spasm in my shoulder; it goes gimpy on me from time to time." He rubbed his shoulder briskly to prove his point, then opened the door to the passenger side for her.

Elinor's mother was probably too sedated to see the absurdity of his answer. Thoroughly exhausted now, she eased herself into the front seat. Her head fell back on the headrest before the Englishman had a chance to close the door.

Suddenly ashamed of her antics, Elinor climbed meekly into the backseat. She had no idea why she was continuing to behave like an idiot; all she knew was that it had to end. Baron Norwood was entitled to try to buy Fair Castle if he so desired; there was no law against it. She had to trust that her grandparents, her stepfather, and her sister—if not her mother—would never allow it to be sold, to him or to anyone else. No matter how shaky their finances.

Subdued now, and somewhat at peace with herself for the first time since she'd laid eyes on the baron from Berwick-on-Tweed, Elinor leaned her head back on glove-soft leather and let her lids droop shut.

It was a quiet ride home.

Chapter 10

"*It's* true what they say: You really *cannot* get blood out of a stone."

Camilla MacLeish should know. She and Elinor had attacked the spot on the floor of the great hall with everything from ammonia to turpentine, and still a faint, ghostly outline remained of the blood that Chester had spilled.

Camilla squeezed the O-Cedar mop dry, then made one last pass over the spot. She handed the mop to Elinor, and they stepped back to survey the job.

"Maybe when it dries?"

"I'll spray a little more bleach on it."

"You can try that," said Elinor to her grandmother. "But don't let me catch you on your hands and knees with a scrub brush again, Gramma Cam. That's what *I'm* here for."

Camilla arched her back with a healthy moan and said, "Not a chance, dear. The only reason I came down was that I couldn't sleep, thinking about the blood soaking into the floor."

In a musing voice she added, "It all seems very medieval, don't you think? As if Chester had been defending the castle from attack—only there were no attackers; just an ordinary power outage."

Hardly ordinary. Elinor frowned and said, "That reminds me. I have to call the electric company." She lifted the heavy galvanized bucket and began carrying it to the kitchen, slopping water on her jeans as she went.

In front of the wall of portraits, she suddenly paused. "Gramma Cam? How long has that portrait of Lady Norwood been askew? Do you recall?"

Camilla followed her granddaughter's gaze. "Since last night, I suppose," she said, sliding a fallen overall strap back onto her shoulder. "I think I would've noticed it otherwise."

Of the six portraits mounted high, the one of Elinor was the only one that was out of horizontal—so much so that the feathered hat she wore over her blond, waist-length ringlets was no longer at a saucy angle. Her full lips, caught forever in an arrogant smile, now seemed to express mostly dismay.

"Maybe the wind shook it out of whack," Camilla suggested.

Elinor was unconvinced. "The walls here don't exactly wobble when it blows." She added, "The ladder fell nowhere near the portraits, so that wasn't what did it."

"A bird might've got in and perched on the frame. We've had that happen before."

"And move it that much? It'd have to be a Canadian goose; that gilt frame is heavy."

"True." The two women stared at the portrait, each with her own thoughts. "Isn't she beautiful," Camilla said after a moment. "I sometimes forget."

"Was she beautiful? Women did not think so. They saw what the men did not: that she cared only for wealth. And where is the beauty of that?"

Elinor snapped out of her uneasy revery. "It's true," she said. "After a while your eyes pass over familiar things without seeing them."

Mop in one hand, bucket in the other, Elinor sighed and added wistfully, "I always assumed that since she's my namesake, I'd grow up to look exactly like her: my hair would turn blond, my eyes become blue; and as for my clothes..."

She brushed her hair away from her eyes with a forearm, then glanced down at her baggy jeans and oversized

T-shirt and let out a rueful laugh. "Shows you what *I* know."

"You're certainly as pretty as she is," Camilla reassured her. "In a darker, more tomboy sort of way. Your problem is, you don't know how to flirt. Whereas my guess is that Lady Norwood was willing and able to flirt if it suited her."

"*I* could flirt if it suited me," Elinor protested.

Camilla laughed. "You? I don't think so. I've watched you interact with every boyfriend you've ever had—except for the one who turned out to be married, and the less said about *him*, the better," she said grimly. "But with all the others? I've not seen a hint of flirting on your part. Maybe that's why your boyfriends always end up being your pals."

It was distressing for Elinor to be told that, even more so when she felt and looked like a bag lady. "What's the big deal about flirting?" she said defensively. "You bat your eyelashes at someone a few times, that's all."

"Oh my dear, there's more to it than that. You have to be willing to promise a man . . . at least, to hint to him . . . that you'd be thrilled to submit to his mastery."

"Submit! Mastery! That's not flirting. That's acting like a cocker spaniel on its back, waiting for a belly rub."

Camilla smiled and said, "I rest my case."

"I'm not going to do that," said Elinor, bringing her chin up. "It's too . . . wily."

"I know, dear."

"I'm the equal of any man. Why should I have to pretend I'm not?"

"Because. That way they don't ever know what hit them."

"Why can't I just be direct?"

"It scares them."

"That's crazy. This is the millenium. Men are supposed to be enlightened."

"That's one theory."

Elinor was more bothered by her grandmother's remarks than she was willing to admit. "You're just being extremely old-fashioned, Gramma Cam," she said at last.

"Maybe."

They gazed at the painting together for another long moment.

Camilla said, "Isn't it odd that Lord Norwood has never said a word about either of the portraits? Your grandfather thinks he's too proud to bring them up." She hesitated, then added, "I believe he intends to make a present of the pair to him."

"What? But they belong in the castle!"

"But in a way the castle belongs—well, your grandfather hasn't made up his mind yet." Frowning through an uncharacteristic blush, Camilla studied the lopsided frame. "I'll get my pruning pole," she said at last. "I think I can just reach high enough to nudge it straight."

By the time the electric company opened for business—and by the time Elinor was able to work her way through the maze of their voice mail—the family had scattered for the day. It was a Thursday; the castle was closed on Thursdays.

Susan Roberts had gone to the hospital to get her husband. Izzy was off at school. Camilla MacLeish was taking advantage of the mild day to divide a few perennials. And Mickey MacLeish, still not recovered from a night in someone else's bed, had decided to crawl back into his own.

When Elinor went in to breakfast, she found Lord Norwood sitting with a cup of coffee and the paper. The buffet had been cleared, but the smell of bacon and waffles lingered, fanning the pangs of Elinor's hunger and resentment. Thursday was big-breakfast day. If she hadn't had to check with the utility—if it hadn't been for the wretched man sitting in her chair—she would've been on time to eat.

"Good morning," she said in a chilly voice. "I don't suppose that Agnes is around."

"Long gone," he said, glancing up from the paper. "Good morning."

She went over to the sideboard and lifted the coffee thermos. "No more coffee?"

"Ah." He held up his cup in apology. "Sorry about that."

"You needn't apologize; I know how to make my own."

His glance lingered until it became a gaze. "You look very fetching this morning."

"Thank you," Elinor said. She had on a cashmere tunic in pale lavender, which she wore over black stretch pants. She'd put on her best perfume, and pale eye shadow to complement the sweater. Elinor knew she looked good; she wanted to look good.

True, she was still smarting from the "tomboy" label her grandmother had pinned to her. But it was also true that after spending the dawn cleaning Chester's blood-stains from the castle floor, she felt a deep need to be clean and fresh and feminine and most of all—alive.

It had nothing to do with Lord Norwood and *definitely* nothing to do with his kiss.

To prove it, Elinor forced herself to bring up the awkward subject of the power failure. "I think you should know that I called the electric company just now."

He'd gone back to the financial section of the *Times*. Now he looked up. "Yes?" he said mildly.

"They told me that there were in fact several outages in the area during last night's wind."

"Yes?"

"Well—I didn't know that. I saw that Izzy's Darth Vader night-light was on, and yet all the other lights were out in the castle."

"And?"

Her cheeks became flushed with annoyance. "I didn't realize that her Darth Vader night-light has its own battery pack now."

"So?"

"So naturally you can see why I thought someone had been tampering with the fuse box."

"Ah. The fuse box. You did say something about that in the parking lot last night—no, I'm wrong. This morning."

"Yes, yes, I'm aware that it was the middle of the night,

and we're oh-so-grateful that you came to pick us up," she said, unwilling to sound grateful at all.

"You'll forgive me for asking, but why, exactly, was I supposed to have been fiddling with the fuses?"

"To scare me, of course. Into wanting to sell."

He laughed out loud at that. "That dent is deeper than I thought."

She deserved that, she supposed. But it still hurt. She bowed her head and stared at the top of the chair she gripped, not so much to focus her thoughts as to resist his dark magnetism. When she looked up at him again, it was to say, almost humbly, "If you want the castle, please . . . just say so. Don't keep me guessing."

"All right. I want the castle."

"You *can't* want the castle!" she cried. "You can't! Yesterday you said you only wanted a good look around."

"That was a rhetorical statement."

"You implied to my family that you weren't really serious!"

"If that's what everyone inferred, it isn't true. I want the castle."

"*Why?* It's so stupid! So expensive! It would be cheaper to build a reproduction, Lord Norwood, honestly. We're not in the Great Depression anymore; labor is no longer free. We have unions, a minimum wage, a genuine shortage of peasants over here! It would be a phenomenal undertaking, a colossal waste of money. Can't you think of anything else to do with your fortune? Can't you buy a Van Gogh, fund a museum, run for office? Why don't you take your cue from someone like Bill Gates. He built his palace from scratch!"

"I want the castle."

"I'll never let you have it!" she cried, railing now. "Didn't you hear anything I said last night? Fair Castle is more than a roof over our heads. It's what binds us together as a family. Without it my grandparents would be in a rest home, my mother in some condo, and me—"

He cut into her tirade. "It's that *me* part that's your real concern, isn't it? The rest is all rationalizing."

"Rationalizing? That's ridiculous! I don't need Fair

Castle; I have a perfectly fine apartment in New York."

"Your grandfather tells me you hate the city; that you escape up here every chance you get. And that your two-year sublet of the flat is nearly up. I don't doubt your love for the castle, Miss MacLeish," he added, tossing down the *Times* and rising from his chair. "But I happen to think you're more selfish than noble."

"*I'm*—!" Elinor was beside herself with frustration. "What about *you*? What's *your* motive? I suppose you plan to turn Fair Castle into a leper colony once you get it back to England?"

Oh, he was fed up with her; she could see it in his eyes. The thought cut through her like a saber, swift and clean. It hardly even hurt. She blazed her angry contempt at him, waiting for an answer to her challenge.

He was more than willing to deliver it. His cheeks were ruddy with outrage as he splayed his hands on the table and glowered at her.

"You cheeky little twit," he said with deadly calm. "What do *you* know about my motives? Not a damned thing. You go flouncing around, tossing off pretty little speeches about love and family, about how many of your generations have prospered here, about what it all means to you—all the while, oblivious to anyone else's claim.

"My ancestors lived in this castle for over four hundred years," he continued, his voice rising in anger now. "Have you any idea how many generations that entails? *Twenty-six*. Twenty-eight, if my grandfather hadn't buggered it. That's a lot of bedtime stories, Miss MacLeish; a *lot* of nursery rhymes."

Elinor fought back. "But they aren't *your* memories," she said hotly. "They're ghosts of memories!"

"Listen! I've had more relatives die in this castle than you will have acquaintances in your lifetime! So don't go all poignant about what Fair Castle means to you personally. Because that won't mean a bloody thing to me! Show me your ghosts—and then we'll talk!"

She shook her head, devastated by his contempt. Tears welled up. "You bastard," she said in a choked, angry whisper. "You want ghosts? Fine. Look around for my father's, in that case. He should qualify. He was killed—maybe murdered—ten years ago!" Her lip began to tremble. "I assume that gives him the right to haunt these halls?" Tears rolled out, unwanted, unheeded. "You rotten—"

He'd done it: He'd broken her. She hated him for that; for prompting the memory, for making her call up the memory.

She was one tear away from breaking down into a fit of sobbing when they were interrupted, amazingly, by Tucker O'Toole.

He hung back at the threshold of the room, obviously reluctant to come in. "Hello? Hi, again," he said with a wince of embarrassment. "I saw Camilla MacLeish in the garden, and she told me to go right in. I heard voices and—"

"You felt a need to add your own?" the baron replied with a glacial stare.

Tucker took one glance at Elinor's tear-streaked face and considerately looked away. "I'm sorry," he said with obvious feeling for her. "This is a bad time."

His gaze came to rest on her adversary. "You must be Lord Norwood," he said, regarding him with cool disapproval. "I understand you're staying here as well?"

"I am."

Elinor watched as the two men sized one another up in silence. They were about the same height and build, but any resemblance ended there. Tucker O'Toole, with his Irish good looks, was younger by a decade and in his prime. Unlike the Englishman, he was surprisingly open about his feelings. Right now, the feeling she saw was hostility.

Lord Norwood, more ruggedly handsome, clearly showed the burden of his extra years. He'd earned himself a fabulous fortune, and it had taken a toll. There was a jaded, weary quality about him. All else was hidden behind a veil of reserve.

The castle wasn't big enough for both men; that was Elinor's first, instinctive reaction. Good. Tucker might be just the ally she needed.

"Well, gentlemen?" she drawled, merely to break the stillness.

Tucker was the first to react. "Guess I'll take my bag to my room and unpack," he said. "I want to get started in the archives room as soon as I can."

"Whereas I," said his lordship with a sardonic smile, "have nothing special planned for the morning. I was thinking of doing a little archiving myself. The room's a treasure trove for the browser."

Tucker nodded curtly. "I'll see you there, no doubt."

"No doubt at all," said the baron.

Tucker picked up his heavy nylon duffel bag and threw it over his shoulder. With a last, sympathetic glance at Elinor, he headed for the stairs.

Lord Norwood took up the financial section of the *Times* and said to her, "If you should see your grandfather before I do, tell him I'm looking forward to going over the schematics with him."

Elinor lifted her chin and looked him straight in the eye. "That's not all I'll tell him."

He slapped the newspaper lazily against his thigh and said, "Here's a lesson I learned early in life, Miss MacLeish: Everything, sooner or later, is for sale. There are no exceptions to that rule. Your grandfather will not see me as the villain you do. So tell away," he said evenly. "It'll bring me closer to my goal."

"The game is joined, my love. Only one of them can win the prize."

"Let them play their hands, each with his own fierce skill. It matters not, Marianne. It will end the same."

Chapter 11

$\mathcal{E}$linor expected dinner to be a tense, silent affair, but in fact it was just the opposite. Chester was so happy to be the center of attention that he affected everyone with his mood.

Like some tame, wooly bear, he sat contentedly with his right arm immobilized in a bright blue sling while all around him women vied to take care of him. Susan fussed and Camilla hugged and Elinor teased—but it was Izzy who got to cut up his food and guide it, airplane-style, into his mouth.

"Okay, Dad, what next? Broccoli, potatoes, or steak?"

He beamed happily. "Gosh, that's a tough one: steak."

Izzy did a dead-on imitation of her mother's frown and said, "All right, but next has to be a vegetable."

Chester, for his part, had his stepdaughter's manner-isms down cold. "Do I hafta?" he said in Izzy's nasal whine. "Broccoli smells so bad."

"Broccoli is good for you. Lots of vitamins. Now don't give me any trouble."

And so it went, in a whimsical reversal of roles that had everyone, even Susan, smiling. Elinor divided her attention between the lighthearted vignette and a discussion that had cropped up at the other end of the table between Lord Norwood, her grandfather, and Tucker O'Toole.

They were talking about ghosts.

If it had been Will who'd brought up the subject so soon after their furious exchange, Elinor would've felt outrage; but it was her grandfather who'd opened the subject by saying, "You mean to tell me that in four hundred years, not a single ghost has had the decency to show up and scare the bejezuz out of one of you Norwoods?"

Mickey MacLeish was feeling mellow and just a little on the puckish side. He took off his ever-present beret and hung it over a chair post, then topped off the wineglasses of his two guests and added a splash to his own.

"You mean to say," he added as he leaned back in his chair, "that there are no legends of the supernatural attached to your clan? What the hell kind of a castle were you people running?"

Elinor's eyes opened a little wider; her grandfather was pushing it. She glanced at Will to see how he'd take the prodding and was amazed, quite amazed, when he laughed it off with grace and good will.

Hypocrite! After his bitter putdown of her claim to the castle; after his impassioned defense of his own claim—to act as if it were all a lark!

"If there were any such legends, they died out long ago," the baron answered with something like regret. His glance slid past Elinor as he said to his host, "And you, sir? Have you ever seen anything?"

"Oh, well . . . that's different," said the old man, glancing at his wife. He rubbed his chin pensively. "Sometimes you think—eh, nothing," he said gruffly. "At our age, you run across your own shadow, and you realize that there but for the beat of your own heart . . ."

He shook his head free of the notion and said, "Hey, at the end of the table—more wine?"

The women waved the bottle away. Then Izzy looked up at her grandfather with wide, innocent eyes and said, "I think *I've* seen a ghost, Grampa Mick."

Camilla laughed and said to Will and Tucker, "My granddaughter is the clairvoyant in the family. Tell Lord Norwood and Mr. O'Toole about the fairies, sweetie."

"The ones who play in the maze?" asked the young girl. "I see them all of the time. Well, I used to, when I was younger. But now they don't show themselves to me, because I'm older. But we're still friends."

"It's true," said Chester with a wink at their guests. "Izzy used to drag me by the hand through that overgrown mess and point them out, one by one. What were their names, Iz? Merilee and James and Ingrid and the one with green hair—?"

Izzy speared a piece of her stepfather's steak and said matter-of-factly, "You mean Fergus. He likes Ingrid, but she likes Pantella. But they're all friends. Well, that's the last piece of steak, Dad. Now all that's left is broccoli. Or *no* dessert."

Chester pretended to grouse. "All right. Shovel it in. But after this I feed myself."

He turned to the cook, who had begun gathering the plates. "Agnes? Can you put my ice cream in a heavy bowl so that it won't slide around?"

Agnes snorted. Presumably that meant she'd think about it.

Izzy spoke up again. "But I mean a real *ghost*, Grampa Mick. Not fairies."

Her statement swept every other crumb of conversation right off the table. It got her the undivided attention of everyone in the room, even Agnes, who became very, very still.

The silence was broken by Susan, who said to her daughter with a nervous laugh, "What ghost, silly girl? You've never said anything about a ghost."

Isabelle tucked her hair behind her ears and frowned in concentration, pursing her lips and staring into some middle distance as if she were replaying a tape of the event. Elinor and the others watched and waited with profound interest—especially Agnes, whose habitually compressed lips had fallen open in an odd expression of wariness.

At last the child said, "Yes. I really think I did. I wasn't exactly sure, but now I am. It was just too real. Not real like this broccoli," she said, stabbing a piece on Chester's fork and holding it up for the company to see. "But real like when you read a book, and you see things so clearly?"

Camilla said with a smile, "That's a perfect description of the imagination, Izzy."

"See *what,* for heaven's sake!" Susan said. "What exactly did you see so clearly? Describe it to me."

Badgered that way by her mother, Isabelle began at once to falter. "Well . . . it's hard to say, exactly . . . it was more like out the corner of my eye . . . a kind of . . . like a . . . it shimmered," she summed up with an unhappy look. "I'm not describing it very good, am I?"

"Isabelle? Where did you see this shimmering thing?"

The question came from Lord Norwood. He was interested in the answer, that was obvious. Elinor could see it in the casual way he posed the question; in the friendly, reassuring smile on his handsome, craggy face.

"In the chapel," Isabelle said promptly; apparently it was easier to say *where* it was than *what* it was. "I was reading a Fear Street book—you know, the one where the boyfriend's a vampire?—and I thought it would be more fun to be in the chapel because, um, it's kind of scary there, you know?"

"Never mind Fear Street, Isabelle," said Susan sharply. "Let's get to the bottom of this silliness. Where in the chapel?"

"Well . . . in the aisle between the front pews. I was on the left side and I saw it . . . like here," she said, groping the air to the right of her without turning her head. "But when I turned to look, it was gone. But it was there," she insisted, digging in her heels the way she was capable of doing. "I could feel it. Almost."

"Feel *what,* child? How can you feel a ghost? This is *very* disrespectful."

Of what, Susan didn't say; but she was close to sending her daughter to bed without dessert. She knew, and Elinor knew—everyone knew—that Isabelle had a wildly active imagination.

By now Isabelle realized that she was getting herself in trouble. She was too honest to lie and say she was making it all up; all she could do was backtrack into a puddle of vagaries and stand there looking uncomfortable.

"I could feel, it was like, maybe cold?" She sighed in

distress. "Or maybe I didn't feel cold. Maybe it was the air that felt cold, and not my skin having goose bumps; I'm not sure ..."

Elinor stepped in to give her young sister a hand. "For Pete's sake, Izzy, you were reading a Fear Street book in the chapel. Of course you'd have goose bumps. Every time I go in there, I feel goose bumps. Lots of people feel that way in chapels and churches. Your reaction is perfectly normal—isn't it, Gramma Cam?"

Camilla MacLeish could be counted on to back Elinor on virtually any position she took, and this was no exception. She said, "I've had that exact reaction. Once I saw a column of vapor rising in front of the pews. I nearly jumped out of my skin, until I realized it was cigar smoke left by your grandfather, who'd just passed through. Remember, Mickey?"

Mickey MacLeish nodded ruefully and said, "I remember the cigars, you bet I do. Those were the days."

He threw Elinor a friendly glance of warning not to snitch on him, then said, "Speaking of which, there's no law won't let me offer my Havanas to men who have no *wives* to cower from. What d'you say we take ourselves off to the library, boys. Tucker? You enjoy a fine cigar now and then?"

Tucker O'Toole had hardly said a word all through the meal. Shyness, thought Elinor at first; but then she realized that he was simply getting his bearings before saying anything stupid.

Think before you speak. Her mother had told her that a million times. Elinor had never bothered to learn the lesson and neither, obviously, had Izzy. She had the sense that Tucker O'Toole was smarter than either of them.

He said, "I don't smoke, Mr. MacLeish, but my father did. It still gives me pleasure to be in the company of those who do. It would be an honor to join you."

Very nice, thought Elinor approvingly. *Score one for the commoners.* She glanced at her mother with a meaningful, thoroughly irritating smile.

Her grandfather said, "Norwood, you'll have to light up for the both of us." He stood up; the guests did, too.

"Take the bottle, take the bottle," he said to Tucker. "No sense letting a perfectly good burgundy go to waste."

Elinor, annoyed at being cut out of the boys' tree house again, said with sweet petulance, "Can't I come, too?"

Mickey MacLeish snorted. "You! What for? You don't smoke, you don't drink, you've probably never even had—"

"Grampa *Mick!*"

"Oh, all right, whatever. It's none of my business," he said, slapping both men on their shoulders. "Let's get out of this wimmin's nest." He turned back to his son-in-law. "Chester? You coming?"

Chester considered. On the one hand, fine drink; smoke; conversation. On the other, a bowl of mint chocolate chip. "I think I'll pass, this time around," he said, rubbing his bearded neck with his free hand.

"Suit yourself," said his father-in-law.

Muttering about sugar junkies, the aging artist retrieved his beret and shuffled in his elegantly baggy pants out of the dining chamber, followed by his guests. Immediately Camilla, who hated to linger at supper when there was gardening indoors or out to be done, excused herself.

Right after that, Elinor's mother left the room to chase after the cook, who seemed to have a new bug up her nose. Susan was barely out of earshot when Elinor said to her sister, "What were you thinking, Izzy? You know better than to say stuff like that in front of Mom!"

"Elly's right, Iz," said their stepfather. "You dodged a bullet there. It could've been a lot worse. Lucky your grandmother came to your rescue." With his left hand, he began practicing his grip on a teaspoon.

"But I did see something, El," said her sister plaintively. "I really did."

"When?" demanded Elinor. It wasn't the kind of thing that Izzy would've forgotten to mention.

"Last night, after supper. I was done with my homework and I wanted to read just for fun. So I put on my sweater that Gramma Cam made and I went into the chapel and . . . and I lit a candle instead of turning on a light—"

"Good lord," said Chester. "You can read by candle-light? Gawd; I'm old."

Izzy's keen eyesight was not the first thing that sprang to Elinor's mind. "You shouldn't be doing stunts like that," she said, sounding a lot like her mother. "You could burn the place down."

"How could I do that?" said Isabelle, a little sullenly. "It's a stone castle."

"It has wood things inside! And flammable people!"

Oh, yes; just like her mother. Elinor made herself pull out of the scold and say lightly, "So how come I didn't hear about this apparition, hmm?"

Isabelle looked more uneasy than ever. "I would've told you this morning, but—"

"But?"

"But it wasn't like the fairies, El," she whispered. "It wasn't *anything* like the fairies."

Her eyes were big, not with wonder, but with anxiety. And suddenly Izzy wasn't ten years old anymore. Chester picked up on it, too. Elinor saw it in his face: worry. Izzy was everyone's baby, the darling of their hearts. She was too young, too sheltered—too loved—to have to know fear. Fear was for inner-city kids. Fear was for pregnant teenagers.

"Izzy, listen to me," said Elinor, beating a soft drumbeat on the table with the palms of her hands to reinforce her message. "Out of all of us, you're the one with the most imagination. Gramma Cam was right, you know. You have tons and tons of it. That's a really good thing; someday you're going to be a professional writer, I just know it.

"But what you saw was—in some ways—what you expected to see. We all know how spooky this place can be. It's usually kind of fun, especially on Fright Night. You remember what a great Frankenstein Grampa Mick made a couple of years ago? All your friends were terrified when he answered the door—and after they went home they could hardly wait for the next Halloween."

Elinor smiled confidentially and said, "But there are times when it all gets to be a little too much. I can go back to New York to get away from it, but this is where you live, honey. Day in, day out. So naturally you're going to see—"

"Ghosts," murmured Izzy with downcast eyes.

"It's like this," said Elinor. "If you lived in the Bronx, you'd have a Bronx accent. If you lived in Louisiana, you'd have a Louisiana accent. But you live in a castle," she said gaily. "You have a ghost accent!"

Isabelle looked up. She got it. Her eyebrows, wide and unshaped, lifted in understanding. "You mean, if I moved out of the castle, I wouldn't see ghosts anymore?"

"Nope!"

Elinor said it with far more confidence than she felt. There were too many odd goings-on in the last few days; too many eerie sensations. Was there a pattern to them? That's what she wanted to find out. And she would; but right now, Izzy needed to be reassured.

"So . . . are you okay on this?" she asked the young girl softly.

Isabelle managed a noncommittal smile. "I think so," she answered. "Maybe I shouldn't read in the chapel."

"Not by candlelight, anyway. Now scram, before Mom comes back," said Elinor. "We'll have dessert together in your room."

"Okay." Isabelle took off, then suddenly fetched up short and turned around. "But . . . El? There's a girl in our class from Georgia, and she still talks with a Georgia accent."

"Oh, sure, for now. But that'll go away. Look at Chester," Elinor said, with a grand sweep of her arm in his direction. "He doesn't have an Ohio accent anymore."

Isabelle cheered up again. "That's right!" Off she went.

Chester, who'd been listening in silence, said, "Ohians don't have accents, El."

Elinor laughed uneasily. "Hey, I was winging it."

Chester lapsed into silence again as Elinor gathered up the last of the dishes from the table. She had a stack of saucers in one hand, a nest of cups in the other and was about to carry them to the kitchen when Chester said, "Elly . . . there's something I've been meaning to say."

The words were ominous enough; but the tone—the tone is what made Elinor set the cups carefully down, and then the saucers, and then take her seat again. She remembered, long afterward, the fearful look on her stepfather's face as he murmured, "I think I know what Isabelle's talking about."

In a low, utterly meek voice Elinor said, "You saw something in the chapel, too?"

Chester shook his head. "Not in the chapel. It was right before I fainted—God, I thought wild horses wouldn't be able to drag this out of me.

"But, Elly," he said, glancing at the door, "there were too many similarities with Izzy's experience. The rush of cold air . . . the sense that there was something just beyond my peripheral vision . . . the, I don't know, just plain creepy feeling. It was just . . . plain . . . *creepy*," he repeated with a visible shudder. "That's what Izzy was trying to tell us, El. I know."

Elinor remembered the dark. Groping her way in the dark. The incredibly crawly feeling she had, cold and alone in the dark.

She searched her stepfather's broad, bearded face for some hint that he didn't believe his own tale. "This isn't funny, Chester," she said faintly. "This isn't Fright Night."

"I'm not trying to pull your leg, honey. I didn't want to say anything because, well, you see for yourself how dumb it sounds. But—"

The sound of footsteps turned his look of pleading into a scowl of warning. "Not a word!" was all he had time to say before his wife marched in, looking for Isabelle.

"Well, I hope everyone's happy," said Susan in a frigid voice. "Agnes has quit. You've all been after her from the start, and now she's quit!"

"Mother, it's no great loss," Elinor said, purposely sounding bored and low-key. "Agnes hated the job, hated us, and not incidentally, hated cooking. There has to be someone out there more qualified than that."

"Really? Suppose you take the time to find her, in that case. I have my hands full with the meeting of the Renaissance Society coming up—how do you suppose we're going to manage, with no cook?"

Chester said, in his typically mild way, "I can't figure why she'd quit. She seemed to be getting the hang of us."

Susan turned impatiently to her husband. "She refuses to work in a haunted house!"

"Haunted house? She refuses to work in a kitchen!" Elinor retorted.

Chester laughed, a little too loudly, and Elinor diverted her mother's wrath by jumping up and saying, "Has she left yet?"

"She's packing her things," her mother answered tersely.

"They're probably *our*—never mind," said Elinor. "I'll fix everything. Leave it to me."

Half an hour later, Elinor emerged from her round with Agnes unsure whether she'd won it or lost it. The good news was, Agnes had agreed to stay on. The bad news was, they had to promise her unemployed son a job as handyman. Elinor had met the son. Of the two, Agnes had the more cheerful disposition and the stronger work ethic.

Well, it couldn't be helped. Anything to avert another crisis. Since Agnes had been too upset to finish cleaning up, Elinor went back to the kitchen to load the Maytag with dishes and scrub the big pots by hand. It was late by the time she peeked in on the library; all that remained there were some cigar butts, dirty glasses, and an empty bottle of burgundy.

Nursing her role as scullery maid, Elinor gathered up the mess and returned to the kitchen with it, and then, after double-checking all the doors and windows, made herself a cup of hot chocolate to take back to her room.

Poor Izzy—who'd given up a while ago on the idea of dessert in her room with her big sister—had come, got her ice cream, and gone. By now she was asleep, hopefully with sweeter dreams than she'd had the night before. Elinor would not disturb her.

What was going on? The question had held front and center of Elinor's consciousness ever since Isabelle's blurted confession at the table. Were the fainting and the blackout and Izzy's vision—and the tilted portrait, for that matter—connected in any way, shape, or form? Or were they completely separate events, each of them explainable in a different way, all of them rational.

True, the electric company had accounted for the blackout. And Chester's fainting spell could've been caused by his general state of excitement over the suit of armor, coupled with his skipping breakfast that day. The portrait on its ear? Maybe Chester knocked it accidentally when he was setting up the ladder. As for Izzy's vision—well, Izzy. She had visions. And Chester, as suggestible as they came, would've decided in retrospect that he'd had one, too.

That left the sense of overwhelming dread that Elinor herself had felt after Will Braddock left the turret. The dread: It had been irrational, pervasive, unlike anything she'd felt before.

The dread. Was it possible to feel it again? Elinor found her footsteps slowing as she passed the chapel. On an impulse, she reversed her course and stood at the threshold of the narrow vaulted room. Still balancing the cup of hot chocolate on its saucer, she hesitated for a long moment, peering inside. Should she go in?

Something about the sweet, familiar aroma of the hot chocolate wafting up to her nostrils made the thought of dread seem silly. There was no place for dread in Fair Castle. It was her beloved home.

She stepped onto the slate floor of the chapel, her soft-soled shoes leaving no echo as she made her way to the front of the pews on the left side. She took a seat, as Izzy had, next to the aisle. The glow from a bronze art deco lamp in the shape of an angel was all the light Elinor needed to see everything clearly. She knew it all by heart, anyway; knew every square inch of every worn brick.

She sat and sipped hot chocolate for a minute or two in the jeweled shadow of the triple lancet window that took up the entire front wall of the narrow chapel. The window, which faced the morning sun, guaranteed that the chapel would shine bright and dispel a dark mood. At least in the morning.

But now it was night. Something made Elinor want the scene to be an exact repeat of the one that Izzy had created for herself. She set the hot chocolate alongside her on the bench, then retrieved a long fireplace match from a deep pewter cup that sat on a walnut table, meant to evoke an altar, that stood under the lancet window. Striking the match against one of the bricks, she lit a thick cylinder of wax that sat impaled on an iron stand, one of several in the chapel that were original to the castle.

And then she turned off the little bronze lamp.

The candle, forced to do the work of modern science, wasn't up to the job. Immediately Elinor found herself straining to see as she made her way back to her seat in the pew. Chester was right. It was no small miracle that Izzy had been able to read by the light of a single taper. Maybe she'd lit more than one. But no. The wicks on the others, Elinor remembered, were unscorched; the candles were merely props for the tour.

So this was it. Izzy and one candle in a narrow, vaulted chapel, dominated by a beautiful stained-glass window. Was it enough to create an apparition?

Elinor tried to remember herself at ten. It was such an impressionable age. She did remember being awed by the centuries of people who must've prayed in the little chapel. And been baptized there. And married there.

And had eulogies said over their coffined bodies there. It had always been hard not to think of that last, sad rite. Even now, at thirty, Elinor was grateful that the wake for her father could not have been held there. She wanted no sad memories directly connected to her castle.

What a chicken you are about death, she told herself, sighing. She knew why that was so; but it didn't make her any more brave. She let her attention drift up to the stained-glass window, though it scarcely showed as more than blobs of blue and red and amber in the dim glow of the candle.

She sighed again, and offered a prayer. *Let them live forever,* she begged. *I love them all so much. We never had* him, *so . . . somehow . . . some way . . . let the others live forever. Amen.*

She closed her eyes to back up her prayer and let herself drift on a sea of pensive melancholy. And after a while, when her thoughts became still to the point of serenity, she became aware . . . that she was not alone in the chapel.

Chapter 12

*E*linor sucked in her breath and held it, too frozen with fear to exhale. Every muscle tightened, every hair stood on end. In the desperate silence she heard nothing; nothing but the thunder of her heart.

Oh, God. Without moving her head, she tried to see to the left, much as Izzy must have done. Her eyes ached from the effort. She wanted nothing more than to bolt and run; but she was afraid.

After a moment she heard a whisper that sounded like the scrape of dried leaves: *sorry*. Then silence. And then, louder this time: "Would you like me to leave?"

Human! Elinor's breath, held too long, slid out on a moan of relief as she swung her gaze to the back of the chapel. "God! Tucker! You scared me half to death!"

He was standing just inside the chapel, looking guilty as a peasant who's been caught poaching rabbits. "I'd intended to go outside for some air," he explained, "but everything was bolted up tight and I didn't want to undo it. I saw a light from here flickering into the hall, and you know the rest: I scared you half to death," he said with winsome remorse.

"No, no," Elinor said, more relieved than she could've imagined. "Come in. I was just . . . sitting." She slid her cup and saucer farther down the pew and scooted over to make room for him.

He came and sat down next to her on the narrow, upright oak bench. He said quietly, "I was thinking of Izzy's story."

"Oh, Izzy," said Elinor with a soft laugh.

"I believed her."

"*Did* you!"

He shrugged off her surprise. "I suppose it's the Irish part of me. She hooked me with the faeries, then convinced me about the vision." He added, "It *is* a chapel, after all."

Elinor assumed that Tucker was motivated not so much by spiritual beliefs as by whimsical ones. She liked that in him, that gentleness. It reminded her in some odd way of Chester.

Smiling, she said, "I feel like a failure, in that case. I've never seen either the faeries or the ghost."

"Hey, let's stick around for a while. The night is young. Who knows who'll show up?"

She laughed. Chapel or no chapel, it seemed all right to do it. "Tucker O'Toole, you're like a breath of fresh air," she told him. "You arrived at Fair Castle in the nick of time."

"I meant it about sticking around," he insisted. His smile was warm and at ease.

She stole a glance at him in profile: what a great-looking guy. Her age, laid back, unpretentious. No wonder her mother had no use for him. He was the exact opposite of Lord Norwood of Dibble, her mother's current number-one choice for son-in-law.

Tough. "By the way," Elinor said, "how'd it go in the archive room this afternoon? Did the nobleman from hell show up as threatened?"

Tucker snorted. "What's with that guy? He treats me as if I'm on a prison furlough. Does he understand that I've come here with a scholarly purpose, and not to steal the family jewels?"

"Family jewels! Surely you jest, sir. Those got hocked to repair the slate roof last year. Anyway, just ignore him. That's what I do," she said, mustering a breezy tone.

It didn't work. Tucker saw right through it. "He got under your skin, though, this afternoon, didn't he?" he suggested softly.

"Well . . . yes," she admitted. "We don't see eye to eye on a very big issue."

"Buying Fair Castle?"

Elinor grimaced. "I suppose it's no secret. Did the three of you talk about it over cigars and brandy?"

"Your grandfather was pretty coy. I had the impression he enjoys having someone lusting after his castle. He kept saying things like, 'I want this place to go to someone who will love it the way I do.' And Norwood kept saying things like, 'I understand completely, sir.' "

"That suck-up!"

Tucker shrugged. "I have to admit, the guy sounds like he means it. What's the story with him, anyway? How did his family lose Fair Castle in the first place? And why the hell does he want it back?"

"I don't know, I don't know," Elinor said in a soft wail. "It seems to have some kind of symbolic importance to him. His grandfather blew the family fortune, and now Will—Lord Norwood—has earned it back, and the castle has become some kind of grail at the end of his quest."

"So he wants to ship it back to England, stone by stone." Tucker shook his head in wonder. "Amazing. How could anyone be that obsessed with appearances?"

"Yes, yes, that's what I keep telling everyone! It's so dumb. He wants the castle for all the wrong reasons; it makes me want to scream."

Tucker shifted his position on the bench so that he was able to face her more directly. His voice was low and sincere and urgent as he said, "Listen, you can't let this guy get to you. I saw your face this morning in the breakfast room; you looked as if you'd been slapped."

Elinor lowered her head and stared at her hands lying listlessly in her lap. "That wasn't his fault, exactly. He stirred a very painful memory. He couldn't have realized it."

"About your father," Tucker murmured.

She raised her gaze to meet his. The candle, caught in

a draft, began to stretch and flicker wildly, throwing jumpy shadows in the air. "You heard me, then."

"I couldn't not hear."

She winced. "I'm not surprised. The good citizens of Berwick-on-Tweed probably heard me."

With a sharp little sigh of resolve, she decided to explain. "My father was killed by a hit-and-run driver as he was jogging less than a mile from here," she said. "That would've been tragic enough. But it's always seemed worse—at least to me—because my dad had just reconciled with my mother after a thirteen-year separation."

Quick to comprehend, Tucker said, "Which explains the big age gap between you and Izzy."

"Most of it, anyway. My dad left my mother when I was five. I don't know what he did for the next thirteen years. I don't know where he went. I know he drank . . . I know he gambled. He was in sales for a while . . . and God knows what else. Once in a while he sent us money. But that was all. I never saw him as I was growing up."

She smiled and said, "And now we come to the happy part. One day, my father showed up again at Fair Castle. It was like a miracle. Deadbeat Dads don't usually turn over a new leaf, but mine did. He courted my mother . . . stopped drinking . . . got a job at Sears. He began going to church again. I was getting my arts degree upriver at New Paltz; I saw him constantly. We were all so happy.

"After half a year, he moved back into the castle. My grandparents threw an enormous welcome-home party. They'd forgiven him completely, and besides, it was obvious that my mother had never stopped loving him. Pretty soon she got pregnant with Izzy, which astonished my mother; she was forty-one. On the day Izzy was born my father's partial manuscript, a murder mystery, was accepted by Knopf. So now the dream was complete."

Here Elinor faltered. She'd relived the dream so many times, and every time, it ended in the same appalling nightmare.

She looked down at her lap again and let out a tight little sigh. Without a word, Tucker took one of her hands in his and held it tight. The warmth of him thawed the icy chill that clutched at her heart. It gave her the reassurance she needed to go on.

"A month later, he was run down. It was my mother who found him ... in a ditch ... alongside the road. She's never got over it, of course. How could she? I don't think she's ever cared for the castle as much since the ... the accident."

Something about Elinor's hesitation made Tucker frown. "*Was* it an accident?" he asked with gentle bluntness.

"Oh, yes. That's what the official report said. It was a foggy morning, a bad time. I can understand that. It's just that there were no skid marks. Unless the driver were blind drunk, he should've braked before or during or after ... he should've braked *sometime*."

"And you're wondering—"

"Who would be blind drunk at seven in the morning? Yes. I've wondered every day for the last ten years."

After a thoughtful moment Tucker said, "Was he in debt, do you know?"

"From the gambling, you mean." Elinor didn't need Tucker's clarification; somehow they understood one another completely. Her grandmother was right. Tucker O'Toole was as wise as he was sensitive.

"No one really knew," she answered. "My father asked my grandfather for a chunk of money just once. Grampa Mick gave it to him, no questions asked. He assumed it was to pay off a gambling debt. But now I wonder whether my father really paid it all off, after all."

"Wouldn't they have come after your father right away?"

Her shrug was bleak. "If they knew where he lived."

"It seems too violent."

"And counterproductive," she said, unable to beat back the bitterness. "How can you collect from a dead man? But then, maybe they weren't too bright."

"Have you ever thought you might be in danger?"

"No, of course not," she said, surprised. "Not for a moment. Not until recen—"

No. It was better not to go down that road. She'd already confessed so much more to this stranger than she ever had to her friends. No. She'd said enough for one night.

"We'll never know, of course," she said softly. "That's the frustrating part." She added in a lighter tone, "Hey, I'm chewing your ear off, and you hardly know me."

"I don't feel that way at all."

Neither did she. They were sitting in a chapel holding hands and discussing her father. How could they not know one another?

"Well, be that as it may," she said, lifting her hand and his in a salute to his kindness, "it's way past my bedtime. I'm wiped out."

She let her hand, still held by his, fall back into her lap; he understood her signal and freed her. Smiling, she said, "Thanks for not making fun. I know my theory sounds paranoid."

In a voice that was all too disillusioned, Tucker said, "Paranoid? Not at all; this is the United States."

Elinor remembered that he was from Canada, a kinder, gentler place.

He got up from the pew and stood in the aisle for a moment, bidding her good night. She thought, *He brings a kind of peacefulness to this chamber. I wonder if Izzy would feel it.*

"Good night, Tucker," she said warmly. "I'll see you at breakfast?"

"Bright and early," he answered, giving the backrest a couple of soft thumps with his knuckles. "I'm already looking forward to it."

He left the chapel, and after a pensive moment or two, so did Elinor.

"Shall we let this happen, Charles?"

"I confess I am surprised to see it."

"Will it further our cause? Undoubtedly, there is an attraction between them. Is it enough to overcome the darker spell already cast? And if it does, what then? I cannot guess."

"One thing is certain. The castle must remain for a little while longer. If it does, all else will follow."

"Ah, Charles—how can this family of dreamers have made such a ruin of our desire? It is they who have tangled this affair into a Gordian knot. Impulsive, whimsical fools!"

Elinor, up early and humming a tune, was sliding the second omelette into the warming oven when Tucker came strolling into the kitchen. He was dressed in Levi's and a sweatshirt, ready to tackle the dusty shelves of the archive room, and he was grinning from ear to ear.

"I just saw a pheasant," he said. "The dumb cluck tried to fly right through the greenhouse. It fell to the ground and then went wandering off, shaking its head. It seemed almost tame; do you raise them on the estate?"

"Estate? What estate? We barely own the parking lot. My grandfather had to sell off most of the land a few years ago. It would've been tract housing by now if it hadn't been for the real-estate crash. Now that the economy's turned around, though, I guess our days are numbered. Every time I sleep here I expect to be awakened by the sound of bulldozers. Coffee?"

"Great. Black. Thanks," Tucker said, taking a seat at the timeworn trestle table that did double duty as a cooking island.

Elinor set a mug of thick Colombian brew in front of him and said, "We don't raise pheasants in any official way, but my grandmother feeds everything out there with wings or fur. We call her Mother of Assisi."

"She's terrific," Tucker agreed. "And by the way, so's this coffee." He raised his mug in a toast.

So there the two of them were, looking and sounding very much like a Folger's commercial, when in walked Elinor's nemesis.

He was dressed in British casual: chinos and a blue button-down linen shirt topped with a navy sweater, obviously hand knit, that had to have cost many hundreds. It was all very proper, all very Savile Row.

And all very annoying. What was he doing there now?

She'd distinctly heard him say that he was leaving for the city at dawn. It was now eight-thirty. And there were only two omelettes.

"Good morning, Lord Norwood," she said with her usual ironic courtesy. "Would you care for a dash of coffee—before you hit the road?"

"Actually, there's been a change of plan," Will said with a nod at Tucker. He pulled out a chair opposite him and said pleasantly, "I have time to linger over a cup or two."

Unbelievable! He was so obviously not wanted, and yet there he sat: square in the middle of Elinor's tête-à-tête with Tucker. She smiled frigidly, splashed some coffee into a cup, and slapped it down in front of him like a waitress at a truck stop.

"Sorry I can't offer to make you breakfast," she said with cruel glee. "We're out of eggs."

"No problem," said the Brit amiably. "Coffee is fine. Is there cream?"

"No."

"Is there sugar?"

"Somewhere."

"Ah. Well. I'll just go on a bit of a rummage, then."

He got up just as Elinor was turning from the warming oven to the table, a heated plate in each of her potholdered hands. They bumped shoulders and Elinor, distracted as ever by the nearness of him, was hard-pressed to hold on to her cargo. "Sorry," he murmured in her ear. "Here. Let me take those."

"N-no, that's all right; I've got them."

"I insist."

Nimble as a pickpocket, he managed to slide his hands under hers and slip the plates into his grip. Like an outraged tourist, Elinor was seized with an urge to cry "Stop that man!" as he laid one plate in front of Tucker and one alongside his coffee, halfway between his place and hers.

It was that second omelette, oozing cheese and smelling of browned butter, that became a bone of contention. It was like a mini-castle in an impromptu tug of war between them.

"It smells delicious," Will said with that dangerously low-key smile of his. "I guess I'm hungrier than I thought."

"There's cereal in the cupboard," Elinor said in a voice like Rice Crispies. "Milk, in the fridge."

"No cream, though, you say," he said with a wistful look at her omelette.

Ah, the cream. Of course; he was British, after all. Wondering how it was that he'd made it this far without having had a heart attack, Elinor said dryly, "You know, there's a Ho-Jo just two miles south of here with an all-you-can-eat breakfast buffet; maybe you should work it into your itinerary. Chester loves it; you can probably drag him along. Heck, take my grandfather. Take the whole gang!"

Tucker, who'd been watching their duel with interest, stepped in and said placatingly, "I have a better plan. Why don't we just split *my* omelette in half?"

"Nothing doing!"

"Good idea."

Before Elinor could intercept him, Will had snatched a clean plate out of the dish rack and was deftly sliding fifty percent of Tucker's omelette onto it. Elinor had no illusions about the incident: It was a power play, pure and simple. The baron was letting her know that he wasn't the type to take no for an answer.

As if she needed reminding.

Determined not to let him have full victory, she gave half of her own omelette to Tucker. Which only made it worse: Now it looked as if she and Will were sharing. Since—symbolically speaking—Elinor wasn't willing to do that, she decided to forego her omelette altogether, claiming she really wasn't hungry.

Will said, "Excellent," and combined their plates.

So now he had it all.

Shit!

Elinor threw a half-despairing glance at Tucker; her plans for a cozy breakfast were as big a shambles as her omelettes. Tucker smiled and rolled his eyes, which made her feel better somehow. Obviously it was Lord Norwood who was being the pain; not her.

And meanwhile, Will was polishing off the eggs before anyone changed his mind. "So, Tucker, m'lad—how go the archives? Found anything of note? Any Gutenberg bibles in there? Any monographs by Conan Doyle? What're you looking for, exactly?"

An angry flush across Tucker's cheeks made it clear that he resented Will's flippancy. "As you already know, I'm writing a book on English social customs in the eighteenth century. Anything that pertains to the period interests me. A friend who'd toured Fair Castle mentioned the archives, and Chester graciously allowed me to peruse them."

"Mmm, mmm," said Will, nodding as he slugged down his coffee. "So you're basically here just to see what you can see, is that it? On a fishing expedition, more or less?"

The muscles in Tucker's jaw flexed and relaxed. "That's one way of putting it."

Why was Will provoking him?

"You plan to get this book published, ever?"

"The book's my doctoral thesis, but—yes; more than likely I'll shop it around."

Will shook his head in wonder. "Oh, yeah. Eighteenth-century social customs—blockbuster stuff for sure. Wouldn't you be better off putting the research into something that pays? Maybe work the material into a historical novel with lots of sex, dukes, and country wenches?"

"I have my own ambitions," said Tucker in a low, deadly tone.

Madder and madder, thought Elinor. Could she blame him?

"Take it from me, Tuck," said the Englishman. "The world has moved on. This is the age of the Internet, not the trebuchet—with all due apologies to Chester."

What the hell did he want the castle for, in that case? What a paradox he was!

"Say, is there any toast?" Will asked cheerfully.

Elinor gave him a baleful look: *Go away.*

"Guess not," he said. "That's too bad. Right now I'd settle for what you Yanks laughingly call an English muffin. Any chance?"

"None in hell."

"There's a pity. Ah, well. Great omelette, anyway." He reached into a basket on the table for a napkin and wiped his lips and then his hands with it. All the while, his gaze never left Elinor's face.

They'd played this game before, this stare-down. Elinor was determined this time not to blink. She felt the color reach her cheeks; she didn't blink. She was aware as he wiped his lips that she'd kissed those lips; she didn't blink. She saw that his hands were well formed, his nails well kept; still she didn't blink. She had an insane notion that if she blinked, she'd lose the castle.

She felt her eyes sting from the strain of her effort; but she did not blink.

Suddenly he laughed. It was a sound as low and seductive as a South American love song. And then he looked away, who knew where. At the teakettle? The clock on the wall? It didn't matter. She'd won. He'd lost. Elinor was convinced, for the first time since his first day there, that the castle would stay where it was.

She was jubilant. Her victory was a little thing, a stupid thing, but it gave her the edge she needed. Yes! Baron Norwood could be driven from the ramparts.

And Tucker O'Toole would help her do the job. Elinor turned to her new ally and said, "You go on ahead, Tucker. I'll clean up here, then brew another pot of coffee and bring some in to you. There are several boxes in the closet that Chester's never brought out; but I seem to recall that somewhere in them is a nineteenth-century translation of an eighteenth-century account of some Frenchman's stay in the English countryside somewhere. Would that be of any interest?"

"That'd be great," Tucker said. "It looks like I've come to the right place. I—"

"Morning, children!"

Elinor's grandmother, dressed in green velour and

blowing kisses, headed straight for the refrigerator and took out a carton of orange juice.

And a slab of bacon and a carton of eggs. "I'm starved," she announced. "Who wants bacon and eggs?"

Chapter 13

The brick hideaway on the other side of the maze was technically too small to be called a lodge, but lodge was easier to say than banqueting house, so that's what everyone called it.

It wasn't really a banqueting house, either. A banqueting house was for enjoying dessert after a fine dinner in a castle and a leisurely tour of its garden. Mickey MacLeish had originally built the tiny two-story structure because he wanted his castle to have all the sixteenth-century bells and whistles. But painting meant more to him than pastry, so he converted the banqueting house into a studio, and that's what it remained. Except that it was called a lodge.

It was not on the tour. It would've been a great place to serve tea to the tourists, but neither Elinor nor her grandfather could bear the thought of giving up their artists' sanctuary to commerce; it was hard enough to find privacy as it was.

The lodge was Elinor's second home. When she was fourteen, Mickey MacLeish gave her the first floor to use as her very own studio, claiming that he had more than enough room, and better light, on the skylit second floor. It was an extravagant gesture, and Elinor had loved her grandfather the more for it. It was only later that she understood how deeply his gift had affected her choice of careers; how seriously it had made her take her art.

Having her own studio had forced Elinor to be disciplined about her painting. Of course, it had helped that her grandfather had to walk past her easel on his way upstairs, always with a comment or two on her progress. (When he did stop commenting, that's when she knew he respected her as a professional.)

Mickey MacLeish came to the lodge less frequently nowadays and not at all in the last week. But Fright Night was coming and there were ghouls to be made; it was time to get cutting.

It's all the baron's fault, she thought, not for the first time. He was throwing the whole family off balance.

But no one more than her. The man was like her own personal train wreck. She could hardly bear to look at him; and yet it was impossible for her *not* to look. And in the meantime, she felt an unbearable tension, as if lives were at stake.

She sighed and took out a large sketch pad. Tonight she and Izzy would do something together; but for now, Elinor had to get out of the house and away from Will. After the omelette debacle, it seemed more important than ever. She had tried to send two clear and deliberate signals at breakfast. One was that she had a lively loathing for the baron and his quest. The second was that she was feeling surprisingly tender thoughts for Tucker O'Toole.

Maybe she was getting ahead of herself about Tucker; but maybe she wasn't. In the archives room she thought there'd been one or two times . . . a look from him . . . a laugh. Had she been flirting with him? She dearly hoped so. It was depressing to think she might not know how. Every woman knew how to flirt. It was just a question of how well.

But then Elinor remembered Yvonne. Yvonne, who'd reduced the boys to stammering monkeys in middle school, and had them all on their knees by high school. Yvonne was a master flirt. She had the long look and the meaningful smile down pat. Her laugh was music itself. And she *dressed*—well, she dressed for boys.

For a while she and Elinor were best friends. But then Elinor realized that her own attempts to flirt looked clumsy and obvious by comparison. So she gave up flirting altogether. And then, discouraged by the fact that she was more or less invisible around Yvonne, she gave up Yvonne as well.

It was easier for Elinor to find boys on her own. She might not be able to keep them, but at least she had a shot at finding them. That bias against flirting and flirty women had lasted until the present day. Of her female friends in New York, not a one was like Yvonne. They were all smart, straightforward women dedicated to their careers, just like Elinor. Of course, not a one of them was married. Just like Elinor.

I'm thirty, she reassured herself. *I have plenty of time.*

In the meantime there was Tuck, and he was interesting, and she was pretty damn sure she had just proved that she could flirt if she wanted to.

And if her mother didn't like it, she could hunt down and marry Lord Norwood herself.

Pushing both men from her mind, Elinor added a log to the wood-burning stove radiating from a corner of the studio, then wrapped herself with her oldest, rattiest, most beloved cardigan, the one that made her feel all snuggly and cozy and in the mood to draw.

She worked at her drafting table in pensive silence for an hour or so, pondering the next story line in her medieval children's series. Maybe she'd do something with the children's castle. Maybe the castle would be under seige. Maybe the children would have to scheme and plot to save it for their parents.

Maybe the villain would look exactly like Lord Norwood. She sketched in a horse, then sat a reasonable likeness of Will on it. Maybe make it a donkey. He didn't deserve a horse.

Maybe she should do a facial study of the villain. She flipped to a clean page, then drew an oval. No good. The chin wasn't square enough. She erased the chin line and flattened it out, shading in a cleft that wasn't quite a cleft.

The eyes: almost always brooding except when he was being ironic. Eyebrows: thick, dark, pulled down in that frown of concentration. Lashes, black and long, damn it. The nose: hard to do in a frontal view. But definitely with a high bridge. Arrogant, that's what it was. Damn nose. She shaded in a sense of it.

Oh, the cheekbones. To-die-for cheekbones. Shade in some gauntness. Not gaunt, exactly . . . more like disciplined. He always passed on dessert. How could he pass on dessert? She preferred a man who liked to indulge once in a while. Maybe even had a little love handle of indulgence. *He* wouldn't have a love handle . . . too lean, too mean.

Hair. Thick hair. Lots of it. Run-your-hands-through-it hair. And then pull. Hard. Couldn't she just. Damn him. *Taking our castle; who the hell does he think he is?*

Mouth, oh God, his mouth. Full, but not too much. Hard, just enough. Tongue, tongue, can't draw the tongue. Oh God. She could taste it, though. No smile. Not now. *No, that's not it.* Make the mouth wider. His teeth would never fit in this mouth. She erased furiously, stretched the line of the lower lip, then the upper.

Is that it? No. What's wrong, then? What is wrong with this picture!

With a cry of exasperation, she threw her pencil at the wall, followed instantly by the eraser. She tore the sheet from its pad and crumpled it into a baseball-sized wad and flung it at the floor. Wrapping her forearms over the top of her hair, she threw her head back in melodramatic lament.

I can't work in these conditions. "I can't!" she said aloud. "Damn, damn, damn him!"

The sound of the side door being opened brought her up short.

"Grampa Mick?"

"No."

She turned. Yes. That's what she'd done wrong with the mouth. She had no clue how to draw a smile that wasn't a smile. Even now, she knew she couldn't do it.

"Your mother said I'd find you here."

"And she was right."

"You don't like visitors."

"How did you guess?"

"The clenched fists?"

She looked down at her balled-up fingers. "Huh. So that's why I can't play the piano worth a damn."

"Isn't it time we talked?"

"What about? *Not* Fair Castle."

"The turret."

"I told you I was sorry about accusing you."

"I don't mean about the electricity in the turret." He laughed and said softly, "Or maybe I *do* mean about the electricity in the turret. There was a lot of it."

"Was there? I hadn't noticed."

"Elinor."

It was the first time he'd used her first name. On his lips, it sounded like a lullaby. She found herself strangely lulled by it.

"Look," she said, sliding off the high seat at her drafting table. "We kissed. Yes. It was done in the heat of the moment. We were—I don't remember what we were doing, I only remember we were doing it heatedly. Arguing, yes, that was it. So naturally, all that . . . heat . . . was in danger of being . . . rerouted . . . and that's where it ended up. In a kiss. Think nothing of it."

"You must be joking," Will said simply. His hands were in his pockets as he stood in front of the door, blocking her exit. A threat, or not? She was desperately on edge, wondering.

He looked around the twenty-foot-square studio with its cozy wood-burning stove and organized clutter of paints and brushes, easels and canvasses. It seemed to Elinor that his lazy glance paused at the daybed before it came to rest on a shelf of her books.

In your dreams, pal, she thought. But her heart was roaring madly ahead, as if it were in a race with her head.

"Your books?" he asked, giving himself a little nudge in the direction of the bookcase.

"Yes, and I feel uncomfortable when people look at them in front of me."

He shrugged. "Turn around, then."

He laughed before she could leap at him and pull off his head. "Just my idea of humor," he said. "You must be too sophisticated for it. *May* I look at one of your books?" he added with careful formality. "The bookstore in town was out of them."

He checked? For her stuff? She was amazed. And—oh, boy, she didn't like this at all—oddly touched. She stripped her voice of emotion as she said, "You have children the right age for them?"

She knew he wasn't married; it didn't mean he didn't have kids.

"No, can't say that I do," he said absentmindedly. He took down one of the twelve picture books published in the series so far and read the title aloud: "*Izzy and the Unicorn.* How about that." He opened the book to a random page and grinned. "You're really good. I'd know her anywhere."

But you wouldn't know the unicorn, Elinor thought with regret. *Not if it butted you on the ass with its horn. Too much whimsy required; not enough technology.*

He put the book back on the shelf and took down another: *Elly in the Moat.* "Uh-oh," he murmured, still smiling. "This sounds like trouble. I hope she gets out okay." He began to read, lingering over the first page or two, obviously taking in the drawings as well.

And meanwhile, Elinor was wondering whether he had children who *weren't* the right age for her stuff. He was forty-one. He could have kids any age, even in college. But surely he'd have mentioned a family. Probably he *had* mentioned a family, over cigars and brandy. All she had to do was ask someone to find out.

No. Why should she? It made no difference at all.

She walked deliberately up to him and took hold of the book still in his hand. "I really . . . really . . . feel uncomfortable," she said, tugging it out of his grip. "Why don't you just take it with you? Better yet, I can save you some time: Elly gets out of the moat."

She closed the small volume with a snap, turned it face-up, and handed it back to him.

"Well," he said with a shrug. "Now that I know how it ends . . ." He wandered away, leaving her standing there with her book and feeling like an idiot.

Pausing at the spiral staircase, he rubbed the knob of

the iron newel post and put one foot onto the first oak tread.

"There's something about a spiral staircase," he mused, looking up at it. "Your grandfather's studio is upstairs?"

"I'm sorry," she said coldly. "His studio's not on the tour. Neither, for that matter, is this one."

"I'm not a tourist," he reminded her.

"Then why are you here?"

There it was again: the smile that wasn't quite a smile.

She decided to confront it head-on. "Look, it's obvious that we have *nothing* in common—"

"Pardon me. Fair Castle?"

"All right. That one thing. But it hasn't exactly made us *simpatico*."

"Ah. Simpatico. That'd be Tucker O'Toole?"

"Well . . . yes," Elinor said with a lift of her chin. "In all honesty . . . yes."

"Oh, come *on*!" It was his first real flash of anger. "Tucker's a whelp!"

"I see. And you enjoy torturing young animals?"

"I enjoy torturing *him*."

"It ill becomes you," she said with a sniff. She sounded exactly like her mother.

His smile was on the malevolent side. "You're right," he conceded. "I much prefer you as my opponent. At least it's a fair fight."

"It's a fight you can't win, your lordship!" she snapped. "Let it go!"

"We'll see," he said quietly.

She was afraid of that: afraid of the quiet in him. He was rich. He was determined. He was oh, so dangerous.

She didn't know what to say to him; she didn't know what to do to make him go away. Frustrated, she said, "Don't you have a *home*?"

He held her look for a long, hard moment. "A man's home," he said grimly, "is his castle."

She took a deep breath, then let it out slowly. "All right," she said, wrapping her tattered gray cardigan more snugly around her. "I walked right into that one. Now

will you just . . . leave me alone? This studio has nothing
to do with Fair Castle, nothing to do with our fight. It's
my sanctuary, my sacred place. It's where I make my
magic. I can't let confrontation and bitterness into it. I
can't. Don't you understand that?"

Maybe he was weary of her; maybe he was bored.
Maybe he was satisfied by her supplicating tone. Whatever the reason, he said at last, "I'll go, then. And leave
you to make magic."

He turned abruptly, kicking the wadded-up sketch
across the floor. Almost automatically he went over to
pick it up. Almost automatically, he began to unfold its
creases to see what discarded disappointment it held.

Elinor was horrified. *"No!"* she cried, pouncing on the
crumpled sheet. "Don't look at that!"

She tried to tear the sketch from his grip, but he held
her off as he studied the cast-away likeness of himself.

A slow, pensive smile replaced the grim one of the minute before. He said, "Pretty good—but you were right to
work on the mouth. It hurts the likeness. You need to
burn the image into your brain. Here: I'll help you remember."

He had her right wrist locked firmly in his grip. Now
he lifted it to his face—trusting that she would not scratch
at him—and then to his lips. Despite herself, Elinor found
her fist going limp, her fingers aching to touch his mouth.
In utter silence, he skimmed her fingers over his upper
lip, then his lower, in a red-hot outline that she knew
she'd take to her grave.

"No-o-o," she said, shaking her head. "This won't
work . . ."

"It will; trust me," he murmured as he guided her fingers over his mouth a second time. He caressed her fingertips with soft, slow kisses, punctuating each kiss with
a single command: "Trust me."

She didn't dare look into his eyes; he'd have her hypnotized in no time. "How can I trust you?" she whispered
with a downcast gaze. "When we are enemies sworn . . ."

"Not enemies," he said. "Opposites. A man. A
woman." He trailed his tongue along the palm of her

opened hand, stopping and teasing at the pulse point on her wrist.

Friendly fire, then, she thought dizzily. It was as deadly as an assassin's bullet. She shook her head in silent protest, unable to repel him with words.

"Don't, Elinor," he murmured. "Don't say no."

He let the sketch fall to the floor like an autumn leaf, and then he lifted both his hands to her shoulders. "There's more than one way," he promised, "to make magic."

He cupped one hand under her chin and tilted her face to his, lowering his mouth in a kiss that began soft and quickly went hard. She was caught off guard by it—by the tenderness of it, then by the urgency of it; it made her almost stupidly pliant in his arms.

Do something; fight; tear yourself away, she commanded her body. But her body just stood there, slowly dissolving into warm honey, as she made soft, whimpering sounds in her throat.

The kiss deepened. His arms slid down, then up, then down the curves of her torso, coming to rest under the shallow hook of her buttocks. He pulled her toward him, all the while battering her with his kiss, in an unmistakable signal that he wanted to bed her.

Why not, why not, why not, said her honey-warm body. She was as wet as he was hard; why not?

Somewhere she'd lost her heavy cardigan; somewhere she heard a zipper. Hers? His? A zipper unzipped, that's all she knew. She herself was now miles above the scene, looking down at the two of them, scandalized by her own behavior, urging him on in his.

He lifted her pullover, the color of cleft flesh, up, up, over her breasts.

Yes, yes, do it, she begged herself in a sudden change of heart. *Make her do it,* she urged him from above. *Get it over with.* It would resolve the tension once and for all.

She felt cool air on her right breast, lifted out of the cup of her bra. Her left breast—cool air. Then the snap of the garment, being undone. Second snap; it thundered in her ears.

From above, she cheered them on. *Yes! This is what you've wanted all along; everyone knows it. Yes!* She was dizzy with him, giddy with him, filled with the scent and taste of him. Watching them, encouraging him, prodding herself . . .

Only wait—footsteps on the spiral staircase. The sound of her name. In her grandfather's voice. Booming and stunned.

"ELINOR! JESUS CHRIST!"

From that high, high place Elinor fell like a shot-down duck, landing with a thud back in her body. She hauled down the pullover, hiked up the zipper, and whirled around.

"Grampa Mick! You were upstairs? I didn't . . . know." Her voice was cringing with embarrassment.

"Well, now you do, for God's sake. And *you*," he said, turning a fiery eye on the Englishman. "Is this how you repay my hospitality? By ravishing my granddaughter while I'm at work?"

"Sir, it was inexcusable," said Will evenly.

Too evenly. It was obvious that he couldn't care less.

"I think you should get out of here, William," said Mickey MacLeish.

"I agree."

"Out."

"Right."

"Now."

No!

Elinor whirled back around to Will.

He'd picked up the crumpled sketch and was handing it to her. "You dropped this," he said with an impassive look.

And then he was gone. Banished. Elinor's grandfather stomped the rest of the way down the ironbound, open spiral and took the sketch from her hand.

He looked at it and snorted. "This is the best you could do? Hell, you may as *well* use the studio for a motel room. This is awful. Look at those beady eyes; his are rounder and farther apart. And that neck. It belongs on a linebacker, not him. What were you thinking? The ears don't even match."

"It was just a quick study, Grampa Mick," Elinor said with some asperity.

"Then *study* him, God damn it! Sit the man down on a chair, take off his clothes, and draw him the way you were taught to do. Not this ... this high-school-crush crap! Gawd."

He handed Elinor back her much-reviewed sketch and said in a growl, "I'll be upstairs. Working on ghouls. All of which bear a lot closer resemblance to human beings than *this* piece of tripe."

He spiraled back up to his studio, leaving his granddaughter alone and free to relive the mortifying scene as many times as she wanted to.

She did.

"I remember well our first time: the taste of your lips on mine, the touch of your fingers to my flesh, the wanton sound of your voice in my ear."

"Marianne, Marianne, even now—"

"I know, I know. I wish it could be so again. But that is behind us, my love. What remains is a gnawing, wretched need to put things right."

"It cannot happen if events move so quickly."

"I fear you're right. She has thoughts only of him now. He has driven out all else. Fair Castle? It is far from her mind."

"We shall change all that."

Chapter 14

$\mathcal{E}$linor dressed for dinner with special modesty. After baring her back to her grandfather and her front to Will Braddock, it seemed the only proper thing to do. The dress she wore, a long-sleeved affair of soft, flowing burgundy, was buttoned from its mandarin collar down to just above the ankles; the only skin that showed was on her face, her hands, and two-thirds of her neck.

She stared at her pale reflection in the full-length mirror, dreading the cocktail hour, appalled by the thought of a dragged-out dinner. How could she face Will after the scene in the lodge? Where was her credibility?

In the wastebasket, with her dignity. Will could've had her for the asking. Presumably he figured he could have the castle now as well. All her fierce resolve, all that blazing hostility—pointless. She'd been as helpless as a handmaiden in his arms; as witless as a wood-burning stove.

She closed her eyes and took a deep breath, preparing herself for the plunge into the cocktail hour, but a knock at her door brought her up short. It was her grandmother, dressed for dinner in peacock blue, and she was agog.

"Your grandfather told me the most amazing story when I got home, dear," she said. Her eyes were bright with curiosity. "Is it true?"

Elinor felt her face flood with color. So much for any hope that her grandfather would be discreet.

"It would be nice," she grumbled, "if you two didn't share *every* little thing."

Camilla MacLeish pooh-poohed the thought, then added a tsk-tsk. "You missed a button," she said, buttoning up the closure directly between Elinor's breasts. "You know how men notice these things."

Elinor was dumbfounded; had she missed the button on purpose? Obviously she wasn't ready to confront Lord Norwood; obviously she would *never* be ready.

"I'm not going downstairs," she said suddenly. "Not until he moves out of this castle." She threw herself into a cushioned chair, crossed her arms, and crossed her legs. Her body language spoke volumes.

"Don't be silly, El," said Camilla. "Your grandfather hardly saw a thing. You know how involved he gets when he's working on a project. The only reason he came down was to pee. So tell me. What did you and his lordship say to one another?"

"Nothing! We talked about my work. He looked at one of my picture books. Then I told him to leave."

"Well, that explains how you ended up half-naked in his arms," Camilla said dryly.

"That's just it! I don't *know* how I got there! I'm not the least bit attracted to him. It's as if he put a . . . a spell on me. I'll die if this gets out to Mother—or to Tucker! You won't say anything, will you?"

Camilla held out her hands, coaxing Elinor from her chair. "Your secret is safe with me. Look on the bright side, dear, your grandfather is a lot less keen on the baron than he was this morning."

Reviving, Elinor said, "You're right! Will may very well think that I set him up!"

"We can always hope for the best."

"You know, I feel a lot better," said Elinor. "Thanks!"

Her grandmother sighed and shook her head. "Elly, Elly . . . you make me feel so old."

They walked out together, and Elinor said, "Why old? Because you're happy and in love while I'm clueless and confused?"

"Actually, I think you've put your finger on it," Camilla told her. "I've loved your grandfather for so many years that I almost can't remember what it's like to be young and falling—"

"No, no, no, no, no! There's no 'falling' going on! You're way off base, Gramma Cam. I'm telling you the same thing I told Will: This is all misdirected rage. It happens."

"Darling, you have it backward. Desire sometimes becomes rage—not the other way around."

"Oh, sure, go Freudian on me," said Elinor, pinching her grandmother's arm.

"Ouch! That hurt, El! Are you trying to prove my point?"

"This isn't funny, Gramma Cam. I am *not* attracted to him."

Smiling, Camilla said, "You would've said the same thing about your grandfather and me if you'd been around when we met. We fought like cats and dogs."

"You and Grampa Mick? I don't believe it. He's always said he knew you were The One the minute he laid eyes on you."

They paused to knock on Izzy's door as Camilla said, "Oh, sure; that's what he says *now*. But at the time he did nothing but provoke me. He thought I overacted . . . he thought I overdressed. And he positively despised my friends. He found them vain and shallow and petty."

"Yikes. How did he ever end up marrying such a hopeless case as you?"

"He decided he had to save me from myself," said Camilla dryly. "First he dragged me through all the museums of Europe, and then he bought the castle and plunked me down in it, and you know? He was right. I was never so happy on the stage as I am in Fair Castle."

Elinor threw the door open to her sister's bedroom. "Izzy! Are you coming or not?"

"*Yes,*" came the hurried answer from around the corner. "But I've lost my string. I just had it!"

"Izzy, darling," said her grandmother, "we're going to *eat* fish, not catch it. Hurry up, dear. You know how your grampa gets."

While they waited, Elinor said thoughtfully, "It's noth-

ing like that between *us*, though. There's something so . . .
remote . . . unyielding . . . about him. Have you noticed? I
almost feel that he's not acting on his own impulses. That
he's doing someone else's bidding. He gets that look in
his eye . . . that strange, distant look . . . as though he has
conflicting desires. . . ."

She shook off the notion with a shudder. "Actually,
who knows why he gets that look. He's probably wishing
he was back home in a pub with a pint, instead of here
with martinis and us."

"Your mother thinks we all get along beautifully."

"In an oil-and-water sort of way."

The two shared one of their private chuckles, and then
Izzy came out, holding a tangle of string in one hand and
a crystal teardrop from a chandelier in the other.

"What's all that for?" Elinor asked her sister.

"It's a new parlor game," said the child as she stuffed
the string in one pocket of her pants, the crystal pendant
in the other. "I was reading a book about it."

"Oh, Izz," said Elinor. She dreaded the thought of
having to hang around for a parlor game. If she made it
through cocktails and dinner, that was worth a medal right
there. But a parlor game? No way.

She tried to discourage her sister. "Every time we play
a new parlor game," she complained, "Grampa Mick
beats you and then you get mad and then Chester lets
you win because he feels sorry for you and then Mother
gets mad at Chester because he spoils you and then she
takes it out on the rest of us. Do you *really* want to put
us through another one of your games?"

"Yeah, I do," said Isabelle with surprising firmness.
The girl fished a rubber band out of some other hiding
place in her pants and then gathered her hair at the back
of her neck for binding.

"This isn't like a game with right answers and wrong
answers," she explained as she looped the band twice
around her long hair. "It's more like . . . like fortune-
telling!" she said, making a sudden connection. "Only
backward."

Camilla straightened the cowled collar of her granddaughter's red sweater and said, "By any chance is tonight a practice for your Fright Night sleepover?"

Izzy flashed a wide-toothed grin at her grandmother. "Yeah. I thought it would be fun, because, like, we were reading about Catherine the Great in school? And Catherine Dyer decided that she's re-incar . . . re-incarn . . ."

"Reincarnated?"

"Yeah! Reincarnated, just because she has the same name as Catherine the Empress. And that's, like, so dumb! So I thought if we *all* show we're reincarnated, then Catherine won't get to be so stuck-up about her name."

"It sounds like a plan to me," said Izzy's grandmother with a perfectly straight face.

They walked into the great parlor, two of them eager, the third one not.

Mickey MacLeish had already poured. Chester, still in his blue sling, was hulked in an easy chair, sipping liquid from a stemmed glass he held gingerly in his left hand. Tucker O'Toole, handsome in a camel hair blazer and black turtleneck, was a little off on his own, standing in front of the high stone fireplace and listening to Lem Samuelson, a neighbor and college professor, describe his recent visit to Quebec. Susan Roberts, as beautifully dressed as Lem's realtor wife, Anne, was in a deep discussion with her, probably over the market value of Fair Castle. They were all there, all the usual suspects.

All except one.

It was possible that he'd made his regrets; Elinor was too embarrassed to ask. She was also too embarrassed—after the episode in the lodge—to go up to her grandfather for her nightly ration of gin. After greeting everyone, she gravitated to Tucker with a reassuring smile and gave him a glancing kiss on his cheek. Why the kiss, she had no idea.

Tucker responded with a surprised, warm greeting of his own. He asked her how her afternoon had gone in the lodge. Had she got any ideas for a new story line?

The short answer to that was: none that was suitable for a children's book. But she told him cheerfully, "Oh, yes; there's always one more story in Fair Castle."

In the meantime, Mickey MacLeish was throwing meaningful scowls her way.

Would her grandfather have been angry enough to throw Will out on his ear? He'd thrown people out before, many times—an offensive tourist, a dinner guest who'd insulted his wife, an electrician who'd tried to gouge them, a drifter who'd wanted to sell them stolen fishing gear.

But Will? Her grandfather might have been high-minded, but he wasn't a prude. Far from it. Over the years he'd told more than his share of off-color jokes. Still, a racy joke and a half-naked granddaughter weren't the same thing. Elinor blushed again at the memory of the lodge.

"I'm embarrassing you."

It was Tucker, trying to look nonchalant but failing. "It's just that you look really sensational in that dress," he murmured. He glanced around the room, but his burning gaze came right back to her. "Sensational."

He was working mentally on the top button, that was pretty clear. Her grandmother was right: Men *did* notice them. Tucker wouldn't be paying as much attention if she were standing there in a string bikini.

"Thank you," she said in some confusion. "You're looking pretty natty yourself tonight. Did that translation we dragged out give you anything useful for your book?"

Tucker seesawed his hand in the air. "There's almost nothing about servants in the account. Which isn't surprising. The upper class didn't give a hoot how their servants lived, much less feel obliged to write about it."

"That has to be frustrating."

"At this rate, I may have to shorten Part Two down to a chapter," he said. "The whole damn project's turning into a bitter disappointment."

She said, "Don't give up hope, Tuck. Besides the stuff that came with the castle, there are tons of other books and papers in the archives room and its closet. Chester bought entire lots, sight unseen, at auctions."

"All of them irrelevant!"

Immediately Tucker's look softened as he said, "I'm sorry; the afternoon was such a dead loss. I was so sure—but hey, enough about my woes. Where's your token martini? Let me get it for you."

He went up to the sideboard and poured her pitiful ounce into a sherry glass. Immediately he was intercepted by Elinor's mother. Susan lifted the glass from his hand with a pleasant remark—dismissing him, basically—and then brought the martini over herself to Elinor.

Elinor winced. Did her mother, too, know about the lodge?

Susan came right to the point. "Would you mind telling me why Lord Norwood has made a sudden decision to go back to England?"

Stunned, Elinor avoided her mother's accusing gaze. "How should I know?" she said testily. "He doesn't keep me in his loop."

Back to England!

"Elinor MacLeish, if you've ruined the one true chance we have—"

"Of what? Selling out the family? What if I have?" Elinor asked with lofty defiance.

Back to England! She said defensively, "You know yourself he was nowhere near making an offer, Mother."

"Of course he was!" said Susan in a low, exasperated hiss. "He'd been through the place with a fine-tooth comb. I'd shown him the bank appraisal from our last equity loan. He'd thought the value was fair. He'd begun making phone calls. And now—gone! It's over. Just like that. No explanation. No reassurances. Just—"

"Yes, yes. Back to England."

Victory. It tasted oddly . . . bitter. Aloud Elinor said, "Does Grampa Mick know you've been negotiating behind his—?"

"Never mind that now! Elinor, this time you've gone too far. If Lord Norwood doesn't return—"

"Has he actually packed and left?" The door to his chamber had been closed when Elinor walked by a minute ago. He must still be around. *Surely* he was still around.

Susan said, "He leaves tomorrow morning, first thing. Obviously something's happened. I tried to sound him out. Was it a business crisis . . . problems at the estate . . . ? He was very vague.

"But then I mentioned your name, and he got this . . . *look* on his face. You know what you are to him? You're a poison pill. You couldn't just be civil, could you. You couldn't treat him like any other guest. You couldn't even treat him," she said with stony resentment, "like *Tucker*. What is wrong with you, Elinor?"

Poison pill. That was awfully strong.

"I need some air," Elinor said abruptly. She excused herself and fled casually from the great parlor.

Without bothering to stop for a jacket, she made her way down the stuccoed corridors to the French door, framed in mahogany and drafty in all seasons, which opened onto the outdoor gallery that overlooked Camilla's faded garden. Stepping out on the long, narrow walkway, she stood at the stone balustrade, looking up at the mid-October night. There, under a cold and starry sky, she tried to come to terms with the shock she'd felt at the news that Will Braddock had washed his hands of them.

On the one hand: hallelujah. With a little help from an aging lion, she'd driven the dragon from the gate.

On the other hand . . .

She shivered violently. It bothered her—in a way that simply amazed her—that Will had turned tail and run. It wasn't that she enjoyed battling with him over the castle; it was just that . . .

She did enjoy battling with him over the castle. Yes. It was true.

Impossible. She might enjoy the battle of wits. Of words. Of manipulating emotions. But that didn't mean she was willing to see the castle go to England. Did it?

No. But it occurred to her that in some odd and profound way, fighting for Fair Castle had made everything worthwhile: had made the castle . . . her family . . . her career . . . more precious than ever. *When something gets threatened, you love it the more,* she realized.

She realized something else. The castle was common

ground for Will and her—even if that common ground was a battlefield. Once Will bought it, he'd go his way and she'd go hers.

She sighed, and her sigh was echoed in the pines that swayed all around her—pines that were free to move, now that the leaves had begun to drop from the maples and alders that hemmed them in. Soon it would be winter. No cars, no tours; nothing to do but keep up the illusion that they would live happily ever after in the castle.

So hallelujah. They'd driven him back. She bowed her head, lost in thought.

"El?"

She turned to see Tucker with one hand on the handle of the French door, obviously reluctant to approach and scare her out of her wits again.

"Your mother was concerned about—actually, that's a lie," he said across the night between them. "I'm the one who's concerned. You looked upset. Are you all right?"

"Yes, I'm fine." She hung back, reluctant despite the cold to go in. Hugging her arms to her body, she said, "As you can tell, my mother is driving me—"

She laughed softly, then tried again. "I guess once a daughter reaches thirty and is still on her own, a mother has just two choices: light a fire or bite her tongue. Things were getting a little warm in there."

But not on the gallery. Elinor shivered again and said in a melancholy voice, "Winter's coming. You can feel it tonight."

Tucker shrugged out of his blazer and wrapped it around her shoulders. "Maybe so, but you don't have to run out looking for it. Come inside, El," he said, coaxing her along. "Talk to me. The music stopped when you ran out."

Touched by his gallantry, Elinor paused in the checkerboard of light on the gallery side of the French door. "Tucker," she murmured, "that's so . . . ."

He turned to snug his jacket more securely over her. "I mean it."

Elinor smiled tremulously, then bit her lip. She'd been

welling with emotion when Tucker found her, and now
he was making her overflow.

He lifted his hand in a sliding caress of her cheek. "I
didn't expect to find someone like you in Fair Castle, El."
He smiled a rueful smile. "I—you must see how hard
you've hit me; I'm as obvious as can be."

Despite her earlier sense that there might be something
happening between them, Elinor found herself overwhelmed by Tucker's revelation. He was making it to her
at a time when her emotions were already in turmoil; it
was like throwing gasoline on a brushfire.

She groped for words to express her own confusion.
"It's all so strange, isn't it?" she said, averting her face
from him in sudden shyness. "We're just toddling along,
minding our own business, and then suddenly . . . everything's different. We haven't asked for it, we haven't
looked for it; and yet suddenly everything's . . . different."

Elinor shivered again, despite being engulfed in a jacket
still warm from him. It seemed to her that the tempera-
ture was falling with every passing second. Unconsciously
she moved closer to Tucker, trying to escape from the
cutting wind.

He put his arm around her and hugged her close in a
gesture that was meant more to warm than to arouse. But
the night was dark and she was cold and he was stirred.
The hug became an embrace, the embrace, something
more.

"Tucker," she murmured as he began to kiss her.

"Tucker—wait," she said, moving her mouth away
from his. She realized they weren't alone. Twice in one
day, with two different men—not alone.

Elinor jerked her head around to face the dark, impenetrable end of the gallery. Had she seen movement there?
She thought perhaps something—someone—moved. It
was the merest shadow of a shadow, maybe a scrap of
litter tossed by the wind. But a lurch of movement, definitely.

It wasn't her grandfather this time; that was certain.
"Who's there?" she said in a low, sharp whisper. Despite
the presence of Tucker beside her, she began to tremble.

There was a heavy, ironbound door at the far end of the gallery; it was never opened. Elinor wasn't sure it *could* be opened. Whoever or whatever was at that end was trapped on their side of the door. "Tucker—" she said, recoiling from the inky blackness there.

Without questioning either her intuition or her logic, Tucker covered the length of the gallery in a few long strides. In the darkness she heard—but could not see—him rattle the door handle.

"Locked," he said. He came back to where she waited, half-fearful, half-baffled, and said, "Maybe you heard a bat. Or a possum on the battlement."

"Let's go in, Tuck," she suddenly urged. "Let's go in."

"Fine with me," he answered with a shudder. "It's frigid out here."

Agnes had outdone herself. From the poached salmon to the crème brulée, dinner was far and away her most edible to date. Elinor decided that hiring Agnes's son Owen as handyman—a form of blackmail, pure and simple— might end up being worth the money, after all.

Elinor's mother should have been pleased with the splash her new cook was making with the guests; but she was not. It was obvious that Will's imminent departure had upset Susan deeply. She was indifferent to the Samuelsons, short with Chester, impatient with Tucker, and positively frigid with Elinor.

By the second course, Elinor figured out that the Samuelsons had been invited for the express purpose of getting William Braddock fired up about Fair Castle. Anne Samuelson, an enormously successful realtor, went on and on—and on—about the property, marveling at its small-scale majesty and its historic aura. She loved its livability, was charmed by its intimacy, liked its flow. On a more level site . . . with the right kitchen . . . well, she'd live in it herself and she really meant it. Truly.

It was a valiant effort but a pointless one. The customer was nowhere to be seen.

Elinor divided her time between Tucker and the excellent food, hearing little that he said, tasting little that she ate.

Back to England. How *could* he? Had that been him at the dark end of the gallery, saying his good-byes to Fair Castle?

And if it wasn't Will, who—or what—then? The sudden fear that had gripped her was not unlike the irrational fear she'd felt as she groped her way through the darkened castle after her clash with Will in the turret. The kiss in the turret. It seemed a million moods ago.

And now, out of the blue, Tucker O'Toole. He was attracted to her and she was attracted to him. It seemed to Elinor that she was under seige emotionally. The carefree vacation that she'd planned had become a cruel joke; the serenity that she needed to create had become a shattered hope.

After what felt like a twelve-course meal, it became time for Izzy's parlor game. The girl had got her grandfather's promise that he'd hang around instead of sneaking off to the library and taking all the men with him, so the great parlor—not as great as it sounded—was full.

As Izzy untangled her string, Mickey MacLeish settled himself and his brandy snifter into the biggest chair, then put his feet up on the tufted leather ottoman that squatted in front of it.

"In my last life," he told his granddaughter, "I was either a pharaoh or a king. But if you care to prove it, Missy Izzy, then you may proceed." He gave the company a wink and waited for the fun to begin.

Elinor could hardly slip away; Izzy would be hurt. So she sat on the loveseat next to Tucker as Izzy had instructed her to do, while the others gathered around in whatever armchairs were at hand.

Not everyone was happy. The professor looked bored by the prospect of humoring a ten-year-old. His wife began making noises about soon having to be on their way.

Izzy dropped to her knees before a wide, low table that normally was buried under stacks of books and magazines. On the table she spread out a map of the world; next to it, a sheet of sketch paper on which she'd drawn a grid of dates dating from 2000 B.C. to 2000 A.D.

"Okay, I'm ready now!" the girl announced cheerfully.

"Ready for what, sweetie?" asked the realtor, who hadn't been paying much attention.

"Ready to tell you who I used to be! It's a game of reincarnation!"

Apparently Izzy's mother hadn't been paying attention, either. Susan looked up surprised and said with some annoyance, "Isabelle, are you sure anyone really cares who you used to be?"

"I do."

All heads swung to the far end of the room. There, standing in the doorway with his hands in his pockets and a look of amused boredom on his face, stood Lord Norwood.

Chapter 15

*W*ill swept them all in his glance and said, "Sorry I wasn't able to be here earlier. Do you mind if I sit in and watch the fun?"

Susan Roberts lit up like a Roman candle. "Lord Norwood! What a delight that you can make the time. Do come join us. Tucker," she said, turning on the charm, "why don't you sit over here, next to me? I haven't had a chance to chat with you all evening. And Lord Norwood can sit in your place."

Elinor, whose heartbeat was bouncing around like a tennis ball in an overtime match, saw through her mother's ploy. "We're fine the way we *are*, Mother. Izzy, let's get started. What're you waiting for?" She refused to look at Will, who took a seat behind Isabelle and directly across from Elinor and Tucker.

Isabelle, innocent and eager, said, "Okay. I'm going to ask myself a bunch of questions, and then I'm going to dangle this crystal pendant and it's going to tell me the answers. If it goes up and down, it means yes. If it goes sideways, it means no. And after I finish, then the rest of you can try."

Poor Izzy. Like the proverbial child raised by wolves, she assumed that she and the grown-ups were all the same species. Nothing could be further from the truth. No one wanted to play her silly game. No one even wanted to watch. There was too much going on in the room. Tension was rippling like waves on a beach between Mickey Mac-

Leish and the baron; between Elinor and the baron; between Tucker and the baron; between Anne and the baron; and between Susan and everyone else *but* the baron.

They were all trapped in a web of civility, and no one was sure who the spider was.

Isabelle suspended the crystal teardrop over the map and closed her eyes. "My first question is, where was I born?" She swung the pendulum by its string in a wild arc to the left and to the right and then let the crystal land with a thump in the middle of the Atlantic. She opened her eyes, checked her alleged birthplace, and said, "Hey!"

Her grandfather laughed, along with the others, and said, "Were you a mermaid, Iz? Or are you just trying to prove you were born in Atlantis?"

Will said quietly, "You weren't following your rules, Isabelle. You have to suggest an actual country. Then the crystal will dip if the answer's yes, or swing if it's no. Or you can suspend the crystal over one country at a time and ask about it. I imagine that's how it's supposed to work, anyway," he added.

"Wow—how do you know that?" she asked him.

"What you're trying to do is a form of dowsing," he said. "It's the same method used by people with dowsing rods to find water."

Over Izzy's head, Tucker locked gazes with Will. "So you're an expert in water-witching as well as computers. That's a little schizophrenic, don't you think?"

Will's smile was thin. "I read a lot."

Lem Samuelson, the college professor, said in his stuffy way, "So theoretically, one is asking one's subconscious about one's so-called past lives. Interesting. It certainly will give one clues about one's self in one's present life."

"Whatever," said Izzy, lost by the psychobabble. "I'll start with—"

"Try Spain," said her grandmother. "That's a good place to look for an Isabelle. Maybe even a Queen Isabelle."

"Good idea!" Izzy hung the pendant over the country and said, "Was I born in Spain?"

Her hands jerked the pendant up, then down. She said excitedly, "I *was* born in Spain! You were right, Gramma Cam! This is so easy!"

Everyone chuckled at her gullibility. Izzy asked herself the next question. Still with the crystal suspended over Spain, she said, "Was I a queen?"

Naturally the pendant bobbed up and down again. "I knew it!" she cried. "Queen Isabelle of Spain. Wait till I tell Catherine!"

"Wait," said Elinor. "You don't know that you were named Isabelle when you were living in Spain."

"Oh, right." Izzy closed her eyes again. "Was I called Isabelle then?"

No contest. Of course she was.

"Was I living in Spain in—when did Queen Isabelle live?" Izzy asked the adults around her.

Her grandfather said, "What! You don't know even that much history? Come on. What made Queen Isabelle famous?"

"Oh, yeah. Columbus. 'He sailed the ocean blue in fourteen-ninety-two.' " She closed her eyes and asked the pendant, "Did I live in Spain in 1492?"

For sure.

Izzy threw down the pendant and clapped her hands. "So there! Queen Isabelle is *much* more important than Catherine the Great. Okay," she said, having completed her personal agenda for the evening. "Who wants to go next?"

Good question. Suddenly all the grown-ups looked like preteens at a school dance: downcast eyes, blushing cheeks, frogs in their throats. Izzy, disappointed in their reluctance, decided to take matters in hand.

"Elly, you go."

"Me? Why me? No! Pick someone else."

All of the others, relieved to be let off the hook, jumped in to second Isabelle's command. Only the nobleman said nothing. He just sat there with that smile-that-wasn't-a-smile on his face, leaving Elinor completely convinced that he was the one she'd sensed on the gallery.

It'd be just like him to resent what he'd regard as an intrusion. And withdraw into the shadows. How characteristic of him. Even if he couldn't possibly have been there.

Jerk.

Well, she wasn't going to let him see she cared. Not for all the castles in England. She flashed him a dazzling, cocky grin and said, "All right, here goes nothing. But if I turn out to have been Ivan the Terrible, I don't want everyone getting mad at me."

She exchanged places with Izzy. Sitting cross-legged on the floor in her burgundy dress, with her back turned to Will, she took up the string and propped her elbows on the low table, then swung the pendant lazily over the map of the world, getting the feel of it. "Hmmm," she said in a musing way. "Where ... was ... I ... born?" She glanced at Tucker, smiled, and then closed her eyes. "Hmmm."

Naturally Elinor felt no pull on the pendant of any kind in any direction; she was about as sensitive as a waffle iron. But that didn't mean she couldn't amuse herself and the company—and yank Will's chain—all at the same time. She opened her eyes and scanned the map.

After dangling the crystal briefly over Egypt—Cleopatra's life sounded pretty cool, until the snake part—Elinor swung the pendant over Europe.

She let the pendant hover over the British Isles. "I feel something," she said in the voice of a mall psychic.

She asked the pendant, "Was I born in Scotland?"

The pendant swung in a lazy arc: No.

"Was I born in Ireland?"

No.

"Was I born in Merry Olde England?"

Ta-dah! Up and down, up and down bobbed the crystal pendant.

Chester nodded approvingly. "That explains a lot," he said, apparently believing Elinor's antics.

"When were you born?" asked Tucker. His smile was more intimate than charmed.

"Wait a sec; I'll find out," said Elinor, giving him a

carbon copy of that smile. She loved the fact that Will was behind her and couldn't see her face. It allowed her to fire Tucker up without letting Will know that she was firing Tucker up. Who said she couldn't flirt with the best of them?

She went back to her pendant. "Was I born in, hmm, the sixteenth century?"

Nope.

"Seventeenth?"

Uh-uh.

"Eighteenth?"

The pendant decided to say yes. Elinor had a definite life in mind now. She began narrowing the decades, then the years within those decades, until she came up with the birth year 1742. Maybe the year would click with Will, maybe it wouldn't. No matter; she had more questions to go.

Interrupting her daughter's whimsical probe, Susan said pointedly, "Find out if you were ever married, darling. *I'd* certainly like to know."

The barb was well aimed. Elinor rolled her eyes at Tucker, reminding him about their conversation on the gallery. The look he gave her in return was so intense that it could have passed for a proposal in some societies.

Aware that she was playing with fire, Elinor continued to stir things up. Her main goal now was to provoke the baron. She didn't know why. Maybe it was because he hadn't had the guts to tell her that the battle for the castle was over and that she'd won.

She asked the pendant, "Was I married?"

Elinor's plan was to make it say yes, just to give her mother hope. But her hands seemed to want to say yes and no at the same time, canceling themselves out. Surprised by her own indecision, Elinor gave the string a forceful yank upward and then let it fall. Yes! Of course she was married!

Concentrate, stupid, she warned herself. Back and forth means no, up and down means yes. She was letting Will distract her, even though she couldn't even *see* the guy.

Ah, but she was aware of him. Her back felt warm, as

if she were sitting too close to the heat of his anger. Will must have known that she was playing with him; must have known that she was trying to provoke him.

"Did I have, oh, seven children?" she asked mischievously.

No.

"Six children?"

No.

Five? Four, three, two? No to all.

"Did I have one child?" One child was all she could handle, she decided.

She felt a sudden, definite, amazing back-and-forth pull on the string: *No.*

Whoa, she thought. *Who's running this thing?* Her elbow must've slipped on the table. Yes. That was it.

"No children?" sighed her mother, disappointed.

Her grandfather said, "What about a name, Elly? Isabelle used to be an Isabelle. Was Elinor an Elinor?"

"Yes, Elly," said her young sister. "Ask!"

Elinor, still a little distracted, said, "I was just going to find out." She knew full well what her answer would be. She was about to claim that she was the reincarnation of William Braddock's great-great-whatever grandmother, the blond beauty whose portrait hung in the halls of Fair Castle, next to the one of her husband.

See what Lord Norwood had to say about *that.*

She glanced at Tucker and smiled flirtatiously, feeding the flames. Yvonne would've been impressed. Tucker leaned forward, drawn by her spell.

Excellent. Let Will know he wasn't God's gift to all women. Let him know that men like Tucker with no money and kind hearts were infinitely more attractive to her than men like Will with their grand fortunes and selfish agendas.

She gave a little wriggle in place, as if she were Victor Borge getting ready to play a comic piano concerto, and then she innocently asked the crystal, "Was I called Elinor?"

Yes. Of course.

Elinor said, "More specifically, was I Lady Norwood?"

Forever after, Elinor remembered the response to that question. There was another strong pull from side to side, and then the string that she held lightly between the thumb and middle finger of each hand began to burn like a red-hot wire, searing her fingers and her soul simultaneously.

"Ow, ow, ow!" she cried, throwing the string and its pendant down on the table. "Hot! The string is hot!"

"Elly, are you nuts?" blurted her stepfather. "Strings can't get hot."

"*Really,* Elinor—" her mother snapped.

Tears of agony welled up in Elinor's eyes as she blew on her fingers to no avail. They continued to throb, sending signals of pain so strong that her arms felt limp. While her family and guests stared in amazement, she plunged first her left fingers, then her right, into a nearby glass of sparkling water, aware that she was acting like a madwoman, aware that she didn't care.

No relief. Nothing in her life had prepared her for the torment she felt. It was as if someone had slid red-hot needles into the thumb and middle finger of each hand and then wandered away. Her fingers began to curl involuntarily from the pain.

It was her mother who broke the stunned silence. "Elly! What on earth is wrong with you?"

Elinor heard rising panic; she had to force herself to sound calm, or her mother's concern would quickly escalate. "It's . . . nothing," she said between gasps. Somehow she made herself say calmly, "I think maybe I pinched a nerve."

In some odd way, that simple explanation seemed to reassure the others. Everyone began speaking at once, offering a story about someone else who'd had the exact same thing happen. In the middle of the cross-conversations Elinor managed to struggle to her feet, intent on escaping from the stares and sympathetic murmurs of the company around her.

And then it happened. The pain went away as quickly as it had come. Elinor stood there, feeling fine; feeling stupid.

"Oh, wow," she said, grinning with relief. "It passed. Thank God for that. Sorry for the spectacle," she added sheepishly. "I never did tolerate pain very well."

The college professor took advantage of the happy ending to signal his wife and get the hell out of there, and after that the party broke up quickly. Will had a plane to catch in the morning. Chester's shoulder had begun to throb. Mickey MacLeish thought that maybe the fish was off a little; his stomach was churning. Camilla MacLeish, who'd been watching Elinor's antics all night with concern, looked troubled and pensive. As for Susan, she was convinced that Elinor had carpal tunnel syndrome and that her career as an artist was now over.

Throughout the good-nights and good-byes, Elinor tried to seem lighthearted and pleasant about the evening. The truth was, she was edgy and fearful. She'd been able to rationalize all the eerie feelings and wild coincidences so far; but that string had been *hot*. Nothing and no one would convince her otherwise.

Elinor was not a superstitious person. The God she believed in was a kind God, not a vengeful one. But even *she* thought that maybe she deserved the needle-sharp pain that had ripped through her after her little performance with the dowsing pendant. She'd toyed with two men's feelings just because she was angry and hurt by Will's decision to up and leave without telling her. Her response had been more vengeful than kind.

So she stood on the landing with both Tucker and the baron, humble now and genuinely sorry that she'd been such a witch.

She extended her hand to Will and gave him a small, mournful smile. "I hope you have a good trip back," she said softly. "I'm sorry things didn't work out the way you wanted."

Or the way *she* wanted either, she now realized—which left her more confused than ever.

Will took her hand in that just-right handshake of his and said in a voice as tentative as her own, "Sometimes the best thing is to step back and reassess. That's what I'm doing."

It was the most information he'd ever given her about how he operated, and it didn't really tell her a thing. Once again Elinor had the sense that he was speaking on more than one level. About his emotions? About the castle? Who knew?

Tucker shook Will's hand, too; but it was obvious that he had no regrets as he said, "Good-bye, Norwood. As you can see, Fair Castle's in good hands."

"I'll bear that in mind," said Will calmly, "as I make my plans."

Elinor had the sense of an older, seasoned knight going off on yet another crusade and leaving a younger, more ambitious squire behind in charge of the castle. Will looked as weary as Tucker looked energized. She hadn't noticed, before now, the flecks of gray in Will's hair, or the way his frown of concentration had permanently creased his forehead. Standing next to the younger, more vigorous man, William Braddock looked every one of his forty-one years.

And yet . . . and yet. There was still something about him that said Lord Norwood would not be denied whatever it was he wanted. He'd earned that fortune back, after all, enough to be able to buy back his heritage. Elinor respected that—even though she'd never admit it to him.

And so they stood there—the three of them—not so much awkwardly as warily, as if there were still skirmishes to be fought and battles to be won, only no one knew who was on whose side.

Finally the silence began to sound a little noisy. Elinor had been unable so far to let the good-byes end: She somehow wanted Will to say, "I was right and you were wrong and I want more than anything to be friends and hopefully lovers."

He didn't say it. Or anything even close. He said, "It's been fun. Good night." And then he turned away from Tucker and her and headed for his chamber, leaving Elinor with no excuse to linger.

Tucker said softly to her, "How're your hands, El? All right?"

"Yes . . . but it was the strangest thing," she said, depressed now and filled with unease.

He lifted one of her hands to his lips, kissing the fingertips, and then he did the same with the other.

And Elinor realized, not for the first time, that she could do worse.

Chapter 16

𝒲ill hadn't been willing to admit that she'd driven him away—not until his plane touched down at Heathrow and he realized that he was back in England with nothing, really, to do.

There was his grandmother to see, obviously. And his broker to meet. The estate was always crying out for attention. But all in all he had nothing, really, to *do*.

Fair Castle had been the focus not only of his trip to the States, but of the last six months of his life. He'd cleared his calendar completely for it. It wouldn't be an exaggeration to say that he'd spent half of the last forty *years* chasing it. He'd always had the desire, and now he had the money, to see it returned to its proper place on that high knoll in Dibble. He'd talked with engineers; he'd met with planning boards. It could be done.

So what, precisely, was the problem?

Elinor MacLeish, that's what. She was the infuriating, exasperating, manipulating . . . *force* responsible for his hasty retreat to Dibble. Dragon, banshee, witch and sorceress: She was all of them, and she was in his castle. How the bloody hell was he going to get her out?

The question pretty much consumed him as he made his way through the evening crush at the airport and then hopped a charter flight to Berwick. He was no nearer an answer as a Berwick taxi ferried him though winding, hilly north country, turning at last onto a road that rolled past artfully placed willows swaying gently in the deepening twilight.

By the time the car stopped in front of the gamekeeper's cottage—a steep-roofed, brick and stucco structure tucked in a corner of his vast estate in Dibble—all that he could come up with after twenty-four hours of thought on the subject was one very obvious conclusion: Money would not buy her.

He overpaid the driver in American dollars and carried his own bags to an iron bench that sat in a cozy, tile-roofed enclosure just outside the front door. There was no need to crank the brass bell; he was expected. The door opened on cue and he ducked inside onto well-worn planks under a low-beamed ceiling.

"Evenin', Maggy; how goes the battle?" he said with more heartiness than he felt.

His grandmother's companion, an intelligent, reassuring woman somewhere at the end of her middle age, said, "Welcome back, sir. Everyone's fine." Her smile was warm and expectant: She was in on the master plan, too.

An old Dalmatian, friendly without being overbearing, approached and waited, tail wagging, to say hello. Will crouched down and rubbed the dog's ears.

"Hey, Pepper," he crooned affectionately. "How's the old girl? Keeping busy?" He stood up and took a deep breath; he still had no idea what he was going to say.

In place of good news, he'd brought a dozen red roses. These he carried with grim cheer toward the austerely furnished parlor. His heels echoed on the bare wood floors, announcing his approach. In answer he heard the motorized wheels of his grandmother's chair humming across the same wood floors, conveying her excitement.

He took another deep breath. "Nana! I'm back and you were wrong," he said, grinning as they met in the hall. "I wasn't robbed and left for dead in the street. Are you surprised?"

He presented her with the deeply scented flowers.

"More pleased than surprised," the elderly woman admitted. She tilted her cheek toward Will for a kiss, then breathed in the fragrance of the roses. "Lovely, dear. Just

lovely. Mrs. Munger, would you put these in water for
me, please? And I wonder if you could bring us some tea.
Thank you so much.''

She handed off the bouquet and turned to her grandson. "I suppose I oughtn't to have worried, William; I
realize Fair Castle is well north of New York City. But
you spent time in the city as well, and one reads such
things about that place.''

"Gross exaggerations, every one. It's a great city; open
twenty-four hours a day."

A look of mild disapproval came over the elderly
woman's lined face. "No one can have respectable business at three in the morning."

"Nana, that's Dibble talk."

"Wheel me back to the hearth, then, and we shall talk
about Fair Castle instead," she said, her pale blue eyes
shining with affection. "I'm desperate to hear every little
detail."

Which is exactly what he'd dreaded. He gazed at his
grandmother, so fragile, so quietly thrilled. Dorothea
Braddock had waited over half a century for this moment.
She'd hoped for it, prayed for it, dreamed of it.

He never knew how much, until he was twenty years
old and on holiday from university.

"Sometimes I dream a little dream," she'd told him. In
her voice was a wistful ache that had haunted him for the
next two decades.

"I dream that I'm back in Fair Castle and that your
grandfather is alive and so is your father. He and your
mother have never divorced and are happy in their marriage. Your sister isn't estranged from everyone. We're all
together, celebrating. I rather think it's a holiday—perhaps Boxing Day. There's a festive air about the place.
There is music . . . and dancing. And a great, leaping fire
in every hearth. The dream is so wonderfully real," she'd
told him. "We are all so joyful. And then, just as your
grandfather is about to ask me to dance—I wake up.

"It's always the same," she'd told Will sadly. "I wake
up."

From the time he was a boy in knickers, Will had

known that his grandmother blamed herself for the dismantling of the Braddock family. His grandfather's suicide; his father's loveless marriage, subsequent divorce, and recent death in a car accident; his sister's depression—she blamed it all on her decision to sell and dismantle Fair Castle.

What Will hadn't realized, until he was twenty, was that she used to dream that little dream about living there again; that she somehow believed that bringing back the castle would make things right.

It couldn't, of course. Will's father had remarried and divorced and married a third time before his death in an alcohol-induced car accident. Will's sister had checked into and out of and back into the best substance-abuse clinics that money could buy. Will's mother had little use for anything outside her London party circle. As for Will's grandfather: Nothing could ever unpull that trigger.

But after Will's parents divorced—and left him up for grabs—Dorothea had taken over the raising of him, and done it well. He owed her everything. He owed her the effort to try to make her dream come true.

Which is why a year ago, flush with the sale of his software company and rich beyond ordinary definitions of wealth, Will had stupidly announced his intention of bringing Fair Castle back to England.

He never should have said so out loud. Not to his grandmother. That was his first and biggest mistake, and now he was going to have to pay for it: by disappointing the one he cared for most in the world.

But his grandmother couldn't know that, as he guided her wheelchair and chatted amusingly about the crazy family that now lived within the walls of Fair Castle—because he had implied, at least on the phone, that the negotiations were going well.

Blame the family, he told himself in desperation now. It was easy. It was safe. It was true.

He settled Dorothea's wheelchair within warming distance of the cozy fire that burned in the blackened firebox, then shut and locked a diamond paned casement that had been left open a crack. He was tucking a wool afghan around his grandmother's knees when Maggie came in with the roses arranged in a crystal vase; Will took them and set them on the foot-deep windowsill closest to where his grandmother liked to read during the day.

Dorothea protested that he was treating her as if she had one foot in the grave. But then she added in a wistful voice, "Do you remember, William, how we used to take Pepper—not this Pepper; I mean her mother—with us when we rode the length of the estate? I was thinking how this Pepper never got the chance. When she was young, I was already laid up with arthritis and you were busy. Now that you've sold your business, you've the time; but she's too old, poor thing. Just look at her."

Pepper, curled on a bed of red gingham and wise to the sound of her name, lifted her head and gazed at her mistress with quiet devotion.

Will was unable to suppress a wistful sigh of his own. "Timing is everything, they say."

"You're right, you're right," said his grandmother briskly. "We must fix what we can, live with the rest. And I *have* been feeling better, now the rain's backed off a bit. Much better! Pepper and I have circled the garden with all due speed at least four times this past week."

Will knew better than to try to talk her into moving to a more hospitable climate. Sixty inches of rain a year had not deterred a multitude of Braddock generations before them; why should Dorothea be any different?

His grandmother straightened her thin shoulders and folded her knobby hands on her lap. "Now," she said, "tell me everything. The owner is still painting, you say, and his wife used to be on the stage? I don't remember that at all; I imagine I was too distressed at the time. Did she perform in the classics? Would I know of her roles?"

Will laughed and said, "Probably not. Camilla Mac-Leish was a chorus girl in a Gershwin play when Mickey MacLeish whisked her off on their fateful tour of England. I will say this: She's still tremendously fit; she looks nothing like her age. I suppose it's all those stairs."

"Whereas we shall have to install one of those stair-lifts. Mrs. MacLeish is a lucky woman," Dorothea said with a resigned sigh.

Like all elderly, she had a keen interest in the health of other elderly. She added, "And Mr. MacLeish? How is *his* health?"

"Still pretty good, although he's had a couple of very minor heart attacks."

"There is no such thing as a very minor heart attack, William," she said dryly.

"I suppose you're right," Will conceded. "He does have to watch what he eats and drinks, and he's been barred outright from smoking cigars. Not that any of it matters if he's in the mood for living well—which he nearly always is. Actually, at the rate he's going . . ."

It amazed Will that he was annoyed by Mickey Mac-Leish's recklessness. Shaking his head, he summed the old man up in a sentence: "He has an artist's temperament."

"Oh, dear."

Dorothea waited for her grandson to go on. When he did not, she gave him a gentle prod. "When you rang me up, didn't you say that the whole family was artistic? Are they all like him? Temperamental?"

"Well may you ask," said Will grimly. He went over to the fire and poked at it. It didn't need stoking—Maggie Munger had got the thing jumping merrily—but Will needed the extra seconds wherever he could find them. He could not bring himself to tell his grandmother that Elinor MacLeish had thrown him out. Or had him thrown out. It hardly mattered which. He was out.

He veered away from any mention of her, beginning instead with her sister.

"The youngest, Isabelle, is ten. She's surprisingly naive, even for an American, and surprisingly gentle. Izzy wants to be a novelist."

"How nice. She sounds quite sweet."

"She is. So is her stepfather, Chester Roberts, never mind that he looks like one of their fierce mountain men. Chester has one overriding passion: arms and armor. I gather he's spent most of his retirement funds on them. It's a point of contention between his wife and him."

Will lifted a log from the wicker basket and dropped it in the flames, then rearranged it with the tongs under the ones already burning.

I hate this, he acknowledged bitterly. *Hate having to tell her.*

"Mr. Roberts's wife isn't artistic, then?" came his grandmother's shrewd question from behind him.

He shook his head. "Susan Roberts is the most practical-minded of the lot. She's the one who keeps the books and organizes the occasional event. I imagine she understands the debit column better than any of them. She's quite keen to sell. I rather think—"

Here he felt his cheeks redden. Grateful for the dim, cozy light in the room, he laid the tongs carefully up against the brick facing and said, "I rather think she has plans for me."

"Plans, dear?" his grandmother asked innocently. "What sort of plans?"

Will cleared his throat. "Of the marriage sort," he said dryly. He turned to his grandmother, unable to keep the grimace from his face.

Dorothea sat up a little straighter in her wheelchair. "And what does *Chester* Roberts say to that?"

"Chester—? Ah. No, it's not to herself that Susan would see me wed."

Plainly confused, Dorothea drew down her brows in a more delicate version of her grandson's frown. "Then to whom, William? Not to the child, obviously. Who else is there?"

"Hmm. I suppose I haven't mentioned Elinor."

"No-o-o, I don't believe you have. You've talked about their cook . . . and about the cook's son whom you dislike so . . . and about some young man doing research there. But I can't rememember any Elinor."

"The older sister? I thought I'd . . . hmm. Well—she's an artist. Not a painter like her grandfather; she does children's picture books."

"Really! How delightful; I hope you brought one with you."

Will mumbled something about possibly having thrown one in his suitcase.

His obvious reluctance to talk about Elinor roused even his innocent grandmother's suspicions. "Is she temperamental, then? Like her grandfather?"

"You might say."

"Well, really, William, you don't seem to be *saying* much of *anything*." Dorothea cocked her head at him like a small, curious bird. "I've never known you to hesitate with an opinion about someone. Is this Elinor so offensive that you can't bear to speak of her?"

Will snorted, more to himself than to his grandmother, and said, "Where's Maggie with the blasted tea, anyway? I'll just go see, shall I?"

He escaped from his grandmother's sitting room, if ever so briefly, and hid in the kitchen while Maggie carefully arranged two bone-china mugs and a silver tea service on a tray that was ferrying Norwood teacups before the Americans threw their first tea party in Boston.

All the while, Maggie Munger carried on a nonstop monologue about her mistress's wonderful new zest for life. Maggie had been attending the elderly woman for nearly a decade, and these past weeks, she told Will, had been far and away the happiest they'd ever shared. Far and away.

Lifting the quilted cozy from the teapot, she lowered her voice and said, "Having her castle back has given her a reason to live, it has. I've not seen Lady Norwood so cheerful in a good three or four years. She does go on about you, sir! She calls you her knight in shining armor."

With a cheerful sigh, the portly companion handed him the laden, two-handled tray. "She's been so lonely by herself here; but now you've got the castle being boxed up for sending, why, the telephone rings every day. Your mum's more attentive and your sister's at least curious. I wouldn't be surprised, I wouldn't, if Penny actually stopped in one of these fine days. It's that much of a miracle."

"Fine, well, whatever," Will muttered, feeling like a royal fool as he stood there with the tea tray, receiving accolades that were not due.

He carried the tray into the sitting room and laid it on a large ottoman covered in a needlepoint rendering of the one thing that he could not bear to look at tonight: Fair Castle. His grandmother had finished the piece with great difficulty while in the first throes of the arthritis that had overtaken her a decade ago.

Her crippling disease was presumed to have been caused by a tiny, germ-bearing tick. To make matters worse, she'd probably contracted the disease on a walking tour through Europe—a tour that Will had arranged and paid for, because he wanted his grandmother to see the world. He'd even paid for two of her friends to accompany her.

And here was the result: a once-fit woman laid up in crippling pain. As always when he thought of that tour, he felt a sickening surge of guilt.

If it hadn't been for that tick, would he now be moving hell and high water to get Fair Castle back? Will couldn't honestly say. All he knew was that his grandmother had taken him in when neither parent had wanted him, and for that she deserved a necklace of stars; she deserved the moon on a string. At the very least, she deserved Fair Castle.

Still loathe to admit his failure to her, he said, "Hold on, I don't see any lemons. I'll just—"

"William Mallard Braddock, you *sit*," Dorothea said with good-natured impatience. "You're as restless as a pony before a storm. Mrs. Munger could've brought in tea. What on earth is wrong with you? Now finish about this Elinor. I want to know all about her. Because I think you're holding something back on me, young man."

Her smile was inexpressibly sweet—and much too hopeful. Dorothea had always bemoaned his bachelor state. Before the arthritis, she used to arrange brutally awkward teas for him with every unmarried woman she'd come across. Even during her abrupt slide into old age, she'd kept up the part of matchmaker, signing her all-too-busy grandson up for parish bazaars and village jumbles on the plausible theory that nice young women volunteered to work in them, too.

But no nice young woman was *the* nice young woman, and so here he sat, forced to come up with a reason why the banshee from hell was not the woman to fit the bill. It wasn't enough merely to say, "She's an American." His grandmother was much too desperate to care anymore.

He could tell her the truth: that Elinor MacLeish had vowed that he'd get the castle only more or less over her dead body. But he wasn't ready—he couldn't imagine ever being ready—to tell his grandmother that Fair Castle was not to be.

And so he sat, like a child caught during math with his thoughts on a soccer field, and tried to explain why it was that he had no use for Elinor MacLeish.

His first foray was just awful. He said, "She's really overly—how shall I say this?—vibrant. They all are. They speak too quickly, too loudly, too often. Their hands fly about as if some puppeteer is pulling strings to them. And they interrupt one another. All the time. A meal can be a madhouse." His grandmother, unable to take his objection seriously, simply stared.

He said feverishly, "They live entirely in the present, you know; and she's the worst of the lot. Won't look ahead, won't read the writing on the wall.

"And she's headstrong," he added, beginning to squirm in earnest. "That's the kindest way I can put it. 'Bullheaded' is more accurate. Point to the sun, tell her it's shining, and she'll deny it to your face. She *will* not see the obvious."

"Well! But is she clever?"

"Oh . . . clever. Clever is in the eye of the beholder. Some might think so. I certainly don't. Although her work is clever. One of her stories features a dragon, and I must say—" He caught himself smiling just in time. "No. Not particularly clever," he said with a shrug.

Undaunted, Dorothea pressed on. "What does she look like?"

"Oh . . . just . . . average. Well, not average, exactly.

She's anything but average. She has this way of lifting her chin in defiance that makes me want to just—" He clamped his jaw down hard in anger, then added, "Well, let me say that no Englishwoman would ever lift her chin that way."

"But what does she *look* like?"

Will was a software engineer, not a wordsmith; it was a real struggle to explain Elinor's gypsy aura. "Well . . . tallish. No, medium-ish. Up to here," he said, slicing at his collarbone with the side of his hand. A sudden, penetrating sense of her warmth seemed to knock him off balance, as did the decided scent of her hair. He was shocked by the nearness of her; she was three thousand miles away.

"Her hair is . . . hmm . . . very thick; very straight," he said in a musing voice. He seemed to be having an easier time picturing her, now that he'd begun mentally drawing her portrait. "Brown hair. A good, rich shade of brown with some red in it; nothing washed out about it. Her complexion is a bit on the olive side, but she blushes easily, so maybe olive is the wrong word. In any case, it's not that wan, porcelain skin we see so much around here."

He found himself rubbing his stubbled chin with his hand, lost in thoughts of her. "As for her eyes . . . I can't really remember the color of her eyes. I remember lavender suits her. She looks a knockout in lavender. What color would that make her eyes? I don't know. Violet? Maybe green? Greenish brown?"

Dorothea was plainly disappointed. "You've never looked into her eyes?"

"Of course I have," Will answered, snapping out of his revery in time to take the tall thin mug of tea that Dorothea had lightened and sweetened for him.

He frowned and added grimly, "But what I see in her eyes is hostility; I never quite notice its particular shade."

"Hostility? Why on earth would she be hostile?" Dorothea asked, surprised.

Hell and damnation. He'd fallen into a trap of his own making. "Why, indeed?" he said, sipping his tea. Shit. Why indeed.

Because she's trying to keep her family together by keeping the castle, he wanted to tell his grandmother. *Does her dream sound familiar?*

He settled for a half truth. "Elinor MacLeish draws on the castle for her children's stories. She doesn't want to give up the source of her inspiration."

"But . . . if they can't afford Fair Castle . . . if Mickey MacLeish's health is failing . . . if the most practical person in the family is eager to sell it, and everyone else is willing—then isn't the young lady being a bit . . . selfish?"

"You might say so." He was being brutally unfair to the young lady in question, but if he laid out Elinor's dream for his grandmother to see, she would simply withdraw from the fray. She was far too genteel to get down in the muck and fight for her castle.

But Will understood—as he hadn't until that moment— that a fight in the muck is what it was going to take.

"William? Is something wrong?" his grandmother said, leaning forward. "You seem so preoccupied."

He forced himself to be genial. "Not at all. There are a million details in a venture like this, that's all."

"Perhaps," his grandmother said with a sigh, "this isn't such a good idea, after all."

He made reassuring sounds and laid his hand gently over his grandmother's, appalled, as always, by the size of her knuckles and the odd twists of her fingers. It took both her hands to hold a cup of tea nowadays, and though she always insisted on adding sugar and cream to Will's tea by herself, he could see that even that simple chore would someday be impossible for her to perform.

Will knew that there wasn't a day that she wasn't in pain. He couldn't take away her pain; all he could do was take away the emptiness that let her focus on it.

He glanced around the small sitting room with its whitewashed walls and faded chintz. It used to be so much cozier, until they cleared away most of the furniture to make room for the wheelchair. Few rag rugs, anymore; no more little wobbly tables laden with books and magazines. No more big plants in big pots sitting under the windows that now were kept clear so that she could see out them from her wheelchair. Everything was on the second floor, waiting for the miraculous recovery that Will insisted would someday occur.

"This cottage is too small for you, nana," he said, not for the first time. "Come up to the big house with me."

"Heavens, no," she answered. "You need your own space." It was her standard response.

"You know what you are, nana? You're a snob. You'll live in a castle but not a big house."

"Oh, tish. I'll live where there are memories, that's all. I know Fair Castle. I know this cottage. I've never lived in that new house of yours, and I expect I never will."

The new house was only two acres away, tucked behind a tall hedge. Traditional in style, it had state-of-the-art conveniences and facilities. Will had assumed that his grandmother would stay there eventually; he hadn't reckoned on her need to surround herself with her past.

"You and your memories," he said with a frustrated smile. He rose to take his leave. "You remind me of Elinor MacLeish."

His grandmother looked up at him and said ingenuously, "And will you marry her, as her mother wishes?"

He laughed out loud at that. It was the most satisfying moment he'd had since his arrival. "Not bloody likely," he said. "I'm beat, nana. Suppose we continue all this tomorrow."

"But . . . you haven't told me how the negotiations went!"

He winced and said, "It's fairly complicated."

"How complicated can it be? I know I don't understand all those things that you do with computers. But I do understand about buying and selling castles," she said, obviously hurt that he wasn't taking her into his confidence.

But he was firm. He leaned over and kissed her on the top of her white-haired head and said, "Tomorrow. If the weather holds, I'll take you in the Land Rover and we'll go up to the knoll. And dream a little dream."

And then, sometime after that, he'd fly back to the States and get down in the muck. He'd make an opening offer that would—as they liked to say over there—blow their damn socks off.

Even hers.

Elinor MacLeish stood underneath the two companion portraits that hung high on the wall with the others in the great hall of Fair Castle. Staring first at the wife, then at the husband, she shook her head. Nowhere in either could she discern a single feature that would link them to their great-great-whatever grandson.

She let her gaze drift back to the blond and beautiful woman of the rakish hat and coquettish smile. Born, 1742. Died, 1780. Too many generations had passed, presumably, between her and Will Braddock. Elinor stood there, ticking them off on her fingers. How many would there be? Ten? A dozen? That was a lot of generations.

She swung her gaze from the portait of Elinor to that of her husband, Charles. The painting of him was less flattering. There was something stiff, almost unwilling about him, as if he'd rather be in bed. Still, if she squinted, Elinor could see a resemblance in the arrogance around the eyes. Maybe.

In any case, it was all she had.

She sighed, then pulled on her coat and slung her handbag over her shoulder. Turning to her date, she said, "I sure hope this movie's as funny as the reviews say it is, Tuck. I could use a good laugh."

Tucker O'Toole, who'd been standing beside her, slipped his arm around her and brushed his lips against hers. "If it isn't, I'll hire a clown. I'll kidnap Letterman. I'll do whatever it takes. I've seen your smile and heard you laugh, El. I want more."

"She sees in him what she cannot find in the other: a willingness to put her first above all else. It is ever so with a woman. We would be the sole desire in your eyes, and when we cannot . . . then we ache, or we destroy."

"You were my sole desire, Marianne."

"And for that, I was destroyed."

"Is it possible?"

"*Charles! I have no doubt that foulest murder was committed.*"

"*When news of your death was brought to me, I was on fire with fever. I remember little of that day, except the fact of your death.*"

"*I can taste the poison still.*"

"*Your father said the meat was spoiled. He survived, but you did not, nor your uncle. I remember well the long nights of agony, knowing that I would never see you again. Weeks passed before I was able to leave my bed. And after that, grief and revulsion kept me from entering hers.*"

"*It is my only comfort.*"

Chapter 17

*O*ctober surprised them with another fine day. Late, bright sun poured through the wall-sized windows of Will's state-of-the-art kitchen as he padded barefoot on the heated tile floor, groping through his jet lag for coffee and something that might pass for a meal.

Yesterday stunk. Today would be worse. He was tempted, for a brief, irrational moment, to call the States and make the offer by phone; but Mickey MacLeish might not be receptive at four in the morning.

And besides, what if *she* answered? What the hell would he do? God. It was like trying to get past the Cyclops.

He stirred sugar into an ill-made mess of brown liquid, then forgot to add cream as he wandered the rooms of his big, new, empty house, sulking because his grandmother had spurned it; sulking because he'd been beat by a woman; sulking because he wanted to sulk.

Damn her! She'd been like some burr under his shirt, cutting, scratching, rubbing him endlessly the wrong way. A part of him had been downright relieved to escape from the castle and jump on the plane. It wasn't until last night, as he tossed and turned in his bed, that he realized Elinor MacLeish was even more irritating from a distance.

And meanwhile, Fair Castle. It hovered ever out of reach, like some dream behind the nightmare of his failure. Beautiful, elusive, haunting. Fair Castle. He wanted it. He wanted it.

And worse: He wanted her. All night long.

In his dreams he'd been able to picture her so clearly; feel her in his arms; practically taste the sweetness of the soft, warm flesh between her thighs.

But now it was morning; he pushed the thought of sex with her firmly from his mind. Wanting Elinor MacLeish was a little like wanting to beat your head against the wall just so you could stop—a pointless exercise in masochism. He'd been thinking hot thoughts about her because he'd been in bed, because he hadn't been with a woman in months, and because he was stiff as a truncheon.

No, by God; he refused to want her.

He dressed with no enthusiasm and got into his Land Rover with even less enthusiasm. His plan now was to lie outright to his grandmother. He'd tell her that he'd given the MacLeishes a generous amount of time to review his offer before they signed. It would give *him* the time he needed to nail down the sale. If she asked him how much he'd offered—well, she would never ask. She wasn't an American, after all.

"I do hate the thought of cutting down the copper beech. I suppose it can't be helped?"

Dorothea Braddock, bundled in dark wool, hovered over her aluminum walker and squinted into the morning sun at the high, grassy knoll, empty save for the single tree she had planted there after the last of Fair Castle's stones had been carted off.

The copper beech was nearly a meter in diameter now, and had thrown its canopy of purple shade over many of their picnics. It wasn't yet large enough to be called majestic; but it certainly was large enough to regret taking it down.

"I think it's grown too big to move," Will admitted. "Although, fifty is young as beeches go."

Will had been amazed to find his grandmother dressed and ready when he came for her; amazed when she insisted that they take her walker along in the car. He began to realize how deep and true her dream really ran; there was nothing little about it.

"I'll tell you what," he added. "We'll ask about moving it. Nothing is impossible—"

"—if one has the money. I see what you mean, dear. It would cost a bomb to move, I'm sure. We shall have to cut it down."

He had to smile. Dorothea Braddock's command of finance was laughably uneven. Compared to moving Fair Castle, moving the beech tree one leaf at a time in a wheelbarrow would seem economical. Still, his grandmother had had the good sense to cling to as much land as she could when the family was down on its luck and headed straight for Carey Street, and for that he would always be grateful. It had given him something to build on.

"Will the Rover make it to the top, or would the path be too potholed?" she asked him. "I'd like to see the view from there again."

"Straight away," he said.

More amazement. They hadn't been to the top of the knoll in two or three years. Dorothea simply hadn't felt up to it. Pleased by her spirit but feeling the pressure more than ever, Will whistled Pepper back to the Rover and then helped bundle his grandmother into it. From there they continued on the neglected path—it hadn't been an actual road for many years—to the flattened top of the knoll where once had stood the castle.

Dorothea insisted on getting out of the Rover on her own, and this she did, slowly but with a firm grip on her balance. Will made teasing remarks about donating the wheelchair to the parish thrift and bringing all the furniture back down from the bedrooms, all the while hovering close while his grandmother navigated the lumpy surface and deep grass of the high knoll.

She found a level spot and then they paused to gaze at the stark, desolate beauty of the sheep-cropped hills around them. To the northeast lay the once hotly contested Berwick-on-Tweed, with its beautifully preserved sixteenth-century ramparts and its dramatic history of backing and forthing between England and Scotland.

Tiny Dibble had been built farther from the sea than

its more fortified neighbor. As a result, the hamlet had no strategic importance and had been spared the frequent sackings of Berwick. Generations had lived in Dibble safely—despite the fact that the first Norwood to build there had been just a touch on the paranoid side.

Inland or not, if the wind was blowing hard from the northeast, it wasn't uncommon to see ocean birds circling overhead, and to taste a briny tang in the air. On a clear day, a thin band of blue on the far horizon reminded one that ultimately, no one in England lived very far from the water, and those along the border, closer than most.

Today the wind came from the west, bringing with it the dry land-scent of the uplands. Will knew every smell from every direction; knew when to wear a sweater up here, and when to bring an oilskin. He knew when it would rain, and when the rain would change over to wet snow. He had been here many times in many seasons, absorbing the beauty of the site, putting his spirit in touch with its spirit.

"It's quite wonderful, isn't it, William?" Dorothea let the words escape on a long, wistful sigh.

"Yes, nana. Quite wonderful indeed."

After a moment she said, "Did you say the archivist is a Canadian?"

Surprised by the change of topic, he said, "Yes. Why?"

The elderly woman frowned and said, "I suppose it's just coincidence, but a Canadian was involved in—well, I don't know what to call it, exactly. An incident, I suppose. Concerning archives."

"Whose, ours?"

"Heavens, no!"

If Dorothea sounded shocked, it was because of the guilt. Will understood that so well. In the haste of the sale she'd let far too many possessions go with the castle. The portraits . . . some archives . . . furnishings . . . even the candle stands and pews in the chapel. She'd never forgiven herself; in her mind, each little loss was one more small sin piled onto the large one.

"I mean the archives at the rectory in St. Anthony's," answered Dorothea. "Father Aloysius gave a man—

whom he found to be a very sincere scholar—full access to the archives at the church. Imagine his dismay when he caught the person walking out with a book of documents. Well, it was all a misunderstanding, of course. The man was on his way to the chemist's shop in Dibble to photocopy some of them. Father Aloysius couldn't allow that, obviously. I said to him—to Father Aloysius, I mean—even though I'm not of his church—that he really ought to install one of those copying machines in the rectory. But apparently he would have to pay dearly for one. With the renovations going on at St. Anthony's, there simply aren't the funds. But now that I think of it, Will, couldn't you get one at some sort of reduced price?"

"A copier? No; no more than he," said Will, distracted. "Do you know what the name—"

"But aren't photostat machines rather like computers? I mean, they're all about *chips*, aren't they?" She said the word with a distrust that bordered on fear.

"Yes, but—in any case, I *program* computers; I don't build them. That's not what my company was about. Software is completely different from—"

He put the rest of his speech aside; they'd been down that road so many times before. Instead he came back to his original question. "What was the man's name? Do you know?"

"Oh, not at all. I'm not even sure Father Aloysius knew. He's terribly naive and much too trusting, you know. He wouldn't dream of asking intrusive questions."

"A man's name is hardly—"

But his grandmother was no longer listening. She winced, then said, "I believe I've rather overdone it for one morning. Might we toddle on back, Will? I was too excited to have my tea, and now I do miss it."

"You bet."

No sooner were the words out of his mouth than he had a flash, again, of Elinor. *You bet.* It was a favorite expression of hers. He sighed heavily and murmured the words again, just to have her near him. "You bet."

Chapter 18

E linor MacLeish was sprawled nearly naked on the sofa of her SoHo sublet, moaning about the heat.

"I live in the only building in New York City with too much of it," she wailed into the phone. "I can't get it to stop! The radiators just keep hissing like rattlesnakes."

"You called the super?" asked Tucker at the other end.

"I did, this morning; he claims they're working on it. But wouldn't they have to shut down the boiler to do that? I think he's lying. By the time you get here Saturday, all that'll be left of me will be a little pool of sweat under my drawing table. I'm *dying*."

"Open a window, goon," Tucker said, chuckling.

"I have—in the bedroom and in the bathroom. But I'm keeping this room closed because I can't *stand* the noise out there. It's always this way after I've been to Fair Castle. From crickets and crows to car horns and sirens—it's too violent a change for my system."

"Maybe an air conditioner?"

"The wiring won't handle it—assuming I could find one this time of year."

She held a bottle of cold seltzer to her neck. "This is unreal. I can't work; my arms stick to the paper. I can't think, can't move, can't *talk,* hardly. I'm in a complete daze." She glanced droopy-eyed at the thermometer on the flea-market end table: an even ninety degrees.

Tucker said, "There's an obvious solution, El. Come back to Fair Castle. It's been dead here since you rushed back to New York. We were having such a great time ... why can't you work on the revisions up here?"

Because of the tone in your voice, for one thing, she thought.

It was too much, too soon. They'd gone out every night, sometimes with Izzy, sometimes without, and by now they were like old friends. Actually—not old friends. Like very new, very intense friends. Too intense. Elinor had grabbed at the chance to cool things down. She needed some breathing space.

The only thing was, she hadn't expected to be breathing ninety-degree air.

She told him with reasonable honesty, "You know why I can't work up there, Tuck. We've been all through this. There are too many distractions at Fair Castle. You. Izzy. You. I'll be there as soon as I hand these in on Monday morning—but not before."

"Tell me again what the problem is with your story? I thought it was great."

"My dragon is too ambiguous," she said. "I need to make him either more kind or more mean, and I can't decide which. Either way, all the drawings have to go. I don't know if I can make the deadline."

She took a long slug of seltzer and suppressed a burp, then added only half-kiddingly, "You can't rush great art, you know."

"I say, make the dragon mean; kids love that. Anyway, I'll see you Saturday, right? We're still on for the play, deadline or no deadline?"

Somehow Tucker had managed to swing tickets to *Rigamarole,* the hottest new musical on Broadway. It was a temptation Elinor couldn't resist, and besides, he'd spent a fortune on the seats; it would've been practically rude to refuse.

"Saturday for sure," she said, even though she was leery about the aprés-play part of their date. She could only hope that Tucker was prepared for a late drive back to the castle.

"What should we do about dinner?" she added. Her thought was to give him some time before the play, not after it. "Assuming that the heat gets straightened out, I could fix us—"

She was interrupted by the rasping sound of her door buzzer. "Tuck—someone's buzzing me; I'll call you back."

She hung up and went over to the intercom, wiping damp hair away from her forehead as she did so. "Yes?" she said tiredly into the speaker.

"Elinor? It's Will. Sorry I didn't ring you up first . . . this was a last-minute . . . look, can I see you for a moment?"

Will. His lordship himself. Oh. *Hell.*

"Ahh-h . . ." She pictured what she looked like. T-shirt. No makeup. No perfume. No *underpants.*

"Ahh-h . . . this isn't really a good time . . ."

"I see. Well. If it's not a good time . . ." Long pause. "Look, damn it, my point will take thirty seconds to make. Buzz me up, would you?"

There it was, that—that *tone* he got. Imperious. British. Infuriating. How did he know she didn't have a man there?

Then again, what would he care?

"All right. Walk up *slowly.*"

She buzzed him in, then made a mad dash for the bedroom. A cold blast of wind rocked her as she hopped around madly, yanking on undies and then a pair of jeans, driving her foot straight through the hole in the the right knee and tearing it still more. A race to the bathroom, splashes of water, smear of toothpaste, rinse, lipstick sort of, no time to blow-dry damp hair *damn* his eyes!

The knock on the door sent her literally reeling. She ran back to it, breathless, her mind a wild tumult of unspoken feelings and unguarded emotions. She was hot; she was sweaty; she was frantic.

She was frightened. He'd caught her off guard.

She swung the door open. There he was. Just the way she'd known in some deep part of her soul, in some hidden corner of her heart, that he would someday be.

"You're back."

"Like a bad penny," he said, and then he smiled that

crooked smile. "Actually, that's my sister's line. I ought to let her have the exclusive use of it."

"You have a sister who's a bad penny?"

"I have a sister named Penny who's bad."

"Aren't you being a little hard on poor Penny?"

"Actually, we'll all a fairly wretched lot."

Wretched. It was such a wonderful word. It described exactly how she'd felt the past ten days while he was gone. She hadn't known it until that very moment. But she'd been wretched. And now he was here. And her heart was going clippity-clop. And she was more wretched than ever.

"I think," she said softly, "that you've just used up your thirty seconds."

Why did she say that? What was she, crazy? Thirty seconds? She could stand there thirty years.

"I called from Dibble yesterday and spoke to your mother—"

"She didn't tell m—! Oh, yes. I knew that."

"Naturally I assumed she'd pass the word to you."

"She may have done. I've been too preoccupied with a rewrite to pay much attention."

He looked at her curiously. "Ah. Well, I understand how that goes. Deadlines and all."

"Yes."

He had no overcoat, had no luggage; she wondered whether he had a cab waiting in the street. Thirty seconds. Thirty seconds of cab fare didn't cost much, even in New York.

"Look, I thought I could do this from the threshold but—may I come inside?"

"Okay," she said, unhappy with the sound of that. She stood aside to let him pass. "But if you can't stand the heat—"

"—stay out of the kitchen? What makes you—? Good God!" he said as he stepped into the middle of her sauna. "It must be thirty degrees in here."

"Thirty? Are you nuts? Try ninety!"

"Fahrenheit?"

"Oh. Centigrade, you mean," she said, embarrassed.

"Yes. The heat is malfunctioning. I'll crack open a window for you."

He was out of his tweed jacket and loosening his tie before she got to the window. Anyone would've thought they were getting ready for a quick nooner—except that it was ten at night, and she herself looked like something the cat dragged in.

Elinor turned around. He saw that she wasn't wearing a bra; it was obvious from the way he instantly wrenched his gaze from her breasts to the television antenna. His self-consciousness should've made Elinor feel superior, but instead she felt a kind of wistful regret that she didn't have big bra-sized breasts. Just this once. Just to make him lust for her, and then she'd have an edge. Or at least an equal playing field. Because the way it was now . . .

She sat on the low rolled arm of the easy chair and clamped her blue-jeaned thighs over her hands, sending him some kind of body-language signal that was an absolute mystery even to her, the sender of it. She smiled inanely. "So. What's up?"

It was obvious that he was in no hurry to tell her. He was literally gritting his teeth; she could see the jaw muscles working, the way they had a way of doing when he was around her. Whatever it was he'd come to say, he didn't want to say it.

Finally he blew out pent-up air and said, "Christ, it's hot in here."

From his pocket he took out a handkerchief and wiped his brow and neck. Still he wouldn't tell her why he was there. Working on a depressingly dead-on hunch, Elinor said quietly, "You still want it."

"Absolutely."

So that's what the visit was about. She thought—for one fleeting, stupid, hormone-driven moment—that maybe, just maybe, he'd come for *her*. Living a life of fantasy had obviously become habit forming. She thought he'd come for her.

"Well, that's certainly your right. Naturally I'll fight you tooth and nail," she said in a soft, wistful voice that echoed her mood more than her words.

He sighed and said, "I don't think you ought to bother."

He stood up, then took his jacket from the back of the sofa and flung it over his shoulder. With his tie loosened and with beads of sweat clinging to his forehead, he looked like an Easterner with a flat tire trying to thumb a ride on a Texas highway.

For whatever reason, Elinor decided to pull over on that highway and open her car door to him. "Nothing personal?" she said, reaching out to shake his hand. "All's fair?"

He stared at her extended hand, then lifted his gaze to her face. His expression was both baffled and burning, and it left her even more wilted than the ninety-degree heat.

"Look," he said. "The plain fact is—"

He stopped himself. "Oh, Christ," he said, flinging his jacket back across the sofa. He took her hand, pulled her into his arms, and covered her mouth in a hard, electrifying kiss that she felt down to her thighs. She might as well have been hit by a bolt of lightning; every atom of her body was charged. Her knees buckled and she collapsed against him, but he held her up while he battered her with more kisses.

Elinor struggled to meet him on that field as an equal, not as a pitiful, vanquished thing. She had to stand up on her own . . . on her own. She stiffened her knees, pressing her body into his, returning blow for blow, meeting the thrust of his tongue, goading him with her own allure.

His hands worked frantically across her back, crushing her close, then caught the hem of her baggy T-shirt and hauled it partway up her back, and then, restless still, let it drop down as he slid his hands through her hair and tilted her head back. He dragged hungry, wet kisses from her mouth to her chin to the curve of her neck, making her reel, making her senseless again. She shuddered and began whispering his name, over and over and over, spurring him, goading him.

A low moan from him echoed into the pulse of her throat, sending her on fire.

After the lightning, the fire. Yes, yes . . . She felt herself going up in flames, but she wanted to take him with her. She caught his hair in her hands and dragged his mouth back to hers, aware that this time, they had gone too far. It was too late to put out the flames . . . too soon to feel joy from watching themselves burn.

He said, "I want you now . . . *now*," and it sounded so like grunting that she felt a dizzying thrill. She was the enemy and yet he wanted her; she despised him and yet she was dying for him. She moaned the single syllable that was his name and then the two of them, in shameful subjection to one another, fell back into the sofa.

He tore at her clothes, already torn, and pulled away her jeans and underpants as she doubled her legs against her chest, shedding both. Off came her T-shirt, hooking on her right wrist; she shook it away, like a sticky wrapper. She was free.

But he was as bound by layers as a knight in armor. He threw off his tie as she fumbled with the buttons of his shirt, then let him finish the job and peel away his undershirt. In quick succession he unbuckled, unbelted, unlaced—would it ever end? She let out a cry of frustration, a moan of pent-up wildness—because she was wild for him—and held out her hands to him in a wanton gimme-gimme way.

"Oh, Will, oh God, hurry, now, hurry hurry," she whimpered as she watched him undress. She didn't dare wait, didn't dare think, or all would be lost.

He was undressed. Shameless in her desire for him, she stared directly at his erection and sucked in her breath. Then he was on top of her, opening her thighs, driving himself in, taking her breath away in the act. It was not savage sex—but neither was it gentle. Dark and dangerous, angry and yet hungry, it was the hot clash of warriors, the sliding compliance of lovers. It was, for all their desire for it not to be, a binding of two minds and two hearts in two bodies.

And when it was done, and he lay collapsed on her breast with his head buried in the lank tendrils of her sweat-damp hair, his heart knocking fearfully against her own, Elinor realized, almost at once, that it had been a dreadful mistake.

Her eyes were still closed with receding rapture as she whispered, "Ah, no, Will. What have we done?"

Even as she said it, she found herself breathing in the deeply male scent of him; found herself threading her fingers through the thick, wet curls of his hair. He was so real. How could he be so wrong?

He didn't answer at first. And then he lifted his head and kissed away a lock of her hair caught against her cheek. "We have done," he said softly, "the inevitable."

She shook her head. "No, no, not inevitable. We should have been on our guard. We should have seen it coming."

"Apparently we did see it coming." He kissed her swollen lip. "I took that detour here." He kissed her eyebrow. "And you—well; you opened your door." He kissed her nose. "Big mistake."

Again she shook her head back and forth dejectedly across the pillow. "No, Will. I'm serious."

He rolled off her and lay on his side, his cheek resting on his propped-up hand, his other hand circling one of her nipples. "I'm serious, too," he said through a smile. "Do you have any idea how much your nipples stand when you're turned on?"

"It was the heat," she said, catching her breath at the instant arousal of his touch. "The heat." What she was blaming the heat for, she wasn't quite sure. She closed her eyes again, aware that the fire hadn't been completely put out.

The arsonist lying at her side was aware of it, too. He said, "I think—I know—I've wanted you since the first day I saw you. Are you saying you haven't felt the same about me?"

"Oh, definitely—ah!—not," she said as he bent his head over her breast and began to lick and tease the nipple. He swung his arm over her to brace himself and moved his focus to her other breast. "I . . . yi . . . I . . . think this is one of those . . . things, that's all," she said, gasping for air now.

One of those crazy things. She tried desperately to convince herself of it as he proceeded to light small little fires all over her body, one matchstick at a time, until she was reduced to the same wanton state as before.

No, no, this is just empty ... mindless ... sex, she told herself. The closer he moved her to ecstasy, the closer he moved her to tears. *I don't know anything about him except that he wants the castle. All I have are the scraps that've fallen from the others at the dinner table. He himself has told me nothing about himself ... his family ... his dreams. He hasn't bothered to get close enough to tell me a thing.*

No. It was just empty, mindless sex.

But it was such *good* empty, mindless sex. He made every square inch of her come alive, come quivering; come, at last, in another orgasm.

Before the first odd, unbidden tear had a chance to fall, he slid into her again, and in half a dozen sure, smooth strokes, he found his own release.

After that they lay in one another's arms in a profoundly silent truce. Elinor had only one question, and it took her a long time to ask it.

"Was that you on the gallery the night of Izzy's dousing game?"

"No," Will murmured into her hair. "I was in my room. On the phone."

And then the first tear fell. And the second. And then the only falling was the two of them, wordlessly into sleep.

Chapter 19

At three in the morning Will woke up. He was on London time, and no amount of jet lag was going to be enough to make him sleep through the rest of the night.

He rolled over on his back, careful not to disturb the woman sleeping next to him, and stared at the lights criss-crossing the ceiling through the filter of the bedroom curtains. Outside it was quiet, for New York City. Only the occasional rumble of a passing lorry broke through the deafening silence of his thoughts.

What had he done? What the hell had he done?

Of all the women in the world—couldn't he have chosen someone besides this one? He thought he'd made his peace with the fact that she'd always be off limits to him. She couldn't be anything else, not as long as she felt so strongly about Fair Castle.

She resented everything about him: the title, the wealth, the power that money gave him. It was understandable. In the struggle over the castle, he had all the advantages while she had nothing more than a bedrock desire to oppose him.

He was turning her world upside-down, and she was outraged. He'd been thinking about it long and hard and had decided that she was a control nut. It explained so much, from her single status to her career choice. She'd gone to great pains to create her own little world—in her art and in her life—and then he'd gone and spoiled it.

Why she was so controlling, he did not know. Maybe

she was born that way. Maybe the loss of her father—
twice, really, according to Mickey MacLeish—had made
her that way. Will had suffered a similar trauma; he
should know. The difference was, he'd channeled his frus-
trations outward, into building an empire, while she'd
channeled hers inward, into her family and art.

And where did Fair Castle fit in all this? For him, the
castle was an end; for her, it was the means.

When he got off the plane he'd decided on the spot to
do the right thing and tell her that to her face. Or at least,
to tell her that the castle was going to be his. And why.

And instead he'd ended up in the sack with her. *Unbelievable*. He'd been like a buck in heat. It was fair to
say that he'd never jumped a woman in his *life* the way
he'd jumped her.

And afterward he still could've escaped; that was the
kicker of it. He'd had his chance—when he woke up with
a start half an hour after their scalding encounter and
remembered the cabbie, then went down to pay him and
retrieve his luggage. God. He'd been so hungry for her,
so completely besotted, that he'd left a freaking cab standing in the street!

So he came back upstairs, still besotted, and nudged the
book that was holding the door ajar, and closed the windows in the now freezing apartment, and came back to
bed with her and found that she'd slept through it all,
completely trusting, completely sated.

Until he woke her up, still on fire for her, and made
her make love again. God. The third time was best of all.
Everything about it . . . the wonder of it . . . the joy of it
. . . the amazing, liberating, *satisfaction* of it. He'd never
felt such calm, he'd never known such serenity as after
he'd made love with Elinor MacLeish for the third time.

He sighed, then rolled his head her way and stared at
her in the dark. His night vision, always keen, was able
to make out every feature of her face: the full lips, parted
in sleep now; the straight nose; the dark eyebrows, one of
them obscured by a hank of hair over it. Such an ordinary
face. Such an extraordinary face. Right now he could not

get enough of it. If he stared at it long enough, maybe he'd understand the hold it had on him.

And yet, did it matter? Once she heard what he had to say to her, she'd have nothing to do with him. He knew that. Before they fell asleep the first time, he'd tasted tears on her cheek. *Why tears?* he'd asked her.

Because this can't go anywhere, she'd told him. *Unless one of us gives up. Unless you—*

He'd kissed away the rest of the sentence, knowing she hadn't heard the worst of it yet. And when she did. . . .

He considered waking her up to make love one last time, so that he could take it through life with him. But you couldn't deliberately set out to create a memory. Memories just *were*.

And so he lay there, drinking in the sight of her, burning her image into his soul, afraid to move, afraid to touch her, because once she woke up, it would be over.

His face softened into a bleak smile. *American hellion.* He'd met no one like her in all of England. He knew he never would. Noisy and naive, headstrong and sentimental, thunderingly idealistic . . . She had no idea what real families were like. None at all. She lived in a dream world. In a dream castle. What would it be like, he wondered, to live there with her.

There? Where? That was the question.

Forget it, he told himself again. *The plan hasn't changed.* And so he lay waiting, his lids heavy, his mind in a state of high anxiety: waiting for her to wake up.

That moment arrived at exactly 6:17 A.M. when a car drove by playing music loud enough to shatter glass. Will cursed the ass behind the wheel; but the damage was done. His reprieve was over.

Elinor began to stir, and then to reach out for him. Her arm slid across his chest, scorching in its intimacy. He didn't move. She sighed—happily, it seemed to him. For an agonizing minute she threaded a finger in the hairs on his chest, then let her hand drift lazily to his crotch, driving him insane with desire as her fingers made their way down.

Every cell in his body wanted to join forces and roll

over onto her; but some tiny, stupid part of his brain was disciplined enough to make his hand reach out and encircle her wrist, pinning it to a safe area of his abdomen.

"Mornin'," he said grimly. It was a warning shot across her bow. He hated like hell firing it.

"Mmm . . . what time is it?"

"Half-past six."

"Good," she said, burrowing her head into her pillow. "We don't have to get up."

"But we do."

"Mm-mm," she said. "We're going to just . . . hide in bed all day."

"What about your revisions?"

"Oh . . . them," she said sleepily. "I have all of tomorrow." She began to snake her wrist free of his grip.

He held it more tightly. "Not such a good idea."

"Not—?" She lifted her head. "Have I worn you out? That'd be a first on my sexual resumé."

But it was quite obvious that he was ready and able, so she said with a faltering smile in her voice, "Or do you just mean, leaving the revisions until tomorrow is not such a good idea?"

He lifted her wrist and said, "No; *this* is the bad idea." He moved her arm gently back to her side of the bed.

"Oh." She lowered her head slowly back on the pillow.

Agony. It was going to be so much more brutal than he'd imagined. In his mind was the thought that if she'd rejected *him* that way right now, he would've gone impotent for the rest of his life.

Her head came back up. "Why isn't it such a good idea?" This time there was no faltering, no smile.

He stared at the ceiling. Another arc of light moved across it, accompanied by a shrill siren. Police? Rescue? Both? He'd rather be the victim at their destination than where he was right now.

"You know how each of us feels about Fair Castle," he said quietly.

"Yes." Her voice was guarded. "The same way we felt about it last night."

"Right. But last night I didn't say—I didn't get the

chance to say—that I've gone and done something about it."

Elinor sat up, pulling the blanket around her. "Something? Like what?" She sounded wide-awake and anything but playful.

It was pointless to drag it out. "I've made an offer," he said. "A fairly generous one."

She said nothing for a moment, but it was clear that it was a blow. Finally she said, "Well. All right. You were bound to, sooner or later I guess. It's too bad, though," she added, obviously disappointed, obviously hurt that he hadn't said so before.

He thought she might lash out then and there; but she was making a valiant effort to keep her resentment under control.

And then he told her the amount of the offer.

She gasped.

He said quickly, "You can see why it was accepted."

"Accepted?" She shook off the news like a spaniel shaking off her bath. "No, Will. I've told you. It can't be accepted. I'll veto the acceptance. I've never hid that fact from you."

They were into it now. He sat up alongside her, aware that they were both naked, wishing he could pull on a T-shirt, not wishing to send a hostile signal. He pulled up his knees and rested his forearms on them, clasping his hands in an absurdly casual pose.

"The truth is, your grandparents *have* decided to accept," he said carefully. "They are the owners, after all. And they've accepted."

"Never."

"It's the truth," he repeated.

"They would've told me. They would've *told* me," she said in a shaking voice.

"I guess they didn't want to upset you. They knew you had a deadline."

"Are you out of your mind? What would a deadline matter at a time like this? It's a trick," she said, yanking the blanket more closely around her. "You're trying to trick me."

She'd pulled the bedding clear off him. He felt like a fool and a heel at the same time. How could a mission so noble feel like a venture so sleazy? He sighed and said, "I'm not trying to trick you, Elinor. Call the castle if you don't believe me."

"I'll do just that," she said, grabbing the phone at her side. She propped it on her lap and began punching in numbers, then slammed the receiver down. "I can't call them at this hour," she cried in frustration. "You know they sleep in."

She dumped the phone back on the nightstand. "Get out of this bed, please."

"Fine," he said wearily. He had no stomach for this. He got up and started dressing.

But she was still in a state of denial. "They weren't selling two days ago; everything was fine two days ago. You're lying!" she said, her voice rising and accusing. "Why would they change their minds? I don't believe you! You're a liar!"

He was tucking in his T-shirt, grateful for the minimal dignity that clothes brought with them. Should he tell her everything? He'd already made a royal muck of the news. He was amazed to see that his own hands were shaking as he tried to buckle his belt. He knew he'd never be able to ride far enough or fast enough to escape the sound of that word being hurled at him like a javelin: *liar*.

He was resigned to being a shit; but he wouldn't be called a liar.

"Something's happened," he decided to say. "They didn't want to alarm—"

"My God, what? What's happened? Grampa Mick—?" Still wrapped in the sheet, Elinor scrambled out of bed, turned on the lamp, and began grabbing at the first clothes she saw. "Tell me what's happened, I've got to get up there—"

Her reaction was so overwrought that he was sorry he'd opened that door. "Nothing like that," he said quickly. "Everyone's fine. For God's sake, calm down."

"*Don't* you tell me to calm down!" she said, whipping her head around at him. She was blazing with fury now, as he knew she would be. "Just tell me what it is that's happened and *leave*."

He was sorry she'd turned on the lamp; it let him see the crushing disillusionment in her eyes. "Your grandmother didn't tell me exactly what happened. She only said that they'd had a change of heart . . . that the castle was beginning to lose its charm for them. I assume she wanted me to believe that they felt they were getting too old for it. But frankly, that's not what it sounded like. It sounded—"

He sighed heavily; he did not want to get into this at all. "It sounded," he said, "as if she was afraid."

"Afraid? My grandmother? Don't be ridiculous. You're reading that into her response. You *want* to believe they're afraid of burglars or killers. You *want* to believe this is a country of outlaws and maniacs."

It wasn't true. He wanted to believe that they were afraid the castle was haunted. That's what Camilla had sounded like, and he had no problem with it. He'd be delighted to take the castle, ghosts and all, off their hands for them. He wouldn't feel like a shit if they were credulous enough to believe in ghosts.

But thanks to Susan, he knew better. Mickey and Camilla MacLeish had borrowed heavily against the castle over the years, and they no longer had the money to pay back the loans. They were deep in debt with no chance of getting out, now that Chester had blown his retirement fund.

But he didn't dare tell that to Elinor, so he said, "Let's face it, Elinor. None of us knows what to believe." He certainly didn't.

But she wasn't hearing him anymore. "I was right in the first place!" she snapped, searching for a second shoe. "You're nothing but a snob. You want your little status symbol, and you'll stop at nothing to get it!"

She found the loafer and jammed her foot into it. "You'll even," she said with a look of true hate, "sleep with the enemy, won't you?"

"Jesus!" he said, grabbing his hair in pure frustration.

"You really can say that? You really can think that after last night?"

Maybe he was wrong, after all. Maybe he'd dreamt the whole wild night. They sure as hell weren't on the same wavelength now; apparently they'd never been.

She said with a trembling lip, "You deceived me! You know you did!"

"Oh, for—I didn't—"

But the bottom line was, he *had* deceived her. He didn't mean to; he hadn't planned to; he wouldn't want to. But that's what he'd done.

"I'm sorry," he said, realizing the folly of trying to defend himself. "I came here with the intention of telling you why I want Fair Castle—"

"I don't care why you want Fair Castle!" she said bitterly. "Not anymore." She turned away, her entire body a study in rejection.

"Right." He sighed heavily and said, "I'll call myself a cab."

"You do that."

He made the call, then went to the bathroom to wash up. When he came out, Elinor was on the phone, he didn't know with whom.

He didn't stay around to find out.

Will had been right: Her grandmother *did* sound afraid.

Afraid, and tense, and completely unwilling to talk on the phone about the decision to sell Fair Castle. Her whole tone was shocking to hear; she wasn't the same woman who'd hugged Elinor two days earlier and told her to hurry back because her grandfather had an extra horrible Fright Night planned for this year.

"I warned you that eventually this might happen, Elly," Camilla said on the phone. "And I told you that if it did, I wanted you to abide by your grandfather's wishes."

"This isn't *eventually*—it's overnight! I won't let you do it! You haven't even told me what changed your mind. What does 'things have happened' mean?"

"Elinor . . . I don't want to have this discussion. Not like this."

"What's going on here? It's like some huge conspiracy that everyone's in on but me! Gramma Cam, don't do this!"

"I will do what I like, young lady."

"Let me talk with Grampa Mick."

"You can't. He . . . isn't here."

"Something has happened to him—what?"

"Absolutely nothing. He *is* here but he's getting ready to take Chester to the doctor to have his stitches taken out."

"Why not Mother?"

"Susan will have to conduct the tours."

"She's behind this, isn't she?" Elinor said. "Now that I'm in New York, she's made her move."

"Hush! This has nothing to do with your mother."

"I knew I shouldn't have left! But I thought with him in England, it'd be safe. Oh, God—"

"I can do without your melodrama," Camilla said testily. "You're only making a difficult decision worse."

"Were you ever going to tell me?" Elinor asked, see-sawing from anger to hurt.

She heard the wince on her grandmother's face. "Yes. Today."

"When? After you signed the agreement?"

"I admit I was dreading this conversation, and now I see why."

Elinor had a horrible thought. "You haven't signed anything *already,* have you?"

"No. Will is bringing the agreement with him."

"Don't do anything, Gramma Cam, please! At least wait until I get up there. I can be there in two hours. At least wait that long."

"What about your revisions?"

"I'll bring them with me. I just want to be told to my face that you're going to do this. You and Grampa Mick owe me that much, at least."

"We don't *owe*—" Camilla sighed and said in a weary voice, "All right, Elly. But we have an appointment scheduled at the attorney's office for three o'clock."

Plenty of time, Elinor convinced herself. At least to find

out what they were afraid of. "Do I have your word that
you won't sign anything before I get there?" she asked,
completely ignorant of legal procedure.

"You have my word."

"Can you keep it?"

"Good-*bye*, dear."

Chapter 20

$\mathcal{W}$ill drove from New York to Fair Castle in a state of coma. His mind and body were functioning independently of one another; his emotions, not at all.

His brain was able to figure out where to cross the George Washington Bridge and how to pay for it in American coin. His body was able to push the right pedals, flip the right signals, and steer the car on the American side of the road.

But his heart—his heart didn't seem to be working at all. All that he felt was a dull ache, a shivering echo of what should have been. Unconsciously he massaged his shirt with the palm of his hand, trying to get the heart beneath it thumping again.

It wasn't supposed to be this way. When he first set off on his brilliant campaign, it was to the thundering cheers of his family, his friends, the local historical society, every businessman in the area, half a dozen politicians, and the village vicar. They'd practically carried him out of Dibble on their shoulders.

His plan had been to take the tour of Fair Castle, then introduce himself to its owners, charm his way into their hearts, and carry the castle—literally—out from under them. In retrospect it was moronic not to have put out some feelers first. But he thought he could dazzle the family; he thought he could dangle a check.

He thought—well, he thought money.

But they didn't care about money; Elinor, least of all.

Only their bank cared. And now here he was, all but twirling his mustache as he drove through strikingly beautiful country past historic West Point and Cornwall-on-Hudson, slinking ever closer to his goal.

It was going to be brutally painful to be with them at all. He never should've agreed to hook up with the MacLeishes and go with them to the attorney's office. As soon as he got to the castle he planned to insist that they take separate cars; and after that he wouldn't set foot in Fair Castle until it was vacated.

Apparently that wouldn't be long. Camilla had told him that she and her husband would look for something in a retirement community, and Chester and Susan would find a house in the area until Izzy finished middle school. No one had said what Izzy's big sister would do, and he hadn't asked.

So Elinor was right. Break down the castle, and you break up the clan. It had happened to his family, and now it was happening to hers. He put the thought aside like a bitter pill and vowed to swallow it later.

By the time he went bumping down the potholed drive that led to Fair Castle, a cold, steady, utterly dreary rain had begun to fall. He turned on the windshield wipers. Nothing happened. After driving nearly off the lane because he couldn't see, he slowed the rental car to a crawl, picking his way around the muddy craters that seemed designed to function as a modern-day moat.

Perfect, he thought. He'd have to go to the solicitor's with Camilla and Mickey after all, making impossible small talk the entire way. Could it be more grim than that?

He parked, then made a dash from the car to the castle and lifted the ancient door knocker—more satisfying, somehow, than ringing the bell—and brought it down in a series of loud raps.

The first time the arched door had swung open for him, it had opened to Elinor in that little black dress, shivering as the wind rushed in from behind him. He'd wanted on the spot to take her in his arms and warm her. Maybe he should have.

No one answered his knock. He remembered that he had a key to the castle in his pocket, given to him by the castle's trusting owner. They were all trusting. Damn them.

He flipped the collar of his jacket over the back of his neck to ward off the rain, and he knocked again. This time someone was there to open the door: Tucker O'Toole.

O'Toole's greeting was a surprised scowl. Obviously he hadn't got wind about the sale of Fair Castle. "Well, well," he said. "I thought you'd pretty much had your fill of us."

Will didn't like the sound of that "us." He ignored the remark and stepped inside with a nod, aware of a surge of jealousy. Elinor hadn't mentioned that O'Toole was still around. But then, Will had been too busy making love to her to ask.

Bloody hell. The sense of her in his arms came in a rush as strong as a full-moon tide.

He brushed the rain from his sleeves and said, "Are the MacLeishes in?"

"She is; he isn't."

"Can you tell me where—?"

"Fuck you."

Will gave him a level look. "I guess that answers my question."

O'Toole turned on his heel and walked away.

"He drops the mask, Charles. He declares his hatred in crude and stark language. After this we may expect him to stop at nothing."

"It does not surprise me. Dare we condemn him? He is our only ally."

"There is no other who can vindicate us?"

"None."

Will stared after O'Toole, more jealous than curious, more curious than offended. He'd seen the way O'Toole hovered over Elinor like some waiter in a failing restaurant; he couldn't imagine a woman of her spirit taking him seriously. But then, Tucker O'Toole wasn't stealing the castle out from under Elinor. Tucker O'Toole was presenting her with a damn broad shoulder to cry on.

Was O'Toole the archivist who'd tried to walk off with the church register back in Dibble? No way to tell. Will had actually paid a visit to the aging monsignor at St. Anthony's to query him further. But Father Aloysius was too old and too overwhelmed by the dust and details of renovating his beloved church to remember.

"The lad was a young, presentable chap," the elderly priest had said. "But a name? I'm awfully bad at them. Bill? Jim? Something like that."

The kindly priest would not have forgotten a name like Tucker O'Toole. On the other hand, if O'Toole were up to no good, he'd certainly use an alias. Like Bill or Jim.

A possible trail led from Dibble to Fair Castle. It could hardly be coincidence. Was O'Toole even a scholar? For all his bookish, romantic, troubadour ways, Will had to say that he didn't think so.

Those wire-rimmed glasses O'Toole wore, for one thing: He didn't need them. Will had caught him reading without them. On the other hand, maybe O'Toole found them helpful once in a while but was still able to read without them—like Will. And some of the books *were* printed in brutally small type.

Bugger it; the glasses didn't prove a thing one way or the other.

Will dismissed the speculation. Tucker O'Toole wasn't relevant. Buying the castle was relevant. Getting himself, and eventually it, back to England was relevant. Forgetting that Elinor MacLeish ever slept, ate, and tormented him in it—that was definitely relevant.

And absolutely impossible. Now that he was actually standing there, the realization hit him with the force of a bayonet: Elinor was everywhere in Fair Castle for him. In the turret. In the library. In the kitchen. In the archives room. In the great parlor, the great hall, in the great, frigging memory of his mind.

He felt a sinking sensation akin to panic. What if he got the castle moved to Dibble and couldn't stand to live in it? What the bleeding hell would he do *then?*

"William, William, William! How *won*derful to have you back!"

Catching Will flat-footed in his revery, Susan Roberts approached with both arms extended and a radiant grin on her face. Will took her hands in his and did the kiss-kiss thing in the air.

"I hope your parents are well," he said, although he felt certain they were not. Camilla had sounded far too unnerved on the phone.

Some of the cheer went out of Susan's face. "They're very well!" she said.

"I'm glad to hear it," he responded, wishing he hadn't forced her into a lie. He couldn't stop himself from adding, "I'm surprised to see Tucker O'Toole still knocking around. His work here isn't done?"

Susan gave him a look ripe with innuendo. "Tucker's 'work' will never be done while my daughter is running around loose," she said. "You may count on that."

"Oh, yes?"

Will pretended not to understand her ploy to make him jealous as they proceeded together to the great parlor, but he was impressed that she was still at it: trying to make something happen between her daughter and him. She was like some Gilded-Age matchmaker gone amuck; she put Alva Vanderbilt to shame. And Will wasn't even a duke—only a piddling baron.

Was it his title or the money? On the whole, he thought it was the title. Naturally the money didn't hurt; but on the whole, he thought the title meant more to someone like Susan.

Baron or not, he was her daughter's worst enemy. Couldn't she see that?

"It makes so much sense for us to sell," Susan was saying, turning on lamps as she passed them in the great parlor. "Take today. Since the part-time help won't be in, there's no one to conduct the tours except me, which means that I had to ask my father to drive Chester to the doctor's, and now I'm worried about him being behind the wheel in this rain."

She went up to one of the narrow casements and stared out at the dark and brooding morning. It was a classic Dibble day; the castle should've felt right at home.

Susan shook her head, murmuring more to herself than to Will. "On a Friday . . . in the morning rush hour . . . on these winding, slippery roads . . . we're in such a terrible location . . ."

Will knew about her husband's accident. Susan was reliving it in front of his eyes. He said, "They'll be fine. The rain isn't as bad as you think."

Unpersuaded, she smiled bleakly and said, "My father hasn't driven very much, and he's arrogant when he does. He expects everyone to pull over and let him pass. Is it any wonder I worry?

"Anyway, after all that," she added, "only two people showed up for the early tour!" She added grimly, "I asked them to come back for the next one; I doubt that I'll see them again."

She pressed the back of her slender hand to her forehead in a graceful show of despair. Something about the gesture reminded Will of Camilla. The difference was, Camilla MacLeish did it for fun. Susan—thin, blond, and beautiful—had all of her mother's grace, but none of her sense of whimsy.

"Shall I bring *you* some tea?" she asked him more cheerfully. "Or would you rather have coffee, perhaps? I assume you've had breakfast. Agnes isn't in today, but I could—"

"I'm all set, thank you," he said. He wasn't all set. He was hungry and unshowered. But he could hardly ask for food or towels without explaining where he'd been all night.

"We'll have a nice lunch before we leave," Susan promised. "You'll come back afterward to stay, of course?"

Will tried to look regretful. "Can't be done, I'm afraid. I'll be turning right around for Dibble this evening."

If I live that long, he thought. He was fading fast. Amazing, the way his dramatic quest had been drained of joy.

Susan made no effort to hide her disappointment. "What a shame; we all assumed that you'd stay on through Fright Night, at least. It's wonderful fun ... all those neighborhood children trick-or-treating ... my father in his ghoul getup, answering the door ... all the shrieks ... Izzy always has a bunch of her friends for a sleepover ..."

"I can't think of any place I'd rather be," said Will. *Except maybe in quicksand with my hair on fire.*

"*Won't* you change your mind?" she pleaded, charming him with gentle courtesy. "It's truly an enjoyable evening. And I just realized: This will be our last Fright Night—our last event, period, since the Renaissance Conference has canceled on us. Well! I guess it's beginning ... to hit home." She looked suddenly teary-eyed.

Oh, dandy. Even her. His last true ally.

He said, "I'm really sorry." He meant it as a general apology for turning their lives inside out.

She waved away his distress. "No, William, don't be silly. We're all pretty much agreed. It's time to sell. Of course there'll be some regrets. That's bound to happen. ... So! Coffee or tea?"

He voted for coffee and asked whether he might be able to see Camilla.

A wary look settled over the fragile elegance of Susan's face. "I think ... my mother is resting. She knows that it's going to be a long afternoon. But—well, I'll see."

She made a self-conscious exit from the great parlor, leaving Will to wonder again what it was that had made the MacLeishes suddenly willing to sell. The money crunch was the obvious, most plausible reason. A castle—even a small one like Fair Castle—required considerable sums to keep in good repair. Two visitors per tour would not do much to add to the war chest.

And yet they hadn't acted as if the bank were breathing down their backs. If anything, Mickey MacLeish had seemed to enjoy dangling the castle in front of Will with no intention of letting it go.

But once Will made his offer, they hadn't even bothered to counter it. They were eager not only to sell, but eager to vacate. It was a stunning turnaround from his initial visit.

Mickey MacLeish hadn't spoken to Will during the very brief negotiations; it was Camilla who'd handled it all. Will wasn't surprised that the old man had hung back in his lair like a wounded lion. The decision to sell must've been devastating to him, no matter what had prompted it. The castle and the river valley had been his personal magic kingdom. Still, it seemed more than a little odd.

Will let out an uneasy sigh. The sense that whatever was amiss could not be defined in dollars or pounds weighed heavily on him. He shifted restlessly in the leather armchair. The air around him seemed damp and chill and hostile, as if the castle had already been abandoned and he were riding into unclaimed territory.

He felt an almost desperate urge to jump up and get on with it. *Closure.* He was desperate for closure, and to put Elinor behind him. But he couldn't just go roaming around the castle looking for Camilla; not anymore. Ten days ago, he'd been a free-ranging guest, like O'Toole. Now he was an owner-to-be. He had no more rights than the two tourists who'd just been turned away.

So he sat put in the parlor, trapped in misery of his own making, and thought how much more excited he'd been when Elinor had lounged defiantly in the chair opposite, wearing a tattered robe and dinosaur slippers and smoking that absurd cigar.

He was surprised to see Izzy poke her head into the room and then retreat.

"Isabelle?" he said, calling her back. She came, but not willingly. She was dressed for play and didn't look sick. "No school today?"

The child assumed a sullen look that he knew was designed especially for him. She lowered her long-lashed gaze and said, "My mom said I didn't have to go to school because today we're selling the castle. To *you*."

God. She sounded like her older sister. Feeling more like a rotter than ever, Will said, "Well, we're going to begin the process, that's all. It will take weeks to do."

It wasn't much comfort, and she knew it. "Big deal! You're still going to take it all apart and move it away from here."

She was daring Will to deny it. He drummed his fingers on the rolled leather arm of the chair and said, "I'm afraid that's true, Isabelle. I'm sorry."

Isabelle shot him a look of such blazing fury that it could have come from Elinor. "You're *not* sorry!" she cried. "If you were sorry you wouldn't do it! No one can be sorry ahead of time for doing something wrong."

Resting his forearms on his thighs, Will leaned forward, intent on persuading her that he wasn't a monster. "Sometimes a person can do the right thing," he said, "and still feel terrible about it."

But it was no good. She was still too young to pick out shades of gray in her black-and-white universe. "You know what I think?" she said in a wavering, high voice. "I think you're the worst person I ever met! We used to have so much fun and now Gramma Cam is crying and Grampa Mick is all upset and Dad feels bad because . . . because he can't stop you from having the castle, because he doesn't have enough money! It's your fault and I really hate you!"

She burst into tears, turned on her heel, and fled wailing from the great parlor before Will could do a thing about it.

Ah, hell, he thought, letting his head fall wearily against the back of the armchair. He closed his eyes and saw Fair Castle rising majestically from the knoll in Dibble, then opened his eyes and saw Elinor sitting in her robe and dinosaur slippers. *Too late,* he told himself morosely. He no longer had a clue what it was too late for.

Susan returned with coffee and breakfast rolls on an enameled tray. She was back to feeling upbeat again.

"What time did your flight get in last night?" she asked him pleasantly. "You seem tired."

"I am, a bit," he acknowledged, ignoring her first question. He'd sooner throw himself from the battlements than answer that one.

"I just saw Izzy," he said, still depressed by the child's outburst. Having a ten-year-old hate him was something new. "She's not handling this very well."

"Of course she is," Susan insisted. "After we move

she'll be closer to school and be able to take part in more
activities. Her life will become much more normal. In two
years she'll have forgotten all about Fair Castle. You
know how kids are."

Actually, he didn't know. When he socialized at all, it
was with other childless men and women. It wasn't hard
to do; there were plenty of people around who had neither the time nor the inclination to design their lives
around kids.

So why was he feeling so rotten about Izzy hating him?

"How is Lady Norwood?" asked Susan, moving the
talk over to his side of the ocean. "I hope you found her
well."

"She's doing extraordinarily well," Will said, reminded
of why he was prepared to let a young girl hate him. "Her
enthusiasm for the project is amazing to see."

"How long will it take to reconstruct the castle?" Susan
asked him. She knew that his grandmother was neither
young nor robust. She knew, as Will did, that time was
critical.

"If all goes well," he answered, "it should be habitable
in twenty-four months or so."

If all goes miraculously well. Those were the engineer's
exact words. The architect had echoed them. The head
mason—well, the mason wasn't even remotely that encouraging.

"Imagine that," said Susan, impressed. "Lady Norwood
will enjoy watching it rise from the knoll. You said the
gamekeeper's cottage isn't far from there?"

"She won't be able to see the construction through her
kitchen casements, if that's what you mean. But yes, once
you break through the woods that surround the cottage,
there it will be."

"Like a dream," Susan said with a smile.

He returned the smile and slugged his coffee and
glanced at his watch. Making small talk was even more
painful than he'd feared. Three o'clock was looking further away than ever. Anything could happen by three
o'clock. Christ, he could change his mind by three o'clock.
All he needed was one more person to burst into tears—

"*Mother!* This is all your doing! How *dare* you force Gramma Cam—"

Back!

"Elinor! For heaven's sake! When did *you* arrive? We thought you were staying in New York until Fright Night—"

Back!

"Oh, I'll bet you did! Where's Gramma Cam?"

"She's lying down, taking a little—"

"Drugged! You've drugged her, haven't you?"

Back!

"Have you gone insane, Elinor? Your grandmother is perfectly fine. She and Grampa Mick—"

"Have been coerced by you or by *this* knucklehead," she said without throwing Will a glance.

Back, in all her fury! Astonishingly beautiful, astonishingly desirable. Elinor MacLeish was back. No robe, no slippers or cigar. She wore blue jeans and a black sweater and her face was radiant with fury.

"You look terrible!" said her mother.

"Do you think I *care?*"

"How the hell did you get here so fast?" Will asked her.

She gave him a scalding look. "I borrowed a car from a neighbor, how the hell do you think?"

"I thought maybe on a broom," he said, scowling. Inside, his heart was doing backflips. Elinor MacLeish was back. And the castle seemed whole again.

"I don't understand," Susan said, turning from her daughter to Will. "How do *you* know—?"

"Yes, Mother, ask him," said Elinor, still locked on him with her gaze of fury. "Ask him how he knows my schedule so well."

Will, who'd shot to his feet when Elinor walked in, now sat back down. He said to Susan with self-imposed calm, "I fail to see what your daughter has to do with my being here."

"Oh! You—!" Elinor was, for once, at a loss for words.

But not for long. "Tell her, damn it!" she suddenly burst out. "Tell her just how low you'll go to get Fair Castle. I haven't had a good laugh for hours!"

She wasn't laughing. Her eyes were glazed with tears just itching to fall and he did *not* want to see them. He stood back up.

"Perhaps I've come too early, after all," he said to Susan, taking a big risk. "If you would kindly tell your mother that I had hoped to speak with her before the signing . . . In the meantime, I think the best thing is for me to leave."

"*Excellent* idea," said Elinor, grabbing the tail of his jacket, ready to haul him away like a piece of roadkill.

By now her mother was apoplectic. "Elinor, for God's sake!" she cried. "He'll have you arrested! *I'll* have you arrested!"

She charged forward to disengage her infuriated daughter at the same time that Will turned to within a breath of Elinor's flushed face and murmured in a low and anguished voice, "Hasn't this gone far enough?"

She raised her hand to slap him—and he was fairly sure, to slap him hard. He caught her wrist midswing as her mother circled them with little twitters of distress, about as effective as a goldfinch trying to break up two fighters in a ring.

Elinor tried again to swing at him; he held her wrist fast. They might've kept locked like that until the castle crumbled if it hadn't been for the appearance of Tucker O'Toole. He showed up in the doorway, took one look, and made a wild rush in Elinor's defense, knocking Will halfway across the great parlor in the process. Someone screamed. Someone else screamed. There was shouting, but Will didn't know what. All he heard was the pounding of testosterone through his body. He'd been itching to take one good poke at O'Toole since the day they'd met: smug, self-righteous young prig. Castle or no castle, it'd be worth it.

He came rushing back at O'Toole, bringing him down backward over the leather sofa. They scuffled, then rolled, held fast in one another's grip, over the edge of the sofa and onto the floor where they wedged in the narrow gap between the sofa and the low book-laden table. The pale scent of old leather and stale cigars mixed with the newer, fresher scent of blood. Blood! Will tasted it, flowing from his nose. Hot with the need for revenge now, he scrambled for dominance, managing to pin O'Toole down in the narrow confine between couch and table.

He sat on top of him, his thighs jamming the younger man securely to the floor. His left hand pinned O'Toole's throat; his right hand came up in a fist.

"Damn you!" Will growled, panting and furious that it had come to this. His fist hovered midair as he calculated which part of O'Toole's face needed smashing most.

But in that simple act of rational thought, Will lost his thirst for the other man's blood. He let out a sound of disgust and, bracing himself against O'Toole's supine body, forced himself up in a reverse deep-knee bend. He felt the pull in both thigh muscles.

"Shit," he said, still breathing heavily, "I'm too old for this shit."

He turned away from his adversary and immediately was confronted with the sight of two women, one of them scandalized, the other one not.

"Look, I'm terribly sorry," he said, as if he'd arrived late for a match at Wimbledon.

He saw Elinor's eyes suddenly open wide and jerked his head back around. Someone yelled to look out—he was looking plenty—but he caught another sharp clip to the jaw anyway as O'Toole came back at him with renewed fury.

Not over yet, he moaned to himself as he tried to fend off O'Toole's wild flailing. *This nightmare of a quest goes on and on.*

They lurched from end table to chair, from chair to couch, leaving a trail of spilling furnishings in their wake. Will heard glass break, and the queer popping sounds of turned-on light bulbs hitting the floor and going dead. Through it all came the semi-hysterical cries of Susan.

"Stop it stop it stop it!" she shrieked, with absolutely no effect.

By now Will, tired of the struggle not to knock out O'Toole, decided that in the long run one good punch would save them all a lot of money. He waited for his chance, then grabbed a handful of O'Toole's shirt to steady himself as he reared back for the blow.

"Tucker, you idiot!" screamed Susan, piercing through the thunder of their combat. *"He's buying Fair Castle!"*

Chapter 21

$\mathcal{T}$ucker O'Toole swung his head around, leaving himself wide-open for Will's punch.

"Buying it? *Fair Castle?*"

Susan's voice rose another octave in shrillness. "You *knew* he was interested, for God's sake! Do you think he's here for tea in the turret? Of *course*—"

"Mother, stop shouting!" Elinor shouted. "You'll wake up the dead! He hasn't bought it *yet*."

Will, the subject of their friendly little chat, felt like a ghost among them—except that he still held O'Toole's shirt in a very real, very vicelike grip. He let out an explosive sigh and jerked his hand away from the younger man, then without a word turned and walked out of the room, desperate for air, desperate to be away from them. He wanted, more than anything, to be alone. To put himself back together psychologically. Emotionally. Physically.

On his way down to the great hall, he saw the single French door that led to the outside gallery; he detoured onto it, grateful for the small overhang that shielded him from the worst of the pouring rain. His system was still in kill-or-be-killed mode, and he was appalled by the fact. He sagged against the outside wall, waiting for the pounding of his heart to die down.

Elinor was fifteen seconds behind him. She burst through the door and stood, oblivious to the rain, ten feet away from him.

"How *could* you!" she screamed, balling her fingers into fists.

He snapped to attention. "Don't come near me now," he growled through clenched teeth. "Don't. I warn you."

"I'll do what I—"

"Don't."

"—want!" she said, taking three steps closer to him. Small steps. And then she paused, eyeing him cautiously, gauging the depth of his anger.

He briefly considered tossing her over the balustrade, and then he looked away. God, she was making his life hell.

Elinor decided after all not to renew their battle—a major victory for him—and turned away in frustrated fury.

She stormed off and he let his eyes droop down again, like a weary soldier on guard duty who's had a scare and then a reprieve. Still, he couldn't just stand there on the gallery until half-past two. He took out a handkerchief and held it under a stream of rain spilling from the battlement above, then dabbed his nose and chin gingerly with the cold, wet cloth. There was blood on his shirt, blood on his tie. The pocket of his jacket was half ripped away and he didn't have a clue who'd ripped it. They were all warriors in there.

He shook his head, dumbfounded by this latest event. He hadn't been in a fistfight since he was twelve years old. He had a vision of O'Toole and him rolling around on the rug in the great parlor: a young and utterly insane archivist, duking it out with a forty-year-old fart of an Englishman.

Thank God it had happened in America and not in the British Isles. He'd never live it down there.

Look out! someone had cried.

He wondered who.

"I heard screaming and shouting. Over Will?"

"Yes," said Elinor, shutting the door to her grandmother's room behind her. "It wasn't pretty." She came over to the bed and sat on the white chenille spread.

Camilla peeled a wet towel from her forehead and handed it to her granddaughter. "Where is he now?"

"Who knows," said Elinor, dipping the cloth into a bowl of ice water on the bed stand. "What does it matter. He'll be back. Like a bad penny."

The phrase instantly called up a picture of him standing in the doorway of her SoHo sublet. She felt her heart twist more tightly than the towel she was wringing of water. Forget it, she warned herself. *For. Get. It.*

Handing the cloth to her grandmother, she turned to the matter at hand. "Now. Would you like to explain to me why I had to steal a car and race up here when I should be in the city, working on my dragon?"

Camilla laid the cloth over her forehead and closed her eyes. "I'm sorry, Elly," she said. "You shouldn't have come . . . there's nothing you can do." She looked small and gray and all too mortal as she added, "We cannot stay here anymore. I want to sell."

"I don't believe that, Gramma Cam. Look at you—you're obviously sick over this. You *don't* want to sell. Is it Grampa Mick?" she urged. "Do you feel you have to sell because of him?"

"Not at all," said Camilla wearily.

It was clearly costing her an effort to say even that much. This was new. And alarming. Elinor knew that her grandmother had had headaches before—usually from working too long in the heat of the garden—but a cold compress and a quick nap had always done the trick.

Elinor glanced at the little silver boudoir clock on the nightstand: almost ten. Five more hours, and all would be lost; she had to do something. And yet it tore at her heart to see her grandmother in pain, so she stood up and said softly, "That's no garden-variety headache you've got there, Gramma Cam. Would you like me to leave you alone for a while?"

In a ghastly echo of her usual good humor, her grandmother smiled under the wet cloth and said, "I won't be much better five minutes from now. Especially with you hovering outside the door, waiting to come back in."

She took off the towel and dropped it over the floating

ice cubes, then made herself sit up. "Help me to that chair," she said to her granddaughter.

Five simple words—each one a separate stab to Elinor's heart. Camilla MacLeish had never asked for help with anything before.

She has *got old,* Elinor realized in a blinding moment. *Overnight. How is it possible?*

They walked slowly together to a pretty but tattered armchair covered in a flame-stitch pattern the colors of stained glass. Elinor helped her grandmother ease into the chair and then dropped to the well-worn oriental carpet.

Folding her legs beneath her, Elinor leaned back on her hands and waited. She'd sat at her grandmother's feet that way hundreds of times, listening to hundreds of stories. Some of the stories had made their way onto the pages of her books. All of the stories had made their way into her heart. It was clear to her that her grandmother was about to tell another one—and that it would have no charm.

Camilla sighed again and said, "Is Tucker still here?"

"You bet," Elinor answered grimly.

"How does he look to you? How does he seem?"

"At the moment, not so good. Not that Will actually— you could tell he really wanted to just haul back and— anyway, there was a slight misunderstanding. Tucker didn't know you'd agreed to sell," Elinor summed up. "Now he knows." She added, "Why do you ask?"

Her grandmother didn't answer at first. Whatever it was she had to say, it was going to have to be dragged out of her.

Or coaxed. Elinor knelt and laid her hand gently on her grandmother's wrist. "Gramma Cam—what does Tucker know that I don't?"

Camilla gazed back at her for a long, unnerving minute. Her expression, usually so wise, so confident, seemed suddenly vague and timid.

Finally she said, "He knows everything now, El. Everything that I know."

Elinor waited. For the first time, it occurred to her that

the impending sale had nothing to do with anyone's health.

With a smile that failed to be reassuring, Camilla said, "You must understand, Elly, that your grandfather and I—but especially I—have always sensed a kind of, oh, a presence, you might say, in the castle."

"Well, sure, the castle has an aura. We all feel that."

"It's more than an aura." Camilla looked around the room as if she were checking for mosquitoes, then murmured, "Do you remember the night Izzy told us that she saw something shimmering in the chapel?"

"Yes . . . what about it?" asked Elinor, feeling goose bumps ripple across her skin.

"Do you remember I laughed and said I'd seen something there myself—right after we moved in—and it turned out to be a column of smoke from your grandfather's cigar?"

"Yes, yes, perfectly well, Gramma Cam! Will you just—"

Get to the point! she wanted to scream. But aloud she said, "It wasn't cigar smoke?"

Her grandmother shook her head. "Your grandfather hadn't been there in over an hour. And he hadn't been smoking."

Now the hair on her arms stood on end. "So?"

Camilla lifted the lid off a ceramic pitcher that sat on the sewing table next to the armchair and filled a glass with water, then gulped it down.

When she finished she said firmly, "What I saw—what I know I *saw*—was the ghost of a woman. She had red hair that fell to her waist and she wore a long, pale dress. I think it was long, anyway; the apparition got hazy somewhere around the knees and seemed to fade away below that. I couldn't see her face. Her back was to me as she stood at the front between the two rows of pews."

Stunned, Elinor said rather stupidly, "Oh. So it wouldn't have been smoke, in that case."

"No, darling. Not smoke," said Camilla with some of her old wryness. "I backed out of the chapel as fast as I could. When I caught up with your grandfather and told him what I'd seen, he wasn't surprised. Chapels were like that, he said. So were great paintings. And masterworks of music. Transcendence, he called it. What I had seen was simple transcendence—a manifestation of the chapel's spirituality.

"I told him, baloney; what I had seen was a ghost. We argued about it and he returned to the chapel with me for a second look. Nothing. Eventually we agreed to disagree. I'm only telling you his side of the story to save you the trouble of going around and making a pest of yourself, as I'm sure you're going to do anyway."

Despite her fearfulness, Elinor had to smile. "And that's what's bothering you? A memory of half a century ago?"

"No—what's bothering me is a memory of two nights ago!" Camilla snapped.

Elinor became still. "The day I left for New York?"

Her grandmother nodded. "I slept very poorly that night, as you can imagine. William had called with his offer by then, and everyone was in an uproar over what to do. The cocktail hour that evening had the look of a barroom brawl; thank heavens Tucker and the help weren't around to witness it. It was very embarrassing, even for us."

Headache or no headache, Camilla was suddenly in a rush to tell her story. Her lethargy seemed in full retreat, replaced by an edgy desperation.

"I had one odd dream after another," she said, her face a picture of controlled agony. "I kept waking up with a start, falling back asleep, waking up again. It was a form of torture, as if I were a prisoner of war. By three in the morning, I was exhausted but still dreaming, dreaming, dreaming!"

She took a deep breath, then went on. "It was the last dream that I can still remember so well," she said, staring at her knees poking through her flannel dressing gown.

"I dreamed that I had an important appointment and I knew I wasn't going to make it—you know the kind of dream I'm talking about? It's always very frustrating. Either you've lost the map or you miss the train or you're at the wrong track or—well, anyway, I knew that this appointment was extremely important. I got out of bed and—I would have to say I was sleepwalking at this point—went directly to the chapel. Frankly, I don't remember any of it. I *do* remember standing at the back of the ... at the back ..."

She faltered for a moment and looked old and little and gray again. Then, summoning some of the iron will for which she was notorious, Camilla charged the rest of way up the hill, with Elinor following breathlessly behind.

"I stood at the back of the chapel," she said, all in a rush, "and was in a quandary whether I wanted to sit on the right side or the left. I heard *music,* Elly. A piercingly sad hymn being played on a wind instrument. And I smelled—no, don't look at me that way; I really did smell—incense. It was as if a thurifer had just preceded me down the aisle, swinging the censer back and forth over the congregation. But there was no congregation. There wasn't even a ghost. There was just me ... half asleep ... weaving in place and afraid that I was too late, I don't know for what. And, Elly, I haven't slept since. I'm so afraid. And I'm so tired ... I'm just so tired ... but sleep won't come. I keep hearing the hymn, over and over and sleep won't come. I think I must be going mad. I know it has to do with the castle. If we can sell it to Will and get out, I just know I'll be able to sleep. Sleep ... I want to sleep so, so badly. ..."

She broke down and began to weep. Elinor stared aghast at the sight of her grandmother hunched up and crying, her thin shoulders rising and falling to the rhythm of her anguish.

"Oh, Gramma Cam," she said, scrambling to her knees and holding the other woman close. "No, no, no, you don't have to cry ... please don't cry ... you can't be frightened by what you saw. You said yourself, you didn't see anything! Anyone can have a tune bouncing around in her head; it can be incredibly annoying. And as for the incense—well, the chapel does smell like a chapel! There could be four hundred years of incense soaked into the walls and pews."

Camilla bowed her head and shook it slowly from side to side. "But I *did* see something," she mumbled, almost too quietly to be heard.

"What? What did you see?" Elinor asked, much too sharply. Her own voice was rising with fear. She made herself sound calm as she added, "Was it that ghost again? The redheaded one?"

Again Camilla shook her head. When she raised it to look at her granddaughter, her eyes were blank with fatigue. "All the candles were lit," she said. "Every one."

Elinor didn't mean to gasp; it just came out. Her grandmother nodded and said, "So you see?"

"Wait . . . someone could have lit them. Was Grampa Mick up and around?"

"When I got back to bed he was snoring as loud as ever."

"Agnes?"

"At three?"

"Could it have been Mother? Izzie again? No, she wouldn't. Tucker! It could have been Tucker! He was in the castle, wasn't he? Maybe he was—"

"Was what—hanging around after midnight mass? Anyway, he hadn't been in the chapel. He came running down from the oratory—that's where we've put him up now, because it's more convenient to the archives room."

"Why did he come running down?"

"Because I screamed. I didn't, at first. It was only when I realized that all the candles were lit. It terrified me, I don't know why."

"You'd had an awful dream, that's why."

"I didn't dream the candles. Ask Tucker."

Elinor couldn't believe that Tucker hadn't lit the candles. "He *must* have been up. He couldn't have heard you from the oratory."

"Of course he could! You know how thin the wall is between it and the chapel."

"What was he wearing? Slacks or pajamas?"

"I told you he wasn't up! He was wearing pajamas. Dark red, with drawstrings. My eyesight is very good, as you know. It's only my brain . . . or else, or worse . . . it *isn't* my brain . . . Oh, dear God in heaven," Camilla said, beginning to rock back and forth in distress again. "I'm so tired. I only want to sleep."

"Why haven't you taken something for that?" Elinor wanted to know. "Just something over-the-counter?" She knew her grandmother disapproved of medication; everything Camilla had ever needed, she'd found in her herb garden. And she hadn't needed much.

A thought occurred to Elinor. "Gramma Cam, *have* you taken something? One of your herbal teas, maybe?"

Exhausted or not, Camilla resented the implication. "I am *not* hallucinating. Not because of something I've swallowed, anyway. If I've gone mad, that's one thing. But I haven't *made* myself go mad."

"No, no; no one's saying you did. Or are," Elinor added awkwardly. "I only meant, there has to be an explanation." She added, "What did Tucker say when he saw all the candles lit?"

Camilla laughed bleakly. "What *could* he say? He asked me why all the candles were lit. I told him that's how I'd found them, and after that, I told him about the original apparition."

"And?"

"He said that—like Izzy—he'd seen things once or twice out of the corner of his eye, but when he'd turn to face them they'd be gone."

"Are you kidding? He never said anything about that to *me*. Although—"

Her grandmother looked up at her, clearly dreading the rest of the remark. "Although what?"

"The night that Izzy dowsed with the pendant, Tucker and I were together on the gallery for a few minutes and he—we both—felt a violent chill. We *were* outside, after all, without coats. But he acted . . ."

Frightened, that's what he acted. Elinor didn't dare say so to her grandmother, so she said, "He acted like me. Goofy. There was a lot of tension in the air that night. It was the night . . . you know . . . of the *incident*. In the lodge? When Grampa Mick found Will and me—?" She felt herself blushing scarlet.

But her grandmother had forgotten all about the incident in the lodge. Her mind was somewhere else altogether. "You see? You see?" she said fretfully. "We've all been aware of this . . . this *presence,* in one form or another. How has it taken us so long to compare our stories?"

"I don't know," Elinor said with a pounding heart. Even she was beginning to be convinced that something preternatural existed in the castle. But she fought the notion—as much because she didn't want to give up on the castle as anything else.

"This is silly," she said, rallying. "The explanation is undoubtedly staring us in the face. We just have to get to the bottom of this."

"*There is no bottom;* can't you understand that?" cried her grandmother. "Too many things are happening; too many things *can* happen. We have to get out. We have to get out. It's what it wants us to do."

She began to shiver violently; Elinor became even more alarmed. "I'll call a doctor—"

"*No!*"

"Okay, okay, I'll . . . I'll make you some chamomile tea. And maybe some toast? Have you eaten anything?"

Again Camilla shook her head, dully now. She'd used up what little energy she had. There was nothing left for chewing on toast.

Elinor studied her grandmother. If she hadn't been hallucinogenic two nights ago, she would be shortly at this rate.

"I'll bring up a tray, anyway," she whispered, bending over to kiss the gray, unkempt head of her beloved relation. "And don't fret, Gramma Cam. We'll do what we have to do. If that means selling—I won't make trouble for you. If Will wants the castle that bad, let him have it," she said, suddenly sick of the fight.

Camilla smiled tiredly. "You're being too hard on him, Elinor. He has a grandmother, too."

Elinor snorted and said, "That surprises me. He acts as if he came down from the mountain fully formed."

"Stop, dear. This isn't about him and it's not about you

anymore. It's about the castle. It's always been about the castle."

"I know; I know," she said, sighing. "But for a while there . . ."

During the night. When she was in his arms. And he was driving her to heights of passion and depths of joy. For a while there . . .

Elinor looked away, compressing her lips in resignation. "You're right," she whispered, utterly subdued. "I'll bring your tea."

She helped her grandmother back into bed, and then she left the chamber. She needed desperately to shower; to wash away the last sticky traces of misplaced passion. After that, she'd get to the bottom of the candle nonsense. And after that, she'd confront the merciless Lord Norwood for the last time.

What would she say to him? She didn't know. She couldn't bring up the castle, and she wouldn't bring up their night in New York. Everything that mattered to her was off limits. What did that leave? Maybe they could talk about the weather. Maybe she could talk about the forecast without screaming or crying or trying to sock him. Or wanting to throw herself in his arms.

It seemed unlikely.

"It will go back, then, Charles! Too soon!"

"I would not have believed it. She has been such a wilful thing; who would have guessed that in the end, she would submit so meekly to her elders?"

"It is because he has broken her spirit. I feel some sorrow: The two of them did burn brightly together."

"It was a fire of straw, Marianne. It could not last."

"How unlike ourselves! I have no doubt that he has offered her words of passion. But you, Charles—you offered me words of love."

"Because I loved you, Marianne."

"And before the seed of your passion became the child of our love, you stood before God and declared me to be your own."

"If only I had done so before man!"

"*Think not of it. We have been granted this one rare glimpse into time to make up for the lapse; we cannot let the moment slip into oblivion.*"

"*Nor will we. Our first order must be to delay this transaction. I see no hardship upon us there.*"

Chapter 22

*I*sabelle sat on her bed with her arms hugging her shins, planning. She waited until she heard the metal rings of the shower curtain being pulled across the circle of brass pipe that hung above the claw-foot tub, and then she sprang into action.

But first she had to make sure, so she crept up to the bathroom door and said in a soft hail, "El?"

No answer. Good. Elly would be taking one of her long do-not-disturb showers, then. Good. She was probably thinking about her dragon. But how she could do that when the whole *castle* was in danger . . .

It was time to act. Isabelle had read a thousand books with a thousand different problems, and all the time, the kids were able to solve them. They didn't just sit on their rear ends and watch TV. They didn't just mope. They took action. And they got the job done.

Lord Norwood had said that sometimes a person could do the right thing and still feel terrible about it. Well, she was going to do the wrong thing and feel really good about it. So there.

She remembered how serious he looked when he was waiting in the great parlor. He was an evil, awful man, and she hated him so much. How could he be so selfish? There were six of *them* who needed the castle for their home, and there was only one of *him*—well, two, if you counted his grandmother in England. But she sounded really old and probably she was going to die soon, but

Gramma Cam was young and beautiful and she wasn't probably going to die until, well, who knows? She could live for so many years yet. It just wasn't fair.

Isabelle retied the lace of one sneaker and walked out of her bedroom on tiptoe, creeping down the hall with her arms flattened against the wall, quietly, quietly.... First she had to check to make sure everyone was where they were supposed to be. She used both hands to muffle the sound of the latch as she lifted it on the door to her grandmother's room, then slid the door open two inches. Yes. Still in bed, resting.

Grampa Mick was driving her dad around, and her mom was in the kitchen making lunch because Agnes didn't feel like coming to work again. Agnes was *so* uncool. But not as uncool as her son, Owen. Owen gave Isabelle the creeps. His ponytail was greasy and his teeth were all yellow.

And even though she couldn't prove it, Isabelle was positive that it was Owen who'd taken the money out of Grampa Mick's wallet when he left it in the great parlor. Too bad Grampa Mick couldn't remember how much he had in it, or even if any cash was missing. He never was too organized about money, Mom said.

Owen didn't work on rainy days. So that left Mr. O'Toole and Lord Norwood. Mr. O'Toole was in the archives room, she was just about positive. But she wasn't sure about Lord Norwood.

She went sneaking up on the great parlor but found it empty. The dining room, empty also. Lord Norwood wasn't in the library or in the kitchen talking to her mom, either. Well, why would he be? He only came to sign his papers and get out. There was no reason to be nice to any of them anymore. Although ... he *did* apologize for breaking all the furniture, and he even apologized to Mr. O'Toole for fighting with him. Izzy saw the whole thing through the keyhole.

She was really glad when Mr. O'Toole refused to shake Lord Norwood's hand. She wasn't exactly positive what the fight had been about—when she'd asked, her mom had just told her to mind her own business—but she knew even without being told. Mr. O'Toole had been defending Elly. He was like the knights in Elly's books, always protecting the ladies in the castle. Of course, Elly was pretty good at protecting her*self,* but it was a nice idea.

If only he'd been able to make Lord Norwood give up and leave! But the whole problem was, no one really fought him very hard except Elly—and now Mr. Tucker—and you had to fight *very* hard, if someone was as rich and as strong as a baron. You had to stand firm. Because if you didn't, he'd just run right over you. Which is exactly what was happening.

But there were people even stronger than Lord Norwood: the police. The police could put him in jail, and then everyone would be happy again. All Izzy had to do was find a reason for them to put him in jail. Stealing would be one reason. So if he stole something—if it *looked* like he stole something—then he'd get arrested and that would be that. Case closed. And everyone would thank Izzy for using her head instead of her fists like Mr. O'Toole.

She smiled to herself as she crept down to the archives room to confirm Mr. O'Toole's whereabouts. Grown-ups could learn a lot if they only read more books.

She strolled casually past the half-closed door. Yes. He was just where she expected him to be, taking down dusty books from the top shelves where no one ever went. Izzy couldn't understand it. He seemed to love to read stuff that wasn't even stories. She'd once peeked at one of the books he had lying open. All she saw were a bunch of names and dates. He might as well be back in middle school. What was the point of graduating, if he wasn't going to read good stories?

Doubling back from the archives room, Isabelle skirted around the chapel and shot up the back stairs to the hall that led to the oratory. Her heart was hardly pounding at all. Looking up and then down the hall, she opened the door to Tucker O'Toole's room and stepped inside.

The room was very neat, much neater than hers—but then, he'd only been sleeping there for two days. In a way it was good. He would notice something missing that much faster. But there wasn't much to steal! Not clothes—he only had a few of those, hanging on the pegs and maybe in the brown duffel bag shoved under the high-legged dresser. Jewelry? She walked over to the dresser without much hope. Just what she was afraid of: nothing, not even a school ring. If he owned a wallet, it must be in his pocket. The binoculars looked expensive; but the camera looked even more expensive.

She picked it up, impressed by its weight. Nikon. Nikons cost a lot of money. Grampa Mick had a Nikon, and when he bought it he told everyone that he had to use the cigar money from the rest of his life. So maybe the Nikon.

She put it back down, then frowned as she turned in place, looking for something that would be valuable enough for Tucker O'Toole to make a fuss about.

Feeling a little squeamish now, she began opening the drawers to his dresser one by one. First drawer: socks, boxer shorts, undershirts. Eee-yew, not what she was looking for. She tried the next drawer down. A couple of old books, maybe from the castle, maybe not; and a laptop computer like her teacher Mrs. Clancy had. A computer! *That* was worth stealing. Except Lord Norwood sounded like he had a zillion of them; why would he bother to take someone else's? She laid the thin gray instrument gently back in place and went to the next drawer.

It was stuffed with pages. Lots and lots of pages. All handwritten in black ballpoint and all in the same handwriting. She had no idea if it was Mr. O'Toole's handwriting, but that seemed like the most logical thing. She had to think fast. The idea was to get in and get right back out—and even then, she'd only be half-done.

The Nikon, or the pages?

She rifled through the drawer of loose pages hurriedly, wishing she knew which ones were the most valuable. They were notes for Mr. O'Toole's book, that was for sure. But which part of the book was hardest to research? Which part would upset him the most to have stolen? She felt bad even having to think that way—Mr. O'Toole was a completely innocent victim in her plan—but she had no choice. You had to do what you had to do.

A sound in the hall made her heart rocket through her chest. Clutching a handful of papers to her breast, she made a dash for the narrow gap between the high head-board and the wall behind it. She squeezed herself be-tween the bed and the wall, bumping her head on one of the wood pegs of the clothes rack that hung above the bed.

Down, down, hide! She twisted both knees to the right and slithered lower until her head dipped below the top of the headboard, then held that position with a painful effort while someone knocked on the door to the room. She shifted her weight; her papers made a little crinkling sound. Horrified, she stopped breathing altogether.

She waited, and so did the person on the other side of the door. Another knock, and then Lord Norwood's voice, not quite angry, demanding to know if Tucker was in there.

Izzy heard the doorknob being worked and closed her eyes, figuring that if she couldn't see anything, anything couldn't see her. Her heart was thumping like a jungle drum. Suddenly she understood why her sister had told her not to go rummaging through other people's things.

She heard the door open.

And then right away she heard the door close.

She let out a sigh and said a prayer of thanks on the spot, then squeezed back out from her hiding spot. No telling when Mr. O'Toole would be back now; she took what she had and ran.

When she got back to her room, she found the door to her side of the bathroom open. In her hurry, she slammed it so hard that Elinor, in her room on the other side, yelled out, "Leave the hinges in place, please!"

Izzy threw her armful of papers under a pillow exactly one and a half seconds before her sister reopened the door of the bathroom.

She was wrapped in a terry cloth robe and brushing through her wet hair. "Didn't you hear me, Iz? I asked you where Lord Norwood was."

Isabelle stared goggle-eyed at her and said, "Why are you asking *me* where he is?"

"Because you're always snooping around and know everything, squirt," Elinor said with a tired smile. "Why do you think?"

"Well, not anymore I don't. *Everyone* here has a secret. They're always whispering and closing doors when I come down the halls. I can't keep up anymore," Izzy said petulantly.

She glanced at her pillows. A page was sticking halfway out. Appalled by the sight of it, she took a flying leap onto her bed, rolled on her back, and flung her arms out wide as if she were setting up to make snow angels.

"What's the matter with you?" said Elinor, drawing nearer.

"Stay away!" cried Isabelle, warding off her sister with an outstretched hand. "I'm tired!"

Elinor stopped in her tracks. "What's the *matter* with you?"

"I want to rest! Could you close the bathroom door when you go back, please!"

"You, too? Has everyone here gone mad?"

"I don't know about everyone! I'm tired!"

"Fine," said Elinor with an exasperated shrug. "Take a nap, then. When is Mother serving lunch?"

"How should I know?" cried Izzy. "You're always giving me the third degree!"

Elinor turned her back on her sister and threw up her hands. "I'm sorry I asked," she said over her shoulder. She looked too tired to argue.

Isabelle leaped out of bed as soon as the door was closed, snatched the papers up, and stuffed them in her knapsack. She raced with it back to the archives room. The door, very thick, was shut. Crouching down, she peeked through the keyhole, but all she could see was Mr. O'Toole's back, which was really too bad; it was much easier to tell what people were saying when you could see their lips moving at the same time.

She pressed the side of her face up against the door and heard Tucker O'Toole's voice, muffled but loud, and

Lord Norwood's voice, muffled but less loud. Still, she knew enough about eavesdropping to know that they were having a serious argument. It could end in a fist-fight—or end, period—at any moment.

No time! She spun on her heel and made a beeline for Lord Norwood's room on the fourth floor. Lucky for her he'd agreed to spend the night. She'd heard him say no to her mom, but then—after the fight—he'd changed his mind and invited himself to stay. It was all very queer. Nothing anyone did made sense. She wasn't kidding when she told Elinor that she couldn't keep up anymore.

On the fourth floor landing she got an unexpected jolt when the door opened nearly into her.

Greasy Owen!

"What're *you* doing here?" she blurted.

He scowled, then said, "Clearing a drain. What's it to you?" He was surprised to see her, probably because no one ever used the back stairs.

"Nothing," she said. "I just—nothing."

He went on his way and so did she. She stepped into the big guest bedchamber, then closed the door and looked around in frantic haste. Where to plant the evidence? Except for one shirt, Lord Norwood wasn't even unpacked! She pulled the papers out of her backpack, then lifted his leather briefcase up onto the bed and tried to snap the catch open.

Locked! She hadn't counted on this. In a blind panic now, she spun the combination wheels madly, trying arbitrary combinations with no luck.

Think! Think! Where were the numbers set originally? The array popped into her vision: four six one. She reset them and then on an impulse tried something she'd seen her grandfather do: change only one number. She moved the last digit first up one numeral and tested the lock, then down one numeral and tested the lock. Still locked. She tried the same with the middle digit. Up one, test; down one, test. Locked. Desperate now, she tried the first digit. Up one, test—open! She'd got it open!

Thrilled to discover that she had the mind of a master detective after all, Izzy lifted the lid of the briefcase and discovered yet more papers, neatly typed and bound in blue. She took the top few documents from the pile and quickly placed Tucker O'Toole's loose sheets on the bottom papers, then sandwiched the new ones with the blue-bound documents.

That extra touch was very cool. After all, a thief wouldn't leave everything on top where it could be seen if he accidentally had to go into his briefcase for something like maybe an address book, in front of someone like maybe her mom.

No, he'd hide it. But not well enough to fool a detective. A detective would know to look underneath the top papers.

What an excellent plan. And all on the spur of the moment, too. Now all she had to do was—

"May I help you, Miss Roberts?"

Izzy's eyes bugged open. She slammed down the briefcase but was far too terrified to turn around and face Lord Norwood. "No. That's all right," she said in a squeaky voice. "I was just looking for something."

"Oh, really?" He walked around to her side and she cringed, because she knew he'd just been in a fight with someone way bigger than she was.

Her instinct was to bolt and run, but another instinct told her to stand still. She bowed her head and waited.

"Did your sister send you here, by any chance?"

Her head shot up. "No, no, Elly doesn't even know. *Please* don't tell!"

He looked as if he didn't believe her. He looked very stern. "Are you telling the truth? Because I see a similar *modus operandi*."

Isabelle didn't have any idea what a motors opera thing was, so she shook her head vigorously and said, "Elly would kill me if she found out. She might even . . . she might even tell *Mom*. Oh, please don't tell, Lord Norwood!" she begged, looking up at him. She began to cry. She didn't want to, but the tears just started coming out.

"It doesn't do much good to weep," he said in an even more severe voice.

This was horrible. *She* was the one who was going to

end up in jail, and he'd get the castle anyway. Oh, how could her plan get so messed up?

She said between sniffles, "I wasn't . . . trying . . . to s-steal anything."

"Right." He flipped the top of the briefcase back up and slid the blue-bound documents sideways. He knew right where to look. "Then what're these?"

"Oh . . . those," she said faintly. "I found them."

"I'm sure." He glanced at the top page and looked surprised. Oh, he knew . . . he *knew* who they belonged to. You could see it in his face.

"Did you take these from the archives room?" he asked her quietly.

She shook her head.

"Then where—? Not from Mr. O'Toole's room!"

Oh-h-h . . . she was definitely going to jail. Oh-h-h . . .

She murmured, "Yes. From his drawer."

"Good lord." He lifted up the pack of papers and began shuffling through them quickly while Isabelle waited, almost without breathing, to hear what her punishment was. She didn't even care anymore if he told Elinor; just as long as he didn't call the police.

At last he looked up from the papers. "Isabelle," he said without smiling at all, "do you have any idea how serious an offense this is?"

She began to shake her head no, then nodded.

"What did you hope to achieve? Did you think Mr. O'Toole was going to find these here, beat me up, and boot me out?"

She shook her head.

"Then what? I'd like an answer, please."

Izzy wiped her nose on the sleeve of her sweatshirt and said, "I thought he would call the police . . . and they would get a search warrant . . . and then they could arrest you for stealing."

Lord Norwood looked surprised, but he did not smile the way her Grampa Mick might have done.

"Oh, yes, you're a MacLeish, all right," he said. "Now listen to me. What you did was very foolish and very wrong. You could easily have been caught by Mr.

O'Toole and properly punished. I know you don't like me, Isabelle. That's your right. But you do not have the right to embarrass me, or to embarrass your family with your foolery. Are we clear on this?"

She nodded solemnly, then said in a tiny voice, "So you won't tell?"

He glanced at the papers again. He looked so fed up. "I don't know."

Izzy wanted to ask him what he was going to do with Mr. O'Toole's papers, but she didn't dare. He was too mad. So she mumbled "I'm sorry" the way she had been taught to do, and skulked out of the room.

At the end of the hall she turned and paused, wondering whether he was going to bring the papers out and take them to Elinor. She waited a fairly long time, but Lord Norwood never came out.

Her shoulders drooped as she turned to go. *I'm gonna get it now,* she thought.

It took Will several minutes to wash up. He was disgusted to realize that he'd had a smear of dried blood on the side of his nose when he made amends with the family and when he tried again with Tucker O'Toole. And, of course, when he delivered his pompous little lecture to Isabelle five minutes earlier.

The plain fact was, he'd been shocked to find the child in his room, setting him up for a fall. It should've been funny—a ten-year-old, determined to sic the local sheriff on him—but when he walked in on her, he was still seething over the encounter with Tucker O'Toole in the archives room.

O'Toole had snarled and spurned Will's overture for the second time in the space of half an hour. Instead of a handshake, O'Toole had offered a tirade about money and power and the corrosive effects it had on society, ending with a blast at upper-class Englishmen in general. Apparently O'Toole himself was a Marxist. Fine. The least he could do was be a civil Marxist.

And now, of course, Will was stuck with O'Toole's purloined papers. Just what he needed. How he was going to return them without incriminating Isabelle, he had no idea. He rubbed his unshaven face and neck dry with a towel and cast a longing glance at the clean shirt he intended to put on after a long hot shower.

But first things first. There was no telling when O'Toole would discover the theft. Will had to move quickly. God. Kids. No wonder he'd never had any.

He picked up the sheaf of papers with their crabbed, laborious handwriting, and was struck by the contrast between O'Toole and him. Two men, both with brains; but one of them spent his time with dusty relics, the other, with cutting-edge technology. Was it any surprise that the money had flowed Will's way instead of O'Toole's?

He glanced at the papers again, reluctant to examine the personal writings of someone else, no matter how impersonal they were. But a familiar if unusual name jumped out at him—MacGilliray, a family well represented in Dibble— and he began to read despite his reluctance.

The pages were a very dry, very dull account of a branch of the MacGilliray family tree in the nineteenth century: who married whom, how many kids, what they ate for supper. All pretty dreary stuff. It was safe to assume that O'Toole's book would not be optioned for a movie.

More to the point, though—was O'Toole writing about *Dibble's* MacGillirays? Will scanned the pages, looking for a reference that would place the family in England. All he found was a mention of the Fourth of July, hardly a holiday over there.

In any case, he had no time to read the account through. He slipped the papers inside his sports coat, flattening them against his body, then made his way quickly to the small oratory that had served as his own bedchamber during his last stay at the castle. If he ran into anyone on the way, he'd have to claim he'd hurt his arm in the scrap with O'Toole; how else explain the awkward way he was holding it against his jacket?

Damn!

The castle seemed unusually subdued, and he made it

without incident to the oratory. He knew the room well. It had exactly four drawers. Closing the door behind him, he crossed the small chamber in three long strides and pulled open the first, second, and third drawers of the dresser in quick succession. A sense of grudging admiration for Izzy's steel nerves came over him as he hurriedly threw the stolen papers on top of the others in the third drawer, then tried to tidy the pile so it didn't look tampered with.

On the other hand, what did he expect? Izzy was an American; as far as he could see, every blasted one of 'em was an outlaw.

"You son of a bitch!" came a voice behind him. The voice was vicious with fury.

Will didn't bother to respond; didn't even bother to look up.

Ah, well, he thought. At least O'Toole wouldn't have to go to the trouble of getting a search warrant taken out on him.

Chapter 23

*E*linor was bent over double, blow-drying her hair, when her mother ran into the bathroom, pulled out the plug, and cried, "*Again!* I can't believe it! Hurry!"

Susan wrenched the blow-dryer from her astonished daughter's hand and threw it on the marble sink surround, then began hauling Elinor forcibly out of her room.

Dressed only in a skirt and bra, Elinor grabbed her turtleneck as they breezed past her bed, and yanked her other hand clear of her mother's grip. "Have you gone bonkers, too?" she asked, pulling the sweater over her head. "Again? Again, what?"

"William! Tucker! Some papers were stolen and he's blaming him—"

Elinor couldn't believe it. "Tucker *is* an idiot!" she said. "Stealing the purchase agreement will never work; how dumb can you get?" (Elinor had thought of the idea herself but had put it aside reluctantly.)

"Not Tucker—William! Tucker caught him stealing research from his dresser drawer."

"Are you *kidding?*"

"William doesn't deny it, and now Tucker is threatening to call the police. I'd ask Tucker to just pack up and leave, but I don't dare provoke him more. He's furious, El. You're the only one who knows him at all well—please, do something, or this afternoon will never happen!"

"Mother, number one, I don't know Tuck that well"—

although it was true that Tucker seemed to know all of
them pretty well—"and number two . . ."

She didn't have to spell out number two. Number two
was why on earth would she help Will to close a deal on
the castle? For the first time since she'd heard that he
wanted to buy it, Elinor's hopes began to rise. She tried
to suppress a smile of joy. She failed.

Susan grabbed her daughter by the shoulders. "*Listen*
to me," she said, fixing Elinor with a fierce look. "This
castle is costing us a fortune. Ultimately, we will not have
the money to keep it going. Not unless you become another Judy Blume. So it's going to be sold anyway—
sooner or later and probably sooner!

"What's more, your grandmother *wants* to sell. If you
don't believe me, go back to her room and look at her.
You selfish, selfish child! This is not a game of Dungeons
and Dragons. This is a serious family crisis and the sooner
you get it through your pigheaded head, the better it will
be for everyone you claim you love so well. I don't know
what your grandmother has seen, and I don't care. It's
what she *thinks* she's seen that counts. She is in crisis. We
have to sell. Do you understand me? Do you under-
stand?"

It was a blast of fire hot enough to singe Elinor's eyelashes. Never in her life had she seen her mother so ferocious. Susan Roberts had always been more the Jackie
Onassis type than a fan of Teddy Roosevelt, and yet here
she was, bearing down on Elinor like a general leading a
charge.

"All right," Elinor whispered, crushed by her mother's
cold logic. "I'll do what I can."

Satisfied, her mother released her grip on her. "It can't
always be magic, El," she said crisply. "That's not how
life is."

Elinor had no answer to that. She wasn't ready to sub-
scribe to such gloom. People needed magic in their lives.
They had to have it. If they tried hard enough, they were
bound to find it. And once they did, they had to work
hard to keep it. To Elinor it was all as clear as Fair Castle.
Magic.

As they made their way quickly down to the great parlor, it occurred to Elinor that when Will Braddock appeared in her life, he brought with him another kind of magic, more than she'd ever thought possible from a man. He'd made her body hum and her spirit soar, all with a wave of his wand. And yet after today he was going to leave and take his magic with him—and Fair Castle besides. Up until last night, she'd been filled merely with anger. Now she felt something like panic.

"It's very quiet," her mother whispered in the hall. She was more alarmed than before. "If he's killed him—"

Elinor dropped her voice down low. "What're you saying? Will wouldn't do that!"

"Not William! Tucker! Oh, what's the difference!" her mother snapped. "Either way the sale would be off."

Susan rushed into the dimly lit parlor with Elinor in tow, both of them expecting the worst. It wasn't that way at all. Will, looking weary, almost bored, was sitting in the rolled-arm chair that he seemed to favor (Elinor thought of it now as his chair, and wondered how she'd ever be able to sit in it after he'd gone). He was unshaved, unkempt, still wearing the bloodied shirt and the torn tweed jacket. He was a mess. And she was pretty sure she was in love with him.

Ah, no. Anyone but him. She closed her eyes briefly, shutting out the unbearable thought, then opened them and swung her gaze to the wing chair opposite. Tucker sat rigidly in it, his hands gripping its hobnailed arms. His fair-skinned, boyishly handsome face was flushed and focused squarely on the man across from him. He looked like a rookie cop who's made his first collar; she was surprised he wasn't holding a gun.

The whole thing would've been laughable if it weren't for the venom she saw in Tuck's eyes. It was obvious that he saw Will as a mortal enemy now.

Will, a thief? It made no sense. She didn't understand what possible interest he could have with Tucker's research. The simplest thing would've been just to ask him. But if her life wasn't very magical just then, it certainly wasn't simple.

No one seemed in the mood to speak, so Elinor decided to break the ice. "I see the *New York Times* gave *Rigamarole* a rave review," she said with a perky smile. "I can hardly *wait* to drive down tomorrow."

Without so much as a glance her way, Tucker said, "I don't think so. Maybe you'd care to take your grandmother. I'm not done with this bastard." He kept his gaze fastened on Will, as if he were expecting him to make a break for a waiting helicopter.

"I assume I'm under house arrest?" Will asked him with a droll look. "Will I be permitted to shower?"

"Very funny, my lord."

"Oh, Tucker, come now," pleaded Susan. "Surely you two can settle this like grown men."

"We tried that," Tucker said, tight-lipped. "You didn't seem too thrilled."

"Because we should've taken it outside," Will suggested pleasantly. "Where I could've done the job right."

"You son of a bitch!" Tucker cried, exploding again. He sprang from his chair, ready for another round.

"Elinor!" cried her mother.

It was her cue. Still unsure what she was expected to do, Elinor jumped in front of Tucker and laid her hands flat on his chest. "Don't, Tuck. He . . . he's not worth it!" she improvised.

"You've got *that* right."

"He'll be gone by three," she added. "I'm sure that until then he'll stay clear of you and your things." She swung around to face Will. *"Right?"*

Will said with faint distaste, "You have my word."

"Your word is worth shit!" said Tucker over Elinor's shoulder. "Come on! Let's go! Let's finish it!" He sneered, pumping a finger at Will.

Will stood up with lazy deliberation. "If the lady would kindly step aside . . ."

"Elly! Oh no, Elly!"

The shriek was high was shrill and as effective as a sprinkler system on the men's hot tempers. Isabelle was standing there—Elinor had no idea for how long—with both hands clamped over her mouth and a look of horror in her eyes. She'd hid under the piano for the earlier skirmish, but this time around she seemed even more upset.

Elinor took advantage of Isabelle's state to subdue both men into a truce.

"I hope you're both proud of yourselves!" she said, rushing to her sister and putting her arm around her. "Tucker, if you want to call the police, go ahead and get it over with. But don't take it out on us or the furniture. As for *you!*" she said to Will, and then she let out a short, pained laugh. There were no words to express the emotions she was feeling for him.

She turned back to her sister. "Come on, honey," she said softly. "We'll just ignore these jerks. Let's go out to the lodge and goof off."

Tucker murmured to Will, "This isn't over, Norwood."

"Alas, my thought exactly," Will said tiredly.

"Oh, don't start again," Elinor said over her shoulder. "Please."

"I have to talk to you, El," whispered Isabelle with tears in her eyes.

Susan wedged in with mind-boggling brightness. "Agnes still isn't in, so I'll be the one serving lunch. Crab-stuffed chicken breasts! Hope everyone's hungry!" she chirped.

Elinor turned to her mother and merely stared. *She's desperate for this sale. That's why she's behaving like a waitress at an I-HOP. How have I not seen how determined she is—maybe they all are—to sell?*

Because I've been selfish. Pigheaded. That's how. She smiled wanly at her mother and said, "It sounds great. You go ahead and finish your preparations. I'll take over the next tour for you."

"Oh, yes, I forgot . . . the tour," said Susan, hardly registering the fact. She went up to the window, nudging aside the blue velvet drapes that puddled on the floor, and peered out through the multipaned casement at the parking lot. "I don't see any cars. It's still coming down hard . . . what's keeping your grandfather and Chester? They should be home by now . . . they had the first appointment . . ."

"El-*lee-ee* . . ."

"Yes, yes, Iz," Elinor said with a shushing gesture. "One minute."

She turned from her sister to Will and Tucker.

"Gentlemen," she said derisively, "there are only three women—one of them ill—and a child in the castle right now. We're waiting for the arrival of an elderly man and an injured one, but that still won't be much of an army to subdue you if you break out in another brawl. All I can do is throw us at your mercy: Please don't fight anymore."

She watched Will go scarlet during her scathing speech. He stood up and said, "I'll confine myself to my room until it's time to leave. Will that satisfy you?"

He gave her a sharp look that was raw with feeling. Elinor was caught off guard by it; it was her turn to go scarlet. She looked away, letting her gaze fall on a trickle of water that oozed alongside the window through stone that needed tuck-pointing. The rain battered the castle; there would be other trickles on other east-facing walls, she knew. The leak was one more reminder to let Will have his way.

Her voice was low and tense as she said, "That would be best, I think."

Will left, followed closely by Tucker, and then her mother fluttered off. Elinor sighed and straightened out a fringed lampshade, then turned to her sister. "All right, Iz. What is it you wanted to tell me?"

Isabelle hugged herself and cocked her cheek against one shoulder. Her face was screwed into a grimace of reluctance as she said, "Promise you won't be mad? Or tell Mom?"

"Yeah, yeah, I promise. What is it?"

Izzy took a deep breath and exhaled it in a tiny voice. "Lord Norwood didn't steal the papers. I did."

Elinor stood in front of the door of Will's bedchamber in a state of high anxiety. Izzy's confession had thrown her for a loop. Baron Norwood had behaved in a manner worthy of his title. He'd been generous. He'd been noble. He'd been kind.

Hell. She seemed to be working harder and harder to hate him less and less. If she loved him, well, that part couldn't be helped. Fate had decreed it. But she had to be able to hate him, too, or else when he walked out of her life, she'd die of a broken heart. It was as simple as that.

She rapped on the door; after a delay, he opened it.

"You were showering," she said, stating the obvious.

He had on black cotton slacks and a white T-shirt; he was barefoot and was rubbing his dripping hair with a towel vigorously, the way men did. He looked untucked and un-British. And yes, she was definitely in love with him.

"I...um...hi," she said awkwardly. Her smile was even worse, a schoolgirl's shy overture to the cutest guy on the soccer field. "Izzy told me everything. And...I wanted to thank you. For what you did. It was very decent of you. Considering how Tucker feels about you, it was downright heroic."

The wary expression on Will's craggy face softened to a merely ironic one. He said, "C'mon in," almost gruffly, as if he were sending a signal that all would stay formal between them, despite his bare feet.

She stood prissily inside the door with her hand on the door latch as he walked into the bathroom and flipped the towel over the shower rod, then took a comb from his pocket and ran it through his hair two or three times. "She told you, then," he said from his position at the sink. "That took guts. She's a good kid."

"A little too gung-ho sometimes," Elinor admitted.

"I wonder where she gets it from," he said in a wonderfully deadpan voice.

He came out into the bedroom then, and she smiled sheepishly, careful not to notice the pineapple-finial bed a few short feet away.

She said, "You have to understand that in Izzy's world of books, the good guys always win."

"And this time they're not going to?"

She colored. "I didn't mean it that way," she said, even though that was exactly the way she meant it. "I only meant, Izzy has always felt empowered. She's an amazement to us all."

"Your sister cracked the combination to my briefcase," he said with respect. "Obviously she has presence of mind. I reckon she's going to be either a criminal or an astronaut."

"Oh, Izzy's fearless. Nothing rattles her except spiders," Elinor told him. "I've seen her stand in the ice-cold Hudson in hip-waders, reeling in a bass the size of a sea otter. She's very focused."

He nodded, then sat on the side of the bed and scooped up an argyle sock. "So you came here to chat about Isabelle," he said, jamming the sock over his right foot.

"Well, not to chat. To thank you, definitely. And to ask if you have any problem with my telling Tucker that it was Izzy who took his research."

Will looked up midroll of the second sock. "Why would I have a problem with that?"

He wouldn't. It was an excuse, and a really lame one at that. She was losing her wits over him. And yet, did it matter? He'd won. She'd lost. She could afford to lose a few wits. The thought was almost liberating.

She shrugged and said, "You seem to enjoy having Tucker hate you. I didn't want to take away your satisfaction."

He laughed—for the first time since he'd come into her bed—and said, "Now that you mention it, I do spend a lot of time that way. Don't know what it is about O'Toole; he puts me off my game."

Will stood up and, she thought, was about to come nearer to her. Instead he hesitated and said softly, "Maybe I'm just jealous."

She felt the heat. She was cool, she was calm, but she felt the heat. "Jealous that Tucker doesn't have a run-down castle to agonize over?" she quipped.

"No."

More heat. It was in his eyes, in the quirky angle of his smile, in the way he stood watchful and alert just a few feet away. As if he were waiting to see which way Elinor would go before he made his own move.

She lifted the door latch behind her.

"Well . . . I guess . . . since you're planning to hide out in your chamber . . . I won't be seeing you, until after you've signed . . . it. The agreement."

Hold on to your anger, she warned herself. It was slipping away, like water through her fingers.

"Elinor." It came out as a frustrated plea, almost a groan. "Does it have to be like this?"

It was the hardest question she'd ever been asked. Part of her wanted to say, "No, of course it doesn't. You're all that matters to me. I don't care about anything else."

But it wasn't true. She had a family. They used to be happy. Now they weren't. It was because he'd arrived like a hand grenade in their midst and was about to send them hurtling in all directions. Even if she could bear to watch the explosion—what then?

"You tell me," she said.

His eyes were dark with agony as he whispered, "I've given someone my word. I can't go back on it."

"Yes. Your grandmother. I understand completely." The worst of it was, she did understand. She was in the same vexing bind herself.

"Camilla is determined to sell," he reminded Elinor, almost in self-defense.

Elinor thought of her grandmother, prostrate with fear and exhaustion, lying on the bed in the chamber below his. Her grandmother was convinced that she was being haunted into a sale, and nothing Elinor could say or do would alter that.

"Yes," she admitted. "I've spoken with her."

"Has she told you why the about-face?"

"Because of a dozen candles burning," Elinor said at last, not without bitterness. "That's why she's selling."

"I don't understand."

"No. I don't expect you to."

"It's not about money, then?"

"Not at the moment. It would be, eventually."

He stood there with legs apart, fists jammed on his hips. "Well. I guess the die is cast, then."

Her heart took a dive. She pulled the door slightly open behind her and said bleakly, "It looks that way."

"All right," he said. "Then let's talk about last night."

Chapter 24

Last night.

Last night was still surging through her body. She tried to focus on the bad parts of last night—his confession about having made the offer, the fact that he'd made love to her before he confessed—but all she could think about were the good parts. Him in her. His lips on hers. The exquisite, maddening touch of his tongue on the tips of her breasts. She was feeling a rush of plain lust, but she managed to say in an offhand way, "There's not a whole lot to talk about. We seem to have good chemistry in bed"—a pathetic understatement—"and nowhere else."

Now he did come near. "That's not true and you know it," he said. "I'll be the first to admit that what happened between us in bed was a nuclear meltdown—"

She winced and closed the door again; Izzy was undoubtedly tiptoeing around somewhere nearby.

"—but meltdown or no meltdown, that's not all there is to it." He was close enough to touch, then close enough to kiss. "There's something more, Elinor," he said. "Something better."

"Better?" she said, averting her gaze from his. "What could be better than the sex? It was phenomenal."

"The fights," he said simply. He cupped her chin in his hand and turned her face toward him. "You're a worthy opponent, my love."

My love. Why did it have to come after *opponent?*

She said over a hammering heart, "So you like fighting

better than you like making love. That's a little weird."

His laugh was low and amused. "Oh, all right. I don't like it *more* than making love. You know what I mean, Elinor," he said, so close to her. "You know we're exciting together."

"Cheap thrills," she shot back, waiting for his kiss. Let him go to England. Let him take the castle. Just don't let him take it without her.

She was surprised when he didn't kiss her. Surprised, and disappointed. She looked at him with a long, thoughtful gaze that was filled with equal parts of pain and desire. His lined face, stubbled with a day's growth of hair, gave him the look of a crusader only partway through a campaign. She thought how handsome he'd look with a close-trimmed beard. On a white horse. With a shining sword in his hand.

Villain? No more. She was lost in longing for him.

"This can't end with the castle," he said. He brought up his other hand and stroked her face, as if he were a blind man trying to see. "You're so fresh, so new, so different from my life," he said in a caress of words. "You make me crazy, but it's such an exhilarating kind of crazy."

"You sound like my mom," Elinor said, dizzy under his touch. "Except for the exhilarating part." *Say you love me, say you love me,* she thought. And all would be forgiven.

He smiled then, and this time, she was right. He kissed her. It was sparing and romantic, really a pledge more than a kiss. If he were on a horse at a jousting tournament, and he trotted over to pay his obeisance to her as she sat in a viewing box, then that's the kind of kiss it was.

She was deeply moved by it and yet . . . somehow . . . she wanted more. Her frustration came out as a tiny whimper deep in her throat.

He pulled away, then took her hands in his and looked at her curiously. The look said it all: *What. What now?*

She responded as if he'd spoken. "I'm wondering," she made herself say, "where this can go."

His eyebrows lifted as he sucked in his breath, then compressed his lips in a grimace, sending the air out in a rush through his nose: the classic reaction of a man Not Quite Willing to Commit.

He shook his head. "Don't know," he confessed.

She smiled sadly. "England. America. It's a long commute."

"Stranger things have happened."

"And God knows," she agreed, " 'strange' is the hallmark of this relationship. It's not every nobleman who beds a woman and then takes her castle. Actually, it sounds more like the days of Arthur than the day of the computer. Maybe you were just born a little late, by, oh, a millenium or so. Maybe you—"

"No, wait. Listen to me," he said, interrupting. "I feel something for you that I've never felt for any woman before. I'm not—"

"Yes. We've established that. I drive you—"

"No, *listen*, you perverse wench!" He held her more tightly to make his point.

She saw the familiar flush of frustration rise up in his cheeks and she thought, would he get tired of me? Of my oh-so-exhilarating ways?

He seemed determined to explain himself. "I've been too busy making things happen in my career to make them happen in my love life," he said. "I've dated on and off—mostly off—and despite my grandmother's relentless efforts, have never had a serious relationship. None that required splitting the housekeeping chores, anyway."

"You don't have to tell me all this," she murmured.

"But I want to; and that's new for me. I'm an intensely private man, Elinor. Even for a Brit. I find your extended family, your shared emotions, well, boggling. But that doesn't mean I'm not—" He struggled for a word.

"Amused?"

"More than that. Envious, I think. You're all so unalike me and mine."

"No stiff upper lips around here, you mean."

He smiled. "None that I can see." He added, "But let me just make sure." He cocked his head and lowered his mouth to hers, catching her upper lip gently between his own, sampling it. "Nope ... nothing stiff about it," he whispered between nibbly kisses. "Just a soft ... sweet ... addictive ... sensation."

His test became a taste, his taste, something more. Elinor felt herself slipping under his spell again, which would've been fine, if Fair Castle were a fairy-tale castle.

She broke off the kiss reluctantly. "That extended family you're so envious of? Guess what. They all still live under this—"

He kissed away the rest of the sentence. "Thick door ... thick walls ..."

"And of course," she said, beginning to melt down again, "we shouldn't forget the tourists ... who'll be arriving ... for the next town."

"They'll wait," he said, threading his fingers through her hair, kissing the curve of her neck.

She lifted her shoulder, shrugging him away. "It doesn't work that way, Will," she said, feeling the first faint tingle of distress. "You're used to being your own man; but around here, we're kind of a team."

"All for one and one for all?" he said, his voice muffled in the folds of her hair.

"That's pretty much how it is."

She thought of her overwrought grandmother in the chamber below them; she wondered where her grandfather and Chester had got lost. Was Izzy all right? Her mother was a basket case. And of course the damn tourists.

Right on cue, the doorbell rang. Show time.

"I have to go," she begged, slipping from his grasp. "Damn them all!"

She made her escape before she could be drawn back into the consuming intensity of his magnetic field. Forget King Arthur; William Braddock was a Jedi Knight.

At the door a good-sized crowd—for Fair Castle, anyway—of six young men and women stood in the rain under six black lawn bags. They'd come up from the city to go hiking, one of them explained, but the day was turning out to be a washout; so they decided, what the hell.

Elinor hurried them over the threshold, stowed their wet plastic, and ushered them into the small reception room adjacent to the office.

"I'll be back in five minutes," she promised. "In the meantime, make yourself comfortable. You may enjoy perusing the photographs on the wall, taken of the castle during its reconstruction here. Also, there's a small gift kiosk," she added, pointing to it with no expectations. "There are souvenirs of Fair Castle—key chains, money clips, mugs—and children's books that feature this castle in them. If you see something you like, just let us know."

She gave them her tour guide's smile and went hurrying off to tell her jittery mother to drop everything and load the dumbwaiter for six teas in the turret, then made a dash to the archives room where, as she expected, Tucker O'Toole was bent over some dusty old translation of some even older memoir which undoubtedly had nothing whatever to say about the servant class in eighteenth-century England.

Keying her voice to a light and merry pitch, she burst in and said, "Tuck! Good news and bad news. Which do you want first?"

The tired old joke went over like wet charcoal on the Fourth of July. Tucker said grimly, "The good. I could use it."

"Okay. Will wasn't trying to steal your research."

"Yeah, right. It was his ghost standing at my dresser and going through my papers."

"I mean it. Will was just trying to put them all back. I hope you think this is as funny as I do," she said, dropping into a chair across from him at the battered oak library table. "But—*Izzy's* the one who took your stuff."

Elinor slid the green-shaded banker's lamp and his gold-rimmed reading glasses to the side and, leaning forward to look her skeptical listener straight in the eye, told him of her sister's attempt to plant the evidence and foil the sale. She made it sound both silly and amusing and was careful not to admire Will's role in bringing the fiasco to light.

And then, apparently still in stitches over the whole

thing, she sat back, crossed her legs, grinned, and said, "Isn't that a *hoot?*"

Tucker's reaction had exceeded her expectations. His expression went from brooding to joyful. By the time she finished telling her tale, he was laughing and acting as if Will were a helluva guy.

"I *knew* he had some other reason for being there," he said. "It didn't make sense, stealing my research. What does he care about life in the English countryside? He *lives* in the English countryside. I suppose you could argue that he had it in for me, but come on. I knew there had to be an explanation," he insisted.

"And you were right," replied Elinor with a straight face. *Give or take a death threat or two.*

She pushed her chair back across the wood floor of the musty, windowless closet—which sounded so much more historic, once they renamed it the archives room—and then she stood up.

"Well, I've got a tour to conduct and revisions to do," she said, bouncing back up. "See you at lunch. Oh, and—about *Rigamarole?*"

Tucker gave her an ironic but good-humored grin. "I know you're dying to go," he said. "But I also know you're under the gun with a deadline. Don't worry about the tickets, El. Maybe your grandparents can use them."

"Hey, you never know," she said on her way out.

Somehow she didn't think so.

"He has intelligence, but he lacks imagination. He cannot find it. Oh, Charles—I despair that he ever will."

"What the boy lacks in imagination he makes up in perseverence. He will find it. You must believe in him."

"But will he discover the manner of my death?"

"Marianne, how can he? There was never a hint of foul play."

"She did it, Charles! I know she did! She had some lackey poison the dish."

"Why did she not murder your father, then?"

"Undoubtedly it was her intention. But my father was much taken with finishing a portrait of his grandson—our

*child, Charles, on whom you gazed but once! I believe it
was by God's design that my father was spared so that he
could raise our son."*

*"Your father was a good man; a forgiving man. When
I myself lay dying, he tried to see me. I learned, during one
of my lucid moments, that she barred him admittance. I
can never forgive her that last cruelty. Did he have our son
with him? I will never know."*

*"Exactly. Do you think that she did not have me killed,
Charles? In truth?"*

"In truth I think she did."

The half-dozen drop-in tourists were a cheerful, lively lot,
as willing to climb stairs as they were to climb foothills.
Some of their exuberance wore off on Elinor. It was good
to see Fair Castle again through someone else's eyes: as
a really neat place with an overpowering sense of history.
The group responded like children to its magic, and Elinor enjoyed taking them around all the more for it.

She led them on a spirited romp through the common
rooms—the great hall, dining chamber, great parlor, library, even the chapel—speaking quickly, catching their
excitement and sending it back to them, wondering
whether it would be the last tour she ever gave. For every
historic fact she fed them (Sir Walter Scott once slept
there), she threw in a childhood memory (her great-uncle,
disappointed in love, tried to jump to his death from the
battlements, but a rosebush broke his fall and he sobered
up and lived happily ever after). By the time they got to
the fourth floor, she'd woven a tapestry of Fair Castle for
them that was rich in detail and textured with love.

They trekked up the worn narrow staircase through the
attic and emerged from the ancient trapdoor to a setting
of bone-china teacups, cloth napkins, and a large polished
tray buried under baked delicacies, all arranged invitingly
on the hexagonal table.

Tea was not everyone's cup of tea, of course, and normally only about half of any group served themselves
from the brass samovar, a Russian antique that Chester
had given his wife on their first anniversary. But the rain

was coming down all around them, and the turret, though barely heated, seemed an especially cozy place to be—a big stone umbrella in the middle of a waterfall.

One by one they poured hot tea from the urn's brass spigot and then chose their treats, the men heaping a mix of miniature croissants and berry pastries on their small plates, the women helping themselves to just as many, except one at a time.

"Very cool, very cool," said their ringleader, the biggest and best looking guy of the lot. He devoured most of a croissant in one bite and said, "I can't believe this place has always been here. I've hiked here before and never noticed it."

"It's one of the best-kept secrets in the mid-Hudson valley. You have to be in just the right position to see it," Elinor explained. "It's getting pretty woodsy all around. We like it that way."

"Aren't you glad I spotted the sign, Doug?" asked his girlfriend, a perky cheerleader who suited him perfectly. She turned to Elinor and warned, "You can hardly see that sign, you know; the brush is really overgrown around it."

"It doesn't really matter anymore," Elinor began. "The castle is about to be—"

She couldn't make herself say it. "About to be closed down for the season," she offered instead.

They nodded agreeably and munched their pastries. The history buff among them—there was always a history buff in a group this size—said, "I thought fortified houses and castles had pretty much disappeared in England by the end of the sixteenth century. You know, with the country more or less at peace and all."

"True," said Elinor. "But you have to understand that the northeast part of the country was quite poor, with many peasants to feed. The difficult terrain was partly to blame; but that area also had a system called *gavelkind*— giving all sons equal claims to an inheritance—which led to a lot of small, uneconomical farms, which in turn led to even more hunger and poverty."

"A castle to keep out a few peasants?" he said. "Isn't that overkill?"

Elinor broke off half of a tiny sugared angel-wing and shrugged. "Organized raids for food—and horses, naturally—were very common. The English raided the Scots, the Scots raided the English. . . . The worst of the back-and-forthing over the border went on roughly from 1300 to 1600.

"Fair Castle, built about the time things finally calmed down, was a little out of fashion by then—but the owner was known to be a conservative man with no great trust in the Scots. Hey, the Scots felt the same," she added. "They insisted on building castles, not houses, well into the seventeenth century."

The baked treat was still warm. Elinor popped it in her mouth, aware that she would carry the memory of munching angel-wings in the turret in her heart always.

"Wait a minute," Doug asked suddenly. "Isn't *your* name Scottish? MacLeish: that's Scottish, isn't it?"

"Yes, it is," said Elinor.

"Guess you guys won the last raid, then," he said, chuckling over his own cleverness.

Elinor gave him a feeble smile and said, "It may look that way."

She had no desire to explain to him why he was wrong, and besides, she was feeling uneasy about virtually every member of her family just then. So she merely added, "Take your time, enjoy your tea, and when you're done, just find your way back down that same staircase to the great hall. I'll be—well, I don't know where I'll be. So Godspeed, and don't forget your plastic."

They thanked her and freely admitted that they had no intentions of going anywhere until the tea was gone—or at least, the pastries.

"Do you want us to clean up our dishes or anything?" asked the shyest one of the group, a heavyset twenty-year-old with dark eyes, short hair, and an interesting, rather pretty face. (It was clear, at least to Elinor, that she had a big crush on Doug the Ringleader.)

"Oh, no, that's not—actually? It *would* be a big help if

you could just set the dishes in the dumbwaiter. It's right next to the stairs that go up to the trapdoor into the turret."

They agreed to bus their own table, in effect, for which Elinor was grateful. The size of the first tour had surprised her; the next one might be just as big. And she still had people to see and things to do before three.

She went straight to the kitchen to ask her mother whether her stepfather and grandfather had returned yet, and when her mother nervously shook her head, Elinor had to try hard not to look worried. Both women knew that nothing had gone as expected in the last couple of weeks. The ominous conclusion—the only conclusion—was that the unusual had now become routine.

Some dire whim made Elinor detour to the chapel before continuing on to her grandmother's chamber. Though she had taken the tour group through the chapel without a second thought, she now hesitated at the entrance of the once holy place, reluctant to go into it by herself. The morning, dreary and dark, did nothing to light up the stained-glass window and draw her inside to bask in its glow. It might as well have been midnight.

She took a single step through the doorway, ready to bolt if she had to, and paused beside the marble holy water font to look around.

The pews, with their elaborate carved detail and red-cushioned kneelers, sat at the ready for worshipers who would never kneel there at a service again, because the chapel was no longer a chapel at all. It was a tourist site. No priest would ever murmur the words *dominus vobiscum* there. No faithful believer would ever answer *et cum spiritu tuo*. The days of ritual—the days of Latin—were long over.

Elinor knew that places of worship were deconsecrated before they were given over for use by laymen. For the first time, she wondered whether the chapel of Fair Castle had been put through such an exercise. If not . . .

If not, what? Would spirits still roam? Was an exorcism called for? Elinor wasn't familiar with the nitty-gritty of religious ritual. But it seemed to her that if the chapel were still in its consecrated state, any disgruntled spirits should've been popping up on *both* sides of the Atlantic. After all, the latest Braddocks hadn't used the chapel for religious services, either. But Will had told them that there were no ghostly legends associated with the castle.

So why the sudden rash of shimmers and shapes over here?

She took a few more steps inside, like a wader into a very cold pool, getting herself used to the idea that there might truly be something there that went beyond mere aura. She took a deep breath. The smell of snuffed candles seemed to linger in the air. Or maybe she was imagining it. She half expected the candles to light themselves. The thought caused a ghastly ripple of fear to roll over her skin. She stopped . . . waited . . . and took another step forward, headed vaguely for the spot where the altar once had been.

Maybe it's the ghost of a priest . . . maybe he's outraged by our taking tourists through here . . . I never really thought about it before . . . although, we've always been respectful of the place . . . it's only natural to be. And besides, tourists go through churches all over Europe . . . even the Vatican . . . all the time. As long as you behave with decency and dignity . . . would there really be a problem?

There was another possibility, one that jarred with her grandmother's description of having seen, so many years ago, the spirit of a female with long red hair. Maybe Camilla's red-haired ghost was not the same as the current ghost.

Elinor's father: Why couldn't it be *his* spirit that was now making itself known? He'd died so tragically . . . so suddenly. He'd just been reconciled with his wife and his grown-up daughter. He'd just had a brand-new baby, one he would never get the chance to love.

Maybe his spirit wanted to see Izzy grow up. Maybe his spirit was a benign and caring one, kind of like a guardian angel. Maybe he'd finally got permission to appear on earth, just as angels did in the movies and on TV. It was a wonderful, heartwarming thought.

But no. It wasn't her father. The fearful sensations that

she'd had in the past couple of weeks . . . the bizarre episode with the scalding string . . . no. Those had not come from a benign spirit. Elinor wasn't sure that the presence—if there was a presence—was altogether evil. But the presence was not of her father. Whoever or whatever had made her afraid and caused her such pain had no great love for her. That, she knew.

She was standing between the two front pews now, in exactly the place where Izzy had seen the shimmering thing and—half a century earlier—her grandmother had seen the apparition of the woman with the long red hair.

Elinor was almost disappointed when after a minute or two, no one showed up. The chapel had been a hotbed of activity during the last few days, and now—squat. She looked around her and rather foolishly said, "Hello?"

Squat.

A little more at ease with the place now, she walked around from one candlestick to another, trying to come up with a plausible scenario for how the candles got lit. She grasped a thick wax cylinder, then lightly touched its wick. Cold, of course. She half expected it still to be warm. Someone *must* have lit them, damn it; candles didn't just light themselves.

But then again, strings didn't heat themselves up to burning temperatures.

She came back to the place between the two pews and stood there, fixed in thought. The candle on the wrought iron stand to the right—that was the one that Izzy had lighted to read her Fear Street book by. Izzy had read for a while and then had become aware of a presence alongside her. When Elinor tried to duplicate the event later on, nothing had happened except the appearance of Tucker, which had scared her plenty, under the circumstances.

But her grandmother had seen *all* of the candles lit, and . . . wait! So had Tucker, when he rushed down to the chapel after her grandmother screamed. But Elinor hadn't thought to ask him about the candles when she saw him, because of the stolen-papers mess that was on her mind then.

And Tucker hadn't said a word. Maybe, like her, he was too preoccupied with the papers to bring up the candles. But still. He should've said *something*.

Elinor was about to dash back to grill Tucker when she noticed one odd little thing: The candle that Izzy had lit to read her book was now shorter than the others. Which would've made perfect sense, except that Elinor's mother had made a point of replacing the candle right away so that it would look as new and virginal for the tours as all the rest.

But now it was shorter again. And that, more than anything else that she had seen so far, bothered Elinor. She tried to push the oddity out of her mind, but it stuck there, like a single stray hair that clings to the forehead on a hot day.

Still puzzling over the implications of the uneven candle, Elinor struck out again for the archives room. If Tucker O'Toole could give her some reasonable excuse for why the candles were burning, who knows? Camilla MacLeish might fall in love with her castle all over again and—who knows? Maybe not sign on the dotted line at three.

But Tucker wasn't in the archives room, so she went off instead to see her grandmother.

She was admitted at once. Camilla, who seemed more grim than calm, had pulled herself together. She'd done her hair and changed into a simple shift of pearl gray silk. The dress was for funerals, Elinor knew. All things considered, she considered it depressingly suitable. It must have shown in her face.

"I know, I know," said Camilla, trying to sound upbeat. "But it's time for us all to move on. We will put this behind us and be done with it. There are retirement communities that let you have your own garden, you know."

"Oh, sure: a burial-size plot that won't hold your herbs, much less your wichuriana roses. What about the summersweet? The montana rubens? The viburnums? How will you decide who dies and who goes?"

"That's not very amusing, dear. Nor is it persuasive. The die is cast."

Will's words, exactly. It was much too eerie. If ever a decision seemed fated, this had to be it. Elinor swallowed hard and said, "Sorry."

Camilla added in an uneasy voice, "Your grandfather still isn't back?"

Elinor shook her head. "Maybe there was an emergency ahead of them at the doctor's," she ventured on their way out.

"I pray God one of *them* wasn't the—"

"Don't say it, Gramma Cam," Elinor said with a shudder. "I can't bear any more sense of dread."

"You're feeling it, too?" her grandmother asked, sounding suddenly small and lost.

"How could I not? It's all around us. The castle is heavy with it. I almost can't breathe. If it weren't for the fun group I just took through here, I don't know how—"

A scream, followed by a series of screams, ripped through her sentence, tearing it in half. Elinor whirled around, nearly knocking her grandmother over in the process. "Where did it come from?" she cried.

"The back staircase, I think," her grandmother said quickly. She began hurrying in that direction, with Elinor one step ahead.

No more, no more, no more. It was Elinor's own little litany, a plea for them all to be spared. If the castle had to go, so be it. *But please, don't hurt anyone else to get it.*

They raced to the end of the hall in time to confront one of the young women clattering down the steps in her hiking boots, her half-shouldered backpack slipping down the sleeve of her jacket. Her face, only minutes ago a portrait of mirth, was now a snapshot of fear.

And Elinor knew at once that her prayer had not been answered.

Chapter 25

"*It's* Amy, my God, it's Amy! She's—it's horrible, call someone, it's Amy, *Amy!*" the girl babbled, and then she began to cry too hard to be understood.

Camilla said, "You go up there, El! I'll call an ambulance and send the boys!"

Elinor hardly heard. She was far too focused, as she flew up the stairs, on what she might find at the top of them. By now she believed anything was possible. Amy, the shy one with the dark eyes, could be rolling on the floor and speaking in tongues, or she could be swiveling her head completely around like someone in a grade-B horror flick.

What Elinor found when she arrived out of breath at the foot of the stairs on the fourth floor was something else entirely. Amy, shy Amy—Amy who was sweet enough to offer to clear away the group's tea things—was lying in front of the open dumbwaiter shaft, her cheek surrounded by a pool of dark blood.

The young historian, his face as white as Amy's, was on one knee and bent over her, uncertain what to do. The cheerleader was completely hysterical. Her boyfriend, the ringleader, was torn between comforting her and rushing to Amy's aid—but Elinor saw at once that there was nothing any of them could do.

She dropped to her knees before the fallen body and whispered words that rang with shocking melodrama in her ears: "Is she dead?"

"I don't know," the historian murmured in a stricken voice. "I can't feel any pulse." He was holding her limp wrist in his hand, his fingers pressed too far outside the pulse-point to know one way or the other if Amy had one.

Elinor laid her index and middle fingers against the carotid artery in the young woman's neck. A pulse. A faint pulse—but a pulse, she was sure of it. Her own heart took a joyful jump in her breast. *Please just let her live.* This time, she sent the prayer straight to the top.

She looked up to see Will running down the hall toward them. Tucker was right behind him.

"Should we move her?" asked the historian.

Elinor said, "No, no, you're not supposed to move an accident victim. We have to wait for the paramedics."

It was hard to hear her own voice over the cheerleader's shrieks of hysteria. Will arrived and said sharply to the ringleader, "Get her away from here! Take her into my room; it's around the corner. Have her lie down."

Doug half-carried his girlfriend away from the scene. The historian, deferring to Will, said in a croak, "How bad is it, do you think?"

Will lifted first one of Amy's eyelids, then the other. He pulled out a folded hanky from his back pocket and said, "Get me a clean towel. Move it!"

"First door to your right," Elinor said quickly.

The historian took off. Will lifted Amy's head with infinite tenderness from the pool of her blood and examined the wound.

"I felt a pulse," Elinor said. "I think."

He nodded. "It's steady enough."

Elinor wanted to believe him, but there was so much blood. It was everywhere: on his hands, on the upper leg of his tan-colored trousers. She was desperately grateful that she didn't have to be strong this time; that she could let someone else make decisions about dilated pupils and moving the victim.

Amy moaned and fluttered her eyes, then became still again just as the historian arrived back with a white towel. Will pressed it against the gushing wound while Tucker,

Elinor, and the historian knelt around him in pointless vigil. So many of them, so unable to help.

Tucker said softly, "How did it happen? Does anyone know?"

The historian knew. "She opened those two doors to see if that was the dumbwaiter shaft behind them. I said it had to be; it was right underneath the attic station. But she was curious. She thought the whole thing was neat. She stuck her head in the shaft and looked up. She said, 'You're right. I can see the bottom of it.' Then she started pulling her head back out of the shaft, but something—it must have been the dumbwaiter—came ripping down and she fell backward and . . ."

He shrugged helplessly and nodded to his injured friend with a blank look. "That's where she fell. I think . . ." he added with obvious reluctance, "I think maybe Kristin might have done something to release the dumbwaiter. That's why she's screaming. She—"

"It shouldn't have gone flying!" Elinor cut in. But even as she said it, she remembered the distant sound of breaking dishes. The dumbwaiter must have come to a crashing stop in the kitchen. Virtually into her mother's lap. Where was her mother?

Don't let her see this.

Why had the dumbwaiter dropped? Normally it was a struggle to work the ropes that raised and lowered it. Was it just one more chapter in their book of bad luck? Or was it something more?

She turned her attention back to the broken young woman being cradled by Will, her head on his thigh as he pressed the towel compress against the wound. The white was already very red. It didn't seem possible that someone could lose that much blood and still be alive.

Blood and spirit. The two mixed so easily, so relentlessly in Fair Castle. First Chester, now Amy. But Amy was an unintended casualty. Whatever presence existed there, it would not be appeased with the blood of a random victim. Even Elinor understood that.

We must sell. Gramma Cam is right. Whoever it is, they do not want us here any longer.

Elinor took her gaze away from Amy and saw a frown of concentration on Will's face that was far more intense than anything the battle over the castle had triggered so far. It gave her, somehow, a sense of profound relief. Amy was in good hands.

She bowed her own head. She knew, everyone knew, that ultimately, prayer helped. And in any case, it was all they had. She distilled her prayers to their essence.

Please, God. Please.

She opened her eyes to see Will removing the towel a little from the wound. At the same time, Amy grimaced and moved slightly, as if she were asleep and twisted in her own pajamas.

He said, "With the rain so heavy, the ambulance will take extra time getting here. I'm going to carry her down. It should be okay," he added when Elinor's eyes widened. "Getting a litter up here and then down again will eat time. I want you to press the towel against the wound. All right. Tucker, give me a hand getting her up in my arms, would you?"

Tucker said, "Right," and crouched down low, slipping his arms under the semiconscious woman and handing her off to Will once they struggled to their feet. Will adjusted Amy's weight in his arms and then he struck out for the stairwell, with the motley crew of well-wishers in his wake, leaving behind yet another blood-stained floor.

It's inevitable, Elinor thought as she tried nimbly to keep alongside as Will made his way down from floor to floor. *Violence is a tradition in most castles. That's why they're castles. We've been leading a charmed life here for the past half century, a life of make-believe. But now Fair Castle is reverting back to form.*

She knew the castle had not been involved in any actual clash of armies. But it was naive to think that in over four centuries, its men had not come to blows with other men—and women. And that its women had not schemed and plotted against other women—and men.

She was learning about the dark side of castles now. And every lesson was written in blood.

The desperate procession continued spiraling down,

with Elinor in awe that Will had the strength and the balance to carry a woman of robust form without dropping her somewhere along the way. A fireman might be able to do it. Superman, yes. But an aging Jedi Knight? It made her want to award Will the castle on the spot—except that the castle had become such a dubious prize.

They made their way to the great hall, where Elinor's mother and grandmother, like stricken maids-in-waiting, attended their needs: dragging a chair forward, replacing the towel, bringing them water that Will did not need and Amy could not drink.

Isabelle, who'd been hanging back in the shadows of their tumult, crept forward and wrapped both her hands around her sister's arm. "What happened, Elly?" she whispered, only half-daring to look at the injured tourist.

"An accident, honey," said Elinor.

If only she could make herself believe it.

After several minutes the wounded woman began coming around, not exactly conscious but clearly not unconscious. Will held her against his breast, heedless of her blood, and whispered soothing words and snippets as they waited for the ambulance.

And Elinor thought, *I love him. Whatever happens to her, to him, to me, to the castle or any of us—I love him.*

The vigil continued. The tall-case clock in the hall—one of many quaint anachronisms in the castle—took an eternity between every tick and tock. Tucker hovered nearby. The women wrung their hands. Elinor watched, on guard for evil, while her sister tried to be brave and stood at her side like a junior sentry. The historian took up a post at the entrance to the great hall and every thirty seconds opened the door a crack—as if he doubted that an ambulance with its sirens screaming could possibly be heard.

"They're here!" he yelled at last—everyone knew it—and he swung the door the rest of the way open with great drama, as if a liberating army had stormed the gate. Two paramedics carrying a collapsible stretcher hurried in. Elinor was grateful that they were different from the men who'd come for Chester; it might keep the inevitable rumors from getting too wild.

Very quickly, the paramedics had Amy bandaged and on the stretcher and were wheeling her over the slate floor of the great hall. The milling group had filled out to include the ringleader and his girlfriend, subdued now, as well as the girl with the backpack who'd rushed to spread word of the accident. Everyone was shaken; but the cheerleader girlfriend, most of all. Elinor's heart went out to her. If she was the one who'd released the rope, then . . .

Then nothing. Nothing should've happened. The dumbwaiter ropes operated on a clutch system. The safety rope that the girl had released was a backup, no more than that. Still, it *was* a backup, and for her to just let go of it was the height of . . .

"Where are they taking her?" the cheerleader asked in a numb voice. She looked devastated. Her pretty, pink-cheeked face was puffy from crying; her blue eyes were little more than red-rimmed slits.

"Cornwall Hospital," said her boyfriend. "I know where it is. Let's go."

The group crowded for the door like movie-goers after a show, leaving Elinor and the others with little more to do than try not to stare at Will's bloodied clothes.

Izzy's mournful voice was the first to break the silence. "Will she be all right, Lord Norwood?"

"I think so, Isabelle," he said.

"But are you sure?"

Will glanced at Elinor, then back at the ten-year-old. "I'm sure." He backed it up with a reasonably confident smile. It was obvious that he was bending the truth out of kindness.

"That kind of wound bleeds a lot," he went on to explain. "Sometimes it can look worse than it is." He glanced down at his clothes and winced. He was proof of his own theory. "If you'll excuse me, I think—"

But Izzy needed desperately to be reassured. "We have a *lot* of accidents around here lately," she said, interrupting him. She carried her soulful gaze from one grown-up to another, waiting to be told why that should be.

"Accidents happen, Izzy," said her mother tersely. "You know that. Without any warning—"

"Oh, there was warning enough," Camilla said, cutting into her daughter's explanation. She dropped into the chair that Will had vacated and patted her flat chest nervously with the palm of her spotted hand. "We were warned," she repeated in a voice that sent chills through Elinor.

Susan, still wearing a white chef's apron over her skirt and long-sleeved blouse, gave the elderly woman a look filled with warning of her own.

Elinor could see that a line was being drawn between her grandmother and her mother. Was it an accident, or wasn't it? That's what they *all* needed to know.

Camilla leaned back in the chair and closed her eyes. Seated alone on the open armchair in the great hall, she had the look of an aging monarch weary of her rule. "I'm sorry, Susan," she said to her daughter. "I wish I could be silent. I know you don't want to think about this today of all days."

It was true. Elinor's mother had been doing her best to stay calm as the household bounced from crisis to crisis, all the while keeping an eye out through the kitchen casement for her overdue husband and father.

But Susan Roberts was a high-strung woman, and she'd been exposed to one bloodletting too many. Right now she was poised on the edge of a breakdown. It was apparent in so many little ways: in the blond hair hanging loose from her bun; in the worn-off lipstick of her pale lips; in the tiny smear of blood on the bib of her apron.

It was the smear on the apron that seemed to unhinge her. Glancing down at the bib, she let out a sudden gasp of horror and began fumbling with the ties of her apron with such loathing that Elinor rushed forward to help.

"I can do it myself!" she cried, but in her hurry to yank the apron over her head she caught the single strand of pearls she liked to wear and broke the string, sending an army of white beads skittering in every direction across the floor of the great hall.

"Oh, *no-o*," Susan said in a wail. She let the apron slip from her hands. "Not the pearls."

She hung her head and began to weep, not because the pearls were falling apart, but because everything else was. "Three o'clock," she whispered through rolling tears. "Three o'clock." It was her mantra to sanity.

Will said awkwardly, "Look, about that three o'clock appointment. I think, under the circumstances, that we should postpone it until after the weekend."

He was right, obviously. Elinor, who, like Izzy, was on her hands and knees hunting down the wayward pearls, looked from Will to her mother for her reaction. She was expecting an outburst, but instead her mother froze in place and said nothing at all. Her look became glazed. A thin, tremulous smile added nothing but unbearable pathos to the fine-boned features of her face.

Elinor winced; a screaming fit of frustration would've been so much more reassuring.

Even Camilla was alarmed. "Susan? Are you all right? You do understand that we can't possibly go ahead at three. By the time we go to the hospital and see how the poor child is doing . . . I'm sure we'll be there a while . . ."

"No. Of course. The hospital . . . I forgot. What was I thinking?"

She turned to Will and said with a sweet, forlorn smile, "You really should take off that shirt and give it to me . . . before the blood dries . . . I'll put it in cold water for you . . . it's quite a nice shirt . . . as for the jacket and trousers, I'm not sure . . . I'll have to read the label on them . . . but I'm sure something can be done . . . to save them. The tie's a goner, though. Silk . . ." She sighed and looked away. "It's hopeless."

Will glanced at Elinor, who was sitting back on her haunches now, watching her mother. He was clearly at a loss; but so was Elinor. This was new. And frightening.

Reading Elinor's confused dismay accurately, Will turned and took a step toward her mother, obviously to comfort her.

"No-no," Susan said quickly, throwing her hands up delicately and fending him off with a terse smile. "Blood

... too much of it ... more to come ... no, no. Mustn't touch ..."

Elinor scrambled to her feet at the same time that her grandmother struggled back out of the armchair, and both of them rushed to Susan's side.

Grandmother and granddaughter began talking together in soothing phrases, their speeches punctuated by a high-pitched *"Mom?"* from Izzy every few seconds. The three formed a circle around their stricken relation, shutting out William Braddock and Tucker O'Toole, who stood helplessly on the sidelines, uninitiated into the comforting rituals of women.

The consoling went on for several minutes, heart-wrenching in its poignancy, until the entire group was unnerved by a series of distinct, sharp raps of the immense door knocker on the castle's arched door.

Tucker made a dash to open it, but before he got halfway there, the massive door swung open to reveal two grown men standing in the pouring rain and drenched to the skin, one of them clearly drunk, one of them possibly so.

Mickey MacLeish was the one definitely in his cups. His towering form was leaning precariously against his bearded son-in-law. His pants were muddied up to the knees. His black beret was pitched at the back of his head, high above a smile that clearly said he no longer felt any amount of any pain.

"Wee-'re ... back!" he announced.

Chester—shorter, broader, with his good arm supporting the old man—said sheepishly, "We were celebrating." He nodded sideways, shorthand for *"He* was, anyway."

The sight of them left the distracted group absolutely speechless.

Chester had to fill in the gap of their silence. "We stopped in at the Train Wreck after they took out my stitches, and ... ah ... one ... ah ... thing—"

"Drink! One drink!"

"—led to another."

"By God, yes. It feels ... *damned* good," said Mickey, daring anyone to tell him that he didn't feel damned good.

He hiccupped. "But never-r fear; ol' Chester was our dresignated . . . diver."

Elinor found her voice first. "What *happened?* Were you in an accident?"

Chester said, "Not exactly," and staggered with his father-in-law to the center of the hall, then tentatively slid his arm free of the smiling, weaving artist. He stood close by, ready to break any fall. Camilla, scowling, came over to give her husband a once-over.

"We got stuck at the bottom of the hill," Chester explained. "It's all washed away. You know the pothole that used to be yea-big?" he said, holding his hands a yard apart. He shook his head. "Not anymore. That's where the truck fell in."

"Told 'im," muttered Mickey. "Told 'im, get frun wheel drive. Anyone lissen? New-w-w. Just an old . . ." He burped out the word "man."

"Grampa Mick," said Izzy, pointing to the old man's muddy pant legs, "you look like you got stuck in quicksand!"

Chester said delicately, "Your grandfather had to . . . uh . . . relieve himself."

"I had to *pee,* is what I had. For God's sake . . . can't we call a pee a . . . *pee?* Good Anglo-Saxon word like that. Huh." He brought his head up from its sideways list and focused his heavy-lidded gaze on Will. "Right? Your lordship?"

Will smiled and said, "It's one of the best."

"Yup, yup. Tha'sss whud I say." He peered more closely at Will, who'd been partly obscured by Izzy. "Hey. Whassat on your leg . . . 'n' your shirt?"

Will had Chester's attention now, as well. "That's blood!" Chester croaked, his voice dropping in horror. "From what?" His gaze raked over them quickly in a double-check. "All of you are all right. How—?"

"There was an accident," Will said quickly. "You just missed the ambulance."

"My God." It hit Chester, finally, that his family was in shock. He rushed up to his wife and said, "Susan . . . honey . . . are you all right?" He wrapped her in a bear hug, then broke away awkwardly, at a loss how to behave in a room full of people, two of them strangers.

Elinor's mother gave him her same blank smile and said, "Certainly, dear. Why wouldn't I be?"

Izzy said in a loud whisper to her stepfather, "They're not going to the lawyer's, Dad."

Mickey MacLeish heard the word "lawyer." That did it.

"The first thing we do," he shouted, "let's kill all the lawyers!"

"Grampa *Mick*!" said Izzy, scandalized.

"No, no, Iz—he's just quoting Shakespeare, that's all," said her sister. "He doesn't mean it."

"He'll be okay by three," Chester promised Camilla. "I'll see to it."

"Three is not going to happen," Camilla said wearily. "In any case."

"Know what the trouble with *lawyers* is?" asked the old man, swinging around and pointing a wobbly finger at the fireplace. "Ninety-eight per-percent of 'em give all the rest . . . a bad name. Uh-yep."

"He's not celebrating *any*thing, Chester; he's upset!" said Elinor as it dawned on her.

Her stepfather shrugged and said, "What do you expect?"

"So he *doesn't* want to sell."

"What do you call five hunerd lawyers at the bottom"— loud hiccup—"of the sea?"

"I call you soaking wet and headed for pneumonia," said Camilla as she slipped an arm around her husband. "Come on. Upstairs."

Mickey MacLeish squinted bleary-eyed at the stone steps that wound and wound and wound. "Nuh. Nuh, I kenna. *Too-o* many. *Too-o* old. Milly, Milly, I'm just . . . too . . . old."

"You're just too *drunk,* you silly old fool. Come along, then. I'll put you in the reception room and bring you down a change of clothes. You can sleep on the couch there."

He burped. "Ahh-h, good. You're so-o good to me,

Milly. I *do* love you. I do. After all-l-l . . . thee-ese . . . years. I love you more'n . . . ever."

He flopped an arm around his wife's shoulder, nearly knocking her down in the process; Chester had to rush to support his weight from the other side.

Mickey began the inevitable slide into melancholy. "*To-morrow, and to-morrow, and*—how many was that?" he asked his wife.

"Don't you dare breathe on me, you awful man," she said wearily.

"*And to-morrow,*" he finished, figuring it out for himself. He collapsed into a muddled mutter as they half-carried him into the reception room, and then his voice burst forth in one last hurrah. "*Out, OUT, brief candle! Life's but a walking shadow, a poor player . . .*"

And then merciful silence.

Demoralized and distracted, Chester said to his step-daughter, "I'd better see to your mother."

Elinor looked around. Her mother had apparently wandered off somewhere. Will had gone, too, obviously to change. Izzy had disappeared. Only Tucker remained, at a respectful distance, watching the procedings.

"Everyone's too preoccupied to go to the hospital," Elinor said to Chester. "I'll drive there myself."

"Drive what?" he asked. "The truck's stuck in the lane."

A wretched thought occurred to her. "Oh, my God. We're trapped in the castle. Will can't get his car out, and neither can Tuck—and no one can get in! An ambulance—!"

"Not a problem," Chester said, quick in his reassurance. "We'll get the truck towed. Don't worry. We'll have it towed. And while you're at the hospital, I'll go out and fill in the hole."

"How can you?" she cried, losing her own battle to stay calm. "You may be healed enough to drive a car; you can't go shoveling dirt—!"

"I'll take care of it."

It was so obvious that he couldn't. She shook her head and said doggedly, "No, no, that won't work!"

Tucker came forward. "If Norwood and I put our shoulders to it," he asked Chester, "do you think we can push the truck out?"

Chester wrinkled his nose and scratched his beard. "Possibly."

Tucker said grimly, "I'll go get him."

He took a step or two toward the main stairwell, then came back to Elinor and said, "Almost forgot."

He held out his hand to her. She opened hers to him. He dropped half a dozen pearls into it.

Chapter 26

$\mathcal{E}$linor MacLeish sat like a sculpture inside the gazebo that was tucked in a corner of Fair Castle's garden. Wrapped in a dress of autumn paisley and warmed by a sweater of earth-toned green, she blended easily with the woods and shrubs around her. October sunbeams slid off her auburn hair, bound in back by a scarf of velour.

The morning was as still as her mood. No bird sang; no breeze rippled the dried leaves that clung to the oaks. No truck roared nearby, no plane droned overhead. The valley was filled to its peak with holy silence. After rinsing the air bleachy clean, the storm had left in its passing this one warm day. Feeble warmth, October warmth; but it was all she would have until spring.

For a long time she sat, aware of little but the subdued glow of heat along the right side of her body where sunlight fondled her dress. After a while her thoughts returned, inevitably, to the bizarre and violent events that had rocked the castle in the last few weeks.

The dumbwaiter accident was the least disturbing of them, despite its seriousness. At least there was an explanation for it: lazy, careless Owen. He'd been told to replace the rope used in the pulleys to lower and raise the elevator, and he'd apparently botched the job by using too slender a cord. An awful accident—but an accident.

Not so the hot string. Again and again Elinor had relived the episode without understanding it. If she hadn't imagined the needle-sharp pain—she had not—then there was only one other possibility. Someone or something was sending her information and making sure she listened.

The idea, once more, made her cheeks warm with distress. Her, a channeler from the beyond? It was laughable. And yet the more she thought about it, the harder it became to deny that a message was being sent.

But from where? From *whom*, for pity's sake? Elinor could hardly remember the sequence of questions, what with her being so busy flirting and all. She smiled wearily at the remembrance of that evening. What a fiasco. It was hard to say which she was worse at—flirting or channeling.

Her mind came back to the questions she had asked the crystal pendant. The questions had revolved around the historical Elinor, Lady Norwood; that much she remembered. If the dowsing pendant was to be believed, Elinor's namesake had had no children. Obviously that wasn't true, as *Debrett's Peerage* would prove.

And then there was the blinding pain from the hot string. It had come immediately after she asked the pendant if the Elinor in question was Lady Norwood. All in all, she had to assume that the answer was intended to be taken as a resounding, infuriated *"no."*

What did it mean? Gibberish.

Was Fair Castle haunted? Impossible to believe, but apparently so. After all the years of laughing and joking about it with tourists, the MacLeishes had got their comeuppance. Should they be afraid? It was hard to feel that way, sitting in the bright light of a warm October morning.

She remembered seeing a television special on ghosts in English castles in which Prince Edward himself had said, "You just have to accept it." If ghosts were good enough for royalty . . .

A haunted castle. The marketing possibilities were endless, she thought wryly. Halloween, for instance, could be a really big moneymaker. On the down side, everyone knew that haunted houses affected resale and scared away buyers.

Except for the buyer in question, of course. Ah, that buyer in question. Her heart was so heavy with thoughts of him. It was almost more comforting for her to think about a vengeful ghost on the loose than it was to think about Lord Norwood.

Lord Norwood. Why couldn't he be plain Will Braddock? Plain Will Braddock, computer jock with a job in the States. Plain Will Braddock, touring Fair Castle and falling in love. Plain Will Braddock, without twenty-eight generations of nobility to appease.

She closed her eyes, shook her head. Why couldn't he be?

"Oh, *there* you are!"

It was her mother, still dressed in church clothes, approaching through the outside door of the greenhouse. "I've been looking all over for you," Susan said as she drew near.

She looked better this morning. To call her smile serene would be an exaggeration; but she seemed resigned to the fact that she would not be rid of Fair Castle for one more night and one more day.

"You should have come," Susan said with a reproachful smile. "It was a wonderful sermon."

She stepped inside the gazebo and had a look around. "I haven't been here in such a long time," she said, as surprised as she was wistful.

She turned in a slow circle, gazing out at a different view through each panel: garden, castle, river, woods, fountain. "It really is in a perfect spot, isn't it?"

"Leave it to Gramma Cam," Elinor said. "She always did have an eye for beauty. Is anyone awake yet?"

By anyone, Elinor meant *the* one. Her mother, who didn't know that, ran through the list before she said, "As for Will, he still seems to be avoiding us all. Can you blame him? First Tucker attacks him, then he finds himself in the middle of . . . of that terrible . . ."

She took a deep breath, trying again for serenity. "Did Amy really seem all right to you last night, El? Really? She still looked so bad yesterday morning."

Elinor, who'd been staring out the panel that faced the castle, turned and gave her mother a reassuring smile.

"Yes, she was doing very well. The X rays were fine.

Naturally she'll have some really bad hair days, what with part of her head being shaved, but . . . she's fine."

"What time are visiting hours today?"

"The same. Two o'clock."

"I think we all want to go. Will they allow us?"

"If she's still there. We should call first."

Her mother nodded. "It was sweet of Will to visit Amy yesterday. Did you two have a chance to chat?"

"We said hello in the hall," Elinor said, looking away. "I almost missed him; he was walking behind a huge basket of flowers."

"That was thoughtful. He doesn't even know Amy, after all. But I suppose . . . holding her during the crisis the way he did . . . oh, it's all such a mess," her mother murmured. After a moment she said, "Chester just told me that the claims adjustor called to confirm this afternoon. It's obvious he's thinking about lawsuits. He'll be over to take photographs and ask us some questions. You'll be around, won't you?"

Elinor shrugged. "Where would I go?" Nowhere. Not while Will was in Fair Castle.

"It's too bad that Tucker's gone off to New York. The adjustor wanted to see everyone. Still, I can't say I blame Tucker for grabbing the chance to see *Rigamarole*. Tickets are ridiculously hard to come by. It's all the buzz."

Elinor said, "I'm glad he found someone to go with. A couple of days in New York will do wonders for him. His mood yesterday was edgier than any of ours. I think all the goings-on are getting to him. I assume he feels he's walked into a loony bin."

"I can't believe he's still hanging around here. If it weren't for your stepfather," Susan admitted, "I'd have suggested he leave long ago. I simply don't care for the boy; he's far too intense. He's very lucky to have Chester in his corner. Your stepfather simply *feeds* off their mutual obsession with the castle and archives."

"Tucker's problem is that he's too immersed in his research, that's all; he's lost touch with the rest of his life. A deadline can do that," Elinor added.

Susan tapped the unopened sketch pad with a glossy-tipped finger. "How *are* the revisions coming?"

A crooked smile. "How do you think?"

Her mother's tisk of disapproval was very much in keeping with her old self. "Then you should turn around and go back to New York. There are a few too many distractions here," she said in a mind-boggling understatement.

"Maybe I should," Elinor whispered. She sat back down and stared at the vaulted underside of the domed roof. An extremely unwanted tear rolled out. She brushed it away quickly.

"Because it's obvious that *nothing* is ever going to happen between you and Lord Norwood," her mother added, working up her usual head of steam. "I have never in my life seen two people less suited to one another. I can't imagine what I was thinking."

"I can't imagine either."

"It's too bad."

"It really is."

"He would've been so perfect for us. Good family . . . money . . . and he wants to keep Fair Castle!"

"But not here."

"Well, true," her mother conceded. After a pause she said in a burst, "You know, I wouldn't have minded the castle so much if . . . if . . ."

"—you didn't have to clean the toilets so often."

"Among other duties." A fretful, faraway look came into her eyes. "Friday when Will said that he wanted to put off the signing, I felt as if the brass ring were slipping right through my fingers . . . as if I'd had it in my hand, and then . . ."

She shook off the recollection and said more briskly, "But the sermon this morning was on the virtue of patience, of all things. I took it as a sign. I can last. Tonight. Tomorrow."

And then he'd be gone. Back to England; back to his own. "I'm sorry, Mother. I know you've built up all kinds of hopes since the arrival of Lord Norwood."

"Too many, apparently," Susan conceded. "But it looks as if at least one of them is going to come true." She smiled a mother's brave smile and stood up. "Well," she said, brushing dried leaves from the back of her skirt, "I suppose I ought to see if your grandfather is over Friday's hangover yet. He was such a zombie all day yesterday; I hope he's learned his lesson."

"How's Gramma Cam?"

"She says she still hasn't slept a wink, but I caught her napping in her rocker just now. Everyone sleeps, sooner or later."

It was such a practical, reasonable thing to conclude. Susan Roberts: the rational one. Alone among them, she kept things moving at a sensible pace. She watched the clock, bought the stamps, led the tours, marked the calendars, paid the bills. She knew who fixed what and how much they charged to do it. She cleaned toilets. She was the one—the only one—who knew where the insurance policy was kept and whom to call after a dreadful accident.

All this, for a bunch of temperamental divas.

Elinor, perhaps the most temperamental of them all, was suddenly ashamed. Filled with self-loathing, she said, "I don't make things easy for you, do I?"

"Oh, my goodness, none of you do," said Susan with a wry smile.

In a fit of remorse, Elinor jumped up and threw her arms around her mother. "I really *do* love you," she said, her voice breaking with emotion, "even if I never say it."

Caught off balance, Susan braced herself against the side of the gazebo. "Heavens, of course you do," she said, amazed by the outburst. "Who said you didn't?"

"I can be such a shit!"

Susan cringed and said, "*Any* other word would do."

"I know, I know . . . but . . . if anything ever happened to you . . . if . . . like Friday . . . with the pearls . . . I don't know what I'd do. What any of us would do. You frightened us so much."

Susan hugged her daughter and patted her on the back as if she were Izzy. "I'm very ashamed of that episode," she murmured. "I wish you wouldn't speak of it."

Elinor said, "Ashamed? How can you be ashamed? I'm

the one who should be ashamed. I'm the one who's been acting like an hysteric. I'm the one who's been making everyone's life hell. I've been so determined to keep us together that I'm driving us apart! I don't know why I'm doing it. I have the best intentions in the world—"

"I'm sure you do, honey."

"But it's *you* who's really keeping us all together. I never realized that about you—not until Friday. I thought it was the castle, somehow, that was responsible."

Susan held her daughter at arm's length. Surprised and pleased, she said, "Then you don't hate me for making us sell it?"

Elinor, no longer trusting her voice, gave her mother a wordless hug.

And when she looked up, she saw him.

His back was to the gazebo. His hands were jammed in the pockets of a navy windbreaker that he wore over khakis. His hair was wet and dark in the bright morning sun; he must've showered late. He looked tall and lanky and a little at a loss. He could've been just another disoriented tourist searching for the parking lot.

But he wasn't. He was a man with a mission that was nearly accomplished. And damn damn *damn*—she was in love with him.

Susan turned her head in the direction of her daughter's gaze and saw Will. "You're as tense as a cat," she said, suddenly wary. "The fur on your tail's sticking straight out. What's going on?"

"Nothing."

He could've stopped to talk to me in the hall. Even with the flowers. He could've said more than hello how ya doin'.

"Did you have a fight in the *hospital?*" asked her mother, scandalized by the thought.

"I told you; we hardly said two words."

Which is about how many he'd said in the course of their fierce couplings in the SoHo sublet. Were they even capable of having long, wonderful talks like the ones her grandparents had? She had no idea. So far their only verbal exchanges had been heated ones—a kind of foreplay, like hot kisses, to sex. It was profoundly frustrating. And

Friday . . . in his room . . . when he'd seemed so genuine
. . . it was still all about sex. Why was *she* calling it love?
She'd never felt sure before. Why now? Why him?

"Elinor, you wouldn't," her mother said in soft warning.

"Wouldn't what?" she murmured, unable to look away
from him.

"Do anything to alienate him. He's had such a struggle
to get this far with us. By five tomorrow it will all be
resolved. We couldn't squeeze in at the attorney's any
earlier, or we would have. Can't you last until then?" Susan asked, unable to keep the wryness from her voice.

He was turning around now . . . he saw the two of them
in the gazebo . . . took a step in their direction . . . stopped
. . . smiled perfunctorily . . . and turned away.

*He's trapped. To go back inside, he'll have to pass within
greeting range. Now that he knows we're here, he'll have
to engage us in conversation.*

How could he have missed them on his way outside?
She would've seen him from a mile away.

"Oh, El—I *don't* like that look in your eye. What's he
done now? What can he possibly have done?"

"Nothing."

And that, at bottom, was the problem. She wanted him
to be as suddenly in love with her as she was with him.
Crazy in love. But he had a name to uphold and a heritage
to restore, and that came first. Her, he might fit around
the edges of his grand project.

How unlike her grandfather. Mickey MacLeish had
found the woman, then the castle. But Will—Will was
determined first to nail down the castle and after that, to
look for someone to stick in it. If there was time left over
from his quest.

"If only you weren't so emotional," her mother said
with a sigh. "You could see him for what he is: our knight
in shining armor. He's taking a white elephant off our
hands, whether you realize it or not."

"Sure."

"Oh, El, come inside with me," said her mother, tugging at her sweater. "I just *know* you're going to do something stupid."

"I won't."

Susan glanced nervously in Will's direction. His back was to them again. He seemed to be sizing up the castle. "Don't talk about anything except what a nice day it is," she urged her daughter.

Feeling both sad and dangerous, Elinor smiled and said, "You mean, don't tip him off that the castle really is haunted?"

Susan's eyes opened wide as she clamped a hand over Elinor's mouth. "Stop it!" she hissed. "Not another word. What if he hears you?"

Elinor averted her head from her mother's grip. "But it's true. Can't you feel it when you move around in there? If not, then you're lucky. You're the only one."

She nodded in Will's direction and added, "You don't have to worry, though; *he* doesn't care if it's haunted or not. In fact, I think he'd prefer it. That way he could think he was doing us a favor."

"This is absurd! The castle is not haunted," Susan said, almost giddily. "No one's actually seen anything—not for decades. And not even then!"

"Right."

Susan bowed her head and pressed the fingertips of both hands to her brow. "I *hate* when you agree like that," she said in an undertone.

She sighed, then looked back up at Elinor. "Never mind. I—you know what? I don't care. You're going to do what you're going to do, and there's nothing I can say or do to stop it. I've been away from the sermon for less than an hour, and already I've forgotten the lessons in it.

"Do what you want to do, Elly," she said, planting a gentle kiss on her daughter's cheek. "But don't do it just for the fireworks. No one's watching anymore."

Susan stepped out of the gazebo and left Elinor alone and feeling—well, like a shit. Her mother was right about her. Despite her constant good intentions, Elinor was far too emotional to be any use to anyone. What had she done lately besides drag her heart behind her on a chain?

She'd fallen in love with the enemy, and it had made her more unpredictable than ever.

Chapter 27

𝓔linor stole another glance at the lanky Englishman standing a hundred yards away with his back to her. Unwilling to look as if she were running from him, she sat back down on the bench of the gazebo and took up her sketch pad. She would seem absorbed in her work. He could slip by if he chose.

She continued to hover over a sketch of a dragon that was little more than a dozen ill-drawn lines, all the while tracking Will's progress from beneath lowered lids. A minute later, her heart lifted high in her breast and then stayed there as she saw his figure loom on the other side of the screened door of the gazebo.

She looked up and said "Good morning" in a soft and obviously besotted voice.

How could he not know she loved him? How could he not?

Will said without smiling, "Am I interrupting?"

"Oh, I'm nearly done," she lied, quietly folding the covering page over her wretched dragon. "I had an *excellent* day in the lodge yesterday. I'll be mailing off the revisions this afternoon."

"Glad to hear it," he said with a faint smile.

How could he not know she was lying?

He sat down beside her and leaned forward with his forearms on his thighs. With his knees spread apart and his hands linked loosely together, he was the image of preoccupation.

"I, ah, wanted to talk to you," he said, staring straight ahead. "Before I leave."

Elinor zoomed in on one word out of the ten. "Leave?"

"A cab's on the way. I've got to get back to Dibble immediately."

"But *why?*"

The furrow in his brow came down a little more. "There's been an accident at my grandmother's cottage. Nothing serious. I hope. But serious enough that I want to be there."

"An accident—there, too? Then it must be *you,*" she blurted.

He did a double take. "What do you mean, it must be me?"

She began to speak, bit her tongue, then said it anyway: "You seem to call down . . . wrath."

"Wrath? You mean, like Job?"

"I mean, like a lightning rod. Look what's happened here—everything! And now in Dibble, too."

"But I'm not *in* Dibble."

"Your people are."

"You're saying—? That the Braddock name is cursed?"

"It's occurred to me."

"How picturesque," he said dryly.

"I knew you'd react that way," she murmured, more sad than offended. "I never should've said it. What happened in Dibble?" she asked, moving their conversation onto firmer ground. "I hope no one was hurt."

"It was a close enough call," he admitted. Concern was written all over him. "My grandmother and her nurse-companion left a paraffin—a kerosene—portable heater too close to the curtains and then went off to bed. Sometime around dawn the curtains caught fire, and it spread through the sitting room. Both women were treated for smoke inhalation. Maggie broke her ankle getting my grandmother out to safety. If it hadn't been for the barking of Pepper—our old Dalmatian—it could've ended tragically."

"It's terrible to think of!"

He nodded. "In any case, the cottage is a mess, so my grandmother and Maggie are moving into my house on the estate for the time being. Luckily my mother was in Edinburgh; she's settling the two women in now." He added, "I doubt she'll stay long."

The coolness in his voice when he mentioned his mother convinced Elinor that her grandmother's theory was right: William Braddock had little use for either his mother or—when he was alive—his father. All of his love, all of his loyalty, seemed reserved exclusively for his grandmother.

She said softly, "Maybe your mother will surprise you."

"I don't see how," he said tersely. "The London season is well underway."

"Ah."

Realizing how harsh he must've sounded, Will added, "My mother was only married to my father for seven years. Now that she's remarried and given up her title, there's nothing to bond her to her mother-in-law except my sister and me."

"Grandchildren are pretty big things," Elinor argued.

He wasn't convinced. "We're not like your family, Elinor. We never will *be* like your family. It's hard for you to understand."

"That's not true. I know how unusual we are. Where in the free world do three generations live happily under one roof anymore?"

"You'll miss it," he said, eyeing her warily.

"Yes," she admitted. "I will."

"And I'll bear the brunt of your resentment."

"No, you—well, I don't know. I haven't thought that far ahead."

He laughed softly. "No. You're a MacLeish."

"Meaning?"

Shrugging, he said, "*Carpe diem.* You live for the day. Each and every one of you."

She wanted to shout, "Hey! You take that back!" But she knew he was right.

"My mother looks ahead," she said in Susan's defense.

"But the rest of us are hopeless. You're right. We do live from day to day."

"At first it made me nuts," he confessed. "But now I find it—I don't know—endearing, I guess."

She let out a tiny snort of derision. "We're not animals in a petting zoo, you know," she said.

"Sorry," he said at once. He leaned his head back on the gazebo frame. "Christ, Elinor," he added, "don't you understand how much I envy you? Don't you wish I could forget—for one lousy day—that I have a family name to redeem?"

"You're talking about your grandfather?" she said, gingerly alluding to the family scandal.

"Yeah."

"I don't see what the big deal of that is," she admitted, grateful to be finally, finally in his confidence. "Over here people just go into Chapter Eleven and come back out swinging. No one holds financial mismanagement against them anymore."

He closed his eyes and sighed. "It's different there."

"Among the nobility, you mean."

"Yes. As for the suicide—it's considered the height of bad form."

He sat up again and sighed. "Not that any of it matters. It's my grandmother I'm doing this for. She blames all of it on herself. The day after she prevailed on her husband to put the castle up for sale, he shot himself, setting the stage for a truly dysfunctional family to strut their stuff."

Distressed to hear the bitterness in his voice, she said, "Don't be so hard on them, Will; don't."

He seemed not to hear her. "You know what they say about the sins of the father . . ." he muttered. "My grandfather wasn't there for my father; my father wasn't there for me. God only knows how I'd do at it. . . ."

"You'd be a wonderful father, Will," she said, maybe too quickly. Would he think she had an agenda? She didn't care; she had to reassure him. "Anyone can see how ultraresponsible you are—maybe *because* of your father and grandfather."

He smiled bleakly, then touched his fingers first to his

lips, then to hers. "Hold that thought," he whispered.

"Will—I know what you're going through. I was angry at my own father for years," she blurted. "It was an incredible waste of emotion."

"Let's be fair here," he said wryly. "I'm angry at both my parents. Neither one of them was in any hurry to claim me after the divorce."

"But anger is so pointless. You've already lost your father. If something happened to your mother—"

"I'm not sure I'd notice," he said without emotion.

"Oh, don't say that!" she said, horrified. "You *would* care. You *do* care!"

He smiled a thin, edgy smile. "I wouldn't care. I don't care."

"But you do!" she insisted. "Not only about your mother, but about your father—even if it's for his memory." It came to her in a revelation: "That's why you're buying the castle!"

Will let out a snort of contempt and stood up, ready to run. "I've got a cab coming. I only came out here because I felt obliged to let you know—what the *hell* do you mean, that's why I'm buying the castle?"

She looked up at him. He was flushed, angry, wonderfully handsome with his wet hair still dripping down his temples. She was aware that she was running a huge risk of alienating him forever.

But she had to tell him what she believed. That, and more. She'd reached a point with him when she wanted to spill out her heart. *Had* to spill out her heart.

She put her sketch pad aside and stood up, laying her hand on his arm. "You wanted the castle to show your father, to please your father, to trump your father—all those things! It doesn't matter that he's died since you began your quest. You started it, and you're determined to finish it.

"It's only natural," she said, wincing under the amazed anger she saw in his eyes. "There's nothing wrong with that."

Please don't turn away.

His response was quick and to the point. "You're insane! I despised my father."

"But you didn't," she said simply. "You can't. He's your father. Just as you can't despise your mother—because she's your mother."

"The hell I can't! Listen to me. My parents had a very indiscreet argument in front of me when I was six years old. I've never forgotten it—will never forget it. Trust me. I have ample reason to despise them."

He turned away from her, despite her prayer, and opened the screen door. Her prayer had failed. He was going.

She watched, stricken, as he slammed the door behind him and took half a dozen steps away from the gazebo, away from her. She couldn't call him back, not without seeming to cling. All she could do was pray: don't go. *Don't go.*

He stopped. Shook his head. Looked at the ground. Swore. Looked over his shoulder at her. Looked away and swore again. And then, looking as grim as she'd ever seen him—and that was grim indeed—he came back to the gazebo, opened the screen door, and let himself back in.

In a voice without emotion, he said to Elinor, "I was sitting at the dinner table when my parents, having decided to divorce, began tidying up the details of their misbegotten marriage: my sister and me. My mother had agreed to take Penny, but as for me—I was negotiable."

His smile was thin and ironic and masking obvious pain. "My mother's exact words were, 'Taking Will is the least you can do, you bastard. After the way you've treated me.' And my father's response was, 'No. It's out of the question. I can't take him. I don't want him.'"

Elinor's face creased into an expression of pained sympathy. "Oh, Will—"

"So are we clear on this?" he said, interrupting her. "I'm taking the castle back because of a promise I made to the woman who raised me. Because of a simple, sacred *promise.* My parents have nothing to do with it. There's nothing Freudian about this!" he said, his voice beginning to rise in anger.

"No, no, I understand that," Elinor said, aware that she'd been too blunt. "I know it's for your grandmother. That's one reason. But you can't deny that there are unresolved issues—that part of you wants to be at peace with the rest of your heritage, and with your parents—or why else would you be willing to go through all this?"

"Please, please! Spare me this New Age crap! I am *not* in the mood! I have a plane to catch, a house to put right, and a castle to move. That's what I'm thinking about now. That's *all* I'm thinking about!"

"But you can't just think about that! You have to think about—"

"*What?* What else are you so eager to put on my plate?"

"Me," she said in a bare whisper. "You have to think about me."

She bowed her head. Wrong time—but when was the right time?

"I—" There was an exquisitely painful pause. "You." Another pause. "You."

Finally, he said in a soft and beleaguered whisper, "Do I have to think about that now?"

"Yes," she answered, trying to decide how to empty her heart and yet have it still work again afterward. She lifted her head. Her eyes were glazed over with tears; she tried to blink them back but failed. "Because I love you," she said as they rolled on by.

His gaze locked on to hers with an intensity that left her breathless—and then, for one fraction of a universe, he seemed to lose focus.

When his soul came back from that quick trip away, he was not the same man. "How can you know?" he asked with humility.

"Because I know," she said. "How can you not?"

The careworn lines of his face softened in a kind of tender agony. "Elinor ... God. You mean so much ... but you don't know me. What a bastard I can be."

She whispered, "Oh, yes, I do."

He smiled then, and she knew her heart was in danger of breaking irreparably. She wanted to touch his face, to feel his mouth on hers. She wanted to take a deep, long breath of him. She wanted to commit his body to her memory before he left.

"I've never told a woman I loved her," he whispered.

"I've never told a man."

"You're younger than I am."

"But much more impulsive."

He smiled. "No argument there."

But still he did not say. She realized that it almost didn't matter. This moment, in the gazebo, was all about her need to tell *him*.

He caught her shoulders in his hands. "You're really convinced?" he asked, frowning with concentration. He seemed so incredulous.

Was it just his British reserve? She gave him a bemused, quirky smile and said, "*Yes*—I really am."

He lowered his mouth to hers in a very, very tentative kiss, as if the rules to a game he'd played all his life had just been changed: as if someone had just handed him a mop to hit the ball in a game of cricket.

She wanted so much to reassure him; to let him know that being in love wasn't as hard as all that. But all she could do was put her heart and soul into the kiss and hope he'd understand that a kiss was not sex, and sex was not romance, and romance was not love. Love was longer than a kiss, deeper than sex, higher than romance. Love lasted. And the only way you could know that was in looking back.

All that wisdom, newly learned, she tried to impart in the sweet, silvery mingling of their tongues in a kiss.

A good-bye kiss. From the other side of the castle they heard the loud, piercing wail of a cab driver's horn. It was time to go.

Will murmured, "My bags are in the front hall. Walk with me there."

She shook her head. The gazebo was a hallowed place now. She wanted to stay immersed in it, not say a hasty good-bye in front of some stranger banging on a horn.

"I'll call you from home," he said, tracing her mouth with his fingertips; and then he walked quickly out of the gazebo.

She watched him cross the garden in a few long strides and enter the castle through the greenhouse. His last words rolled across her mind, somehow subduing hope. *I'll call you from home.*

From home. Despite the hold that Fair Castle had on him, if it wasn't in England, it still wasn't home.

Chapter 28

The place smelled of scorched fabric and charred wood. All Will could think of, as he wandered from room to room in the boarded-up gamekeeper's cottage, was that burned curtains smelled hellishly like burned clothing.

It could've been so much worse.

He walked back through the low-ceilinged hall to the sitting room where most of the damage was done, and surveyed it one more time. Much of the wide-planked floor would have to be replaced. The massive beams above the paraffin heater were badly charred, though they were still structurally intact. The lead-framed window casements were gone, of course—stove in by the fire brigade. (The casements had lasted three hundred years. But nothing lasted forever.)

All of the window treatments and all of the old and overstuffed chairs with their small down pillows were too badly damaged to save. The chintz, the shawls, the needlepoint rug—all bound for the dustbin. Will tried to photograph the room in his mind, so that he could give his distraught grandmother a piece-by-piece account when he went back to his house after his mournful chore.

He walked over to his grandmother's favorite armchair, a comfortably saggy affair dressed in faded roses, and lifted a corner of its burned-out, waterlogged cushion. Not a prayer of saving it. He sighed and picked up one of several framed photographs that lay collapsed in a heap

on the small sewing table—itself perhaps salvageable—
that stood next to the armchair.

It was a snapshot of him as a little boy, in knickers and
an argyle vest, taken when he was on holiday from school.
He knew what it was because he remembered the metal
frame; the photograph itself was unrecognizable. Most of
them were.

He picked up another frame, this one surrounding a
photograph of his father, dressed for the hunt. His father,
too busy with political and social obligations to have much
time for either of his children. His father, whom he
claimed to despise.

Elinor's words echoed in the empty cottage: *You
wanted the castle to show your father: to please your father;
to trump your father—all of those things!*

Was she right? He didn't know anymore. Maybe. He
didn't know.

He patted his jacket pocket, reassuring himself that the
photo *he* most treasured in the world was still there. He
reached inside and felt its corner, just to make sure.

Still there. Still his. Still time.

Elinor's dragon was in big trouble. He'd just saved Izzy
and Elly from a forest fire, but now the forest fire had
leaped from treetop to treetop, getting between them and
the sea, where the dragon had originally planned to take
the two sisters until the fire burned itself out.

What to do, what to do.

Nuts. The story was becoming too frightening for a picture book. Elinor had begged for, and got, an extra three
days for her revisions. Now she was wasting them moping.
She'd made her dragon bad, good, and in between, and
none of them seemed right to her.

The fact was, until she knew how Will felt about her,
she wouldn't know what to do about her dragon.

Was Will cold and uncaring? He'd gone ahead and ex-
ecuted the sale agreement through a power of attorney.
His action had promptly sent Elinor into a tailspin, her
grandparents into a state of melancholy, and Chester into
a funk. Only her mother seemed relieved—and even she

was tiptoeing around the castle, feeling guilty about feeling relieved.

Or was he kind and chivalrous? Will was fulfilling his promise to his grandmother, after all, which was chivalrous. And he sounded sorry about having to do it when he'd talked with Elinor on the phone, which was kind.

Or was he simply somewhere in between? Will was a human being, after all, not a character in a children's fantasy. He had good intentions and mixed motives, just like every other human being.

One thing was certain. All he had to do was utter three little words, and Elinor would turn the dragon into a hero with a few quick strokes of her pencil. But so far he hadn't uttered them.

She tried the words out loud, just to taste them in her mouth again. "I love you."

She stared gloomily at her good-bad dragon with its fierce red eyes and flaming breath, then took a colored pencil and stabbed it in its rear end. "Jerk!"

An hour later, Elinor had abandoned her drafting board for the refrigerator. She was rummaging through the fruit bin when Tucker O'Toole strolled in with a grin on his face.

"Hi, Tuck!" she said, looking up from the fridge. "Welcome back. Did you have a good time in the city?"

"Couldn't have gone better," he said with refreshing enthusiasm. "*Rigamarole* was great. Fantastic choreography ... great score ... great dancing ... incredible energy. You should've come."

"No, it's better that you were forced to look up an old school chum. People have a tendency to fall out of touch. Apple?" she asked him. "Brand-new harvest." He nodded and she tossed him a Cortland, then took one for herself.

"So what's going on around here?" he asked, pulling back a kitchen chair.

He seemed in no hurry; it was a remarkable change from the guy she'd packed off to New York. Elinor felt a brief pang of regret that she hadn't grabbed the chance to go with him. It might've been fun. Instead she'd hung around, waiting for those three words from Will.

"*Nothing* is going on around here," she said with a sigh. "Including my revisions. Everyone's been in a blue funk since the papers were signed. Except Mother, of course."

Tucker stopped midbite. "What papers?"

Elinor bit into her own juicy apple and took a squirt in the eye. "*What* papers. The sales agreement—what papers do you think?" she said, wiping the stream of juice from her cheek.

"But that's impossible! Norwood's in England!"

"Sure, but all he had to do was give someone power of attorney. Which he did. The closing's in a week. And they may move *that* date up. An all-cash offer lets you do stuff like that," she said glumly.

A thought occurred to her. "How'd you know Will was in England?" she asked. It came out before she had a chance to think about it.

Tucker hardly heard her. He was upset. Extremely upset. "I called the castle," he said, finally getting to her question. "Izzy told me."

"Oh. Well, in any case, we're all clearing out of here soon. Will told my family to take as long as they needed, but everyone's too depressed to hang around. They want to be relocated before the snow flies. My mother's been on the phone with her realtor chum all morning."

"But you can't *do* that!"

She shrugged. "Jump before you're pushed. Isn't that how it's supposed to work?"

"It's not his castle!"

"It will be."

"Will you *listen* to me?" Tucker said, his face red with rage. "Fair Castle never *has* belonged to Norwood! *For the simple reason that he's not a Norwood!*"

"I—what?"

"He's a nobody! He's not a baron; he has no legitimate claim to Fair Castle! We've got to stop this!"

Elinor was absolutely dumbfounded. Her heart went off on a wild run and her cheeks felt hot with dismay. "What are you *talking* about? Of *course* Will's a Norwood! The castle's been in his family for hundreds of years. He knows every generation. He's counted them. Ask him. He's as obnoxious as can be about it!"

"Shit!" Tucker hurled his apple like a fastball at the kitchen wall. It splattered into applesauce from the force of his pitch and drooled down the whitewashed stone. "You couldn't just wait a few days! I would've had it all worked out; I could've showed you all the proof you'd need!"

"Proof? That's what you've been doing all this time? Trying to prove that Will's not a Norwood?"

"Obviously!"

"It's not obvious to *me,*" Elinor said, wincing under his fury. She added, "If you were so close . . . if you're so determined . . . then why did you go to New York?"

"You shoved me out the door, that's why! I would've looked like an idiot, clinging to the archive shelves by my fingernails. As it is, you were making jokes about prying me loose."

"Well, why didn't you just *tell* me what you were doing?"

"How could I trust you? First you hate him, then you're hot for him, then you hate him—"

"That's not true!" Which it certainly was. Reeling from Tucker's allegation—which she did not believe—Elinor said, "His mother had an affair? That's what you're claiming? Or that he was, what? Born out of wedlock before she got married?" Elinor wasn't even sure what constituted a bastard in legal terms.

"How should I know about his mother? I'm an archivist! I found evidence—clear, irrefutable evidence—that Charles Braddock was a bigamist!"

"Charles Braddock! *That* Baron Norwood? The guy on the wall?"

He may as well have said Mickey MacLeish.

"But Charles Braddock was married to Elinor. *My* namesake Elinor!"

Tucker's expression turned into an angry leer. "The blond and beautiful Elinor Hammond was the second one on the baron's train. Charles had been married a year to someone else by the time he agreed to the sham of a wedding with Elinor."

"But . . . but it's Elinor's portrait that hangs next to him in the hall—not someone else's!"

"Oh, well, that's proof conclusive, then," Tucker said in a scathing tone. He jumped up from the chair and began pacing the kitchen in frustration. "How naive can you get, El? Anyone can paint a portrait and slap a plaque on it. You have to look for documentation. *Documentation.*"

"But . . . but surely anyone can forge a document, as well," she argued.

"That's right," he conceded. "So you have to go one better."

He wasn't even talking to Elinor anymore—just going over a personal checklist in a room she happened to occupy. His eyes were unfocused as he mumbled to himself, "You have to find a corroborating document . . . preferably cross-referenced . . . and multiple points of evidence. That's what constitutes proof to a historian. That's right . . . especially if the references turn up in opposite camps . . . behind enemy lines. That's when you know. That's when you know you've got 'im."

"Got *who?*"

He brought himself up short and gave her a penetrating, burning look. "Elinor . . . you've been a good friend . . . maybe . . . maybe even more than that," he said, dropping into the chair next to hers again. He took her hand in both of his and squeezed it tight, sending a thrill of urgency through her.

His face, fair and flushed and earnest, was close to hers. "Can I trust you? Can I trust you to do the right thing?"

"Of course you can," she said, her breath coming in shallow waves. "Because if what you say is true . . ."

"Then Will has no use for Fair Castle! Right! You'll have it back. There's no way he'd want what didn't belong to his ancestors in the first place. It'd be dishonorable, and he prides himself above all else on his honor. You can trust me completely on this. I know what I'm doing. I stumbled across the first piece of evidence when I was

working on my book, and now I'm a heartbeat away from
finding the corroborating document. El, I'm convinced it's
in this castle!"

"What document?" she begged. "What are you looking
for? Would you just start at the *beginning*? You're overwhelming me, Tucker!"

"Yes, okay, I know. All right. How's your English history?"

Still dazed, she said, "Just talk. I'll tell you when you
lose me."

"Good. Mary Tudor—Bloody Mary. Homely, humor-
less Mary the First, daughter of Henry the Eighth by
Catherine of Aragon. You remember her?"

"Sort of. She came and went. She was a religious zealot,
wasn't she?"

"She'd have to be," Tucker said impatiently, "to try to
reverse the Protestant Reformation that her father put in
place. "Okay. First off, the woman marries a Catholic like
herself, Philip of Spain. Then she brings back the mass,
reestablishes the pope's authority, and returns whatever
land the crown has appropriated from the Catholic
Church during Henry's reign. Pretty impressive stuff for
a woman who reigned for only half a decade. In five years
she did a pretty good job of turning England on its ear
again."

"She was on the throne when the castle was built," Elinor said, starting to make some connections.

"It was no coincidence. The Norwoods, devout Cath-
olics, came into their own during her reign. Okay. Fast-
forward two hundred years. Charles Braddock—Lord
Norwood—still Catholic, marries Elinor Hammond. Big
wedding. Big guest list. *But*."

"He was already married?" Elinor whispered.

"To a Catholic. In a very secret ceremony, is my guess.
I suspect the woman he married was pregnant. It's a cli-
chéd reason to wed, of course, but this was the eighteenth
century; pregnancies happened. In fact, I have no doubt
that that was the case. Anyway, if the marriage *was* secret,
then it was for love. That's the one great given in this
story: It had to be for love. Whether the real wife was

pregnant or not, Charles loved her. Otherwise nothing makes sense."

"Why do you say that?"

Tucker shrugged. "The baron's second marriage—his bigamous union—to Elinor Hammond was a very public event. I found extensive accounts of the ceremony, the wedding feast, the guests, the weeks-long celebration before and afterward. I have a list of his guests, for God's sake. They included the Earl and Countess of Onset, an Irish bishop, a couple of other barons, and several baronets. The wedding was a really, really big deal in Dibble.

"Now let's say Charles had publicly married someone else first who then, say, died. That first wedding—if it were not secret—would also have been a big deal. Charles was a wealthy man, and very keen on his status. He was a peer, and he had money and he had power. Yet there are no records anywhere that such a wedding took place."

"Oh." Elinor, who'd been caught up in the story so far, didn't bother to hide her disappointment now. "So you're really just fantasizing about the first marriage. Because if there are no records . . ."

He hesitated, then said, "Oh, but there is. Or was. At least one. I found an entry in a church register of births, deaths, and marriages; I won't get more specific than that. It had been blotted out—who knows when? Sometime over the past couple of centuries. Obviously someone else knew about the first marriage and wanted to expunge the record. If only I could've got a better look at it!" he added in a burst of frustration.

He got himself under control again. Very calmly, he said, "The chronological place in the register matches exactly the time period in which I think the first, secret marriage took place."

"Wait a minute," Elinor said, confused. "If that's all you've got—a blotted-out entry that you can't even read— then what's the basis for your theory that there *was* a secret marriage? What sent you out looking for such an entry in the first place?"

He became vague. He looked away and said, "People talk. Locals talk. Legends get passed on. This one had an obvious ring of truth to it. I've never doubted it."

"You believe a legend that old? Hold it. So you've been to Dibble?" Elinor asked him, surprised. He'd never mentioned it. .

Tucker flushed a dark shade of annoyance and said, "I've been to England. It's a small country."

"Not *that* small," Elinor shot back. But he had a look in his eyes that she preferred not to challenge. She didn't want him to stop taking her into his confidence, so she added placatingly, "So you think there's a document in Fair Castle? In a secret vault or something?"

It was absurd. The castle had been broken down completely and then rebuilt again over here. It wasn't as if anyone had left a stone unturned.

"Yes," he said. "I think the document is here. The legend claims that there was a marriage certificate hidden away somewhere by the first bride. She never actually lived in Fair Castle, but she had access to it. Some versions say the priest who married them was the bride's uncle, and that's why he was able to get around the banns and give her an actual document."

"Then why didn't he object when the second marriage took place?"

"He may have been killed," said Tucker without a hint of melodrama. "Maybe they thought—wrongly—of the document as insurance because they saw what was coming with Elinor Hammond. Or maybe they just didn't have the chance to drop it in a safe deposit box," he said acidly. It was obvious that he resented Elinor's skepticism.

She couldn't help it; there were too many *ifs, ands,* or *buts*. "But why not hide it in her own people's castle?" she suggested.

"Did she have a castle?" he asked. "We don't know that."

Both fell into thoughtful silence. *I think he must be as mad as a hatter,* decided Elinor, amazed by the entire conversation. On the other hand, he sounded so sure about the legend and about his findings.

After a moment, Elinor settled for saying, "It . . . ah . . . seems like a long shot."

He didn't take offense, which surprised her. "I know that," he said. "But I'm just so convinced . . . that somewhere in that archives room . . . maybe stuck between the pages of a book . . . or in a secret pocket of a binding . . . *somewhere* . . . that document exists."

"Do you know the first bride's name?" Elinor suddenly asked. It would be so much more believable, if only he had a name.

He shook his head. "I assume that when I come across a marriage testament with Charles Braddock, Lord Norwood's name on it, I'll know I've hit pay dirt."

He had no idea how droll he sounded. Elinor stared at him, marveling at his conviction, fascinated by the lure of the hunt.

And then, very suddenly, Tucker's scholarly puzzle took on a human face. And the face belonged to another Lord Norwood altogether.

"Oh, but what about Will!" she said. "Are you really prepared to confront him with your findings? To tell him that he descends from—"

"Do you think he'd care?"

"Of course he would. He's a peer. He's in the middle of a huge effort to rehabilitate the family name."

"Is that what he'd care about? Or would it be the money at stake?"

"The money? You mean, he'd have to forfeit the estate? But the legitimacy of the line of descent wouldn't matter after all these generations, would it?"

"English law is complex on the issue; but, yes, absolutely—"

Agnes came into the kitchen then, and Tucker clammed up. "Why don't we take this someplace else," he suggested with a meaningful look. "And let Agnes have her kitchen back."

The stocky cook planted her fists on her hips and glared at the apple mess on the wall and the counter. "And who do you think is going to clean up here? Cinderella?"

"We will, Agnes," said Elinor, pouncing on the apple fragments. "After all, you're the *cook*."

"Not a damned scullery maid."

*   *   *

"Strange, is it not, Charles? One man struggles to move a pile of stones to its rightful place on the wild coast of Northumberland—while the other one struggles to prevent the first from succeeding."

"How is it that the second one cannot perceive you, Marianne? We see that he tries. We know that he cares. And yet he cannot find the key."

"I have told you the reason. It is simple enough. He lacks imagination."

"More than that, my love. He lacks the capacity for joy. He is venemous in his obsession."

"It's true. His single-mindedness has made him cruel. He has injured one innocent in his effort to keep the castle intact a while longer. Is he capable of worse? I think he is."

"Ironic, that the power denied him should be possessed by a family whose tie to the castle is merely whimsical."

"So he is our ultimate legacy. Ah, Charles—how wretchedly bittersweet."

"As our love was, Marianne. And our lives."

Chapter 29

*W*ill had God on his side.

His search for a temporary caregiver was short and sweet, thanks to Father Aloysius. The elderly priest was able to recommend a young woman of highest character who'd be able to move into Will's house immediately to tend to Dorothea and poor Maggie Munger.

To repay Father Aloysius for the trouble he'd taken, Will offered to take the priest to dinner. Somehow his invitation got accepted, adapted, and converted into a large dinner party that Will had no desire to host. In the first place, he didn't have the pots. In the second, his mind and heart were on the other side of the Atlantic.

But he let himself be swept along on a wave of false cheer, and eventually found himself sitting opposite Father Aloysius at a dining table he'd never had to use before. Around the table were seated the usual suspects: the vicar and the vicar's wife, the chemist and the chemist's wife, Dorothea's physican and poor Maggie Munger, and last but not least, Maude.

Maude was his grandmother's idea: a librarian in her early thirties who was more genteel than all the rest of them put together.

Will was bored to tears. What he wanted was one of Mickey MacLeish's stiff martinis, not a dose of dull sherry. What he wanted was to jump with both feet into one of the MacLeishes' screaming matches over sex and

politics, not to wait his turn to hold forth on the merits
of canned versus sun-dried tomatoes.

What he wanted was Elinor. He wanted her in his arms,
he wanted her in his bed, he wanted her—it was pointless
to deny it—in his castle. He was on fire with longing for
her. Two days in Dibble? It felt like two years. He kept
trying not to think of it, but his mind kept going back to
it: being sunk into the hot, dark cavern of her flesh. He
wanted, with every cell of his being, to go back and sink
there again.

"And so, Aloysius, *will* you be able to find suitable
wood for the damaged truss? It's a large timber."

The vicar was sympathetic to the priest's efforts to restore his church to its original condition. He'd gone
through a similar ordeal himself.

Father Aloysius sighed and said, "Oh, it's big, without
a doubt."

Will felt his cheeks burn hot. A priest and a vicar,
within eavesdropping distance of his lustful thoughts. He
waited for the lightning bolt to knock him off his chair.

The elderly priest cut a slender bite from his lamb and
said, "They may have to scarph two smaller timbers together. It's quite distressing."

"Iroko would be a good wood for that."

"So the head carpenter was telling me."

In the gazebo, when he'd said good-bye to her . . . it was
incredibly wrenching. He felt as if he were tearing out
part of his heart and leaving it there. She looked so beautiful . . . a creature of the forest, breathtakingly still. For
once. She was waiting for a commitment from him. Why
hadn't he given it to her?

He had no idea. Maybe because she was telling him
truths, and he hadn't wanted to hear them.

"A good many of the roof tiles need replacing, I'm
afraid," said Father Aloysius, patting his lips with a ser-
viette. "I shall have to advertise for used ones in good
repair."

She was infuriating. But then, that went without saying.
It was still much more exciting than . . .

Will glanced at his dinner partner and gave her a kindly smile. She smiled timidly back.

Than Maude.

"With any luck, the interior will be completed by Shrove Tuesday."

"Oh, excellent," said the vicar. "It's an important season, liturgically speaking."

"Yes. We do some of our best business then," Father Aloysius said with a good-natured chuckle.

So: He hadn't told her he loved her for the simple reason that he was pouting. How truly adult.

He loved her. He loved her! He'd loved her from the moment he'd seen her. It was only now, looking back, that he realized it. He loved her! He sat, stunned, in his chair—whacked by that bolt of lightning after all.

He wanted to rush back to the States and throw himself at her feet. He wanted to impregnate her. He wanted her to bear a dozen of his children. He wanted to carry her off to England on a white horse and crown her queen of all that was his. He wanted her. For now. Forever. He loved her!

"William, dear, are you all right? You haven't eaten a thing."

There were problems with that plan, though. She wouldn't leave her family. That was one problem. And she had a career. That was another problem. Or maybe it wasn't. With faxes and FedEx and satellite dishes, how could that be a problem? He'd get her the best scanner in the industry. He'd give her the studio of her dreams. She could have easels. She could have paint. She could have anything! If she would only marry him.

"William?"

The family. That was the bigger problem. He would simply have to move the entire family to England. Yes. That could be arranged. After the castle he'd move the family. Chester could be constable of the castle. He'd love it. Mickey could paint landscapes of the English countryside. If England was good enough for Thomas Gainsborough—yes. And Camilla. Camilla could have an even bigger garden, in bloom for a longer time. Even in the

north country. As for Izzy, she wouldn't mind; it'd be an
adventure. And Izzy's mother would absolutely, positively
love the concept of country gentility. He was willing to
bet the estate that no one at his table had ever even *considered* taking the Lord's name in vain.

He looked up with a serene smile.

"Good God, what's wrong with you, son?"

It was the vicar, and he looked alarmed.

"Hum?"

"Are you feeling well? My lord—you're looking a bit
queer."

It was the priest, and *he* looked alarmed.

"I'm sorry?"

Will looked around. It was extraordinary. They were
all looking at him as if he'd gone mad. And maybe he
had. He grinned and stood up, more or less in acknowledgment of the fact, then sat back down and said, "*Excellent* lamb. Simply excellent."

That was pretty much all he had to say through the first
couple of courses. Not until cheese and greens did he
reenter the earth's atmosphere—and even then, only because he heard a magical word invoked.

"Elinor, I believe."

His head shot up. His grandmother, wearing her best
wool dress and her best brave smile, was watching him
appraisingly. "Isn't that what you said the young lady's
name was, dear? The one who does the children's
books?"

Big grin. "Elinor! Yes! She does the most delightful—
they're so incredibly—ah! I know! I'll get one of her
books to show you all."

He pushed his chair back so abruptly that it tipped
over. The librarian let out a little squeak and recoiled
from him in terror. Was he really behaving that oddly?
Could be!

He kept on grinning his foolish grin and said, "In the
meantime, I have a photograph of her I can pass around.
It was taken of everyone at dinner one evening. You can
see a bit of the dining chamber, and some of Chester's

collection of armor on the wall. A completely bizarre assortment, but never mind; he likes it."

He reached in his inside jacket pocket for the dog-eared snapshot and handed it to the librarian. "Here you are— I'm sorry; what's your name?—Maude, yes, of course. Just have a look and pass it around, would you? That's Elinor, next to the old fellow in the beret. And I'll run fetch her book. It's my favorite: *Elly in the Moat*."

Maude looked as if he were handing her a grenade with the pin pulled out; but she accepted the photo with reasonable grace and even managed to say as though she cared, "And who are all the others?"

"Ah, yes, yes," he said feverishly. "The whole clan's there except Elinor's mother, Susan, who took the pic."

He ran through the lineup as Maude politely shared the photograph with the village chemist who sat on her left, and then he said, "Back in a jif!"

He was at the foot of the varnished stairs when he heard the chemist say something that stopped him in his tracks: "My word. I've *seen* this chap. Recently, too."

The only chaps in the photograph were Mickey Mac-Leish, his son-in-law Chester, Will (scowling at Elinor), and Tucker O'Toole.

Suddenly tense, Will retraced his steps to the dining room. In a voice as carefully calm as he could keep it, he said, "Which one do you mean?"

Will had no doubt that the chemist would point to O'Toole, and he was right. He said, "Would you happen to remember when and where you saw him?"

"Well, now, let me think. I suppose it had to've been Sunday early. I was walking the dog, which I don't do on weekdays and Saturday when I have to open the shop. Norma walks the dog then; isn't that right, dear?"

Norma said, "Yes, I always walk the dog on weekdays and Saturday when you have to open the shop."

"The lad was pulled over to the side of Braintree Lane with a flat and was rummaging in the boot for a tire jack. I asked him if he needed help. He merely stared at me, not very kindly. Americans! Personally, I'm convinced it was the Boston Tea Party that started them down the slippery slope of their bad manners. Be that as it may, the lad never said boo. Just went back to fixing his flat."

"He's not an American," Will said briefly. "He's a Canadian."

The chemist shrugged and added, "I expect he was in a hurry. It was starting to rain, after all. But that's him, all right," he said, tapping the photograph. "I never forget a face. Do I, Norma?"

"No, dear," his wife agreed. "You never forget a face."

Will took the photo and handed it to Father Aloysius. "Father? Does the fellow seated across from me at the table look at all familiar to you?"

The elderly priest pushed his bifocals over the bridge of his nose and pruned his lips in concentration. "Don't know . . . the light's a bit weak in here."

Will reached over to the rheostat and undimmed the chandelier. A hundred and eighty watts of light transformed the cozy setting into an interrogation room. The priest shook his head uncertainly. "It could very well be the Canadian who was so keen on walking out with my register. It's hard to say for certain, of course. Jim? Bill? Jim? Which was it again?"

"Tucker," said Will in a voice that was now grim. "Tucker O'Toole."

"This is odd," said the vicar. "Do you suppose he's come after the register again, Aloysius? You really ought to think about keeping it in a vault for safekeeping. It's not the same as in the old days, you know. There's a black market for every kind of antiquity. Thieves abound."

"I will not do that," said the priest with lofty resolve. "The register is as much a part of the history of St. Anthony's as the graveyard behind it."

"Well, they've stolen a headstone or two from your graveyard *and* mine, which goes to prove my point."

"Now, Paul, we've been all through this," said the priest, looking around him uncomfortably. "We don't want to bore—"

"Father, could I have a look at that register anytime soon?" Will asked suddenly.

"Certainly. Would tomorrow morning suit you?"
"Tonight would suit me better. Right after dinner."

Elinor and Tucker were up to their earlobes in old books, manuscripts, and papers. Boxes stood in haphazard, tippy stacks all around them. The day had been spent in a frantic search for the legendary document, and by dinnertime the air was thick with dust particles that leaped and danced every time that someone slammed a book shut.

Elinor rubbed her red, itchy eyes, then shook the little bottle of Murine that she'd brought into the archives room hours ago. Empty. Hours ago. Her nose was stuffed, her sinuses ached. Her skin felt coated with very old dust, as repellent to her senses as the silverfish she swatted every few minutes.

"How do you do it?" she asked Tucker, flicking away another dead bug. "This is abysmal work."

Tucker hardly heard her. "You have the wrong mindset. There's treasure here," he said, spread-eagling a book and letting its pages hang down. "All we have to do is find it."

"But we've been through all the shelves and all the boxes. There's nothing here. There really isn't. I hate to say this, Tuck, but you've been caught up in a wild-goose chase. What you heard was a romantic old wives' tale. Stories like that get twisted and exaggerated as they get passed down. They're fascinating stories; but there can't be any truth to them after enough generations pass."

"Maybe. Maybe not."

"And we don't have all the archives associated with the castle, in any case. A lot of them stayed behind in Dibble. Frankly, I've never understood why we got *any*thing," she said, petulant in her weariness.

"You got the archives for the same reason that you got the portraits and furnishings: because Lady Norwood was distraught at the time she sold the castle and had no use for them, and later your grandfather didn't want to open old wounds by offering them back."

"Really? He never told me that."

"You never asked."

Tucker pulled out another manuscript from a box marked *Amsterdam, 1875–1890*—which couldn't possibly be relevant—and began fanning through its bound pages. Elinor wanted to scream, "Can't you *read?* Chester bought that lot last year at an auction in Pennsylvania. The box has never been in England, much less in Dibble!"

But he was a man possessed, and Elinor felt bound to oversee his search.

She lifted a box of old books and dropped it on top of a very unevenly stacked pile. The box slid off with a crash to the floor; books, papers (and for some reason, brochures for Disney's EuroWorld) went spilling out, sending clouds of dust spiraling up Elinor's nostrils. She launched into another series of violent sneezes.

"Oh, *damn,*" she said, blowing her nose into a sodden hanky. "Tucker—Tucker, do you really hate Will that much?" she asked plaintively.

Because that's what the search was all about, she was convinced: the fierce desire of a poor-born Canadian to humiliate a well-born Englishman. It had nothing to do with scholarly research, and nothing to do with academic curiosity. Tucker wanted Will's head on a platter. What Elinor couldn't understand was why.

Tucker laid the manuscript down on top of some others and took up another one. He said in an amiable voice, "I don't hate him. That's nonsense. We're not exactly soul brothers, but—I'm just curious, that's all."

Elinor stuck the wet hanky into the pocket of her jeans and said in a stuffed-up voice, "There's something that's been bothering me, Tuck—ever since yesterday, when you told me about the legend."

Tucker paused. The room became quiet. Even the dust particles seemed to pause middance. Tucker said quietly, "What might that be?"

Her hazel eyes stared into his green ones. "Did you come to Fair Castle because of your book, or because of the Norwood legend?"

He didn't insult Elinor by laughing off her question. "To be honest? Because of both. My visa was up in England, and I had to come back to Canada, anyway. It wasn't so hard to make a trip down here to check out the castle—which will make a great little postscript for my book—and research the chronicle at the same time."

Oddly relieved by his candor, she said, "I've been thinking about it—about the legend, I mean. I admit it's fascinating; but what can possibly be gained by proving it? It's too late . . . it would be cruel to tell the Norwood family—"

"Cruel! You have a strange idea of cruelty!" he said, slamming the manuscript down on the desk. "Cruel is when people are denied their birthright. Cruel is when their land is stolen out from under them. Ask any Native American about *cruel*."

"What do Native Americans have to do with the Norwood legend?" she said, as puzzled as she was taken aback.

"I'm trying to make the point that it's the squatters who're cruel and the displaced parties who suffer," he said, his eyes blazing with anger now. "I ought to know: I'm married to an Iroquois!"

Elinor didn't really hear the Iroquois part. *"Married!"* It came completely out of the blue. "How can you be—? After the way you—?"

Married!

It was obvious that Tucker knew he'd been indiscreet, and possibly stupid. The flush of anger became a flush of embarrassment. He looked away, as if he were trying to read the answers on someone else's test, and then looked back at Elinor.

He was calmer now. "I'm not really living with her any longer. But I understand—because of her—what it means to suffer injustice."

He's a liar. That's what Elinor was thinking. He'd kissed her and dated her and never once had he mentioned a wife. Elinor had no idea now what to believe. She studied him for evidence of deceit; but there was nothing in his boyishly good-looking face with its sea green eyes to tell her where he'd been lying and where he hadn't.

All she knew was that she no longer trusted him.

"Well, it's none of my business, of course," she said. "Sorry for the bug-eyed reaction. I was just a little surprised, that's all."

Her mother had been right about Tucker all along. And Elinor, again, had been wrong.

Uneasy now, she decided to bail out then and there from the bizarre search for an imaginary document. It was time to go to her grandfather and have him gently show Tucker the door. No good could come of his crazy obsession. Elinor had been trying to watch out—God only knew why—for Will's interest. But this wasn't the way to do it.

She stood up. "Tucker, you know what? I don't think we're going to find any proof in the archives. We've gone through everything—some of it twice—and it's just not here. Maybe it exists; but it's not among the archives. I'm tired. I'm filthy. I hope you don't think I'm a quitter," she added to placate him.

She had to get out of the small confines of the room. It was making her crazy.

He looked at her for a long, unnerving moment before he said in a voice of chilling calm, "Sure. You clean up and go on to dinner. I'll amuse myself here for a little while longer."

Very little, Elinor thought as she left the room with an apologetic smile. She didn't like this at all. The sooner he made his exit from the castle, the better. Shuddering with relief, she headed for fresh air, soap, and hot water.

A call came when Elinor was in the shower. Izzy dragged the phone into the bathroom to her. "It's long *distance,*" she said in a stage whisper. "From Lord Norwood!"

Izzy sat on the toilet and Elinor sat on the tub, wrapping a towel around herself awkwardly with one hand and trying to shoo her sister away with one bare foot.

"Hi," she said in a soft croon. She kicked Izzy in the thigh, but her sister wasn't budging. "This is a surprise. It's, what? Midnight over there?"

"Yeah, it's late," Will said. He sounded secretive, as if he were calling her from under the blankets in his room.

"But I wanted to catch you tonight. Actually, I'm calling you from the rectory of our local church. My house is filled with anxious women, and I didn't want to add to the anxiety level."

"Oh, that's too bad," said Elinor. "So they're still jumpy after the fire? You can't blame them. It's a scary thing, having a fire in your house."

She covered the phone with her hand and muttered "Out!" to Izzy.

Her sister sucked in her lips.

Distracted, Elinor said to Will, "Why are you in a rectory at midnight?"

"It's nowhere I want to be," he said. His voice sounded tense and unhappy. "I've been doing some amateur sleuthing, and it turns out I'm no damn good at it. That's not why I'm calling. I'm calling to let you know—this sounds insane, but you have to know this—Tucker O'Toole was in Dibble this weekend."

"What?"

Izzy's eyes got wide. What was she missing? She jumped up and pressed her ear near her sister's. Elinor shoved her away.

"I learned it purely by accident tonight. One identification was quite positive. The other was iffy and I wouldn't give it credence, if it weren't for the chemist— the pharmacist—being so sure. Tucker's been here more than once."

"Not this weekend—no way! He went to see *Rigama-role*. He had a great time; he described it!"

"He couldn't be in two places at once, Elinor. And he was in Dibble."

The church register. It must've been in Dibble. And that's where Will was now, in the church rectory. In the middle of the night.

"I . . . I don't understand," she said, stalling desperately. "What could Tucker possibly want in Dibble?"

Did Will know? If he did, would he say?

"Elinor—I hate like hell to tell you this without proof— but you've got to be on your guard. I'm fairly sure that it was Tucker who set the cottage on fire."

"*Tucker?* That's insane! That's not why he was there!"

She heard a confused laugh at the other end. Will said, "You have a better reason?"

Oops.

Chapter 30

"Well, I don't know," she said, swallowing hard and thinking slow. "Maybe Tucker was—I suppose he could've been—in the rectory doing research for his book?"

There was a brutal pause. "I didn't say Tucker was in the rectory. I said he tried to burn down the house."

Oh God. Getting in deeper. "Oh, right; I'm getting mixed up."

"Elinor—are you all right? You sound distracted."

"I *am* distracted," she said, this time without hesitation. "My sister is in my face, making a pest of herself. The next sound you hear will be her death rattle."

Izzy gave her sister an ooh-I'm-scared look and, quick as a chipmunk, jumped into the bathtub and hid behind the shower curtain.

"Izzy! Damn it! Out! Right now! I'm not kidding!"

Will was even less patient. "Ignore her, would you, for God's sake? This is important."

"I know it is, but it's also bizarre. How could he burn your house down? You never said anything about arson." She began flailing at the shower curtain. "You said it was a kerosene heater."

Will's impatience began doing a slow burn of its own. "If you climb through a window and move a heater closer to flammable curtains, then that's arson."

"Is that in fact what happened?" Elinor asked, grabbing her sister's wrist and yanking her out of the tub.

"It must have been. Both women have decided on reflection that the heater was not where they'd left it. The ground beneath the casements was generally torn up by the firemen, but there were one or two untouched bootprints there that didn't match theirs—or the groundskeeper's. We think. The prints have since been washed away. Needless to say, my grandmother's terrified. She's putting on a heroic front, but frankly, I've felt the need to hire a security guard."

Elinor shoved her sister back into her bedroom, then locked the bathroom door. "I'm sorry about this," she said into the phone. "This is the payoff for ten years of spoiling Izzy. She doesn't take any of us seriously."

"I want you to take *this* seriously, damn it, Elinor! If he's capable of arson, he's capable of anything! Are you even listening?"

"Yes, I am, I am. But why would he—?"

"I don't know," Will said. "It makes no sense. We have a visceral dislike of one another, it's true. But for him to fly to England to lash out at me seems far-fetched."

Even Elinor had a hard time buying it. "There's another consideration—money. How could he even afford it? He doesn't strike me as having very deep pockets."

"Ever heard of VISA?" Will said. "Still, I'm having a hell of a time believing it: that he'd try to burn out my grandmother. Where's the motive? What's the point?"

The point might have been to draw Will back to England so that he couldn't sign the purchase agreement. Could Tucker be naive enough to think that would work?

Yes. She remembered Tucker's response when she'd told him that the papers had been signed anyway: "That's not possible!" he'd said.

Well, it *was* possible, and Tucker was now working frantically on Plan B.

Should she tell Will about Tucker's determination to bring him down? She didn't know. Her head was spinning. "The register—tell me about the register," she said into the phone, reaching for her clothes.

"You tell *me* about the register. How did you know Tucker had been in Dibble examining it?"

"I just learned it this afternoon. It's got something to

do with a line of descent," she said, as truthfully as she dared.

Think, think. Could she take Will into her confidence without telling him he wasn't—might not be—a Norwood?

She couldn't see how.

"Did you find anything . . . interesting in it?" she asked Will. "Anything that might give you a clue as to why Tucker was there?"

"I told you. Amateur sleuthing is not my thing. It's not like looking for a bug in a software program. I'd have to be psychic to know what he was looking for in that register."

"Were there any . . . blotted out entries?"

"Of course there were. The register had several of them. It's not as if they had a delete-key back then. Why do you ask?"

"Tucker did mention something about a scratched-out entry," she said, hanging on to the truth by the skin of her teeth.

She'd wrestled into a shirt and had the phone jammed between her ear and her shoulder and was pulling on her jeans when Izzy crept back into the bathroom through the door on Elinor's side.

"Hold on a second," she told Will. She grabbed her incorrigible sister by her sweater and said, "Did Tucker call you on Sunday?"

Expecting, obviously, to be beaten, Izzy was thrilled that she'd been made part of a Very Important Conversation instead.

"Yes!" Her eyes were wide-eyed with expectancy. Next question?

Elinor obliged her. "Did you tell him that Will was in England?"

"Yes!" she cried.

"Oh." There went a possible piece of incriminating information. Elinor didn't know whether to be elated or disappointed. Too much data was being thrown at her too fast. She wasn't able to process it.

"Will? Maybe Tucker wasn't there this weekend, after all. Just how sure—?"

"Wait!" cried Izzy. "No, I *didn't* tell him that Lord Norwood was in England. Because I didn't know. All I saw were the bags sitting in the hall. And that's what I told Tucker: that Lord Norwood's bags were by the door."

Izzy was as eager to please as a puppy. "Is that what you wanted to know?"

Oh, God. It was not. It meant that Tucker, undoubtedly calling from Dibble, had been making sure that Will was rushing home. And that meant that Tucker had known there was a crisis at home to rush to.

And Elinor couldn't tell any of it to Will, not without tipping him off that he might not be a Norwood at all.

"Will, can I call you back?" she pleaded, shoving her sister out of the other bathroom door and locking that one behind her as well. "Things are a little hectic here right now," she explained.

"I'll be home only long enough to pack a bag," Will said. "I'll try calling you sometime on the road. I'm taking the next flight to New York. There's an early flight out of Edinburgh, a later one out of London. Meanwhile, the weather's ferocious and getting worse. But the airlines are fairly intrepid. I'll get to Fair Castle—one way or another."

"I'll be waiting," she confessed.

"Just . . . be careful. I don't know what Tucker's up to; but obviously the stakes are high, or he wouldn't be acting like a maniac. I'd have the law at your door in the blink of an eye but I can't prove a damn thing!"

How ironic; Tucker was in the same boat.

"I'll be fine," she said, basking in his concern. "There are a whole bunch of us here, and only one of him. Tucker's a little obsessed, but I truly don't think he's a threat."

"How long does he plan to stay? Has he said? Can you ease him out without riling him?"

"I'm going to have my grandfather ask him to leave in the morning. In the meantime, at least the castle's fireproof," she quipped.

Will's anger was palpable. "Don't even joke about it!

If anything happened to you—my God, Elinor—just don't do anything to provoke him. Leave him to me. I'll be there."

"No, really, Will; you're overreacting. By the time you get here, he'll be long gone. Are you sure you even need to come?"

She meant it, of course, as his cue.

"*Yes*, I'm sure!" he said, sounding wonderfully amazed by the question. "I love you, Elinor. *I love you.* Very much."

Finally. "Ah, Will," she said, wildly elated and totally frustrated at the same time. "Why didn't you say so in the gazebo? I've been holding my breath since you left!"

"You can breathe easy, then, darling," he said, his voice dropping to a caress. "I wish to God I'd told you when I had you in my arms. I wish I'd—"

He laughed, sighed, and said, "This isn't the way I want to do it. I want to see your face. I want to kiss your mouth. I want—"

Her heart had just achieved liftoff when Will suddenly muffled the phone. She heard echoes of his voice, and echoes of someone else's voice. When Will came back to her, it was to murmur, "I'm being kicked out of the rectory, darling. The housekeeper wants to lock up. I'll call you again. Be careful. Please, please, be careful. I'm not a believer in intuition; but the thought of Tucker O'Toole in that castle is making my blood run cold."

Elinor, who *was* a believer in intuition, hardly had need for it now. Tucker O'Toole had made it very clear that Will was the target, not them.

In any case, the telephone sex was put on hold, so to speak. Will's good-bye was hurried and strained. But it was enough—for now—for Elinor to know that he loved her. She wrapped the three words around her the way she would a warm sweater on a cold day. She might not have come out of her blissful revery at all, if it weren't for Izzy's persistent tapping on the bathroom door.

By now Elinor was at the end of her patience with Izzy's nosiness. She opened the door. "*What.* What is your problem?"

"Did someone try to burn down Lady Norwood's *house?*"

Izzy's voice was high and shaky; her eyes were wide with shock. It occurred to Elinor, for the first time really, that something truly dangerous had occurred. She'd been both thrilled and distracted during Will's call; but now she was listening to his words through her sister's eyes.

She said more soothingly, "They don't know. It looks a little bit suspicious."

"*Tucker* did it?" her sister asked in a scandalized tone. "He was there?"

"Izzy, Izzy—have you ever noticed how you worry about everything? Even things that have nothing to do with you?"

Isabelle wasn't buying it. "But it does have something to do with me! He's in our *house!*"

"But our house is made of stone," Elinor said lightly.

"But the furniture could burn! We could burn! That's what you said when I lit the candle!"

Unbelievable. No matter which way Elinor stepped, it was into a cow-pie.

She chose her words with care. "It's very rude—not to mention, illegal—to accuse people of crimes without any evidence, Izzy. Listen to me. Tucker *is* going to be leaving." She made up a reason why. "Everyone will be house hunting starting tomorrow, and he can't just stay here alone. Chester was very nice to let Tucker go through the archives so thoroughly. But now Tucker's finished, and he'll be leaving. Tomorrow."

"Tonight! Make him leave *tonight,*" Isabelle begged.

"I'll tell you what," Elinor said, aware that Izzy knew enough to be a loose cannon at dinner. "If you promise to forget everything you heard—which was only bits and pieces anyhow—I'll see what I can do. But you have to leave this to me."

Isabelle nodded gravely, then crept closer to Elinor and wrapped her arms around her waist in a search for reassurance. "Before they came, everything was fine," she said in a mournful voice, leaning her head on Elinor's breast.

"They?"

"Lord Norwood and Tucker. They came at the same time. And Dad got hurt at the same time. It all happened at the same time."

"It did work out that way," said Elinor, hugging her sister and rocking her gently. She rubbed her chin on the top of Izzy's head. "But things will be getting better now. You'll see."

Mickey MacLeish was more than willing to throw the bum out.

"You want it, you got it, Elly. I'm in just the foul mood to enjoy it, too. Your mother's been hemming and hawing to the man for a week now, but he won't take the hint. Where is he?"

Elinor glanced around the library guiltily, then lowered her voice. "He must be in his room. I've looked everywhere else. His car's out front, so he can't have gone anywhere. I'm surprised he didn't show up for dinner."

"So'm I," Mickey grunted. He laid down his *New York Times* and hauled himself out of his chair. "He's never offered to buy a single goddamned quart of milk, you know that? Talk about ingrates. Oh, he started out all right, but lately . . . taking advantage of Chester that way . . . of all of us . . . smoking my best cigars . . . sitting around on his duff . . . never saw anything like it . . . when I was his age . . ."

And on he groused, never even asking why Elinor wanted Tucker out of the castle; he was just happy to be kicking a little duff. His mood was utterly black after spending the day being forced to look at brochures of retirement villages, and having to decide whether or not to build something new and dull where his old and exciting castle had been.

Elinor felt almost sorry for Tucker as she left her grandfather banging on the door of the little oratory.

The next call from Will came at six in the morning. He'd opted for the earlier flight from Edinburgh, and there he sat: The airport was shut down in high winds and driving rains. Worse, the delay would play havoc with his connecting flight out of Brussels. He was hopping with frustration.

"So much for the space age," he told her in a wry voice. "I should've just booked on a steamer. I should've just—I can't stand this," he burst out. "I can't stand being away from you like this. I want to be near you. To watch over you. This is maddening. This is infuriating. I want . . . I want . . . I don't know what I want. I want you with me. Always. Marry me. Elinor, marry me."

That woke her up.

She let out a surprised laugh, then sighed happily. "I . . . would . . . love to marry you, Will," she said, her eyes rimming with emotion. "You know that I love you."

"I'm so desperate for you. I'm sorry. It's on the phone. I know. The gazebo was the place. This isn't the place. This isn't the time. Marry me."

"I'll marry you."

"I mean it. Marry me."

"I mean it. I'll marry you."

His laugh was nervous, edgy, not yet ready to believe. He was plainly feeding off the noise and frustration of the crowd of grounded passengers around him. Elinor focused on his every rambling word, filing it away in her heart. Years from now, they would laugh about the phone-call proposal the way people laughed about weddings where the minister didn't show or the limo broke down. But for now, it was a moment of tender frustration for them both.

She closed her eyes and pictured him vividly, his hand clapped over one ear, his body turned away from the milling throngs and foreign chatter. He was so close—she could hear his breathing, sliding out in a series of sighs—and yet he was so far away.

He said, "I know this has been a whirlwind courtship—who'm I kidding? It hasn't been a courtship at all—but I also know that some men and women are meant for one another. I've read it more than once; I've never believed it. Not until now. I love you, Elinor . . . I'll always love you . . . I was incredibly blind not to see that. It's obvious that I *chose* not to see that. You were . . . a complication.

I didn't need any more complications. It was easier for me to just label you an enemy and try to roll over you. But now I see that without you, my life wouldn't be empty of complications—it'd be just plain empty. There's such a depressing difference. Am I babbling? I think I must be. But I want to be there, and I can't, and my heart is so damn full. . . ."

For once in her life, Elinor did not interrupt. She clung to his every word, every sigh, every smile. And when at last they hung up, she lay in bed, hugging her pillow, replaying the tape of her memory. Years from now, they would laugh.

But not today.

Eventually, Elinor, awake and curious, tiptoed down to the oratory to check on Tucker's progress. He was an early riser; he should be up and packing by now.

She was wrong; he'd already gone. She found the door to his chamber wide-open, the bed in a tumble, the four drawers agape. The floor was littered with unwanted research notes, the ashtray piled high with Twinkies wrappers. A can of Coke lay spilled on the nightstand. Everything about the room suggested sudden flight. Somehow she didn't think they'd be getting a bread-and-butter note from him.

The question was, did he leave in a rage or with something to hide?

He's found the marriage document was the first thought that went through her head. The second thought, hard on the heels of the first, was: *No way. He's been looking for weeks. Why now?*

She backed out of the room and made a beeline for the office off the great hall. If Tucker was fleeing the castle, he might be tempted to take a travel kitty with him, courtesy of the MacLeishes. He knew where they kept the cash from the tours; there'd never been a need to lock it up. Elinor was even more worried about checkbooks and credit card numbers, kept in the same desk.

But she never got as far as the office. In the great hall she nearly tripped over the heavy frame that once had surrounded the portrait of Elinor, Lady Norwood—or whoever she was. The frame was still intact, but the oiled canvas was slit on three of its sides, slumped over the bottom of the frame like a dead body.

Elinor crouched down and folded the portrait back gently. She stared at the coquettish smile and bright blue eyes beneath the outlandish hat. A medical examiner might have stared at a corpse in much the same way: with a dreadful mix of curiosity, excitement, and compassion.

Was the woman an innocent victim of centuries-old rumors? Assuming there was a secret marriage, had she known about it and then gone ahead and married Charles anyway? She might have been desperate. *She* might have been pregnant. No one could reasonably expect to know. If historians couldn't agree on what to say about kings and queens . . .

And then, at last, Elinor's intuition kicked in. *The marriage document.* It must have been hidden behind the portrait the whole time. Of *course.* It made perfect sense. The portrait had come over with the rest of the castle's furnishings and archives; it had been hung on the wall, perhaps by Mickey or Camilla, without a second thought. How ironic. How wickedly ironic. Someone had had a very warped sense of humor.

Who? Surely not the first, betrayed wife. How would she get access to the portrait, which must have been painted after the first wife's day in the sun had passed? Unless—unless the first wife were a friend of the family? A relative? A houseguest? A servant! She could've been a servant who'd so hypnotized Charles that he was willing—at least in front of a priest in a secret ceremony—to declare her his wife. Servants dusted portraits all the time.

As for the priest who'd agreed to bend his church's rules and marry them without announcing the banns: He had to be a relation of the probably pregnant woman. A kindly uncle, according to Tucker's legend, or a cousin. Why he'd permitted Charles to marry again without speaking out against it—that, too, they might never know. Maybe he died. Maybe he *was* killed. Maybe he just didn't care; it would be his niece that he wanted to save from damnation, not Charles.

What Elinor wouldn't give to know.

She jumped at a sound behind her. She turned to see her grandmother staring aghast at the mutilated portrait.

"Tucker must've done it before he took off," Elinor explained. She added quickly, "Don't worry; I'm sure we can remount it in a smaller frame."

"I've just come from his room," said Camilla, still in her terry cloth robe. She looked frail and frightened all over again. "If we had banished him last night, this never would've happened!"

She crouched down beside her granddaughter for a closer look at the oil painting. "Why would he do this, Elly? What's the matter with him?" Fear wavered in and out of her voice. "We let him live among us . . . he seemed like such a clean-cut boy . . . I've never been so wrong about someone in my life."

Elinor said cautiously, "It turns out that he's been looking for a document all this time—the equivalent of a marriage certificate. I think he found it, tucked between the portrait and the back covering piece."

"A marriage? Whose marriage?" asked Camilla.

Careful, Elinor told herself. Cow-pies everywhere.

"Even Tucker didn't know the whole answer to that," she said, keeping it vague.

"Was this for his book? It seems like a lot of trouble to go to for a book," Camilla said with some of her old wryness. "I mean, why didn't he just ask, for pity's sake?"

She was beginning to work herself into a fit of pique. "Really; was it necessary to be so dramatic? This is pure vandalism. Are all researchers this obsessed? What an unpleasant group they must be."

She got back to her feet with an effort and stared down at the painting, shaking her head. "We would've let him take down the painting and look behind it. All he had to do was ask."

Elinor couldn't resist saying, "But would you let him actually keep what he found?"

Her grandmother shrugged. "Why not? What do we need with more old papers?"

But Tucker wouldn't have known that. He'd had a last, desperate inspiration, and he'd acted on it. And now it was over, at least for the MacLeish clan.

God only knew what Tucker had in mind for Will.

"I confess it pleases me to see her thus: underfoot and in tatters."

"Do not waste eternity with thoughts of her. She was a hag, Marianne, a spiritual hag: dried up inside, and without the capacity to love. She had no soul."

"I know that. All she had was a willingness to steal. She took my husband, she took my name, she took some peasant's child and presented it as her own. Did she kill the mother? I'd not be surprised. Thief! Fraud! Neither mother nor wife! I wonder, still, how she lived with herself."

"She is done with! Think not of her, Marianne! Think rather of the boy, who is urgent now in his pursuit. He will be heedless; he will spill blood."

"He is a poor excuse for a man. I am grieved that there is no other to vindicate us."

"Tonight, my love. Vindication will come tonight. You and I, at last and forever, will declare our true love for one another."

Chapter 31

*T*he day progressed with no sign of Tucker—but no sign of Will, either.

"I'm still in freaking Amsterdam," he growled into the telephone.

He'd missed the Brussels connection and had flown instead to the Netherlands, where he was currently stuck at the gate and waiting out a mechanical delay. About the only good thing Elinor could say for the space age was that airports came equipped with phones for calling people you loved and telling them how stupid air travel was.

"I'm fine. Everyone's fine," she said, reassuring him. "By now Tucker's back in Ontario."

Planning, probably, to blackmail you. The idea popped up as unexpectedly as a jack-in-the-box. Elinor pushed it back down and snapped the lid tight over it. She would not let it taint the call. Money was Tucker's predictable motive. But Tucker was tomorrow's problem.

Will said in a soft, intimate voice, "How's your dragon coming?" He could hardly speak words of desire to her while he was fending off a line of travelers jockeying for his phone. But there was such love, such longing, such genuine interest in the question that Elinor got goose bumps anyway.

"Great! I worked all morning on it. Thank God I got the extra time. Suddenly everything just fell into place. He's turned out wonderful. I do love him," she said softly.

They talked for a bit about the book. The last thing

Will said before he hung up was, "I think it's fantastic that you can work on your career anywhere."

Which naturally started Elinor wondering. If he'd had more time, she would've asked him the question that had been on her mind ever since his proposal: *Once we're married, where exactly are we going to pitch our tent?*

She would not be asking the question lightly. The castle was going to England, she knew. But she wasn't prepared to abandon her own country—much less abandon her family—for England. It was her deepest prayer that Will would understand that.

In the meantime, her parents and grandparents were house shopping, and Elinor and Izzy had the castle to themselves for the afternoon. They played Scrabble, they watched Oprah, they made S'mores for an early supper and then had pizza delivered for dessert. They had stomach aches at the exact same time. It was almost like the good old days.

Almost.

Maybe it was because Elinor felt so close to Will; but his words of warning seemed to hover everywhere in the air around her. She heard them in the somber tick and tock of the tall-case clock: *Be-e careful. Be-e careful.* She heard them in the nervous ticking of the Viennese picture clock: *careful careful careful.* The mantel clock, the calendar clock, the elephant clock—every clock in Chester's eccentric collection echoed the same dismal warning: *careful!*

It was oppressing, and Elinor wanted to feel joy. Damn it! She was in love.

The trick was to erase the memory of Tucker. It was easy to do in the room from which he'd fled. The oratory was small and easily put right. But the archives room, with its boxes and boxes of acquisitions, was now an unholy mess. And the space on the wall where the portrait had hung seemed shockingly bare; Elinor had to avert her gaze every time she passed through the great hall.

The sun sank fast, which made things worse. A long June night was called for; but all they had to work with was a late October one. True to the season, it began to rain. Elinor heard its steady, dreary drumbeat on the copper roof of the mud shed as she cleaned up the mess from making S'mores.

Things will be better once everyone's back from dinner, Elinor told herself. And in the meantime, she tried to keep the conversation cheerfully silly for Izzy's sake.

When the telephone rang, Elinor was decidedly relieved; the quiet had become unnerving.

"Gerald Furness here," a flat voice intoned over a television blaring in the background. "I was there on Sunday—the claims adjustor handling the dumbwaiter incident."

Incident? Not accident? "Oh, yes, Mr. Furness. This is Elinor MacLeish, Susan Roberts's daughter." She explained that her mother was away for the evening.

He got straight to the point. "Our examination shows that the replacement cord for the dumbwaiter was the correct diameter for the clutch system."

"Really." Everyone had assumed that Agnes's inept son had screwed up when he replaced the fraying cord. "What *did* cause the dumbwaiter to drop, in that case?"

"The clutch itself seems to have been tampered with."

"Oh, but that's not possible!" she blurted. The words were barely out of her mouth when she realized that it was all too possible.

He ignored her predictable protest. "Because of the tampering, there will be further investigation. I'll need to speak to Mrs. Roberts about that."

He added, "I'll also need to speak with a Tucker O'Toole and a William Braddock. Is either one of 'em back yet? I've left several messages to please have them call." He meant please the way the IRS means please.

"Mr. O'Toole's come and gone, I'm afraid permanently. I can give you his home address." She said it without enthusiasm; undoubtedly it was a fictional one. "As for Mr. Braddock, he should be back very late tonight."

"Have him call me tomorrow morning. Please."

Susan Roberts did not take kindly to the news of tampering. Her high cheekbones became cherry red with emotion, her voice tightened with fury when she heard the news from Elinor.

"Are you telling me that that lowlife actually sabotaged the dumbwaiter? That he put an innocent tourist in danger so that we wouldn't sell the *castle?* Because he needed a little more time to search for that marriage paper? Are you *serious?*"

Chester, for some odd reason, was anxious to be fair. "I doubt that he thought a tourist would use the dumbwaiter, Sue."

Susan rounded on her husband and said, "Oh, *well,* that makes it better, then. He intended one of *us* to be killed."

"You have to admit, it would slow down a sale, dear," said Camilla wryly.

"That outrageous man! He *knew* we used the dumbwaiter shaft to talk between floors. If I could, I'd throw him down the shaft myself! How could he! To hurt a sweet, innocent person like . . . it could have been Izzy! My God!"

In the meantime, Mickey MacLeish was pursuing another line of thought altogether. "How do we know," he said quietly, "that it was Tucker O'Toole?"

Everyone turned to him. His wife was the first to speak. In a voice as still as his own, Camilla said, "Whom did you have in mind, dear?"

The artist, who'd been leaning back on the sideboard, put down his nightcap and folded his arms across his chest, the way he did when he was studying one of his works in progress.

"Not so much *who,*" he said, "as *what.*"

Camilla's face went pale. "Mickey! Don't! Please—I can't go through this again."

Mickey turned to his granddaughter. "Elly, did the claims adjustor say how, exactly, the clutch was tampered with?"

Elinor shook her head. "He was very brief. He was really just putting us on notice."

"And all because of that horrible man," said Susan, more fretful than angry now. "He's gone off and left us with his mess to clean up. There's bound to be litigation, and we don't even know where he lives!''

Chester said mildly, "Could William have done it?"

It was a bucket of cold water in Elinor's face. "That's outrageous!" she cried.

Her stepfather said doggedly, "Well, we *don't* know it was Tucker."

Elinor's mother rallied to her side. "For God's sake, Chester—think about it! A peer of the realm versus someone from the Canadian backwoods? You're blinded by your bias. You were so thrilled that someone cared about those boxes of dusty archives—"

"*I'm* blinded! What about you? Wave a title in front of you and—"

"What's wrong with Canadians?" asked Izzy, who'd somehow managed to sneak back into the room after being banished twice. "I have a pen pal in Manitoba. She's really nice."

"I am only throwing this out for discussion," Chester persisted. "I'm only trying to say, we don't really know it was Tucker."

"Who do you think knifed the portrait and stole the document?" asked his wife, astounded by his refusal to back down.

"We don't know that he stole a document. That's Elinor's idea."

"Why else would he rip the canvas?" Elinor argued.

"Maybe there was nothing there—"

"Or maybe Grampa Mick really got Tucker mad last night and he wanted to show us!"

"Oh, God . . . what if it *was* another manifestation—?"

"All right, that's *enough!*"

Mickey MacLeish had grabbed the reins of their runaway buckboard and yanked hard, slowing them all to a halt. He waited a moment for everyone to catch his breath, then said calmly, "Isabelle, go to your room. This conversation is not for children.

"As for the rest of us," he said, monitoring his reluctant granddaughter's exit, "let's review what we *do* know. We do know there have been a series of unexplainable events.

The first of them—the *only* one of them, up until now—
occurred, according to Milly, over fifty years ago. Since
then, the castle has more or less been quiet. We've always
felt a profound sense of its history; of the many lives that
were lived here. We consider that sense to be merely the
castle's aura. Are we agreed so far?"

Everyone nodded.

"And then suddenly we were set upon by a burst of
phenomena: Izzy's sighting of something shimmery in the
chapel . . . the lighted candles there . . . the sensations of
extraordinary cold both in the chapel and on the gallery
. . . and the episode of the hot string. . . . Have I forgotten
anything?"

Elinor raised her hand. "The executioner sword falling
on Chester."

"That was because of the power outage!" her mother
snapped.

Mickey MacLeish gave his middle-aged daughter a verbal rap on the knuckles. "Sue! We're keeping open minds
about this! The falling sword may have been an accident,
but it was part of the series of unusual events. The dumbwaiter 'incident,' obviously, was another. And the torn
painting. Anything else?"

All were silent.

"All right," said Mickey. "The next question is: Is there
a common denominator in all of these occurrences?"

Chester said, "The last three things, and the lit candles,
can be explained rationally." Which didn't answer the
question.

Elinor murmured, "Tucker was here for all of them."
Which did answer the question.

"But Tucker couldn't have caused the shimmery thing
that Izzy saw," her stepfather said.

"And Tucker couldn't have made the string feel hot—
or the chapel feel cold," her mother admitted.

Her grandmother added, "And technically he wasn't on
the premises when the sword fell—though he'd been here
earlier that day."

Someone sighed, followed by someone else's sigh. No
one seemed inclined, or able, to solve the mystery.

"What it means," Mickey MacLeish said after he downed the last of his brandy and put it aside, "is that Tucker has friends in very high places."

"Oh, don't, Mickey," said his wife, blanching. "Don't *you* believe in them."

"Why not, Milly?" he asked, surprised. "You've been tryin' to convince me for fifty years."

"Only when I thought she was—"

"Nice, Mill? They aren't usually nice. *Casper* is nice."

Elinor stared openmouthed at her grandparents. Their conversation was entirely surreal. She'd been doing her best to put all thoughts of the supernatural aside—she was in love; it wasn't so hard to do—but now they were being dragged back and propped up before her.

"Good Lord," said Chester in a low, incredulous voice. "What are we going to do?"

"We're going to sell the castle and let it be someone else's problem," said Susan sharply.

Chester had another thought. "If Tucker's gone, does it mean he's taken it—her—them—with him?"

"I suppose it depends on where the connection lies," his father-in-law mused. "Is the, ah, entity connected to him—or to the castle?"

Camilla said bleakly, "Tucker wasn't born when I saw her in the chapel."

Mickey said, "Okay. The connection is to the castle, then."

No one wanted to hear it.

After a depressing interval of silence, Chester said, "What is it about Tucker that brought her forward again after all these years?"

Camilla sighed and shook her head. "I haven't got a clue."

But Elinor had a clue. What no one seemed to have noticed was that the occurrences started when Tucker and *Will* were thrown in the castle together. Izzy, unwittingly, had figured it out first. The magic combination of ingredients that had precipitated the string of events began on the day *both* men arrived.

As for the entity itself, Elinor had a pretty good idea

now of who it was. But if she explained her theory to her family, it would start the Norwood ball unraveling. She owed it to Will to wait for him and tell him first.

Only a few more hours.

"Well, I'm going to bed," Susan said. "We can't just sleep in shifts until the sale actually closes. If things get too weird, we'll move temporarily into something furnished. I assume that with Tucker gone, things will finally settle down."

She sounded very brave and businesslike until she added, "Are you coming to bed, Chester?" The question had a frightened, pleading quality that made itself felt in the room.

Chester, clearly feeling protective, said with gruff nonchalance, "Maybe I will. I've been meaning to catch up on my reading."

He put his arm around his wife and off they went, followed by Elinor's tired grandparents. Elinor sat alone for a long time, absorbing the sounds and smells of the only home she'd ever known. The rain was still falling, quiet and steady, saturating the air around her, calling forth the faintest echoes of mildew. She'd always liked the smell of the castle on a rainy day—that slightly musty scent of antiquity—but tonight she smelled only decay.

Had the castle turned on her, she wondered? Or worse—had she turned on *it*? Would Will expect her to live in Fair Castle after he moved it back to England? She didn't even know. And she was no longer sure she could.

She curled up on the sofa, dragging an afghan over her to ward off the chill. Eventually she fell asleep to the manic ticking of the clock on the mantel: *careful careful careful careful.*

Chapter 32

"*E*lly. Elly, wake up!"

Elinor charged from the sofa half-asleep but ready for battle, only to find that her sister was holding her back by the skirt.

"Shh-shh," Izzy warned in a hush. The child turned off the dim lamp by the sofa, plunging them both into darkness.

"What's going on?" Elinor whispered over a pounding heart. It wasn't that Will had arrived; that was obvious.

Izzy cupped her mouth to Elinor's ear and whispered, "I came down to ask you to come sleep with me because I was scared. And then when I went past the chapel, I could tell there's candles lit again." Elinor felt her sister's thin body shudder as she added in the same desperate whisper, "Somebody's in there."

Elinor slipped an arm around her and whispered back, "Okay. Don't worry. We'll just call the police."

She got up and groped her way cautiously to the phone next to one of the armchairs opposite. She lifted it up. The unlighted numbers on the handpiece told her what the lack of a dial tone merely confirmed: The phone was dead. It had happened before in wet weather; she wished with all her heart that this was one of those times.

She went back to her sister's side and whispered into her ear, "I have a better idea. You stay here. I'll go see. Be real quiet. Don't wake anyone up and scare them for nothing. Okay?"

A shadowy nod from Isabelle: The child no longer trusted her voice. Elinor said unnecessarily, "Shh," and then she began the torturous tiptoe past the careful-careful clock and out of the great parlor toward the chapel.

Izzy was right. A dull golden glow emanated from the chapel onto the slate floor of the hall where Elinor made her way cautiously, sidling close to the wall. She felt melodramatic; she felt foolish; but she kept close to the wall.

There was no doubt in her mind that she was going to find Tucker in the chapel, doing something bizarre. The question was, would he turn dangerous if she demanded to know which bizarre thing he was doing? She paused outside the entrance, utterly unwilling to look within, utterly unable to walk away and alert the household.

She took a long, deep breath, as if she were getting ready to dive into the sea and explore a cave there, and then turned decisively into the chapel, pausing under the arched doorway before a scene more strange that any she could have imagined: Tucker O'Toole was on all fours in the main aisle, pawing the end of a pew.

All around him, the chapel was ablaze with light. Every candle was burning. The deco angel lamp was turned on. Even the flashlight that lay on the floor was turned on, its bright beam shining in her direction like a runway light, guiding her forward.

Elinor took several steps, despite an overwhelming sense of dread that tried to pin her to the spot. Amazingly, Tucker seemed unaware of her. He was—she didn't know what he was doing—stroking the ornate carving of the pew ends with his right hand, it looked like.

Shadows danced and music played. Music! Where was it coming from? Behind her, alongside her, above her—heartbreakingly tender music, all of it nudging her forward, despite her desire to hang back and run. A flute, a recorder—some wind instrument, anyway—tugged hard at her spirit, calling up a sense of holiness from deep, deep within her. Her eyes glazed over with tears; through the watery veil the dozen candles became three dozen, sending a kaleidoscope of candle flames shifting and twinkling below the jeweled hues of the stained-glass window.

The haunting notes settled into a pattern of melody, and Elinor knew, with the inbred certainty of a woman, that she was there to witness a wedding.

She focused her blurred vision where the bride and groom should be, and she was not disappointed. Between the two front pews a silvery, incandescent shimmer wavered and struggled to find shape and at last succeeded. The large mass of emanating light seemed to break into two distinct columns: a taller form, but not very tall, and a lesser, more free-flowing form. And yet the evanescence held fast at its center, as if the forms were holding hands.

The haunting notes became more faint. Elinor strained through her tears to impose a distinctness on the columns, because she knew that when the music ended, the vision would, too. The taller form remained featureless, but the smaller form seemed to resolve into a flow of red hair encircled with a crown or a wreath, and a long gown suggesting azure more than any other color. Elinor caught her breath at the sheer loveliness of the vision.

The melody—surely a hymn, though she did not recognize it—lifted to a piercingly tender plane and then began to modulate, and she knew her fleeting glimpse of eternity was about to end. It was so painfully beautiful, so achingly romantic, that she whispered, "No . . . please," imploring that it remain for just a little while longer. Until she could see . . . until she could understand . . .

But it was not to be. Tucker O'Toole broke free from his trance and, turning his head sharply toward Elinor, let out a snarl that scarcely seemed human.

And with it, the vision wavered and faded away—Elinor knew, forever.

"Between the pews," she said, devastated. "Oh, Tucker, between the front pews! Didn't you *see*—?"

"The *front* pews! But I looked!" he said in a croak.

He scrambled to his feet and made a wild dash to the back of the chapel instead of to the front. Elinor let out a cry, fearing an attack, but he was after the flashlight, not her. He snatched it up, raced back to the two front

pews, and began shining the light on the end carving of
the left pew.

That he was insane, Elinor had no doubt; but he
seemed to have forgotten all about her again, so she
watched, mesmerized, to see what he would find.

Nothing. He swore and, still on his knees, shifted to
face the end of the pew on the right. At the top of the
long bench, where the backrest ended in a graceful scroll,
he shined his light, examining it with fierce attention.

"Yes," he said at last; it came out in a serpentine hiss.
He threw down the flashlight and took out a Bowie knife,
then opened the blade and began poking at the carved
wood with it.

Elinor heard the click from where she stood. Some
mechanism behind the decorative carving obviously
sprang open; Tucker was able to swing one of the carved
floral elements up and away, revealing what must have
been a chamber inside the pew. He probed the compart-
ment with his middle finger with no luck. Again he swore,
then took up first his flashlight, then the knife, and felt
around with its tip while he shined a light on the secret
nook.

She saw his body go rigid and knew that he'd found
something. With infinite, tender care, he used the tip of
the knife to drag something from the unreachable depth
of its hiding place. When it was nearly out, he stuck his
finger in the hole again to ease it the rest of the way, then
caught what she could now see was a rolled parchment
between his thumb and index finger.

Still kneeling, he shifted his weight to his calves and
spread the scrolled paper on his thigh, holding it open
awkwardly with his right forearm as he read it by the
beam of his flashlight. In the lurid halo of light she saw
his face: grotesque, crazed, and triumphant.

Tucker had his document at last—and Elinor was
standing between him and the exit.

She took a step backward but bumped into something
soft and human. She cried out.

Izzy cried out.

"What are you *doing* here?" Elinor said in horror to her impetuous sister.

"I wanted . . . I wanted . . ." Izzy's breath came shallow and fast; she was thoroughly petrified.

Her gaze was focused behind Elinor, who turned in time to see Tucker making a lunge for them both. Izzy let out a squeal and took off between two of the back pews instead of heading for the door. Elinor, appalled that her sister went the wrong way, simply stood there, an easy prey for Tucker. He grabbed her arm and twisted it roughly behind her, sending a stab of pain through her shoulder so fierce that she lashed out automatically and kicked him hard in the shins.

It was enough to surprise him into loosing his hold on her. She wrenched herself free; he grabbed at her again, catching her sweater. It stretched like a bungee cord before she broke away a second time and raced for the front of the chapel where Izzy had taken refuge. Why she ran there, she had no idea; now there were two of them trapped.

He's not going to hurt us, she told herself. *He's a scholar. Scholars don't kill.*

But then he picked up the dropped knife that lay at his feet, and she thought about changing her mind.

He stood there, hulked over his weapon, flashing it nervously in his hand.

There's no way, Elinor decided, *no way that he's going to use that knife.* Her heart was roaring in her breast; but her head kept telling her that Tucker was a scholar.

"Tucker, what are you doing?" she asked in as soothing a voice as she could muster. "This is all so unnecessary. You have the wedding document now. That's all you wanted. And . . . and who did the bride end up being, by the way?"

He laughed harshly. "You'll appreciate this: She was the daughter of the artist who painted the bitch's portrait."

"Really! You recognize the name?"

"Marian Bankes. She's buried behind St. Anthony's Church in Dibble."

"And the priest?"

"Her uncle."

"She was pregnant, of course," Elinor said. "So you were right."

"About everything."

"Except the document being hidden behind the portrait of Elinor."

He snorted. "I never thought it was there."

"But you ripped open the canvas—"

"I was cutting it out to take it with me as a souvenir; but I heard someone coming and had to take off."

So. Wrong again. Her instincts were about as sharp as a volleyball.

Still, she was convinced that if she engaged Tucker in a dialogue, she could defeat him. Somehow. "You lit the candles that terrorized my grandmother, didn't you?" she asked, drawing him on.

His smirk was repulsive. "Just one, at first—I was trying to recreate the scene of the kid's so-called sighting. Mickey had already regaled me with the story of Camilla's encounter when she was a newlywed here. So I thought maybe there was something to it all. I wasn't taking into account your overactive imaginations."

He had a laugh over his own susceptibility. "Anyway, the experiment was a big yawn. So I lit the rest of the candles, for the simple reason that I needed more light to see the carving on the pews. I was kneeling in the outside aisle, looking them over, when Camilla came in, took one look at all the lighted candles, and let out a blood-curdling scream."

He shook his head. "What a pathetic bunch you are. Anyway, it was simple enough to crawl to the back of the chapel and come up behind her as if I'd just arrived."

"So you've never seen anything. Not even now."

"Now? Now I'm all set," he said with mad cheer, waving his proof in the air. "Although, I have to say, I burned out a parlor for nothing."

Elinor slipped her arm around Izzy, quietly easing her sister behind her.

"And the dumbwaiter?"

He hesitated, then said, "That was another mistake."

His admission gave Elinor hope. He had a conscience, after all. "What made you decide the document was in the chapel?" she asked.

He grinned. "Ah, you think your ghosts led me here. Sorry, El. Logic led me here. The pews came over with the castle. I'd already examined every other stick of furniture in the original inventory. And you know as well as I do that it wasn't in the archives. I just decided to examine the pews one last time. I'm surprised Chester didn't think to look for hidden compartments. He's supposed to be the antiques expert."

He laughed harshly and said again, "It was *not* your ghosts."

Elinor didn't believe him. Obviously he had realized that there was a lot of unexplained energy in the chapel. Which of course had been the whole point of the apparitions—to lead someone to the proof.

But what did it matter whether he was willing to admit it or not? Here they all were.

"So what's next?" she ventured. "Blackmailing Will?"

The question caught Tucker off guard. He said sharply, "What the hell for?"

Elinor felt her sister cringe behind her. She backed down quickly and said, "I'm sorry; I thought that's what this was about."

Could it really be about Tucker's dumb *book?*

He seemed to be mulling an answer. Elinor thought she saw something, a shadow of movement, in the hall behind him. She watched without seeming to watch.

Tucker said thoughtfully, "I think I have enough now to have the body exhumed."

Elinor stiffened. If she'd had any doubts about him, they were gone now.

"M-Marian's body?" she asked. More shadows in the hall.

"Of course. And Charles's. DNA testing will prove that Will is not related to either of them."

"Can . . . they do that? After centuries?"

He ignored her. "God only knows whose loins he

dropped out of. Not from the bitch Elinor; her hatred of men is well documented."

Someone was getting ready to jump Tucker from behind; she had to be ready to help.

"A pity those Norwoods never did their homework," he mused. "Didn't they ever see *Roots*? Well, I did," he said, waving his parchment again. "Out with the old, in with the older. *I'm* the legal descendant to Fair Castle. The DNA will prove that, too."

She riveted her attention back on Tucker. *"You!"*

"Are you even *listening*? Never mind the stories that I grew up with; now I have legal proof!" he said, angrily rattling the parchment. "If the Indians can claim the Black Hills of Dakota, I sure as hell can claim the estate in Dibble."

To soothe him, she agreed wholeheartedly. "There does seem to be precedent—"

Suddenly from the darkness of the hall burst two aging heroes: Chester Roberts and Mickey MacLeish. Her stepfather pounced with his healthy arm around Tucker's neck and her grandfather dropped to his knees and wrapped his gangly arms around Tucker's legs.

They didn't know he had a knife.

Tucker turned and lashed out at Chester with it, slicing at his face, then turned in the next heartbeat to Mickey and drove the knife into his biceps. The first man staggered, grabbing his bleeding cheek, the other one dropped and rolled on his side.

Elinor, horrified by the carnage, bolted forward with no real plan except to get in the way of the knife, while Izzy ran off to one side.

Her mother rushed in, her grandmother, too, to tend to their fallen protectors. The chapel was overflowing with MacLeishes; but Tucker O'Toole had the knife.

He was so clearly willing to use it. Elinor saw the flash of bright steel, then felt hot rips across her forearm and the top of her right hand. She stared at her arm, dumbfounded by the flimsiness of her flesh, and when she looked up again, Tucker had Izzy.

Chapter 33

*E*veryone froze.

Tucker's hand was over Izzy's mouth, the bloody knife flat against her throat. Izzy's eyes were huge.

Elinor whispered, "Tucker, don't—don't touch her. Please. Don't cut her." Elinor's chest was heaving, her brain in shock, her breath coming out in long, ragged strokes.

Careful careful careful.

"Take the paper. Take whatever you want. No one will say anything. Take it all. No one will say anything."

Careful careful careful.

"What you've done ... it could be worse ... you can still get away ... only leave us ... leave her ... please."

Careful careful careful.

Tucker's breath was deeper and more ragged than her own as he yanked Izzy another inch closer to his chest, the knife a fraction closer to her throat. Every time he took a breath, he thrust her skinny body closer to the knife.

This was it, the end of the dream; no matter how it turned out, the end of the dream.

Without a word, Tucker began to edge away from the immobilized group, sliding Izzy along with him in a clumsy *pas de deux*.

Isabella, ballerina: his hostage.

He was in the hall now, about to writhe out of their sight. Elinor couldn't bear to let that happen and neither could the others. If they followed him, what?

Careful careful careful.

"Hey, Tuck. She's small fry. Your quarrel's with me."

Will. Somewhere in the hall. The dragon was in the hall, sounding friendly and reassuring.

She watched Tucker's face contort into a twist of pure hate. *"Out of my way, bastard!"*

Will's voice again: "I'm unarmed. Come on. Chance of a lifetime. Look. I'll make it easy for you. I'll sit on this chair. How's that? Hey, I can't handicap the game more than that. Oh, all right. Want me to close my eyes? I'll close my eyes."

His voice was soothing, mesmerizing, and utterly dangerous. Something in it drew Tucker like a heat-seeking missile. He hurled Izzy aside and lunged out of Elinor's view. Izzy staggered into the chapel and into her mother's arms. Susan grabbed her weeping child and held her tight, leaving Camilla to comfort the wounded soldiers.

Elinor hopped over and around them to get to the hall. The men were locked in combat there; Will had his hand wrapped around Tucker's wrist, the knife in Tucker's hand poised above them both. Will slammed Tucker's arm once, twice, into the wall. The knife fell and Elinor snatched it up, dropping it into the bowels of an earthen vase that sat in the hall.

A fair fight, now. Something in her was gratified to see it. Something in her—primitive, warriorlike—rose up over her shocked sensibility to cheer Will on. The men lunged, staggered, grappled, then fell away. They locked arms again, struggling for supremacy, backing into Chester's poor knight in armor, sending it sprawling in pieces across the floor for the second time during its short stay in the castle.

They were in the main part of the great hall now. The arched door to the outside was ajar; Elinor ran to close it, then threw the bolts at top and bottom. Tucker would not get away, not if she could help it. She stood loyally by, watching the fight through half-shut eyes, wincing with every blow, dreading their pain, ignoring her own, but never doubting that Will would be victorious.

But Tucker surprised her. He landed two hard punches

that sent Will reeling. He ran for the door, ready to flee, but got tripped up by the odd ancient bolts. Will came back after him, still unsteady, and Tucker broke free, then sprinted toward the stone stairs that wound up through the castle's center.

They fought their way up step by step, sometimes engaging, sometimes split apart, but always moving relentlessly upward. On the second floor, Tucker split off and ran to the single door that led to the gallery—the same gallery where Tucker had surprised her with a kiss and from which she had been banished by Will. Tucker fled outside, obviously hoping to make his way down the wall of the castle to his car. Thick vines of ivy clung to the stone; it would work.

With her stepfather now alongside, Elinor dogged their heels, unwilling to let Will from her sight.

The rain had let up to a thin drizzle, leaving everything wet, cold, and slick. Wet, slippery leaves, the last of the year, covered the gallery deck, making their footing unsure. From inside, the dim wall sconces threw halfhearted light over the sight of Will pulling Tucker back from the balustrade onto which he was trying to climb. Both men were clearly exhausted, weaving in place like two drunks.

Give up, Tucker! she wanted to scream. *Can't you see it's not his fault?*

Once again Tucker caught Will off guard, kneeing him in the groin with a vicious thrust. Will buckled and Tucker threw one leg over the balustrade. His parting shot to Will—"This isn't over, asshole!"—came out in a low growl, and then he was over the side.

Still in pain, Will staggered to the stone rail and sprawled over it, in relentless pursuit. Elinor and Chester ran to the balustrade and peered over. It wasn't impossibly high; Tucker scambled down and then dropped to the ground from five feet up, landing on his feet with a grunt. By the glow of a garden lantern, they watched as he made a final bolt for the parking lot and his waiting car.

But fate had other ideas. Tucker slipped—as Elinor herself had often done—on some wet, unraked leaves and lost his footing. He fell, quite hard, against one of Camilla's stone flowerpots, catching his head on the rim and rolling onto his back where he lay still. Will, catching up to him in a few long strides, dropped to his knees beside him.

The last thing Elinor saw before she ran back into the house and down the stairs to the outside was the sight of Will bending over his adversary to give him CPR.

"He was his own worst enemy," said Camilla MacLeish as she picked up her husband's beret from the ground alongside the car, then handed it to him before climbing into the backseat with him.

Mickey MacLeish whacked the beret on his thigh to clear off the dust and settled the cap on his head with his good right arm. He did it awkwardly; he was left-handed.

"Here's what *I* want to know," he said, frowning. "How in hell—"

"Mickey!" she admonished. "Some respect!"

"—heck did he think he was going to go back to Dibble and claim a birthright from that long ago? He might as well have tried to claim the Roman Coliseum."

Chester pulled down the mirrored visor on the passenger side and contorted his mouth as if he were going to shave his right cheek, testing his flesh again now that the stitches were out. He grimaced at the deep pink scar and flipped the visor back up, shutting out his image. "Definitely going to grow back the beard," he muttered to no one in particular.

Susan checked the rear-view mirror to see that her daughters were in the truck, then put the Escort in gear, leading the two-car motorcade at a dignified speed from the memorial chapel tucked in the mournful heart of the Peace Dale Cemetery.

"Suppose he *had* got someone to take his case to court," she said. "He couldn't have won. The castle's here, the rest of the estate's there . . . Will bought most of the land back—and certainly is buying the castle—with his own money, not inherited wealth . . . the courts would take forever . . . and then, too, where would he sue? Ontario? New York? England? As for digging up *bodies*—I don't think so," she finished with a shudder.

Mickey MacLeish let out a petulant snort and said, "Speaking of which, it was a really lousy Halloween this year."

"We had our Fright Night a little early, that's all," Camilla said in her dry way.

Chester shook his head. "Too bad. He was a bright kid. Lots of enthusiasm."

His wife sighed and said, "Only you, darling."

"Isn't it odd that none of his relations knew what he was up to?" said Camilla, musing aloud. "Twelve years on a genealogical hunt, and no one had a clue."

"He lived in his own little world."

"And all because of an innocent high-school assignment to make a family tree," said Chester, leaning back on the headrest.

Susan said, "Who can tell what sparks an obsession? At least it wasn't some poor woman."

"True."

They were silent for a few moments as they wound their way through a valley of bony trees and shrubs, and evergreens that had come into a season of their own. A homeowner with a wide, cleared lot was burning twigs and brush; the smoke lifted heavenward, unbothered by wind.

"It was a very nice service," said Camilla. "I'm glad Elinor thought of it. It gives us closure. It lets us put it behind us."

"She's a good kid, our Elly," said Chester with a loving stepfather's pride. "She'll make him a good wife. Of course, I *was* beginning to wonder," he added.

"She can be headstrong," Elinor's mother agreed.

"And impatient."

"Much too emotional."

"And she's too damn fond of yellow in her work," her grandfather said.

Off in a thought of his own, Chester eventually chuckled and said, "He'll be able to handle her."

"She'll be able to handle *him*," said his wife with a sideways look.

She changed the subject. "Agnes has a marvelous buffet planned for later. How wonderful she's been."

"It helps that Will doubled her salary," said Camilla wryly. "Do you suppose we should offer to pay the increase ourselves? We have the money to do it."

"Hell, no!" her husband said. He added more seriously, "The important thing now is to make Lady Norwood feel welcome for her visit. There will be memories—painful ones—for her when she sees the castle again."

"Same as us," said Chester.

"But they're surely outnumbered by positive ones, or she wouldn't be so anxious to spend the next two weeks there," Camilla said.

"Same as us," said Chester.

Mickey MacLeish stared out the window of the car and said, "I think she knows she won't be around by the time the castle's reconstructed in Dibble."

"Mickey! Don't talk that way!"

The artist turned to his wife. "Ah, Mill—we *have* to be able to talk that way. Who knows how long each of us is going to be around? Nobody. I don't care who you are. And the sooner we admit it, the sooner we can begin living the . . . the best possible life . . . the sooner we can take the time to stop, and look around, and maybe say I love you? To the ones—"

His voice broke a little and trailed off. He lifted his good arm around his wife's shoulders and bent his silver-haired head next to hers. "I love you, Camilla MacLeish," he murmured in his rich baritone. "It does seem like yesterday that I said so for the first time."

Camilla inclined her head toward his with poignant grace. Her lip trembled and her eyes glazed over with tears. "Me, too, Mick," she whispered. "Me, too."

Chester sighed and reached over for his wife's hand, squeezing it gently, and Susan smiled and squeezed his hand back.

*   *   *

At two o'clock precisely, Will and his grandmother pulled up in front of the arched door of Fair Castle.

Izzy stuck one last piece of tape on the "Fair Castle Welcomes Lady Norwood" banner that hung above the hearth in the great hall, then ran to the window to peek while the rest of her family gathered in welcome on the other side of the arched door.

Izzy gave them a blow-by-blow report. "Lord Norwood is opening her door . . . helping her out of the car . . . she has a cane . . . and a blue coat . . . and a blue hat . . . her hair is short and white . . . she's looking up at the castle . . . smiling . . . dabbing her eye with her glove . . . shouldn't we open the door?"

"Not yet," said Izzy's mother. "Let her take in the castle without us distracting her."

"She's pointing to your pots of mums, Gramma Cam. She likes them. I can tell."

Camilla smiled. "Well, good. I'm fond of her already."

"They're coming up the walk, Mom!" said the child excitedly. "Can I open the door yet?"

"Yes, Isabelle. Now you may."

With great ceremony Izzy swung open the heavy door and peeked around it. She fluttered her hand in shy greeting, then stepped back, letting the grown-ups do the rest of the work. Camilla and Susan stepped forward, crowded behind by their husbands. And behind them, suddenly as shy as her much younger sister, waited Elinor.

She hadn't seen Will in two weeks. During that time, not a word had passed between them about either love or marriage. It was Elinor's idea, and at the time it had seemed like a good one.

"I pushed you into it," she'd told him. "I was impatient and impulsive and all those things you accuse me of being. And then when Tucker became a threat to us all, you felt even more urgency. I don't want that, Will. I truly don't. Let's put it all on hold for now."

And he did. Which amazed and disappointed her. If he'd really been in love with her . . .

Her heart was pounding in apprehension as she waited to be introduced to Lady Norwood. If Will had been serious about marriage, clearly his grandmother would know it. And if she knew it, Elinor would know she knew it.

Will looked up just as burly Chester stepped out from in front of her, murmuring, "Sorry, I'm hoggin' the stage here."

"Elinor."

"Hello, Will."

Looking for reassurance, she stared into those slate blue eyes of his. But all he gave her was one quick glance—as if he were double-checking his decision—before he presented her, with great formality, to the baroness.

Faltering, Elinor stammered a welcome. With downcast eyes she said, "I-I'm very pleased to meet you, my lady."

If she was feeling downstairs to Lady Norwood's upstairs, it certainly wasn't the fault of the baroness. The elderly noblewoman was as gracious as could be. "Elinor! How delighted I am to meet you at last. My grandson has shown me your children's books, and they are enchanting."

Elinor made herself look into Lady Norwood's eyes. She found friendliness there, and enthusiasm for her books—but she didn't see hugs there, or good wishes. Feeling less confident than ever, she stepped back, all but bobbing her head in a curtsy.

No one else shared her awkwardness, that was obvious. Mickey MacLeish, erstwhile lord of the manor, was prepared to hand over the castle with grace and dignity, and so was his wife. Susan, Chester, even Izzy—all were curious and friendly and filled with good will for the frail, charming woman who'd raised Will practically from scratch.

Elinor watched as her family did their thing; but she felt as out of place as a martian at a cotillion.

In any case, the last and final tour was underway, so Elinor made some excuse about seeing to the table and then fled upstairs and didn't stop until she got to the turret.

The turret was the safest place to be. Lady Norwood

was not about to climb through the attic with her cane to view a river she had no wish to see. Elinor needed the space and wanted the time to compose herself.

Was her godawful theory actually right? Had Will felt pressured to match her emotions, and was he thanking his lucky stars that she'd let him off? She found her breath coming in panicky gasps as she stared without seeing at the ribbon of water that split the valley in two.

Now what? Now what? She couldn't very well tell him she was taking their relationship off hold. How would she even phrase something like that—"Good news; you can propose now"?

She bit her lip. What had she *done?*

"Hey."

It came from below her. She looked down to see Will standing on the wooden steps that led through the floor of the turret. He looked up at her and said, "Is there room for one more?"

She said in a faint voice, "Oh, yes."

He came the rest of the way up, stepping onto the floor and dropping the hatch closed after him. "I never did get that tea in the turret," he said sadly.

"I know. But the samovar's all packed up."

He frowned. "Isn't that a little premature?"

"We did the knickknacks first. They're what take the time."

"I guess you're right."

He looked glum. Her heart fell.

"Well," he added with a half-shrug, "I'm glad Chester didn't pack up his tools."

He reached in his pocket and pulled out a cold chisel, then slid a hammer out from behind his belt. Without looking at Elinor, he went over to the wall opposite from where she stood, then reached up and traced his fingers over the *E* and the *L* that she had carved in the stone when she was a girl. Lining up the chisel a few inches above the *E*, he whacked it hard, sending the sound of steel on stone clanging through the turret.

She watched, astonished, as he took another hard swing, and another, moving the chisel down the stone until he had a line that slanted from upper left to lower right. He lifted the chisel and started another line, lower left to upper right, then reversed the first two lines. And when he was done, he had a *W*.

He turned to her with an endearing grin. "Damn. This is hard work. How old were you? Eight? I'm impressed."

"Your cuts are deeper," she whispered, bemused. She knew, now, where he was going, and her heart began to lift in her breast like a helium balloon into the sky.

He sighed and said, "Now for the last initial. Damned if I have a clue. Wait. I know."

He worked quickly, not turning around, banging hammer on chisel, chisel into stone, until the letters *W-I-L-L* were formed above Elinor's *E* and *L*. He made two more cuts—a plus sign—between his name and hers, and then he laid down the tools and stepped back to survey his work.

"That oughtta last," he said, satisfied.

After that he turned to Elinor, took her hand in his, and said, "I don't want to play your silly game anymore. I do love you. I'll always love you."

He reached in his pocket and took out a ring—a thick band with a cabochon stone in it, obviously old—and slipped it over her finger. "I love you and I want you to be my wife. For now. Forever. That promise is carved in stone. Will you marry me, fair maiden, and share my bed?"

Elinor's voice was low and filled with joy as she said, "Aye, my lord. I will."

Epilogue

*I*t loomed on the hill like a Disneyland dream: Fair Castle.

The tower glowed pink in the afternoon radiance of June, with flags snapping smartly from each of its four bartizans—oversized banners of Northumberland and New York, of England and America. In between them, smaller flags portraying coats of arms flew in heraldic glory from merlons on all four sides of the embattled parapet.

Everyone loved a wedding.

Huge armfuls of ferns and flowers, hand-cut by Camilla MacLeish and jammed into galvanized vases, filled every open window on the first and second floors. Over the arched door hung bunting of silver lamé that Camilla had braided through garlands of green. In the middle of the bunting, Chester had mounted two big bells of papier-mâché, fashioned by Mickey MacLeish and painted robin's-egg blue by Izzy. Where the bells' clappers should be, Izzy's mother had been inspired to hang upside-down lilies of white.

Everyone loved a wedding, the MacLeishes, most of all.

A trio of musicians—she in a pale green dress with a scalloped hem, the men in tights and tunics—played Renaissance tunes under a canvas gazebo set up for the day near the back entry. Tender notes from flute and harpsichord wafted over the grounds and down the gently rolling grass, tumbling one after another into the river, to be carried along to a faraway sea.

"What lovely music," someone said.

"The flowers are truly divine."

"I've never seen so many people so happy."

"Yo! I've never tasted such wine."

Everyone—absolutely everyone—loved a wedding.

The men gathered, as men liked to do, around linen-covered card tables set up with bottles and glasses and wedges of lime. Mickey MacLeish was one of the first. He raised his glass to the bride and groom chatting with guests a few yards away, then slapped an old friend on the shoulder.

"Well, Ed? What do you think? Looks a lot better without the asphalt parking lot alongside, doesn't it? Garden looks like it's always been there. They did a great job."

His old friend agreed, and Mickey added in a low voice, "I'll tell you, I won't miss having those tourists underfoot all day. I'd be walkin' through the great hall in shorts and no shirt, and *boom,* right into a gaggle of blue-hairs. Very embarrassin'. Anyway, I had a great old time this spring when they were tearing up the asphalt. One of the men even let me play on the backhoe for a morning. I should've gone into construction, by God. Missed a good career, there."

Ed said, "Trade in your beret for a hard hat? Come on. We'd all be the poorer for it."

Mickey threw his arm around his friend and touched his glass to his. "I thank you, sir. Life, they tell us, is an incurable disease. But I've been damned blessed with mine. Milly, Milly!" he suddenly cried out, then, with a wink, raised the same glass to his wife.

A shy four-year-old, enchanting in pink, came up to Mickey's old friend and tugged at his sleeve. "Grandpa? I have nothing to do."

Ed smiled and said, "Nothing to do! Tell you what, Samantha. You go over by the rest of the kids. See where Izzy is? You go over there. She's telling everyone a story."

The little girl crossed the lawn and dropped down hesitantly on the edge of the circle of children gathered around Isabelle.

"But the prince was very unhappy in the castle," Isabelle was saying. "Yes, this very castle! He was sad because he was a prisoner of the mean old witch! And the beautiful maiden that he loved, she couldn't come there, because she was poor and she wasn't allowed.

"She didn't have much money," Izzy told her wide-eyed audience, "but she knew how to do one thing— *magic*. She knew how to make herself invisible so that the mean old witch couldn't see her, and she was able to sneak in the castle and visit with the prince."

"What did she look like?" asked one of the children.

"She was *very* beautiful, extremely beautiful. She had long red hair—down to here!" Izzy said, jabbing at her hip, "and she wore lovely gowns of silver and blue."

"Could the prince see her when she was invisible?"

"Oh, yes," said Izzy with a faraway look. "He could see her very well. And now they're so happy."

In a cushioned wicker sofa with a good view of the children, Camilla MacLeish and the dowager Lady Norwood were putting their heads together to plan their next project.

"I think that area—from the walnut tree down to where the willow used to be—would be perfect for a terraced garden," said Dorothea, cupping her gnarled hands over her cane. "There's so much sun there now."

Camilla expressed surprise and then delight. "You're right! I've never thought of landscaping there; the area's always been too shady."

In her gentle British tones, Dorothea said, "What a dreadful storm that was! It's a pity the wind split the willow in two. I know you must miss it."

Camilla tucked a stray hairpin back into her friend's chignon and said, "What I remember about that night was your birthday cake and Will's funny stories. And besides, now that the greenhouse has been restored and expanded, you and I will need something new to tide us over the winter."

"It *would* be grand fun, wouldn't it," Dorothea said with a warm smile.

"The perennials will have to be very tall, I think. Otherwise we won't see them over the grade from the kitchen."

"Oh, we'll need delphiniums, surely . . . and rose mallow . . . foxglove . . . I wonder how well burnet would do there?"

Chester set the mint juleps on the table in front of the two elderly gardeners and beat a quiet retreat. "They'll go on for hours like that," he told the unattached woman who stood nearby, seeming a little at sea.

She gave him a friendly smile and said, "Oh, we all have our hobbies. Personally, mine is touring castles. I've been all over Europe in search of them."

"Really?" said Chester, stroking the beard that covered his scar. "So have I. Which did you like best?"

Ten minutes later, his wife came up and slipped her arm through his. "Chester . . . darling . . . I wonder if you could give me a hand with the caterers. Poor Agnes is swamped." With an apologetic smile Susan said to their guest, "I'm *so* sorry to have to steal him away."

The latest Lady Norwood, watching her mother at work, smiled and said to her husband, "Gramma Cam and Nana aren't the only ones tending their gardens."

Grinning, Will quoted a little Oscar Wilde in her ear: "Men always want to be a woman's first love; women like to be a man's last romance."

Elinor fell into a demure curtsy before her new lord. "And therefore shall we both be content."

He laughed out loud at that and slipped one arm around her waist. "Let's walk down to the river for a few minutes, wench, and hide behind the forsythia. I have a burning desire to kiss you senseless."

"*Deal.*" She swept up the train of her *peau de soie* gown. "Do you think anyone will notice we've slipped away?" she asked him with an innocent batting of eyelashes.

"Don't care. If I have to explain one more time that the castle's staying right where it is . . ."

Something in the way they laughed and the way they looked made their guests slip respectfully out of their path as they sauntered down the rolling stretch of lawn to the banks of the Hudson River.

All the while, Elinor spoke in an easy flow of low, intimate sentences; and Will, he looked enchanted.

They ducked behind the forsythia and he took her in his arms and kissed her—exactly according to plan—senseless. Elinor laughed and pulled away and let herself be drawn into his arms again for one more kiss, one more taste of the life that was yet to come. It was a delicious form of rapture, sexy and unsatisfying at the same time.

More than once, she sighed and said, "We should get back to our guests." And every time, he talked her out of it. His nearness intoxicated her. The murmur of his voice, the smell of his skin, the taste of his mouth on hers left her reeling. Part of her didn't even *want* to be satisfied: the longing itself was too delicious for her to wish it would end.

Eventually, grudgingly, they turned from the shimmering, magical river to rejoin their guests. Elinor was well aware that most of the people strolling on the lawn were from her side. Will had flown in his grandmother's old nurse and companion, as well as Father Aloysius and the vicar from Dibble. Several other of his friends and relations were there as well. His sister, Penny, had been there and gone. But his mother was not, and Elinor couldn't help feeling the loss for him.

He knew it. "A broken leg at her age is no small thing," he said. "She'll be off her feet for a while. Spring skiing! The woman is a wonder." He smiled and said, "Don't worry. I do *not* believe that she did it on purpose to get out of coming."

"Will she welcome grandchildren, do you think?" asked Elinor, not quite sure what to expect from the woman she still hadn't met.

"You know, once I would've said no. Grandchildren would make her feel too much her age. But now—after the accident—I have to admit, she seems more ...

thoughtful somehow. More at ease with herself. At least, she's sounded that way on the phone."

"People slow down. She'll have more time . . ."

He shrugged. "Maybe."

It wasn't a yes; but it wasn't a no. He was coming along. "It's funny, isn't it, how things turned out," she mused. "The castle is staying, your grandmother's staying, but you and I are going."

He looked surprised. "Madame, the New York brownstone was *your* idea."

"Oh, and I love it," she said quickly, "I really do. It's where we should be now. With me writing and you forming another start-up company . . ."

"All right," he said, scrutinizing her face. "As long as you're sure."

She laughed. It was fun keeping him off balance. "We'll still be close to everyone," she reasoned. "We *can't* live in the castle, Will. There's no room. And besides, I want you to be able to chase me naked around the house sometimes. There's a time and a place for everything—and it's time for us to have our own place."

"Hmmm," he said, nodding. "I agree. Especially about the naked part."

She flashed him a wicked smile that prompted Will on the spot to kiss it away. When he let her go he said more seriously, "There's something I have to know. Do you mind that my name is probably MacGilliray or Jones or something, and not Braddock?"

She thought that was funny. She thought *he* was funny. "It's Braddock enough for me," she said with a lilt in her voice. "I love you, Mr. William MacGilliray-Jones-Braddock-Lord Norwood. You could be plain Joe Blow. I would still love you tonight, tomorrow, forever."

Will kissed her lips, then, and said softly, "My love. My own true love. Come on—let's toss that bouquet and go."

No one believes in ghosts anymore, not even in Salem, Massachusetts. And especially not sensible Helen Evett, a widow who lives for her two teenaged kids and who runs the best preschool in town. But when little Katie Byrne enters her school, strange things begin to happen. Katie's widowed father, Nat, begins to awaken feelings in Helen that she had counted as dead. But why does Helen get the feeling that Linda, Katie's mother, is reaching beyond the grave to tell her something?

As Helen and Nat each explore the pain of their losses and the joy of their newfound love, Linda Byrne's ghost plays a bold hand, beseeching Helen to uncover the mystery of her death. But what Helen finds could make her the target of a jealous killer and a modern Salem witch-hunt that threatens her, her family...and the magical second-time-around love that's taking her and Nat by storm.

BESTSELLING, AWARD-WINNING AUTHOR

ANTOINETTE STOCKENBERG

Beyond Midnight

Once upon a time...

A lovely lady fell asleep in a charmed ring of flowers and dreamed of Comlan, king of the fairy realm. She spent a few magical hours by his side, enjoying the company of the handsome king whose golden hair and green eyes could turn the head of any mortal maid...and whose charming attentions captured her heart.

But the year is 1850, and Amy Danton knows better than to believe in fairy tales. However wonderful Comlan seems, he is nothing but a figment of her imagination.

But then, across a crowded ballroom, she sees him— the man of her dreams...

"An exciting romance...this novel has everything a romance reader desires...a beautifully poignant fairy tale."—*Affaire de Coeur*

Once Upon a Time
Marylyle Rogers